The End of All Things

The End of All Things

Sherlock Holmes and His London Through the Eyes of Scotland Yard

by Marcia Wilson

Edited by David Marcum

MX Publishing

Sherlock Holmes and the Scotland Yarders
by Marcia Wilson

1. *You Buy Bones*
2. *Test of the Professionals: The Adventure of the Flying Blue Pidgeon*
3. *Test of the Professionals: The Peaceful Night Poisonings*
4. *Test of the Professionals: Leap Year*
5. *The MoonCursers*
6. *A Sword for Defense*
7. *The Narrow Path: The First Storm*
8. *The End of All Things*
9. *A Fanged and Bitter Thing*

Further adventures forthcoming . . . .

Author Foreword
by Marcia Wilson

Looking back, it was a strange time. High school in the late 1980's meant Tolkien, King, Christie, and Poe were always checked out of the school library, but we had multiple copies of Sherlock Holmes on the shelf. If students were going to apply for English-oriented scholarships, by gosh, we were going to read the good stuff, and that meant short stories with murder and mayhem. In emulation of the masters, our choices were usually ACD or . . . Hemingway. It wasn't much of a contest. Hemingway didn't have a demon glowing Death Hound on the moors.

High school segued into college, but we had *Mystery!* re-runs on PBS, even if we had to visit people to watch it, and besides Jeremy Brett, we had Christopher Plummer's compassionate Holmes against Jack the Ripper, a role that shattered the domination of Rathbone and Bruce. Our classmates swore it was necessary for our sincerity as fans of Sir Arthur to see it.

If that sounds like pithy stuff for high schoolers, my generation had a flexible relationship with media – or even power grids. Even if they existed, they weren't exactly as reliable as the sun coming up every morning. The further into the West Virginia panhandle you got, the bigger the library room in the house. Even the poorest of houses, be they on blocks or wheels, had at least one shelf of sanity to rely on when the power was out, or the brownouts made hash of anything but AM radio. When a flood took out the local libraries, it was devastation.

There was media, but there wasn't enough – there's never enough – but as far as the books printed in the wake of Sir Arthur . . . it really was never enough. You were lucky to find something in a thrift store or library sale, and your odds were no worse than combing the bookstores in the mall. Oh, for the days when there was more than one bookstore in a mall. If something was found, readers had to buy it on faith that it wasn't a waste of their time.

Look, our standards weren't low, they were desperate. We made a lot of poor book-buying choices, which were hastily returned to the ecosystem of flea market sales for some other poor shmuck to buy up. One girl, bless her, would donate the books after carefully penciling in every sin the authors made against Canon, history, plot contrivance,

1

and attempts to pair Holmes up with a romantic partner. I like to think she cackled as she returned the much-improved dreck to the public. She always cited her sources . . . .

It shouldn't be a surprise when we wound up obsessing, ever so slightly, with what little we could find that wasn't terrible, and (*Hooray!*) didn't go against The Canon. I wonder if anyone has ever tried to list all the knockoffs and illicit print runs out there. Probably not – I'd like to think nobody could be that crazy.

Fan fiction was the outlet for a crying need that had hit breaking point. Paper fanzines of decent quality were even harder to find than a decent paperback on the shelf – you have never bought a pig in a poke until you've combed through a hand-printed zine catalog, squinted at the type, and decided to spend your allowance on what sounded the most promising – and too bad the cover art was rarely as good on the inside.

Fanzine editors lived in the twilight, trying to put out their passion projects between the obligations of home, family, and keeping a roof over their head, as well as hanging on to entire drawers of receipts to make sure a rival 'ziner didn't get spiteful and report them to the IRS. (That actually happened.) Zines were non-profit only, which is partly why the zines we could afford were always shipped Media Mail on whatever paper was on sale. If you were very lucky, you got your order in three weeks.

Maybe we shouldn't talk about the pastichery in animation . . . .

The Internet found its feet and bloomed with forums and places to hide and talk about the lack of stories, and that led to posting paper zines online, and people began writing fresh stuff, online, and showing it for reading and/or critiquing. Almost overnight there were clubs, groups, and social organizations that could get their fix on the stories between the boom-and-bust world of conventions and newsletters.

There were friendships made that I miss to this very day. The sheer power of a small number of people who were intelligent, thoughtful, and mindful of Canon encouraged so many of us. They helped with research, knew how to spell, and learned different languages in this world. They reviewed books, scrounged supplies, and let us know if someone was copying our plots just a little too much for comfort. Plagiarism and how to address it was a real eye-opener when it came to intellectual property that wasn't yours to begin with, but you could claim the OC's (Original Characters) were yours, and debatably, your unique perspective on the people, places, and things created under the pen of Sir Arthur.

I was a fan of these fans. They were amazing and – honestly – damn good writers. *Damn* good. They were role models. They read the whole Canon, and they kept track of everything, and they led us to places like *fanfiction.net*, where we could post with a minimum of fussing.

I could write about anyone I wanted, but it was partially out of respect for these writers that I began to veer away from making just one more story about Sherlock Holmes and Dr. Watson. I loved the stories, but part of their appeal was their world. And there was a lot to that world that was relevant today. Methods may alter crime, but motives rarely do.

At the time, there was a pretty well-represented group that was pro-Watson, and they wrote some of those "damn good stories" with Watson as the protagonist – or at least, a powerful, equal voice. The Granada series was a huge influence, as well as the Russian series, and throw in some of "the radio show" for good measure.

These fan writers may have loved the tight scripts and drama of the Rathbone and Bruce approach, but as they grew up, they said, collectively, "Man, that was bad for Watson!" There were other words, much less polite. Burke and Hardwicke were a positive force for the shift in the thinking that pointed out Watson was *not* an idiot and we couldn't do a decent job showing how smart Holmes was by surrounding him by idiots. This had already been tried, during Classic Dr Who, and nobody had been left happy about it. Nobody blamed the actors for doing their job too well.

Fine, I thought, *there are a lot of really good writers writing for Watson. I can do that.* But I also caught on that if Watson illuminated Holmes by writing of the man from his point-of-view, *maybe I could write about Watson through other people's eyes.* The question was: *Who?*

Enter a re-visit to the Granada Series, and "The Norwood Builder".

I make no secret of the fact that I am heavily synesthetic. Face blindness comes with its own challenge, and I have to train myself to recognize people. With an irony that approaches opera-grade comedy, I literally could not tell Holmes from Lestrade in Granada's "The Norwood Builder". Also, Lestrade made me angry when I was a hero-worshipping teenager watching the show with other hero-worshipping teenagers. *How dare Lestrade challenge Holmes? Couldn't anyone see Holmes was the smartest man in the room?*

Older adult me revisited that part of my life and went *Oops!* because there were some of those Fanfiction Demigods that rather liked Lestrade and had plenty of backup reasons. I wish I could remember the name of the one who mused, *"Colin Jeavons is the only actor who could be bulldog-like and also ferrety."* I was doing a lot of research at my job, and that included the Victorian era and law enforcement. Somehow it all started clicking together, piece by piece.

A writer whom I regret losing (her entire message board went the way of LiveJournal – only, it vanished for good. Poof. No trace) challenged me on whether or not Lestrade was stupid. He knew more than he let on, she said, and I . . . kind of said, *"Oh? Prove it."*

Ouch. She did, lining out events in "The Boscombe Valley Mystery" and "The Second Stain" and a few other bits and pieces, and I ate crow. A lot of it. I was wrong. Still, I could at least write with this new perspective. Bad as it was to be wrong, it would be worse to stay with it.

Add to this a sleep disorder that can politely be called *insomnia*, and a marriage turning into a nightmare of violence, and no health insurance – but writing was the cheapest therapy out there . . . Lestrade slowly woke up and came to life. I'll blame Colin Jeavons for knowing what the writers wanted out of the scripts. It's on him.

"Trust your characters," my old English teacher would say, sternly, so I did. I wrote short stories that could connect with others to make a fuller piece. A necklace is made one bead at a time. I wrote at night. I had to. I needed to stay awake, listening to any sounds that might be my ex-husband's return to stalk us – tampering with my car, crawling under the house, draining the well his own children needed to drink from, and taunts to the police that tried their best, but could only work within the limits of the system. They failed, but it was the system that failed. They cared, and they shared my rage that when the ex was finally brought to justice, it was too late for one of his victims.

There is only so much a policeman can do against so much collective injustice out there. If Sherlock Holmes had existed on that force, they would have begged for his help against my ex-husband. They knew he could go where they couldn't, and they would know when not to ask the awkward questions about how information was collected. They would have sniffed and said, "Well, that's a pity," and shrugged and did things according to the law – *their* law – but not expecting civilians to follow the same oaths they swore.

I empathized with Gregson's ability to buck the rules, and I empathized for Lestrade's inability to do so. The Yarders took on their own lives and, without knowing it, the job had changed. I was now sitting back and watching the stories unfold, writing them as fast as they told them. They had a lot to say. They still do, but the stories are whispering now. We are safer, there is no need to listen for danger. I am learning how to sleep.

More years ago than I'd like to recollect, I received an email so startling I forwarded it to my sister before a family dinner at the pizza parlour. It wasn't a fantastic day. Before long I would be needing their help to flee across the country in the middle of a winter snowstorm. The mood was glum. We were subdued.

My sister looked at me over the table and said with uncharacteristic bluntness, "You impressed that man."

That man was David Marcum.

Marcia Wilson
February 2025

Scotland Yard's Story
Editor Foreword
by David Marcum

Back in 2008, it was still a different Sherlockian world from today.

In those days, the quest for more excellent Holmes adventures beyond the pitifully few sixty Canonical adventures was still quite difficult. Each year, only a few slipped through the needle's-eye clutch of the moribund major publisher model. (In fact, if one is still publishing by that route, then this fact remains true.) But there were many Holmes adventures waiting to be revealed, and they just needed an outlet. Is it any wonder that the Internet was that path?

Holmes pastiches have been around since William Gillette's 1899 play, *Sherlock Holmes*, showing that Our Heroes' adventures did *not* have to pass across the first Literary Agent's desk. Some amazing and accurate adventures appeared on the radio in the 1930's, courtesy of visionary Edith Meiser. And the door kept getting wider, with more radio shows, films, and the occasional book giving us more traditional, authentic, and Canonical Holmes.

But it was not enough.

In 1998, *fanfiction.net* was created, allowing another outlet for sharing Holmes's adventures, wherein those who had discovered them could get them directly to starving readers immediately, without facing the impossible discouragement of the faceless soul-dead major publishing model. I was fortunate to discover the site a few years after that, and began to visit regularly to read and print and archive stories about the True Holmes. There are thousands of Holmes stories located there, but many are parodies, or anachronistic, or related to modernized and offensive simulacrums, or with incorrect ghost-busting leanings. Others were clearly written by individuals who have no clue about Sherlock Holmes, or have hijacked him for their own agendas. These stories may be ignored, even if they have to be waded through – for buried in the muck of this backyard goose lot, for those who take time to look, are some true and rare jewels.

And in April 2008, the beginning of a couple of stories were posted, "An Ordinary Meeting" on the tenth, and "Truth is the Critic" the next day, both as written by an author going under the curious sobriquet of *aragonite*.

"An Ordinary Meeting" gives details of Lestrade's first consultation with Sherlock Holmes, and "Truth is the Critic" is written from the perspective of the Scotland Yard inspectors as they read *A Study in Scarlet* – and providing their reactions when see how Watson has described them. These were well written and interesting, and this approach really hadn't been attempted before.

(To be accurate, there had been some stories about the Yarders, but they were inconsistent. For instance, M.J. Trow's long Lestrade series veers wildly from legitimate mysteries to unreadable parodies, with particularly bogus attacks on Sherlock Holmes, and Trow inexplicably gives Inspector G. Lestrade the first name of "Sholto".

In "Truth is the Critic", *aragonite* was already painting the Yarders – Inspectors Lestrade, Gregson, Bradstreet, and Hopkins in particular – in well-rounded and respectful ways that hadn't been seen before. They had their own life stories beyond The Canon, and weren't just the inspector *du jour* appearing in this-or-that Canonical tale. Who knew then that this new author, slipping quietly onto the scene, had such an overall vision for these individuals, with fully realized details about their personal lives, their backgrounds and histories . . . and a plan for a massive overarching adventure that would span decades in their lives?

Over the next few months, more stories quickly followed – "A Cookout in Cornwall", "Route to Madness", and "Just Inspector Will Do" (my all-time favorite of these works, relating the events on the Paddington platform when Mary Watson awaits her husband's return from the Continent in mid-May 1891. I re-read it every year on Reichenbach Day.) But on April 17th, 2008, *aragonite* raised the stakes, publishing the first chapter of a novel, *A Sword for Defense*, the first of a massive story arc relating what Watson and Lestrade and the other Yarders faced in the months after Holmes's supposed death at the Reichenbach Falls.

While keeping one story going would overwhelm many authors, *aragonite* – whomever he or she was – had even greater ambitions. New stories and chapters began to be posted at a feverish pace. A week after *Sword* started, another serialized novel began, *You Buy Bones*, telling how Watson, in early 1882 and fresh from his first year living with Holmes in Baker Street, comes across a monstrous crime that directly and personally affects the Scotland Yard inspectors. And a few months after that, *aragonite* started another novel that served as a prequel leading to *Sword* called *The MoonCursers*, telling of Lestrade's

7

own terrifying adventures in late April and early May 1891, occurring at the same time Holmes and Watson were playing cat-and-mouse with Moriarty, on their way to a fateful encounter in Meiringen.

Over the course of that summer, nearly every day brought some new chapter: Sometimes another episode in *A Sword for Defense* or *You Buy Bones* or *The MoonCursers*, and at other times a seemingly stand-alone story that that filled in some crucial and interesting aspect about the Scotland Yarders that only made the overall painting richer and deeper.

Imagine if Charles Dickens were writing and publishing three serialized novels at once, and adding in short stories too. And they were going straight from being written to being posted for public consumption as soon as they were complete. And clearly the overall storyline wasn't being generated along the way – there was a *plan*, for little threads mentioned here and there about Lestrade's boyhood or Bradstreet's family had massive importance much later.

Over many months during this time, *aragonite* was also constructing another massive work, *Test of the Professionals*, which related the events after *You Buy Bones* and served as a set-up for *A Sword for Defense*, telling us much more about Lestrade's past, his unfortunate and dangerous life-long connection with Professor Moriarty's agent, the truly evil Jethro Quimper, and the escalating and terrifying events surrounding his courtship with Clea Cheatham.

In August 2008, with all of this going on, *aragonite* started another brilliant novella, *A Secondary Stain*, the *other* events of "The Second Stain", in which Lestrade was not as clueless as he appears in Watson's manuscript, actually working behind the scenes to assist Holmes's investigation. It was the brilliance of this story that finally prompted me to write a fan letter.

Using the fan fiction website's messenger feature, I emailed an extensive message to *aragonite* in October 2008, and soon received a wonderful and informative reply.

First, I learned that *aragonite* was really Marcia Wilson. In subsequent communications, I learned that *aragonite* – which curiously I'd never looked up before then – is calcium carbonate used by marine organisms to build their shells and skeletons. Since aragonite can be found in cave formations, and since Marcy is a caver – the evidence of which can be found in some of her stories brilliantly dealing with caverns and London's Lost Rivers – I suspect that's why she chose the unusual pen-name.

Over many emails over many years, Marcy has explained to me that she wrote so prolifically in those early years because she had insomnia, and that was a very productive time to write. She also could *see* all of these scenes, and almost couldn't write fast enough to convey them. In her very first reply to me in October 2008, she explained, how she approached telling the Yarders' story, and why she named Inspector G. Lestrade *Geoffrey:*

> *I've never liked the playing down of characters. It's a lazy way to pump up the character in your mind. I have to be very careful not to wander into the Fangirlyverse. Usually I deal with it by giving a character a name I dislike, and for some reason, I dislike Geoffrey so naturally I stuck it on the poor guy.*

She also explained that:

> *I was so bleeding tired of writing against another person's notions on Holmes and Watson that I just went to another character that I rather liked. (When I was younger, I hated Lestrade. He should have been kowtowing to Holmes' genius like all of us!) Later on, I realized that it took a pretty remarkable man to refuse to see Holmes in a reverent light. [The] clues about Lestrade were subtle and interesting. There had to be a reason for someone who was supposed to be such a good cop to stay a police inspector after his initial promotion. I made him a Celtic Breton out of a half-thought. I was seeing Colin Jeavons in my head, and he's so Welsh he's probably half-Neanderthal! Being a Breton or a Channel Islander would have made [Lestrade] an English citizen, but he would not have been accepted as an equal in race or status by many people.*

Our communications continued, as did her writing. By early 2009, *A Sword for Defense* was complete, and the next book in the ongoing saga, *The Narrow Path* had commenced. Those were great days to be a Sherlockian and to be reading *fanfiction.net,* as there were other great authors there as well – *Westron Wynde* and *KCS* among them, all with powerful and correct understandings of the *True Holmes.* These authors were writing for the fans, and also for each other, and I was privileged to be in contact with many of them. In a few years, Marcy and *Westron*

9

Wynde – who turned out to be amazing pasticheur Sarah Bennett, whose works are slowly being made available from Belanger Books – began to take down their online works and publish them in real books. (It was at this time that I let Marcy and Sarah read my first Sherlock Holmes pastiches, written in 2008 and at that point seen by no one but my wife, and with their encouragement I started publicly publishing my stories too.)

Marcy initially published *You Buy Bones*, along with some related short stories, in 2010 (from Lulu Publishing. That version is now out of print.) Next came *Test of the Professionals: Leap Year* (2013, also from Lulu and out of print), also collecting the original online novel and working in some supplementary material.

In 2015, I came up with the idea of *The MX Book of New Sherlock Holmes Stories*, and of course Marcy was in the initial list of invitees. Since then, much of her writing has been turned to contributing stories to these anthologies, having submitted nearly two-dozen. Through these books, she became associated with MX Publishing, who issued a new edition of *You Buy Bones* in 2015, as well as splitting *Test of the Professionals: Leap Year* into three planned smaller volumes. The first two, *The Adventure of the Flying Blue Pidgeon* and *The Peaceful Night Poisonings*, were published by MX in 2016 and 2017, respectively. Unfortunately, due to a combination of events, the third part of *Test* – the much larger piece called *Leap Year* that relates the exciting conclusion to that narrative – was not published.

So for the wider public, those who were never able to read Marcy's massive *ouvré* on *fanfiction.net*, her available works consisted of these three novels, and her well-respected stories in the MX anthologies. (Unfortunately, Marcy, Sarah Bennett, and several others were forced to pull their Sherlockian content from *fanfiction.net* several years ago after some of their works were stolen – copied-and-pasted and then republished under other author names by way of Amazon's self-publishing program.)

In late 2024, I was in the process of working toward assembling and editing the final volumes, Parts 49, 50, 51, and 52 of the MX anthologies, a process which would continue into early 2025. While looking around in my computer files, I found something I'd forgotten: Years earlier, I had saved and formatted the files for five of Marcy's novels – those relating to Watson and Lestrade's adventures during The Great Hiatus. Since the late 1990's, I've printed and archived every traditional Canonical Holmes adventure that I've found online –

thousands of them – and I have over 175 binders of pure Holmes adventures – including all of Marcy's now-withdrawn stories. But luckily I had these novels as Word files. And I had an idea . . . .

I contacted Marcy, who hadn't had time in several years to think about publishing more of her works, and asked if I could shepherd these five novels to publication – *pro-bono*, just because I was passionate about other people reading these incredible stories. Marcy was willing, and so I started editing with great enthusiasm – even as I was supposed to be editing the final MX volumes, stories for which were rolling in every day.

It soon became apparent to me that to publish these five novels without readers knowing the events of the missing *Leap Year* would be a confusing mess. Too much happened in these books that continued from what happened in *Leap Year.* Clearly, that missing volume would need to be edited and published too. And while I was at it, why not re-edit the previously published three books – *You Buy Bones, The Adventure of the Flying Blue Pidgeon*, and *The Peaceful Night Poisonings* – into an overall cohesive narrative?

MX Publisher Extraordinaire Steve Emecz, THE Sherlockian publisher and the Sherlockian Gutenberg – the man who made Sherlockian publishing accessible to real people instead of guarding a narrow doorway, or deciding that Sherlockian publishing should only be available for a very narrow cadre of self-described elites – was enthusiastic, and ready to proceed immediately. But I needed to actually finish editing the nine books first. It was a joy, and a labor of love to do so.

I had read all of these books serially as published, hopping from story to story as new chapters appeared, back in 2008-2011. But to read the story now, in one place, in order and available in its entirety, made it even more amazing – and exciting for the thought of new readers able to discover this magnificent world: *Sherlock Holmes's London, as seen through the eyes of the Scotland Yarders.*

Even as I dug deeper into Marcy's Scotland Yard adventures, I was remembering the other stories – the previously mentioned *A Secondary Stain.* Her Yarder's Christmas novels, *Gunnysack Goose for Christmas* and *A Mouth of Ivy.* Short-story collections like *Devilry* and *It's All in a Name.* Other novels and novellas like *The Muse of History, Ghosts in the Making, Courage Rises, The Kings and Queens of London*, and the World War I narrative, *The Days of Our Years.* I had amazing fun editing the first nine books that are being published in

11

2025, and with any luck, I hope to be able to edit the rest of these, along with a collection of Marcy's MX anthology contributions, over the next year or so, in order to fill in Marcy's *Great Scotland Yard Tapestry*.

There are certain authors who "own" other Canonical characters by taking hold of them and defining them. The late Carole Nelson Douglas was Irene Adler's chronicler. Michael Kurland gives us the best portrait of Professor Moriarty. Will Thomas has absolutely defined Barker, Holmes's hated rival on the Surrey Side. The late Gerard Williams claimed Dr. Mortimer (even if only for two books), and Susan Knight is easily becoming the definitive voice of Mrs. Hudson.

But Marcia Wilson tells the True Story of the Scotland Yarders – and presents an amazing viewpoint of Holmes and Watson along the way.

I've said it many times before, and can't say it any better now:

Marcia Wilson has found Scotland Yard's Tin Dispatch Box.

David Marcum
January 2025

SPIRIT LEVEL©2015

The End of
All Things

Author's Note

Let's put this mess in perspective.

A Sword for Defense

The story opens three months after Sherlock Holmes's "death". Colonel Moriarty emerges with a challenge before Scotland Yard: to expose John Watson as a liar about his version of the Battle of Maiwand. Although it takes a lot of poking around, Lestrade learns that Watson served at the same time as his twin brother, who behaved impulsively and died after the war. The key evidence is tied up in the condition of Watson's sabre. It is illegal for a man in the Medical Corps to draw his weapon save in self-defence, yet he faced a criminal charge of lifting it in anger.

Watson is curiously unforthcoming about assisting the police in clearing his name. He concentrates on his upcoming fatherhood, an event he and Mary are meeting with great expectations. He appears to be doing no more than work on his writing career, his medical practice, and staying in touch with his friends of the past. He has privately released his version of Holmes's death, but has not yet published it. Those who have read it are talking. While it takes Lestrade a while to catch on, Watson is asking for help in a very indirect way. Pursuing a clue, Lestrade finds traces that Watson and his twin brother had been working for Colonel Hayter in an attempt to ruin Colonel Moriarty's unspecified but patently criminal activities within the service. To defend himself or to prove that his brother had been the offender would be to expose Hayter's well-meaning subterfuge.

Events seem caught at a standstill, but Lestrade faces down Moriarty's campaign of slander against Watson before witnesses. The Colonel departs in a strangely content mood. Gregson realizes this has all been a test for the Colonel: A test of the Yard's mettle to see how easily they could be distracted or swayed or bribed. He knows things are about to grow worse. Lestrade discovers two dress sabres: One clean and unscarred, the other battle-marked and scored deeply with Ogham writing. Lestrade can go no further than the literal decipher: Cave of the Dead Druid. *It means gibberish to him.*

In the meantime, Sherlock Holmes is seeing the world at a frantic pace. It is hardly the stuff of legends. There are rumbles of war, and thoughts of the world he has left behind are his sole motivation for preventing it. Sick and alone in body and spirit, his active mind is trapped by his circumstances to absorb everything he can of his new experiences, while waiting fruitlessly for word from his brother.

For a while things appear to be calm, but Lestrade is growing morose. He confesses to his father-in-law that his nightmares will not stop. He constantly relives the circumstances of his worst encounter with Moriarty's most powerful agent, Jethro Quimper, a man who once tried to drown him in a fishpond. The dreams are re-lived events to the drowning and his fighting for life in the dark Thames while a voice whispers to him that "The hour is come but not the man . . . ."

The Narrow Path

The season – and prospects – have worsened in London. Gregson, Lestrade, and Hopkins meet under clandestine camaraderie and speak frankly about the future. A recent scandal involving graft and funeral homes for Afghan war veterans have caused discomfort throughout the Yard, but so far is being kept from blowing open to the public. Lestrade and Hopkins have been working together so the young man can benefit from the older man's experience and previous connections with the affected parties dating back to the actual war-time. At the palaver, Gregson advises Lestrade to stick close to Watson. He isn't safe with any Moriarty running about. Lestrade gives in to Gregson's dictatorial commands with little protest. He is starting to show the signs of strain from the events of the year.

Disease runs through the cold winter streets. Clea Lestrade falls ill. Mary Watson's health wavers.

The Watsons are proud parents of a baby boy, Arthur. Watson has agreed to stand as police surgeon while Dr. Roanoke steps down. Lestrade catches another, apparently idle clue from Watson: Comparisons of Professor Moriarty to a previous criminal mastermind, Jonathan Wild. Drawn to dig up Inspector Patterson, now retired, Lestrade finds a shell of a once-strong man. Patterson says only one man was ever strong enough to go up against Colonel Moriarty and live: Watson's friend and patron, Colonel Hayter. Someone is listening and watching them. The price of asking for Patterson's copy of the Holmes's reports leads to an attack by a corrupt police inspector who soon kills himself in custody. Soon after, another inspector with a tie to both men is attacked to keep silent about a seemingly innocuous conversation. Running back to London, Lestrade and Hopkins barely prevent a third attack upon Watson's home by more hired thugs.

A brutally murdered man is found with Colonel Hayter's professional cards in his possession, one addressed to John Watson. Hayter does not know who the man is, but Lestrade traces him to be an employee of the paper company that made the card. He had stolen the cards for some reason and was murdered. Gregson's suspicions are bearing proof: The Yard is being distracted from their true duties to solve this mystery. The lowliest and least trustworthy allies of Moriarty's gang are being sent as cannon fodder against the Yard. Hayter and Lestrade independently note that Watson's published adventures of Sherlock Holmes appear to have some unknown agenda . . . Watson neither confirms nor denies their questions. He is content with things the way they are.

Hopkins' work with the funeral home investigations has led to further scandal and the shocking find of a barrel of human fingerbones. Watson positively identifies them as adult human, while encountering his closest rival, Dr. Pennywraith, for the first time. He also sees Patterson recognize the murdered man as one of his informers against the Moriarty gang, and wonders if a man so prone to fainting would be a weak link for the Yard. Weak or not, Patterson has rejoined the Force. Geoffrey gets a letter from his grandfather addressed to his father-in- law's house. The letter only says he will be in to visit when he can, but Lestrade knows his grandfather is trying to warn him about something.

Clea Lestrade is at her wits' end with her husband's fading strength, but can only be advised to speak with Mrs. Watson when she returns from her visit to the country. The appearance of Clea's mother-in-law bodes ill. She warns of the failing health of Geoffrey's father in a way that makes Clea hesitant to even tell him.

Hopkins' work has reached a nadir. Something is fishy in a forgotten graveyard under new restoration. Watson struggles with his depression to attend his assistance, but when the cold winter weather is like this, he is reminded of Reichenbach Falls everywhere he looks. He notes that Lestrade and Bradstreet, usually the closest of friends, are awkward and brittle in each other's company.

Disaster strikes when the ground opens up under Lestrade's feet and he collapses into a grave. It is the last straw. At this point, his health tips over the line. His family moves to Clea's father's house to avoid his quarantine, and his grandfather is left to take care of him. Watson gives a brief comment on the effects of too much strain to a shamefaced Yard. Gregson warns Bradstreet that he'd best keep any questionable news to himself.

Chapter I – Christmas Passed

John Watson grimaced all the way to the bottom of his soul as a wagon loaded down with some of the worst-smelling stuff in the experience of man trotted past him on the busy High Street. The driver was wrapped so deeply in mufflers (all around his nose), it was a wonder he could see. Black, faintly glistening mounds of what looked like congealed oil quivered. The horse had realized if it kept going at a good pace, it would have a chance of outrunning the stench.

Long moments afterwards, the odour lingered like a particularly miasmic fog.

He shuddered. After the unseasonable pre-Christmas rain and snowmelt, the overstressed pipes to the Thames had needed outright replacement. While that meant work for the hard-ups and usual coarse laborers, it was still an appalling job. The Ministry of Health had swept down upon the matter like an outraged archangel.

The closer they grew to the 1900 mark, the more the city donned awareness of the future. Sanitation ought to be a good part of it . . . .

The doctor shrugged his heavy medical bag into the other hand and continued on.

Kensington had been an intelligent move. Initially it had been a difficult area in which to relocate, and Paddington had been a necessary change. But now he was back to a part of London that held much of his first fond memories of the city.

In a way it was like one's first school. A few sentimental thoughts are inevitable. Either had been adjacent to the St. Marylebone of Baker Street.

Baker Street.

Watson stopped for a moment, aware of his tactical error. Time hung upon his hands for another two hours, and Mary would not be back from her charity for at least that long. Arthur was with her of course. An infant was a guarantee to draw sympathy.

Two whole hours – !

He thought for a moment, but it was all an act to himself. He knew where he was going.

Orchard Street was practically a stone's throw away.

Baker Street was only a quarter-mile in length . . . .

He hadn't seen Mrs. Hudson in almost two months . . . She'd not been home when he sent her that basket . . . .

"Dr. Watson!"

That voice on top of a most infuriating week, dissolved the frail scraps of Watson's hopeful mood just as he was about to step down the kerb.

He turned his head slowly.

"Mr. Patterson," he nodded quietly.

The Inspector drew up, panting lightly in the crisp air. At least the high spots on his cheeks were from exertion and not from any of the ailments roaming London now. "I tried to find you at the Coroner's," he began by way of apology. "I do apologize. I was on my way home when I saw you here. It was a surprise."

"I believe you, sir." Watson made a snap judgment. "How may I be of service?"

"The Wardrobe Man." Patterson flinched at his own voice and glanced about using only his eyes. It was un-nerving. "Do you have a moment?"

Watson silently mourned his lost opportunity to see Mrs. Hudson. "I do. Do you fancy a drink?"

Paddington Street urchins pelted down the kerbs like mice, shrieking with glee and clutching objects to their thin coats that were doubtless stolen. Whatever they *had* stolen, it was a loss to the vendor, but the children needed to eat too. Losses were losses. The poor looked out for each other to a level that was surprising to the better class, and this concentrated effort had meant planning and scheming most would think a child incapable of.

Triaged Potier watched them go through the glass of the little window, and his smile was wry. They were gone like leaves in the wind, and the Bobbies would not try to find them very hard. Not unless someone complained loudly.

Old Potier frowned between his grey brows and beard as he lifted the teapot in his padded hands. One would think (he mused glumly) that the *English* of all people could appreciate the worth of good clay. Kemper-fired pottery this was not. He shook his head as he went ahead with the fixings of a decent cup. He should have brought some pottery with him.

He was not a small man among his own people. Quite average in fact. Here he was considered little, and it never failed to amuse him. He'd sailed with native Rus, where the men and women were nothing less than two and a quarter yards. Remembering those large, cheerful blond giants brought another smile to his face as he found the little pot of chestnut honey under the cabinet. A-ha. Barely used. Jafrez' English wife would not have a palate for the bittersweet stuff. Well, she had few enough faults that he could see.

22

"Awake, *mab*?" He called, tapping his knuckle on the wooden door that led to the old study. His grandson looked up blearily from the blankets, and the old man chuckled softly. "Surely you can eat something."

"You sound awfully certain of that," Geoffrey answered in a voice as pale as his face.

"Start you on the tea and toast first. I put some cinnamon in with the honey. Should kill every stubborn hold-out of a germ inside you."

The boy looked better than he had. A pale face was better than a white face, and he'd ceased to sweat rivers into the sheets two days ago.

Geoffrey reached out for the cup and looked relieved that he wasn't about to drop it. He sipped the lukewarm beverage gingerly, wincing between each sip as his mouth protested being used again.

Potier put his own cup to good use and for a few minutes there was no need to talk – never had been with the old devil. He had a suspicion that the boy found the quiet soothing. After his experience, small wonder.

And there was no point in saying anything. He'd missed the entire twelve days of Christmas in his illness, with only Potier for company. Potier didn't think his company was that good. His own sailors had pointed out he was a terrible man to be trapped with for more than a week. And missing Christmas also meant missing Martin's birthday. The boy had been born right on the edge of the holiday.

Potier had offered to shop, and Geoffrey consented painfully. It wasn't pleasant to have someone else do it for you.

"What shall Martin have then?" Potier asked as he went down the list.

Geoffrey finally stirred. "Nothing practical," he said sourly. "He wants a sheet of vellum. I'd ask the stationary shop for odd scraps so he could get a feel for his pen first."

"Well, of course," Potier nodded. "But you're his father. You don't have to give him anything you don't want to."

"I want to," was the faint answer. "He wants that apprenticeship so badly. It crushed him when Clea said to wait a few more years."

Potier nodded his understanding. They'd talked about everything once he was capable of it. "Mothers are like that. She'll change her mind once there's another one on the way."

"That's not likely," Geoffrey said flatly. "She and Nicholas nearly died at his birth."

Potier hesitated over his cup. "It was so close?"

"It was."

Potier pondered that without another word on his lips. His daughter Jeanne had borne too many children, it was true. Geoffrey had personally witnessed the strain on his mother. Despite it all, three Lestrades never survived to see adulthood.

23

Four dead children, four live ones.

Geoffrey was staring out the window, even though there were nothing to see in the icy courtyard but sleeping plants and a glazed stone walk. If being so very ill had done something for him, it had pushed him to a level of exhaustion his nightmares could not reach. His mind was finally resting but not his body.

"*Tad-kohz*, what were you going to tell me when you came?"

"I can't see my family because I want to?"

A sigh. "*Tad-kohz* . . . you wanted me to know you were coming, but you didn't want the letter to get to my house. You sent it to the Cheathams on purpose. And you aren't a letter-writer. You write Breton as badly as I speak it."

Potier snorted, and chuckled despite himself. "Right you are. Between the two of us, we'd make one literate Channel man." He set his cup down and poured more. "It's true I have news, but it can wait. It can wait until you're better off."

Geoffrey grunted. There was no point in pressing the old rascal ahead of time.

Potier straightened slowly. "I'm going to get a paper," he e announced. "And that vellum. Can you think of else you would need?"

"Nothing comes to mind," Jafrez said wearily. His eyes were closing again as the door clicked shut.

Charles Cheatham was utterly blind, had been so for years, but he stepped out of the cab with his usual grace, stick tapping firmly on the kerb to confirm its level. Aida took the signal and hopped down first. Her weight made the entire cab shudder and then rock on its springs. The old wrestler's sharp ears caught a muffled word of awe as the large dog poised for her master. The poor man had been paid extra for his time – and allowance of the dog. Usually they had to pay as if she was a human passenger – she took up about the same amount of space. In dog-years, she was also fast-approaching his age, and he felt a courtesy to her was a small price to pay for her willing loyalty.

Cheatham threw up the money toward the sound, earning another gasp of admiration, and he tried not to smile at the obviousness of the trick. Somewhere, an urchin clapped. "Chokehold Cheatham", he was still known by his professional trade, and Paddington Street saw him as another celebrity to enjoy. One of their own.

"'Allo, Charlemagne!" A most familiar voice sounded from far below his shoulder.

Triaged Potier beamed up at the man, knowing the blind man could sense he was looking up from the way his voice was pitched. "You're

24

looking well – not that many people can look worse than my grandson right now."

"Is he still poor-off?" Charles Cheatham wondered.

"Pulling out of it, I'm pleased to say. Come to visit, or bear news from the great outside?"

"Perhaps both . . . I'm afraid the news was mixed up again." Charles Cheatham admitted as he pulled a packet out from beneath his coat. "This was addressed to your grandson." He cleared his throat. "I also have a few things from the family."

"Ah, good. We can trade."

Potier frowned as he took the thick envelope, pushing the door open with his shoulder at the same time. A Plymouth address looked back at him. His heart fluttered at the thought of his daughter, but then stilled as he saw the sender had been another police Inspector. "I don't know if he can read this," he warned. "The lights still hurt his eyes."

"The messenger was *adamant* that the contents reach him," Charles Cheatham supplied as he leaned on his stick. His large body blocked most of the hall and what sunlight was trickling through.

Potier blew through his beard. "Very well. At least he's back on his feet . . . of a fashion."

"Of a fashion?" The old wrestler repeated as he followed the sounds of the smaller man's foot-falls up the stairs. Aida trotted jealously between them.

"He's out of bed, and he made it to his usual spot by the settee." Potier stopped talking and hefted the tray. China made a crinkling sound as it shifted and he opened the door. The smell of a fireplace mixed with a blend of light, sweet, and spicy plants caught Cheatham's nose. Clea's beloved plants. Lemongrass from the East. Lemon balm, a besom of cinnamon sticks, and a bush of rosemary.

"Allo, *mab*," Potier said cheerfully. "Time for another dose, and you have a visitor."

Lestrade had been dozing, half-drugged by his close proximity to the fireplace. Potier was one for believing in sweating an illness out of a person. The detective was beginning to think that his grandfather had cleaned out the market on white snakeroot. He was drinking close to a half-gallon of the weak brew every day, and it was all going straight out his skin.

"Who?" he asked slowly, blurred and feeling worn out from the sheer effort of skating along two days of consciousness – thin ice, indeed. He slowly took in the man-mountain filling the doorway, not to mention the over-sized dog that liked him without good reason. "Oh." He began the long process of sitting up. "Mr. Cheatham? Is something amiss?"

25

"All is well in Little Venice," the old wrestler assured him. "A missive was sent to my house in your name by mistake. I thought it simpler to bring it here."

Lestrade tried to peer at the inked lines but his head throbbed. "I'm sorry, the letters are blurring."

"I could try to read it," Potier offered. "This modern English isn't something I've ever had much practice with. I managed to do fine without it most my life."

His grandson snickered wearily. "Says the man who made his living in questionable means with ships, during a time when the English were supposed to be the greatest sea power."

Charles Cheatham chuckled softly, deeply amused. "I can help you if you can spell it out for me."

"Very well. Let's go to it." Potier fished for reading-glasses in his waistcoat-pocket and snapped the paper out flat. For a few moments he was stone-quiet, concentrating on the letters before him. "It is a man named Inspector Browning, Potier began carefully. "They are wondering if you would be free to serve as a . . . *translator*. With a case of murder in Plymouth at The Sea-Eagle Tavern . . . tomorrow at noon"

"A translator?" Lestrade's eyes opened up again – and just as quickly winced shut. "In Plymouth . . . ." He swallowed softly. "A translator in what language?"

"Brythonic," Potier said very softly. "I suppose they don't know the right word."

Lestrade reached for the water-glass and drank slowly. "They never do. It's like the difference between *Scotchman* and *Scotsman*." He swallowed painfully. "Is it any clearer than that?"

"Not in so many words . . . Mr. Browning adds something a bit queer, though, here at the bottom. He says that he hopes to renew your . . . oh, dear. *Acquaintance?*"

"Acquaintance."

"And that he has fond memories of your case together over the Joey Coiner's case."

"Joey Coiner?" Lestrade repeated. "I never worked with him on – " His lips clasped shut. "I see."

"I don't," Potier answered.

"This sounds like one of those little codes you and Clea are always passing back and forth," Charles noted.

"It is. Joey's slang for a tuppence kind of counterfeiting, and Coiner itself is street for making false money . . . But them together and . . . ." Lestrade closed his eyes, exhausted with the effort of thinking. "He's

26

warning me there's something wrong," he said at last. "More than meets the eye."

"Forgery sounds bad enough," Charles protested. "Is it another term then for a false face?"

"Counterfeiting can apply to a lot of different things. But this . . . a case of murder in Plymouth . . . needing a translator . . . ." Lestrade shook his head and was sorry he did. It made him hurt all over. "They could easily get the priest for that!"

"Most of the Twelve Families are still in Plymouth," Potier agreed with a dark flash of his dark eyes.

"*Still?*" Charles Cheatham asked with a deep chest-rumble. "I would think they would have escaped those terrible Quimpers."

"No," Potier said sadly. "The Glenan died out from lack of sons, but the others – the L'estrades, and Kerbers, the Kasts, Diders, Arzhurs, Germains, Gilberts, Baldwins, Bartholomews, Beneads . . . Well, you may as well just say the Donasians are gone. There's but the two of them left, and they are too old." He noticed a flinch from his grandson. "They all serve at the Damson Estates in some fashion."

"I doubt the L'estrades are doing so well themselves." Lestrade reached for something to smoke, and found his little tin case.

"I doubt they are either," Potier admitted. "There was just Marcus to carry on the name the last I checked." Another flinch. "You want to go, ya? We need to think of some way to get you there without killing you."

Charles Cheatham shook his head. "You have my sympathies," he said sincerely. "I foresee difficulties ahead for you."

Potier hesitated, and let himself breathe out. "I am afraid it is more difficult than that." He put the papers down and rubbed his eyes. "I should tell you why I've come."

"It's about the family, isn't it." The tone was too dull to be accusing.

"Your father is not well."

"That could mean different things."

"They don't know what he has. Perhaps cancer. Perhaps. He eats little. He drinks little more. There is no appetite and no strength."

The silence could not have been larger in the middle of the ocean.

"I could not tell you earlier, when you were so ill . . . and there was no possible change we could have made."

His grandson only rubbed his temples, not speaking.

Charles Cheatham cleared his throat. "I took this from under the Christmas-tree on my way out," he confessed. "I was going to take Clea's, but she said if you wanted your gift from herself, you would have to come up and get it in person."

Potier chuckled wickedly. "I like that girl."

Geoffrey shakily took the small box, surprised at its weight. He shook it once and something clopped within the confines. He shrugged and carefully prized open the wrapping. Someone had dyed ordinary twine a more festive dark green and stamped the butcher paper with simple block prints of six-sided snowflakes and red apples. "Who is this from?" He wondered. "There's no name."

"Your boys," Charles told him.

"They did this?"

"You must have been truly ill, Geoffrey. Otherwise I'm certain you would have heard the cook's screams of outrage when she caught them in the kitchen. They carved up her best potatoes to make ink-stamps, and Martin had made vegetable-dyes with the red cabbage, turmeric, and whatnot he could rig off the shelves . . . which, I might add, had been on the menu. When she finds out they robbed her best sprigs of dillweed to make miniature Christmas-trees in the homemade wrapping papers . . . well, there might not be much of a holiday spirit in the works." Charles Cheatham tried not to sound too proud of his grandson's shenanigans, but it leaked through his beard. Cheathams were naturally dissident by nature. London survived, barely.

To do him credit, Patterson was not interested in drinking. He ordered a beer and sipped on it as he studied his surroundings from under his eyelashes. When his wrists moved, the hints of appalling marks of violence peeked out from beneath his cuffs. Watson was a man of formidable will, but not noticing those ragged silver scars was a test of his determination.

"I never knew all of my informants," the detective confessed. "It was safer that way. I didn't want to betray anyone . . . and I didn't want them to betray me. Most of them thought Patterson was an alias . . . ." He smiled without any feeling whatsoever.

Watson waited patiently. He'd chosen a single slender glass of Bordeaux, and it would satisfy him until the single nightcap before bed.

"I didn't know him. The Wardrobe Man. I called his Louis. He said he was a ropewalker. I never checked him for marks, or the smell of tar . . . that was safer too. Mr. Holmes would scold me for that often . . . He said I needed to *see* and *observe* in equal amounts, but I was afraid of seeing too much. I don't know if I'm making any sense."

"You are," Watson said gently.

There had been a time when he knew only anger at the sound of Patterson's name. But Watson had not understood his own capacity for compassion until he realized the raid had been an error any man could made. Even Holmes, for all his brilliance, had tripped on that brilliance every once in a great while.

"He'd lost someone he loved to the gang. I knew that was the truth. He likely obfuscated all the other facts but . . . but he was reliable, Doctor. A reliable man and a good one. What I can't understand is . . . why would he be found dead with a pack of Colonel Hayter's cards in his pocket . . . and one of those cards would be addressed to you?"

Watson breathed slowly, taking a sip of his wine. He should have asked for bread to go with it. "On my last visit to the Colonel, I gave him one of my cards . . . it was a sort of a joke. The paper had been of a rather inexpensive sort, but it looked very pricey. Felt like it too."

"He was planning to return a bit of humour upon you?"

"I suppose. You should ask him to be certain."

Patterson looked down. "I want to find out who Louis really is . . . was. If I can do that . . . perhaps I'll find another link in the old remnants of the gang."

Watson pursed his lips. "How do you intend to do that?"

"I'm not certain. I'll need help."

Watson slid his fingers over the smooth glass. "You have it, sir."

Chapter II

"You're a little too quiet," Potier observed. For himself, Charles Cheatham said nothing. The old wrestler had gone into his "at-ready" stance, leaning his hands upon the knob of his stick with his back erect and blind eyes slitted half-shut.

Lestrade did not pretend otherwise. "I was thinking of the Donasians. There's only two left?"

"Last nephew lost in some skirmish for France somewhere." Potier shrugged wearily. "Why?"

"Oh, I suppose it's nothing."

"From you? *Mab*, you'd worry sand to nothing. There's something melancholy in your eyes right now."

"I was thinking of opportunities lost," Lestrade admitted. "Before I was sent to live with you . . . well . . . it wasn't much of a secret how the others felt about me."

Potier grunted.

"The Donasians offered to take me in. Raise me in place of the son they'd lost."

"Yes, I know. It wasn't long after you were born . . . ."

"No," his grandson said. "They offered again . . . before I was sent to live with you."

Potier swallowed. "That I did not know."

Why didn't they let them? Keeping the boy where he was plainly not wanted . . . that suited no one.

It was a raw confession to make, especially in front of one's own father in law. Potier wasn't certain he'd have that sort of nerve. He grimaced as his grandson slowly stood up under his own power and made his way to the window to peer out. His breath steamed on the glass, and Potier watched as he huddled within his dressing-gown.

Fevers were like furnaces. The heat their produced was high but demanding in fuel. The little box his sons had carved rolled back and forth in his palm. The soft *clop* noise from inside emanated with each turn.

"Are you going to open up their present?" Cheatham beautifully ignored the subject. In that moment, Potier felt his respect for his fellow grandfather grow. It meant something deep to the English society. It meant Charlemagne cared enough about his grandson to be solicitous.

It was a shame that Jafez was too battered by his closer kin to notice.

"I'm afraid I already know what it is . . ." was the obscure mutter. Finally, the boy returned to the settee and turned the wooden rectangle

30

over. Nicholas' work with a hot nail flattened to a chisel-point: Delicate burnings of the wood traced a light rope of vines and small birds that might be wrens or sparrows . . . it was a little difficult to tell with so many vines in the way.

"Well, don't keep us in suspense," Potier urged. "I want to see how clever my boys are."

That broke the ice. Geoffrey snorted while Cheatham chuckled in the same tones as the other grandfather. He thumbed the little sliding door open.

"Oh, bother!" Geoffrey blurted. "He didn't."

"I don't understand," Potier confessed. "The calligraphy is very fine – he made his *Tad* business cards, Charlemagne. Hand-lettered. A bit shaky on the downwards, but otherwise stands perfectly respectable."

"I just gave him these cards for his birthday," Lestrade grouched. "I didn't expect him to do this."

"Wait," Charles Cheatham broke in without warning. The blind man was tilting his head to one side, his better ear aimed to the window. "Someone's knocking," he reported.

"You could hear that?" Potier was impressed as he rose to his feet. He peered through the glass. "Ah, there's that newsboy. I was waiting for him to show up . . . ." He patted his pocket for money as he left the rooms for his way downstairs.

Two minutes later, he was wishing he was completely ignorant of the English language.

"What is it?" Charles could sense something was wrong, even if he couldn't see it.

Potier swallowed dryly. "Poor news," he whispered. "Give me a moment. I need to find a way to tell him."

"Thank you, dear."

Mary paused with the teapot to put a kiss upon her husband's brow. "Not at all. What do you think?"

"It is beyond description," John confessed. "I haven't had such a cup since I was in India. She grew the tea herself?"

"Mrs. Forrester always was an achieving sort of woman." Mary smiled proudly. "We plucked the new leaves ourselves."

"But new growth? And tea? They must be indoors somewhere."

"Very true." Mary was so glad to be back home she melted into her usual chair. Her feet thanked her within their constraints. "She has to rotate the bushes so they all get the same amount of sunlight by the windows."

"I never thought I'd be drinking fresh tea in England."

"Just you wait, John. She's plotting something to do with coffee too."

31

"That ought to be a test of her resources. So much effort for only one pound of coffee a year . . . ." John lifted his cup in a salute of respect to his wife's distant friend and former employer. "I would ask how your trip was, but it would seem anticlimactic after this."

Mary chuckled. "It was most restful." She reached for her sewing-basket and began layering "things to fix" into her lap like so many tablecloths. "And you? Have affairs died down?"

A flinch that crawled over every inch of her husband's expressive face was her answer. "It has not been boring, I assure you."

"No more blackguards and fiendish-looking ruffians?"

"Blackguards no, but your husband rather looked like the latter when he staggered out of Barts during the dawnshift. I don't think the human race was designed to be subterranean for very long."

"Do you enjoy working for the Yard?" Mary's voice was deep for a woman's and pleasing. It softened even the bluntest of her questions.

"It is more absorbing than I dreamed it would be," he confessed. "Life is strange, Mary. Strange beyond my imagining."

"How so?"

He shrugged with his good shoulder and rose, holding the precious cup in his hands as he moved to the fire. Mary watched as she sewed. It was second nature to her skills. John had watched his wife stitch neat seams while directing the Maid, debating the butcher's bill, and list the week's shopping budget off the top of her head without missing a single stroke of the needle.

"I never regretted taking the Queen's Shilling, you know," he said at last. "But I was young. There were so many things I did that . . . well, they were performed without much thought. Even when there might have been a time to regret it later. Of all the experiences I had in my life, I think I was only disappointed at Maiwand. Even then, it was not so much a disappointment in the Army . . . as it was in myself."

"However do you mean?" Mary asked.

"It was the first time in my life I'd ever dealt with a failure I could not accept." He sipped slowly, resting the cup within its small saucer. "I suppose I thought I was being clever, or adaptable. I always held that no disappointment was too great to endure. And I did endure being invalided out . . . but it was a bitter sensation. A bitter sensation." His mouth worked in a wry expression. "Is it not typical for a young man's arrogance to dwell on being dismissed from his regiment instead of being thankful for his life?"

Mary smiled as she glanced down to her needle. "As you said, you were a young man."

"It did teach me, though," he said softly, mostly to himself. "I didn't know it at the time . . . but it did teach me."

Mary thought about it. There were not many secrets between them. She knew her husband had faced many disappointments in his relatively short life: Loss of his parents, slow and painful loss of his only brother, his last close relative. The consecutive loss of the family's small property from that brother's dissolution. But he had faith in himself and faith in rightness. That had carried him through many griefs.

Losing Mr. Holmes had been on par with the loss of his health. It was no exaggeration to Mary's mind that Holmes had been like an extension of her husband – a portion of his being that was permitted free reign. The poor man had been brilliant as a diamond, but heedless of his personal safety. In watching out for him as a friend ought, John had been able to channel that sense of importance he'd learned for himself in the Army.

And then he had married.

Mary did not regret having a husband who was so firmly devoted to his wife. Nor had she felt Mr. Holmes had resented his withdrawal from Baker Street. He had simply . . . eased himself out of their lives, so gradually the couple had not been fully aware of it.

She remembered so well the day he'd emerged before the wedding with a wrapped box.

John had nearly had a fit at the sight. "Holmes, you needn't – I told you!"

"When have I ever done something I needn't?" The patrician brow had lowered with all the poise of a stern schoolmaster. "I do this because I wish to, my good Watson."

John sputtered helplessly. "Holmes, for Heaven's sakes, I told you anything you would give us would be . . . superfluous! You already gave us everything we could ask for when you brought us together!"

And a wicked, most mischievous gleam had sounded in those clear grey eyes. "Dear me, Watson. That was only the first gift. And I thought I was doing so well with breaking out of that 'emotionless machine' mold you've described . . . ."

John tried to fume around his growing smile, but it was difficult. In the end he had accepted the box – a small woman's watch that matched John's in every style.

"Aren't you glad now you failed to deprive your good wife?" Mr. Holmes had asked with an almost innocent expression.

Not knowing Mary was standing behind him in the hallway with Mrs. Forrester, John's response had been rather abrupt. The women still laughed at the memory.

The first gift . . . .

His silent and undemonstrative blessings upon the Watsons had been his *ongoing gift.*

He never tried to compete with her in John's heart. He was assured of his standing with her husband. Assured enough that he never questioned it.

And she had returned that favour as often as possible. When the strain of his mundane cases and the fog of London threatened to pull him down, she could see how his eyes would light at the hope of a case. She would have him go without complaint. Urged him for his own sake, and the paleness of his face. To bring that light back into his eyes was reward enough.

Mr. Holmes had answered those little moments of generosity on her part. He had slid the danger away from her husband, and at the very end, tricked him to spare him his own fate.

His last gift.

And like his first gift . . . one that continued to give.

John would finish his tea, go up to the nursery, and hold his son a moment before heading to bed. Mr. Holmes's gift.

Mary would always be grateful for the man who only told the truth when he said he was not ruled by emotions. A more emotional man would have been more selfish.

"Ha!" John exclaimed with a blend of relief and joy. "There it is!" The door-bell had just rang.

Mary didn't know what he was so excited about, but there was no need to stop the stitching while she waited for enlightenment. Soon enough, John returned, a copy of the evening paper in his hand.

"Dear, I sold my latest to *The Gazette*! Can you guess which it was?"

Mary cast he mind frantically while her husband paged through frantically. "Was it another adventure?" she guessed.

"No, nothing so predictable! It was for the artifacts found upon the St. Mary's Chapel!" John beamed with his face flushing as she watched. "Wait until you read it! I spent ages on the researching notes! It – " Something caught his eye and Mary saw his face drain of healthy colour. His eyes grew large, as if he was having difficulty believing the evidence before his eyes.

"John . . . ." Mary felt herself rise, and she was suddenly, instinctively afraid of calling him "James" at this moment. "Whatever is the matter?"

"I didn't know . . . ," he was murmuring. "I didn't know this was happening . . . ." Shaken, he lifted the sheets of newsprint up. With a sinking feeling in her breast-bone, she took in the lines of black print.

Inspector Gregson was lighting a cigar in the hopes the ritual would help him think. At the very least he would be calmer – a man took what he could get without complaint. In the cold privacy of his office, his neat, clean space was reflective of his personal goals: Take what was messy, and clean it up to the point that it made sense.

The bluff, white-faced man felt better soon after he had drawn the tobacco in. It was expensive weed. A gift from his own Louise in the hopes she could sway his tastes to something less foul than his chosen brand. Gregson felt guilty about that in a small, unclear way. Louise was extremely sensitive to strong odors, having a nose a perfumer would envy . . . but the foul bitter tobacco of his childhood was one of his few fond addictions and a memory of his past.

Louise did know why he preferred the worst brands in London. She never complained to him, but there were nights when he deserved it. He tried not to smoke in her presence as an apology. Hard enough to have a sensitive nose and live in London.

A soft tap – one knuckle against the wood of his door – and Gregson pulled the cigar out of his mouth. "Come in," he said gruffly. Had to be Hopkins. Subtle and to the point. That was the boy.

Boy. He's no boy. Done more with his years than any of my *family at that age. He was born old . . . .*

Hopkins poked his head around the doorway for a moment before stepping inside, shutting the door after him.

"Sorry to bother you," he murmured. "I came to tell you . . . ." Hopkins held Gregson's eyes wearily. "You were right on the money. Bow Street's up on charges for leading the labour strike."

Gregson groaned around his flavoured smoke. "Bradstreet?"

"He wasn't in the mess." Hopkins gnawed on his lip, looking too old for his years. "He was off researching and nowhere near the strike when it happened."

"I suppose that's good news," Gregson muttered, but sourly. "Well. Not like it's the first time the Runners went on strike, is it?"

"I suppose it's no longer guessing." Hopkins leaned his back against the wall and toyed with the engagement ring on his finger. "Want to bet that's why he's been pulling away from us?"

"Wouldn't take that bet for season tickets," Gregson sniffed. "Bradstreet's smarter than Lestrade – barely – but he isn't smarter in a lot of things." Angry now, he stubbed out his cigar to cold ash. "Fool thought he was protecting us by keeping us ignorant. I'll show him what ignorant means . . . Bloomin' fool! Barking mad blooming fool . . . ."

"It doesn't matter," Hopkins protested wearily. "He wasn't in the strike, so he won't be charged with the strikers."

"Unless they think to ask him if he knew anything about it," Gregson spat. "He's too honest to direct the truth, Hopkins. And he's too stupid to understand that the prosecutors will be looking for signs of *dissent*, not *proof*. They'll ask him if he knew about the strike, and the fool will say yes to protect his honour, and there go his little'uns without a means to be fed."

Hopkins caught the irony that the childless Gregson was angry on behalf of the Bradstreet children. He was smart. Smarter than most, and smart enough not to say anything about it.

The big man suddenly growled under his breath and put his head into his hands.

"Lord," Gregson quoted the motto of the *Punch* magazine, "'What fools these mortals be.'"

Chapter III – History Repeats

Charles Cheatham no longer missed the use of his eyes. If he had lost one input, he had gained more of an understanding in his senses than most people. At the same time, he had a rare advantage against his fellow man, for to the casual opponent "blind" was as good as crippled.

The Cheathams had once been staunch Celts. The blind had never been useless among those fiery folk. Their blood and identity was diluted into the Normans and the homogeny of the Industrial Revolution . . . but there was still some stubborn spark of their old ways left.

He listened to the description as Potier read it off the print in his halting English. His ear was amused at the unconscious similarities between the old smuggler and his staunchly law-abiding grandson. The content of the newspaper was much less amusing.

"Inspector Bradstreet is one of Geoffrey's oldest friends," he said at last. "Hazel was the first friend my daughter had outside the family once we moved here."

"I know how this works." Potier rolled the paper up in his hands. Charles could "see" the little man in his mind, spry as a cricket, pacing back and forth in the bottom of the stairwell. "*This* is why they pulled away. *This* is why Jafrez has been wondering if he'd done something wrong . . . Why *Brodstreet* didn't come to visit or send a note after the quarantine . . . ."

"How bad do you think it is?"

Potier stopped for a moment. The silence grew thick as the damp in a spring day.

"They weren't on strike out of a sense of mischief," he said at last (Cheatham sensed the smuggler was in a quandary. "Not the Runners. Even we knew about them. Good, hard-working men just like the rest of the policemen. Fewer scandals . . . They've been around longer . . . I suppose that makes them more of a threat. People follow who look up to." He sighed. "They were probably trying to just get a little bit of money to live off . . . Times are hard."

"Yes, I know . . ." Charles Cheatham said calmly. "As I recall, many policemen have been in this difficulty."

"At least *they're* no longer in debt," Potier muttered.

"Who?" Charles asked sharply. "Who do you mean?"

Potier held his silence for a bald minute. "It's in the past, Charlemagne. Jafrez had to work a little extra to pay for Nicholas' birth. That's all."

37

The old wrestler took in what he was hearing, plus the inflictions. There was more to it than what was being said, but Potier was asking him to let it be. His hands rubbed over the knob of his stick. "Well, what now?"

"I'll tell him," Potier answered simply. "Not else I can do . . . and then help him pack for Plymouth – Well, I'll pack. He can rest while I'm packing for him."

"You're so certain he's up for the trip?" Charles' ear had caught the laboured breathing of his daughter's husband from the start of his visit.

"He'll breathe better in Plymouth than he will here," Potier said with the finality of an old patriarch. "And he can see well enough if he isn't trying to read. So long as we keep to that . . . Well, we should be operative."

"You'll be going with him then." Charles was relieved.

"Of course. I have much to do before they put me in an unmarked grave . . . ."

John had not examined his motives in bringing Patterson over to his practice for a cup of tea. It was more a sense or instinct than anything else.

He knew he had been right by the way the man looked about him in the foyer. The starved-looking eyes darted about in that lean face, settling on the strangest objects: A nosegay of Mary's flowers. A small wooden rattle given him by one of the Yarders. Even the pattern of blackwork on a lace doily took Patterson's attention.

Mary descended from the first floor with Arthur in her arms. The Queen of her domicile, she was hardly timid.

"You're perfectly on time, dear," she smiled. "I have a marvelous pot of Oswego brewed up. Shall it ward off the weather I see on your shoulders?"

John ruefully smiled at the thin seeps of cold evaporating off his good wool coat. "Mary, I wonder that you haven't been recruited for the spiritualists. You are positively uncanny." In the presence of a guest, the kiss was only on the cheek as he put his hat upon the rack.

"I just cleaned out your office, so I trust the orange-fumes aren't a trial." Mary shifted Arthur to one side. "There's hot bread and new butter. One of your guests brought over a conserve of nuts."

"You are determined to take out my waist." John took Patterson's coat off his shoulders. "Mary, this is Inspector Patterson. We'll be making use of that freshly renewed office."

"Good evening, Mrs. Watson." Patterson said awkwardly.

"Good- evening to you, Mr. Patterson. Do you fancy a nut conserve? Or would you care for strawberries with your bread?"

"I . . . the nuts would be fine, Mrs. Watson . . . ." Patterson went from awkward to stammering.

The Old Mews:

"Good Lord, Stanley." Gregson had no recourse but to shake his head with a sad expression. "Can't you do better than that?"

"You . . . ." Hopkins was no gull. He gnashed his teeth and narrowed his eyes. "Hitting the target on the seventh try isn't a bad odd, Tobias. Considering I've never mistaken a bloomin' truncheon for a bloomin' atlatl before."

"*Manners*. Where do you young folk learn them?" Gregson ambled slowly over to the painted square of soft pine and bent, joints popping, to pick up the truncheon in question. Before long their little forays into the backways of London would be impractical. With softening weather came powerful odours and an atmosphere that was less-than-healthy for a policeman.

Until then . . . gossipers were unlikely to spread rumours about two daft coppers playing a game of target with their truncheons.

"What are you going to do when the target is running, Inspector? And chances are, it'll be running away from you."

"I would hope," Hopkins agreed sourly. "They can hardly be shooting at me while they're running away."

Gregson laughed so hard his eyes burned. "Let's take a breath," he advised.

Hopkins found a fairly clean spot on a bench that had begun its days as several fruit-crates. Gregson rolled himself an awful smoke before joining him.

"On your feet all day, Hopkins, will just finish what began to your feet back when you were in those Constable crabshells."

"Well, just you try chasing down retired members of the Burial Board when they're the only ones alive to remember all those little details you need!"

"Lord, have mercy on us all." Gregson struck his match on the side of his calloused hand. "You had to go through the Burial Board? I am so sorry."

"They aren't all that bad, and I'm glad they're there . . . but I don't envy them their work."

"Nor would any of us." Gregson smoked a bit more in silence. A flock of sparrows took off from under the high eaves of the abandoned stables. "You're no use to any of us if you go Lestrade's route."

"Well . . . ." Hopkins made a grumbling sound under his breath and did not look at the older man. "Not sure practice in the Old Mews would be any better . . . ."

Gregson smiled from the other side of a thick cloud of smoke. Hopkins imagined mosquitoes dropping dead from a yard's length.

Unbelievably, Gregson saw something through the wall of tobacco. His face froze in the most open expression of surprise Hopkins had seen in months. The younger man turned around just in time to see Bradstreet coming slowly up.

"Hello, gentlemen." Bradstreet's voice was hoarse, as if unused . . . or . . . overstrained. As he came closer the light fog swirled away from his face, showing a haggard ghost of a man. "I thought I'd check out the territory before I paid Lestrade my respects."

Gregson was a moment finding his voice. "He's . . . doing much better." The bluff man coughed. "That old reprobate is taking care of him."

Bradstreet blinked and the tiniest smile echoed over his thick moustache. "And you approve of that scalawag taking care of one of our men?"

"Why not? If he's caught up in that, we know where he is and how much trouble he isn't getting into. A man like that, I prefer to have his whereabouts before I lock up my silver."

"I thought that was pewter," Hopkins said not-so-subtly under his breath, and got a friendly fist below the ribs for his cleverness.

Bradstreet's smile grew a bit more, but it was incapable of crossing a certain point. "I'll be sure to see him then." He sighed like a very old man and pulled off his hat, letting the dirty air cool his face. "I owe him quite a long apology."

"I don't think he grudges you your leaving while he was possibly contagious . . . ."

"Rubbish." Bradstreet snapped. "Pure rubbish, Gregson. You know what I mean." With a hard look he turned back on his heel and walked out the way he came in, firmly jamming his bowler back to two inches above his browline.

"Well, I don't know what you meant," Hopkins said frankly. "Must be one of those 'Before your time, pup' moments."

"You are a good detective," Gregson praised in that infuriating manner that no one else could equal. Lestrade might be the terror of the Yard for his rare volcanic explosions, and PC Murcher was a legend for his berserker skills in a raid, but Gregson was the man everyone feared just a bit. His cold analysis could pick you apart and hold you out to dry in the air before you even knew what was happening.

Hopkins got to his feet and went for his truncheon again. He loosened his throwing-arms back and forth in silence while Gregson smoked.

"Aren't you going to ask me for details, Hopkins?"

"Why should I?" Hopkins wanted to know. "I imagine there's enough people I can trust to ask."

"Bloomin' Hell . . . ." Gregson sounded like a mule just after small boys blew pepper up its nose. "It goes back too many years for most of those fools to even know why Lestrade's a pariah."

"Rather a strong word, isn't it, Gregson?" Hopkins ignored him as he continued his practice.

Gregson made that mule-sound again. "Strong I doubt. Know anything about the scandals of '77?"

"Corruption scandal. Yes. Cleaned out a bunch of rats. Caused a fuss." Hopkins threw Gregson's truncheon first. It sailed end over end and struck the target above the bull's eye but by the long side of the weapon. He groaned to himself.

"Ask yourself how they were caught in the proof of their scandal, Gregson."

Hopkins had just thrown his truncheon. It went wild and into a pile of muck behind a broken wagon that was too rotten to even be burnt by the hard-ups. He turned to stare at Gregson.

"You're saying *Lestrade*? That wasn't in any of the reports we read."

"Wouldn't be either. But somebody had to pretend to be the gull . . . and he fit their bill neat enough that he was the one who got all the evidence on 'em." Gregson frowned. "He did the right thing, but it was rough going for a while . . . By then, Bradstreet was the only friend he had. Cooper'd already been killed . . . ." Gregson's calm, callous gaze factored all the murky knots of human emotion and tragedy without hesitation or even compassion. "I would imagine Bradstreet now knows what it feels like to be the one on the outside. And he's probably wondering if he'd been enough of a friend to Lestrade back then."

"I *know* you have a pea-jacket around here, *mab*!"

Lestrade had been roused out of another drug-inspired doze to find his father-in-law gone with the just-as-large dog. As usual, the absence of a Cheatham made his small rooms feel spacious. Banging and wooden thumps along with a chatter of vocabulary that somehow belied the myth that Bretons were an insular race filled the walls.

"What in the world did you just say?" Geoffrey demanded as he leaned his body into the doorway. (It was propping him up. Clea could scold him about the hair-cream on the wood later.) "And what does it have to do with a salt-panner's chewing tobacco?"

41

Old Potier sniffed. "If you don't know, then we still need to work on your language, boy."

"I'm not so sure. Bear in mind I try to use a little bit of it around the wife and children."

Potier giggled. That was, going by previous experience, a bad sign. "So where's that pea-jacket?"

"What would we need a pea-jacket for?" Lestrade wasn't going to help – not just yet. He caught a yawn and felt his jaws crack. Watson would kill him if he found him out of bed and on his feet. "We're not heading off to the Channels again – for which I am thankful."

"No, but you never know with Plymouth. People do cross the Channel from there."

Lestrade growled something. "Grandfather, if you knew what I had to pay so I'd have a good winter pea-jacket tailored so that it would actually let me lift my arms over my head . . . ."

"Well, good for you. What is the problem?"

"The *problem* is, I usually ruin whatever coat I'm wearing if I'm around you!" Lestrade crossed the room and wearily began returning the scattered clothing from the floor to back in the wardrobe, dresser, chest, and laundry-rack.

"Oh, you'd rather be well-dressed and dead?"

"Well-dressed and alive is better . . . ." Lestrade felt dizzy after re-folding a loose indoors-coat and sat down on the edge of the guest-bed. "You're lucky I'm feeling better," he warned. "In fact, I feel too glad to be alive to fight you on this."

"Just tell me where the jacket is, and I'll leave you be."

"Somehow I doubt that . . . ." Lestrade slowly knelt and yanked out a wooden box on runners. "Here it is. When are we leaving?"

"As soon as I send my friends a wire . . . ."

"Lord, don't tell me you have friends over *there*." Lestrade decided he might as well help. Clea might overlook a smear on the door, but she wouldn't forgive a shambled wardrobe. Potier was so busy thinking of the troubles ahead he couldn't be expected to concentrate on cleaning up after himself.

Chapter IV – Searching

Mary woke to Arthur's sleepy chirps. Still smothering a yawn, she saw to the start of the baby's morning and had him dressed for the day before taking him down the stairs. John's empty space in the bed (long vacated some hours after midnight) spoke of another troubled bout.

He would work his way through it. He always did. Mary had suspected the closer they drew to the anniversary of Mr. Holmes's death, the more difficult it would be.

She pondered it all as Theresa buttoned up her dress from the back, absently thanking the girl. There were times when she wished to be as bold as Mrs. Lestrade. Practicality had the little woman use the more scandalous front-buttons, but she hid them from the public scorn by wearing a pullover-sort of apron that belted in the back. A lady wasn't expected to sacrifice respectability for independence.

Mary held Arthur in relief when it was done. Below them her small garden was bathed in slowly melting ice. Why must everything in this be so *atypically* hard for John? That was a question she wanted answered. It wasn't as though it weren't difficult enough with losing one's best friend off the Falls.

John hadn't told her everything. He hadn't needed to. Mary was an intelligent woman, and she liked to think.

The Reichenbach had seen many victims, mostly suicides. The gendarmes were accustomed to dealing with another human life taken in the force. The Falls were horrific, but the water below was a fairly small pool and an even smaller channel. A cascade that ferried water to the lower elevations of Switzerland. It was predictable in its moods.

Normally.

Why did the Professor stage his attack upon Mr. Holmes in the wake of one of the worst rains in Switzerland's recent history? Why did he pick the day when the cataract was swollen past the point of reason – where one could hear, John said, boulders rolling down the mountain?

The next day the water had been close enough to normal that her husband had gone in it, searching for Mr. Holmes remains. His failure still weighed on him, and Mary understood. The sanctity of the dead was a deeply personal issue for John. In his mind, it was only right to bring his friend home.

John spoke rarely of his experience in the military when it came to the massacre, or to death itself. He kept his anecdotes to the quiet, fond sort of respectful recollection that gave the Berkshires and Northumbrians the obeisance they deserved.

But once . . . he had let something slip.

"A man may travel all his life, but he ought to have the right to return home."

There was something about his work at the Yard that was touching close to the past. Mary studied the slow drip of sooty ice upon her alpine strawberries as she thought. It was touching on the problem with the Colonel . . . and also . . . something deeper.

Plymouth:

The Sea-Eagle looked (and smelled) about as reputable as Lambeth real estate in the height of flood season. Lestrade muttered something under his breath that Potier caught with a smile.

"Fond memories, *mab*?"

"If you can call it that . . . I believe that was the first tavern I was ever thrown out of."

"*You*? What the devil were you doing?"

"I have no idea. It was a hundred years ago . . . ."

Potier let his battered travel-bag down on the floor under the table and put himself down with the same lack of grace. "You're looking much better," he said critically. "Getting out of London was a good idea for you."

"So it's mentally healthy to find another crisis?" Lestrade asked skeptically. "When the old one gets stale?"

Potier grinned ferociously. Lestrade had seen that exact same look stare down an obelisk of a Cornishman in a bar even worse than this one back in his childhood. "So what does this Browning look like?"

"Well . . . like . . . *that*." Lestrade peered through the crowd and suddenly nodded.

Ordinary Norman, was Potier's first impression. The man was average height with the weak chin and strong forehead the old smuggler associated with the Normans, and a slight slump to one shoulder that looked like an old injury. His blue-green left eye blinked often in the cigar-smoke of the tavern, and he moved with his poor shoulder pointed first like a wedge through the people.

The eyepatch made him stand out a bit, but Potier reasoned it was because he chose policeman's blue instead of the traditional black.

"Browning, it's good to see you." Lestrade stood slightly as the newcomer bent to shake hands, and then all three of them were seated

44

around the table. Potier signaled for some of the blackberry ale the chalk-board was advertising with such confidence.

"As you, Lestrade. What's it been . . . how many years since the Riot?"

Lestrade's lips twitched. "About five-and-twenty . . . Long enough . . . allow me to introduce my grandfather, Triaged Potier."

"Hello, Mr. Potier." Without turning a single hair, blinking, or blanching, Browning shook his hand over the table-top. Potier decided he liked the man. Anyone who could ignore the infamous name of The Seagull was someone he wanted to know. "Pleased to meet you. I've known your grandson since the milk-years of '66."

"Nothing milky about the Hyde Park Riot," Lestrade grunted. "You were lucky you only lost one eye."

"That's why I have a spare." Browning grinned saucily. "And it's just as good as the old one." He pointed to the eyepatch, which Potier could now see had been cut from a blue policeman's coat. "But I'm not always frivolous. I have a fancy patch I wear on formal occasions. Mrs. Browning stitched the Guelphic Badge in gold thread in it for me so everyone knows I'm on duty."

Potier definitely wanted to get to know the man better now. He had the mental image of Browning trading jokes with Charles Cheatham on the subject of eyes.

"Haven't seen you much since the Riot, Lamps," Browning confessed. "Sorry for that. But something came up and I had the instinct you should know about it."

"Go on."

Browning took a deep breath. "Your father's going to be charged with murdering Mr. Ivo Quimper."

Lestrade suddenly knew what it was like for his brother Paul to live colourblind.

John said his goodbyes to his last morning patient and gratefully turned his back on the world of preventative measures against septic infection and sewer-gas poisoning. His notes from Hopkins' burial case could now – and now at last – take his undivided attention.

What a relief it is, he thought, *to be able to simply sit and absorb quiet information in peace.*

Or as quiet as such ghoulish information could be . . . He looked ruefully at the crooked furrows of three different detectives' hands crawling up the margins like so many strangling vines and wondered if Gregson's would improve with a stiff drink. *Education is no guarantee to penmanship* . . . Not for the first time, John wondered at the incongruity of how the extremely intelligent and well-schooled so often had a handwriting that would have gotten them expelled from their first classes.

Perhaps it was the fear of making a simple error and being understood? It would certainly embarrass their families . . . John supposed an execrable style was a way of avoiding the whole "*I* before *E*" rule if the "*I*" looked like an "*E*" . . . .

Enough of the nonsense. Time to start with the problem. He sharpened his pencil on the little knife kept by his inkwell and began taking notes. Patterson had been right to call upon the abnormality of the Wardrobe Man's hands. They weren't quite like anything he could remember seeing before, but over the course of the night Watson had let his mind percolate on the issue. It was a trick of his, to never completely put a problem from his mind. He'd always felt that if it was a matter of remembering something, it would surface eventually.

Tannic stains . . . but nothing that one would find from a tannery.

Hands weren't stained like a peat-cutter's hands were either . . . nor were they adorned with a bog-cutter's scars and callus . . .

Still . . .

Still and still . . .

He was just barely missing something . . .

John drummed with his fingertips on the blotting-paper, an absent staccato that would have reminded his friends of a military drill. Something small . . . the most minute detail . . . it all hinged on the tiny missing datum.

"It's fishy." Browning said under his breath. "Fishy as a flounder."

Lestrade remembered too late that the man was in possession of the worst metaphors north of Piccadilly Circus, but the alliterations almost justified being forced to listen to him. He nodded. "Perhaps you should tell me in your own words? I can always read the report later."

"I don't know about that." Browning said tightly. "You may not want to read the report and just stay . . . ignorant."

Lestrade stared at him. Ice prickled up his spine. "Keep going," he said at last.

Browning looked both ways before sinking further into his collar. "This is how it goes." He tugged at his necktie in reflex. "Murder site, couldn't be plainer. Dead as dead, is the Lord of ye old manor, understand?" At Lestrade's nod he continued. "Servant guilty as sin. Pool of blood, his footprints in the blood, blood on his hand . . . scrape on his right hand like he'd picked up the weapon – "

"What was the weapon?"

"Baroque candlestick. Awful thing. Sharp bits everywhere. Nick on the skin here – " Browning showed the webbing between the thumb and forefinger. " – like he'd squeezed it up and then hung on to do the deed." Browning met his gaze. "The old man, he beat him off a good one before he was finished."

Lestrade swallowed hard. "What part of this is fishy?" he asked hoarsely.

"The Foreign Office has picked it up."

Lestrade heard his own swallow click loudly in his throat. Potier set himself back with a soundless whistle of suspicion.

"The Foreign Office wouldn't *care* about a rich landowner in Plymouth getting murdered!"

"That's so . . . So why would they be interested?" Browning pursed his mouth. "Everyone knows the Quimpers were into all sorts of nice things . . . and the son worst of all. But still . . . you had Ivo. No matter what name he went by, he was still Ivo Quimper." Browning sipped his drink slowly. "There's talk of war with France again. I don't think there's that much to it, I've got family over here. The Foreign Office decided that Plymouth is a place to eye because 'sa leading port that was between England and France, and Quimper's keeping of French servants . . . ." He gracefully ignored the outraged snorts at the table. "Add to the fact that the Bretons aggressively supported France during the war with the Prussians – "

"For which we were amply rewarded," Potier said icily. "I lost all but three of my cousins when the French sent us to the front lines and deserted us. I lost their fathers, my uncles, and twenty of my neighbors' sons, youngster. *Twenty.*"

"The Foreign Office believes what it chooses," Lestrade pointed out. "Bretons aren't trusted by English or French. Why should that change?"

Poiter growled and drowned it in his drink. "So what do you think is happening?"

"There's some sort of political tie with this family that has the Foreign Office concerned." Browning spoke with a finality that sank like a stone about the table. "Whenever there's a threat of war with England . . . Well, you've seen it."

"I've seen it," Lestrade agreed softly. "So to all appearances, my father had cause to murder Ivo Quimper?"

"Thomas Lestrade wouldn't kill a grass snake," Potier sniffed.

"Like I said, it's fishy," Browning said seriously. "And making it all worse is the fact that he is either unable or unwilling to speak English. The local police aren't happy about letting any of the relatives in to speak as a translator, but you'd be another matter."

Lestrade flinched. His father could speak English. But he had never been more than diffident in his use of anything but the language he was raised in. He wouldn't even unbend enough to speak to his English-raised son. Perhaps it gave him some protection from unwanted attention.

"Would anyone criticize Jafrez for performing the duty?" Potier hit it right across the yardarms. "He *is* his son."

"Not anymore." Browning spoke with chilling honesty. "Perhaps in extenuating circumstances, but everyone knows he's a dead man to his family. Your grandson has proven himself as someone who'd choose duty over everything else . . . every time."

The compliment, such as it was, gave no particular sense of warmth. If anything, it made Geoffrey wonder yet again how his wife's family could even tolerate him.

"First thing's first." Lestrade cleared his throat and pushed his drink aside. "I'll be the translator . . . but I want more than that. I want to see the location of the crime with my own eyes. I want to see the murder weapon, and I want to hear the testimony of everyone involved."

"That's risky," Browning protested. "You'll be threatening your reputation as a professional."

"I don't think so. Tell them I need to line up what I'm being told with the facts as I see them. Part of the translation process. Remind them that there are four base languages, major dialects, and about twelve provincial differences in the language. Remind them if you must that it's been over twenty years since I was very conversant in the way Thomas Lestrade speaks."

"I'll try it." Browning looked a little happier. "Perhaps it shan't be too hard. All I have to do is say 'Celtic language' and you just look at the eyes glass over."

"Why not?" Potier sneered into his glass. The ale rippled from his breath. "People've been complaining about Celtic languages since Caesar's time."

London:

Mary pressed the study-door open to balance the tea-tray in her hands. She was just in time to see her husband leap to his feet as if a match had lit under his shoe.

"Mary!" He exclaimed as he only now noticed it was tea-time. "Where is the old address book?"

"I . . . well . . . ." Flustered for a moment, she had to think. "I believe I put it in the book-case under the Directory."

48

"Thank you!" With a spring that heavily favoured his better leg, John ripped open the door, rattling the glass in its housing, and thumbed down a stack until he yanked out a much-deteriorated journal. "There it is!" Without pausing to explain what "it" was, he flipped through the pages until he was past the half-way mark, and then slowed down, frowning in his haste as he searched.

Mary silently set out the tea and waited.

"Peat," John was muttering. "Not peat cutters. Peat *excavators*. Difference in marks. Similar stains. Ketoids shifted further down for the delicate work . . . excavating . . . excavators . . . experts . . . ."

Mary wordlessly set John's plate with sandwiches and a boiled egg.

"I might have known!" John exclaimed. "I might have known! If that isn't a mark to the smallness of the world!"

"John, would you like some dill with your egg?"

"Eh?" John looked up and blinked, confused as a frog under a lantern. As if remembering what country he was in, he glanced about. "Oh. I'm so sorry," he apologized.

"Not at all. You'll have time to eat before you send out your telegram to whoever it is you've found in that book." Mary delicately poured the tea in their cups as she spoke. John excited was a John renewed. He had found something, and he would pursue it with all the natural ease of a soldier given a foe to battle. "The errand-boy comes in twenty-five minutes, and that should allow you your tea."

Bright-eyed, John took his place and took a discourteous gulp of his tea. "An old acquaintance may be coming to visit us soon, my dear. I daresay you'll enjoy the experience. He's harmless enough, but a brilliant sort, and just the sort of expert we need on this case."

"An old acquaintance?" Mary's eyes sparkled. "Would it be from one of the adventures?"

"Yes."

"Is it an adventure you have written up?"

"Yes."

"Hmm . . . is it an adventure that is published?"

" . . . .No. No . . . it is not published yet. I'm rather waiting for . . . a few loose ends to knot themselves up first."

Mary stroked her delicate chin as she thought. "Have I read this adventure?"

"Yes . . . ." John was smiling for all he was worth as Mary parsed the question down.

"Hmm . . . Dear me, John. There are still so many possibilities . . . How many years ago did the Adventure occur? No, wait. That would be too revealing. Perhaps if you quoted me a memorable line from your friend's lips?"

John set his cup down to prevent spilling what was left. He was shaking with the effort of not laughing. "Very well . . . I shall quote something he said . . . something that was almost the first thing that crossed his lips when he first set eyes upon Holmes." John collected his composure for a moment and took a deep breath. Mary was all a-tenterhook.

"'I covet your *skull*!'"

Chapter V – Hungary

Another illness. Simple exhaustion from running the trains and an obvious lack of resistance to the belching factories of Eastern Europe.

He would stay here, at least for a while. Buda-Pesth was not a place where a man could hide in plain sight – there *was* no plain sight. A juggler may well hide in a carnivale.

At least, that had been his belief before he stepped down from the train onto a platform to find Cholera had come to visit before him.

There were disadvantages . . . strong disadvantages . . . to running so swiftly that he had no time to investigate the lay of the land before he came to it.

And yet . . . it was a price to pay. A statistically small price . . . If he did not know where he was going, then neither would his enemies.

So he went to ground in Buda-Pesth, a city split by the Danube and who wore a name that meant, so provincially, "District-County". He'd been struck by the strange contradictions – strange to his mind at least – that a river could split more than a city. It split a people into two very different minds and populations.

The Thames had united its people, not divided them. It was dirty, filled with brine with the tides, murdered people in its cold grip, and caught corpses on a daily basis. And yet it would *never* occur to an Englishman not to love the Thames. The dredgers pulled up filth and crime and relics of human sacrifice from thousands of years in the past . . . a dark legacy for a dark river . . . but it was not a river to judge or condemn. The Thames resonated somewhere inside the English soul, went as deep as bone, and if the Thames ran salty, well, so did the blood in the Englishman's veins.

Here he rested on the side of Buda. The "older side" where the Monarchs of Hungary resided as well. It was a peculiar paradox to Holmes that Pesth was the side of the government and the rising industrial class. Such a separation was hardly bound to assist in communications and foster good feelings.

He shook his head as he pulled the simmering tea-pot off the fire. When Cholera ran, one boiled everything . . . even the milk. He had no troubles with taking his meals in the form of endless cups of black tea and even blacker coffee that was, in the words of the Persian dealer beneath him, "strong as death, black as hate, sweet as love."

He could easily reside on liquids while he was here, and ignore the more dangerous if tempting foods. Strong vinegary dishes were served up to stave off the disease. Blackberry cordials and desserts postponed as well as prevented the deadly effects. Elder-flowers were served in teas and washes while men and women boiled endless kettles, pots, pans, and utensils every day.

Pesth . . . he should have taken his rooms there. It would have been more comfortable for his peace of mind. He would have hidden himself in that bustle, which reminded him more of London's swirls than this older, staid and – Dare one think it? Complacent? – form of Hungarian civilisation.

Still . . . Buda had some appeal. It had the old mosques and shrines . . . and there were still the marks of the Turks here, like water staining through the ink of a complex letter. Shrines within thickly choked vineyards and tiny mosques cut within the rock itself, rubbing geographic elbows with the intricate tramline that rose at forty-five-degree angles up a four-eighty-five line to the fortress that oversaw the city . . . and much of the world.

There were hot springs. The Germans called this side "Ofen" for "oven" because of them. They spoke of how the sun would sink to his kingdom beneath the earth in the old days, but his passage warmed the waters that flowed out of his nightly realm and warmed the water that came back to the land of men. He wished he were brave enough to enjoy the old baths. A steam bath would be his only solution until the epidemic broke.

Roman carvings intrigued him. Roman baths and architecture . . . it would be a matter of minutes to take up pencils and paper and adopt the guise of an idling artist. The symbols were strange, flavoured by the intricate Hungarian language that wrote right to left. In this land, priests still demanded the burnings of pagan embroideries and old languages were hidden in plain sight, underneath carvings and mouldings of houses and meeting-houses and even other churches. He smiled to see the disguise. It was as subtle and graceful and simple as the Turks who served coffee with a single rose petal floating on top of the brew: The rose petal was what the brain remembered, not the colour of the coffee or the strength of the roast.

Semi-barbaric and splendid was the consensus of Europe. He found he had to agree.

He huddled inside the goosedown blanket provided by a tavern-keeper too old to be concerned with any gossip. Outside the open window he could see men and woman milling about and preparing for one of the saints that was unique to that part of the world. He suspected it was not a canonized saint, whoever it was . . . the figure was black and warped-looking wood, with an almost Mongolian style to the carving.

Watson would be furious with him to be squandering his health in window-sill watching while he hovered in this sort of afterlife of an existence . . . . *"Holmes, you* truly *will wind up dead, and if you do you will*

52

surely be defeating your own purpose, would you not?" Watson scolding him even as he saw to his health. *"Professor Moriarty was a mathematician . . . He would be ultimately satisfied that his equation has finished!"*

Holmes doubted he was shallow enough to want to cheat the desires of a dead man . . . yet Watson would be right. Watson, steady, reliable Watson, who preferred to observe humans with an eye that still loved them. Watson who could see something fine glimmering in most, and if he couldn't, he was willing to believe that there was something above the base behind their surface appearance.

And yet, he was not enough of an idealist that he viewed Holmes with blinkers. He knew he was a trial as a friend, and more than once had described himself as a "most long-suffering" individual.

There were rare friends and even some enemies that liked you for your pleasing qualities, and kept you despite your less than sterling examples. And then, there was Watson.

Of his friends, they were few and seldom. Musgrave and Trevor had been bright spots in his life (even with Trevor's demented dog and Musgrave's bone-deep diffidence). They had accepted him for who he was . . . all drawn to his life by circumstance and some degree of coincidence.

Watson was by far the best of his friends because he seemed to understand that there was no untangling the skein that made Sherlock Holmes. The threads that made him a difficult person also made him the thinking machine that was meant for the benefit of many. The threads wove together, contrasting cords that spun the irrevocable rope.

It made him smile, though he was tired to the bone. He could rest here. He *would* rest here. No place had brought him peace like it had at the top of the world . . . but even that peace had segued into a form of internal torture. He needed to be back among his people, and he needed to finish his work while he remained dead to the world. Buda-Pesth was a pleasant distraction . . . but still . . . distraction.

He was looking forward to spring. If he survived this . . . he would be seeing the first anniversary of his death.

Very soon.

Soon felt so far away.

Chapter VI – Plymouth to
West Station

London:

Inspector Hopkins was starting to stumble in his step. He knew it was the lack of sleep, but still . . . it was hard to rest. Beats had to be regulated. A vicious thief with a knife had been cutting his way through London in a swath. Someone *else* was claiming to be knowledgeable about Leather Apron – they would have to get another file cabinet for that sort of lunatic. *The Gazette* had decided to touch on an old case of Gregson's that actually had more of the late Sherlock Holmes in it than any of the Yarders (and a horrible case it was too) . . . .

The fuss over the Bow Street mess was settling in tiny bits, but Bradstreet was nowhere to be seen by the casual eye. Morton had come by to deliver a warrant for Surrey and reported he'd seen him with some of the old historians for the Robin Redbreasts. [1]

"Lord, what next?" Gregson had exclaimed around a pungent cigar. "Someone else is writing a book that won't be read by anyone but burglars, insomniacs, mad historians, and their descendants?"

Amusing as Gregson could be, it was only a brief rest from the monotony of the week. One solid week of uninterrupted wading in filth for a few scraps of clues . . .

The young man closed his office with a faint sense of unease and barely paid attention to his own goodbyes by the main entrance. For a wonder, the weather was mild and soft and he should have been paying attention to that as well.

He was more tired than he thought.

Hopkins was a sharp, intelligent young man with boundless energy, and initiative, but even a man the late Sherlock Holmes found "promising" could bow to pressure. He found himself inside the walls of The Elegant Barley and with an unusual amount of comfort in its sponsor, John Barleycorn.

He didn't know what his fiancée would think to find him whiling his time away in a tavern. Kate's family answered problems with some sort of activity or they joined a cause. Their energy was admirable. His uncle and mother were hesitant to approve, as they weren't wrapped up in the more conventional pastimes . . .

Kate was a breath of fresh air, but the longer their engagement grew, the more he found himself worrying about . . . things. She wanted him to bicycle. He couldn't afford a Norfolk suit for such a jaunt, and he certainly couldn't wear the usual morning-coat and pinstriped trousers to the park!

Like most of the Yarders, Hopkins already owned more than three suits – an extravagance to their peers considering their income. Most men went through the year with only two, and the poorest wore all their clothes at once. Yarders were expected to be professional, adapting to each situation, and always respectable in appearance to whomever they dealt with, and the uncompensated price was in cloth and exorbitant laundry bills. Not to mention shoes. Hopkins wondered if he still walked the same length as he had back on the constable's beat. A twenty-mile day seemed mild in comparison to what he'd been trodding lately!

Glum about how expenses never went away in his mind, Hopkins bought another drink. A barley-based liquor to nurse in tiny sips while people jostled, talked, argued, fussed, quarreled, and joked far too loudly. His eyes burned while his vision bleared. Halos emerged around the candle-bowls the owner staffed at the tables to prevent gas-fire.

" . . . *with the dead*," a man muttered. Hopkins' ears sharpened to needles and arrowed to the owner. "*Not right. Not civil. Even the Papists would say no to this. Indecent.*"

The conversation floated away with the speaker. Hopkins swallowed. He was trembling inside. Finger-bones glowed in his eye-lids. He thought of how Dr. Watson's clear brown eyes had sunk into the room, facing off Pennywraith. Put the whole room in a chill, he had.

He pushed up from the table without formulating a plan. For a moment, he rested his weight upon the plank, but his own pressure bothered him and he stopped. Pressing himself away and moving to the door without checking to see if there were any familiar faces. Normally the police came here to unwind at the end of the beat. He didn't look for any of them in the clot. His skin crawled with his need to be away.

The cool air felt good on his face . . . on his hot, dry eyes. He closed them for a moment, listening to London rush around him. It felt good. Despite the chatter of the passed holiday about him, he could feel a growing inward calm. A faint smile tugged at his mouth, making him look (in Lestrade's words) ridiculously young. Thoughts of home and a late supper added to the pleasant haze. His last clear memory of the night was stepping to the curb to hail that cab tolling up. Thinking to write a letter to Kathy before going to bed.

Plymouth:

55

The murder room was a horror lit by dull gaslight. What it must look like in the hard eye of the sun didn't bear worth thinking. Old Potier kept his composure as he hung behind the policemen. This blood-darkened room was not *his* element.

Inspector Jacobs (lean and grayish as beech saplings) had met them at the door, nodding once to show he knew they existed. "Inspectors." Potier he noted but said nothing. It gave the sensation of a test, passed.

It took a while for the old smuggler to acclimate himself. He was accustomed to rival families, war, clandestine night-raids, and all sorts of nightmares. This was alien and unspeakably gut-churning. The room had been decorated with every thought to comfort and expense . . . and then made filthy with blood and gore and pain.

"Just in time, Browning," Jacobs said in a low voice to their escort. "We were going to send him off to the basement." The "him" was a sheet-covered form, twisted in a grotesque position of death. Potier was glad he could not see it. He guessed the window had been left open to freeze the room in hopes of delaying Nature on the body.

Browning nodded without speaking. "Jacobs, you may have already met Inspector Lestrade – ?"

Jacobs nodded again. (What nodders these people were.) "Met over the Grand Forgery case, wasn't it?"

Lestrade returned the handshake gravely. "You're wanting a translation, I understand? If there's a matter of questioning my – "

"Oh. No, sir, I assure you there isn't a problem with that at all." Jacobs lifted both hands in a swift placating gesture.

" . . . I was about to say, I brought back-up." He jerked his chin to Potier, who decided a pretense of his skills would be a good idea. He smiled and took the handshake from Browning. (Good Heavens, the man had hands of ice.)

"Well . . . ." Jacobs cleared his throat and passed a look to Browning that was . . . awkward. "The truth is, we don't need to ask many questions of him . . . We know he did it . . . The signs are clear as can be . . . but . . . we can't figure out *why* he did it."

Lestrade swallowed dryly.

Browning said it: "A past history . . . perhaps?"

"Wait." Lestrade lifted his hand up. His voice was hoarse and strange. "I am not questioning the case. I'm here to assist in the way Inspector Browning requested."

Something dangerously close to pity sparked in Jacobs' pale eyes. "Very well, sir. The horsemaster is in the estate cell." He nodded, almost apologetic as they blinked. "No room at the inn, so to speak. Rough bunch of sailors are sleeping it off at the gaol. And the estate cell was built to hold humans for crimes."

"Two-hundred years ago," Browning pointed out, too softly to be offensive.

"Not much choice. I haven't ruled out a temporary loss of mind." Jacobs was not being deliberately shocking, but it seemed as though he was created for the purpose.

"One moment . . . before you take him downstairs . . . ." Lestrade nodded at the sheeted corpse by their feet. "Would you mind if I took a look?"

"No, not at all." Jacobs' mouth twisted in a complete lack of surprise but worlds of understanding. "I would imagine we'll get plenty of those requests."

"Pardon?" Browning asked as Lestrade hunkered down on his heels, Potier following.

"He wasn't a popular man, Browning, but I daresay death will bring him many visitors."

Potier swallowed hard as his grandson pulled the sheet back from the face. It was stuck with dried blood and part of the skull had caved in with something sharp and with small spikes that dug into the flesh and left triangular wells of blood and bruising. The eyes were open.

He looks . . . looked *. . . like his son almost exactly.* Lestrade was caught in the observation.

"I am surprised," Potier said in his mother's tongue, underneath the murmur of the two standing Inspectors.

"How so, sir?" Lestrade whispered back in Breton.

"The priest was wrong." Potier stared into what had been the face of the man who had forced himself on his daughter so long ago. "Evil *can* be killed."

"He'll be a *tor-penn* [2] a good bit longer," Lestrade warned as the sheet was returned to the awful face.

"What's this cell they speak of?"

"It was built with the estate, back when the manor lords had more control . . . and their word was law." Lestrade's composure remained, but his dark eyes were very controlled as he swept his hands up to describe a slender, cylindrical cell made of stone with a single window and a heavy door. "I think it was used to hold gardening tools when I was a boy."

"And they put him in that?" Potier lifted his thin eyebrows in a dry opinion. "He ought to be flattered that they think so highly of him."

Lestrade shook his head and rose to his feet. His twisted foot – the foot his own family had given him – pressing against the floor for balance.

57

Barts:

"Hopkins?"

Hopkins heard the voice, but didn't know what all the fuss was about. It kept insisting on his name . . . over and over.

"Stop it," he mumbled without opening his eyes. "s'till dark out."

"Inspector." Another voice. Gregson? What would Gregson be doing? He still had the night-duty. "Stanley, try to wake up. We need to see how badly you've been hurt."

It was slow going, like drops of water filtrating through loam, but finally the words sunk into Hopkins' awareness. He was hurt? He must be. Gregson wouldn't contrive something like that.

And if he was hurt . . . he must be in a hospital.

That quickly, sound flooded his brain. Hospital. Noise. Noise like the tavern, just with more screaming and cursing. Smell returned: Carbolic and gangrene.

"Gregson . . . ."

"Good, Hopkins." Gregson swallowed loudly. Hopkins heard it over a man's loud demands for brandy. "How are you? That was quite a knock you got."

"How?" Hopkins tried to open his eyes, but they weighed like walnuts. "When? Where?" His breath was gone.

"Horse took a swing at you, that's '*How*' . . . '*When*' is just as you were leaving The Barley, and as to '*Where*' . . . ? How's the breathing?"

"A little . . . ." Hopkins tried to think about it. "Sore?" he guessed.

"Strange luck, I told you," Gregson snorted. "An inch closer and he'd be wrapped like a mummy and force-fed that awful brew of yours, Doctor."

"All's well that ends well, Inspector." Dr. Watson sounded a bit annoyed. "Can you focus your eyes this time?"

"This time?" Hopkins repeated. "What . . . do you mean?"

"Just open your eyes, please." Gentle but firm, Watson was not someone to disobey. Hopkins struggled and finally, a crack of yellow light blinded his eyes. "Ah, good. Dilation normal for both pupils." The light went away, to Hopkins' relief. "We've been sitting up with you the past six hours, waiting for the sense to return to your head, Inspector."

"How . . . bad?" Hopkins was starting to wish his memory wasn't returning. He felt eerie. His head floating while his body dragged behind, scraping painfully upon something sharp.

"Not really bad, Hopkins. It was just a rap on the ribs and head . . . Gave you a good nosebleed, and you kept asking us about the cab driver."

58

"We kept telling you that the cab driver was fine but you didn't understand us," Gregson added. "I told you not to spend too much time with Lestrade. You're getting more bull-headed and less intelligent all the time."

Hopkins felt a smile crack through the pain. "So glad . . . we can mark my regressions . . . but . . . what did you tell . . . family?"

"Rest easy. We didn't tell them the *truth*. They think you're nobly sitting up with a sick compatriot. Dr. Watson's a fine one for spinning tales. He's got your uncle convinced you're the next best thing to St. Francis of Assisi."

In the hallway (thankfully deserted), Watson stopped and traded a dark look with Gregson. "He was most fortunate, Inspector."

"I know." Gregson's hands twitched on his pocket normally stuffed with cigars.

"What does Morton have to say?"

"The cabbie had no idea what was happening." Gregson put his back against the wall and folded his arms across his chest. "He just sensed someone'd come up behind him . . . then they were walking past him to the horse . . . ." Gregson mimed a hand striking down, flat and sharp against an invisible horse-rump. "Thorn between the fingers, stabbed like a sewing-needle. Horse took off like a shot straight at Hopkins."

"If it's not a random case of malicious wounding, then it's surely something deeper. Has anyone tried to mischief on him before?"

"Oh, certainly. Nothing like that, I assure you."

Watson rubbed his chin.

"That makes mischief on Lestrade, on you, on Montgomery . . . now what, Doctor?"

Watson shook his head and said nothing. Defeat slumped his shoulders, and with it . . . anger at admitting his defeat.

Plymouth:

Potier had cast a sharp eye about their room at the tavern (not The Sea Eagle, thank the Triple God), and resigned himself to airing out the bed before they used it. He wasn't about to share his lodgings with biting little freeloaders. Once the covers were turned for inspection, he breathed easier and sat on the edge of the mattress, hands loosely in his lap.

His grandson was standing by the window, still in his outside-clothes and staring blankly through the bottle-glass at . . . well, this part of Plymouth looked like a choked-up brown garden, so Potier decided Jafrez wasn't looking at anything.

Potier didn't blame him . . . not one bit. Not after seeing the murder room. Jafrez hadn't blinked, which earned his respect. The boy – no, not a boy, hadn't ever been a boy – had been as good as his word. He had obligingly presented himself as a translator to his own father and some work had been accomplished from that . . .

. . . and then Jacobs had taken the notion to take them all, including the murderer . . . back to the place of the crime and continue the questioning. Potier's mind refused to dwell on that now. When he tried to focus on a bit of memory here and there . . . his own brain betrayed him, skipped wildly to anything else: Thoughts of his grandchildren . . . his daughters' children and their children . . . thoughts of Jeanne learning to sew and tat lace for her bridal gown.

He saw her in his mind still, donning the brown cap of widows after her husband was stretched by the drop. A brave girl aged too soon, forbidden to see her last son and her son's sons.

And Thomas . . . Tripledie . . . Thomas . . .

"You're quiet, *mab*," Potier said roughly.

His grandson stood where he was, by that pitifully small window contrived of green glass bottles set into a wood box-frame aimed at the moon.

"*Tad-kohz* . . . ." Jafrez said quietly, "I know what to do as a policeman. But I don't know what to think about this." His gaze had slipped away for a moment. He corrected himself to stare back out. "The full moon was last night . . . Crime always goes up with the full moon. Have you noticed that?"

"Couldn't help but notice it," Potier admitted. "Seamen, smugglers, and older rascals rise up with the moon-beams and ride the tides . . . What's on your thoughts, son?"

Lestrade no longer flinched inside to hear Potier call him "*son*" or "*mab*". It had grown almost familiar.

"I'm doubting myself. That's what it is."

Potier did not snort, or sniff, or all those other reassuring blustery things old men did when something utterly stupid struck their fancy. "In what way?"

"Oh . . . ." Lestrade finally turned away, to the old man's relief, and wearily limped to his gripsack. "I don't doubt the report. It's plain as paint! But there's something about it I can't . . . ." His hands tightened as he lifted out a clean change of clothes, folded into neat squares. "Usually I see things in my head when I'm going over a crime. I might be wrong, but I can still see things. I can believe what's happening. Now I can't, and I don't know why. I *promised* I wouldn't let my emotions override my duty. *And I won't.* I'm here as a translator, and I'll do that."

Potier had found one of his home-grown, hand-rolled cigars. He rooted deeper in his belongings until he found another one. "Heh. Here we are. Have one of these and you'll feel much smarter."

"Oh, for . . . That went out with the barber's leeches, you old pirate!"

"I grew this myself. Don't scorn a gift."

"I'm not scorning any gift!" Lestrade snapped tiredly. "But I'm flattered that you think I'm man enough for one of those things." He pulled his own tin out and sank down into a basket-chair. "I'll take that, though." He suddenly decided. "I owe Gregson *something* for all the tea he's made me drink."

Potier chuckled, remembering brightly painted language on that subject, and struck a match on his thumbnail. Lestrade tucked the cigar in his case and lit his preferred brand off his grandfather's tip. They smoked for nearly a minute in utter silence before Lestrade rose and put his collar and cuffs into the little box reserved for day-soiled linens. Potier kept silent as he washed the city off his neck and wrists and face and took a comb to his hair.

"I swear I found another grey hair since all this started," he said at last.

"I don't see how you could tell with all the soot," Potier traded back his own light joke. "Just you wait, boy. It always starts at the sides," he tapped his temples, "And sweeps backwards like a tree-blight."

"Will you stop calling me 'boy' when I finish tarnishing?"

Potier laughed. "My *mamm* called me 'babe' until the day before she died."

"You don't have to stick with tradition, you know." Lestrade wearily sank into the basket chair again and pulled his feet out before him. "I don't understand," he said. "Say it in any language, and I still don't understand." He rubbed at his temples. "If I'm getting caught up in this already, I won't be fit as a translator."

"You had a day bad beyond belief," Potier grunted. "I don't know how I would react if my own father didn't recognize me, but I don't think I'd be comfortable in my skin."

"It's not that he didn't know me," Lestrade protested. "He thought I was you. If his mind has gone back to the past, what will the court say? A murder is a murder . . . Jacobs is already talking of Dartmoor!" Pale afresh at the thought, Lestrade gnawed on a fingernail. "Two of the family in Dartmoor." He swallowed hard. "And that'd be the best the jury can declare. They'd just as easily aim for the rope. You saw those marks. Nothing could hit Ivo Quimper like that unless pure rage and hate was behind it."

Worked up now, Lestrade stood again, went to the fire, back to the window, to the fire again. He wanted to walk outside, pretend he was on the beat again but it would have been sheer foolishness.

"There's more than this bothering you, Jafrez. Don't keep the pus inside the boil."

Lestrade shuddered at the ripe old analogy but said nothing.

West Station:

Colonel Moriarty put aside another letter and reached for the next. Behind him his guest was pacing in slow, restless movements against the book-case. Despite the fact the other man was uncomfortable inside, the colonel was able to ignore the sounds on his carpet.

"I am surprised." Moriarty said at last. "I confess, that isn't the sort of news one expects right now. I doubt I've even thought of the man for . . . several years now. Perhaps five or six times since he retired but that was . . . What? Four years ago? Five?"

"Almost nine years." Was the answer. "He lived quiet as a mouse once he stepped down. The question is how to *address* this."

"Address this? I'm not certain we should do anything about it."

"A murder like this affects us all. I don't care about his shifting loyalties right now. They're no longer in question."

"You're right about that, but are you surprised this day actually did come? It's the timing, not the action that has me . . . ." Moriarty put his letter down and rose, going to the social sphere of the brandy. "Concerned," he finished at last.

A low grunt was his answer.

NOTES

1. Bow Street Horse Patrol. They were called Robin Redbreasts from their red waistcoats. The Metro absorbed them in 1836.
2. Pain in the neck. Pain in the head

Chapter VII – Dr Mortimer?

Plymouth:

"Y ou're wondering," Potier said cannily, "how much more your wife will put up with this." He refreshed his match and puffed quickly until it was caught up before taking up his small flask. "I've worn that expression quite enough. I deserved that expression most of the time. But bear in mind I was little like you. No one ever dared me down from a fight. Surcouf's pesky blood talking, I suppose." He grinned. "There was a time when I was the shortest moon-curser in the North Sea. Not that you would know that by looking at me today, *Nann*?"

Lestrade grinned too. The tension shattered.

Potier stretched back on the bed with a comfortable sigh, arm folded behind his head. "Out casting my nets during the day . . . and at night I was sailing with the moon. I lived wild and both my wives were saint enough to put up with me . . . I suppose it helped that they didn't see too much of me. But yes. I didn't do what I did because I wanted to worry them . . . or make them afraid. Or leave them widows. I did it because I was wild and no one could prune me into a right shape."

"Interesting way of saying that," Jafrez sighed. "I've felt that was all they tried to do to me when I was a boy."

"Well, it wasn't your fault you looked so much like me," Potier snickered. "I imagine they must have panicked when they saw you."

"Ha." Jafrez smiled faintly.

"You're not like me in that, *mab*. You're far more responsible than I was. You don't have that crazy moon-blood in you."

"I don't *know* what I have, *Tad-kohz*." Lestrade's hands twitched at his sides. He was never silent for long, even when deep in thought he gave the appearance of internal motion. "I do know that I have so much to lose," he added softly.

"Clea won't leave you."

"That doesn't mean what I'm doing is fair to her."

"Fair? You've never believed in 'fair' before." Potier's brows drew up and together as he tapped ash into the fire. He leaned back to study. "You only believe in justice."

"You know exactly what I mean. I don't know what to tell her . . . that her estranged father-in-law will be hung for murdering a man who is the father of a man she hates and fears with every inch of her being." Lestrade measured an inch of space between his thumb and forefinger.

63

"There are those in her family that will see that as proof they're doing well to ostracize her. Bad enough she married a policeman who can't promote past inspector. Or that her closest friend is staying away from her thanks to a stupid scandal over the Bow Street Strike. Or that I've come home to her half dead at least once a year since we've been married."

"The important thing is you do come home," Potier pointed out. "Heed this old veteran: *You come home.* You may not rise in your profession, but better to dig deep in respectable soil than fall over because you've over-reached your length."

"That sounds like pruning again."

"What do you expect? Potiers farm when they aren't fishing."

"Or running the tides."

"Or running the tides."

They were both silent a moment, listening for the night-sounds of London that weren't there. Plymouth was different even in this – at least it was this far from the shipyards. A rabbit screeched as something grabbed it, the killer itself soundless.

"He killed the man that did the worst wrong to his wife . . . your mother," Potier said at last. "Clea isn't going to fault that . . . nor are her brothers and Charlemagne. They would have easily done that with their own hands. There's enough of the Celt left in them to agree to that."

"Years so late? *Mamm* and Armoricus did their best to keep that secret to themselves. It was easy because early births run in the family, and Armoricus looked just enough like Thomas that it'd be enough to satisfy anyone."

"Somehow he learned, ya?" Potier shook his head. "His health is failing. Could be cancer, or something just as bad, and he learns this truth . . . and this is how he reacts. Wouldn't he want to spend the last part of his life righting an old wrong? A wrong against my daughter? I've never doubted he loved her, *mab*. Never that."

"No. I never doubted that either."

Lestrade put his back against something wooden and strangely carved. It looked like a ship's figurehead someone had given up on halfway through the work. "Something's off," he returned to the old subject. "And I've lost my way."

"You've been good to hold up this long. Can't expect you to pull your usual fifteen hours until you recover." Potier rose up and went to the day-basket. "Let us see what Mrs. Collins packed, ya? She has a good hearty appetite, like a dancer should."

"Dancing, my foot," was the response. "She and Clea together would wear out a team of Greek athletes."

64

"It's true not many women would have the . . . withall to put a menu into a supper-basket." Potier lifted up a sheet of paper thoughtfully. "Are you *certain* your landlady doesn't come from good solid peasant stock? " He elevated a loaf of unsliced bread. "She's never made white bread once in my presence."

"Your presence has nothing to do with it." Lestrade found the inevitable terrine of stew, so thick it could be eaten with the edge of a knife-blade, and set it by the fire to re-warm. "The women of London are protesting white bread as it helps tooth decay. Wholemeal bread helps clean the teeth." He sliced off the heel and chewed without trouble as he fished in his travel-bag. "Remember when Old Baldwin was holding that nut-cracking contest?" He dredged up a memory from his childhood in Brittany. "None of the *gentlemen* could do that. They'd be using a hammer to crack their nuts."

"Cheating," Potier chuckled. "They were *hazelnuts*. I could open those with my gums."

"Oh, for . . . ." Lestrade lifted his tiny canister of *Jewsbury and Brown's* ruefully. "I think the boys have been in the tooth powder again."

"You're upset that they're cleaning your teeth with your tooth powder?"

"Nooo . . . It's not *their* teeth that's the trouble . . . ." Lestrade opened the little lid and poked through it suspiciously. "I caught them trying to clean Mrs. Collins' cat's teeth with my usual tin last month. They argued they were trying to make its breath better . . . but I told them no, not *my* tooth powder, use their own." A troubled expression crossed his face. "There's less in here than there was last time . . ." he muttered. "I keep this tin in the travel-bag . . . I suppose they thought I wouldn't notice . . . ."

"Bless the saints." Potier was well used to boys, having been one, but he too was caught between a grimace and a smile. "Does the cat have better breath?"

"I have no idea. That thing is large enough to frighten the Thames rats." He gave it up with a single laugh. "*Tsk*."

No fool with his energies, Jafrez ate and put what was left of the tooth-powder to good use, falling to sleep soon after. Potier stayed up a bit longer as he nursed the fire along, smoking his tobacco and thinking . . . .

Things had smelled like trouble even before they stepped out of that damned tavern.

Potier had been glad to be out of The Sea-Eagle for starters. Strangers were always eyed (discreetly or not so discreetly) in a tavern. In their case . . . he and Jafrez were no doubt "somewhat familiar" to the tired men and handful of women populating the little dive. There was a fairly good chance that the boy cleaning up the floor-sweepings was one of the Baldwins. He had the trademark fair hair and square face of that family.

There was no avoiding the families, but Potier had no desire to advertise their presence with songs and flowers. It would just be . . . brainless. Judging from the way Jafrez huddled down inside his coat just a bit, implying he was even smaller than he truly was, and passing sweeping glances from beneath his bowler . . . they were both thinking the same.

First, Browning had glanced about with his one eye as if looking for something. Failing to find it, he made an almost-shrug motion and led the way down the tiny road (more like a muddy stream breaking the monotony of the field-grasses), and it was not in the direction of the Plymouth station.

When Jafrez pointed that out, Browning answered something unclear to the effect that the gaol was full, and his father was being held on the estate.

With that, Jafrez snapped his mouth shut with a click so loud it must have hurt his teeth.

Potier had not been in Plymouth in some years. The risk of seeing his estranged family was painful. Still . . . .

The little old man trotted after the other two, holding himself back with effort. After a quarter-mile up the winding trail from the tavern to the outskirts, Browning opened up a little to talk.

It was in English, a language Potier found illogical as much as infuriating. A trading language? A trading mishmash. A linguistic case of Bubble-and-Squeak, [1] *and it was to his grandson's credit that he had the brain power to be fluent in the ridiculous language.*

"Well, now, why can't we call you a Janner?" [2] *Browning was asking as they hustled up a winding slope around and even more winding path . . .*

"Haven't lived in Plymouth long enough to be called a Janner," Jafrez was arguing. "Have to be considered a bloomin' native to be a Janner!"

Banter aside. Old Potier was certain what sort of thoughts were running through his grandson's mind as they followed Browning. The look on his face matched the feelings the smuggler had when he had gone to the ti-ker *in hopes of positively identifying his brothers' drowned remains.*

He kept his eye on Jafrez as the two policemen traded apparently light conversation. Browning was still trying to say Jafrez was a Janner and Jafrez was saying he hadn't lived nearly long enough in Plymouth for that esteemed title.

Plymouth had always appealed to the smuggler, but not this soft green veldt of planted clovers and rolling mists with lazy herds of sheep eating their way through the veldt. He loved the noisy hustle of the ship-yards, where everything was for sale and the rest negotiable. Where men and women took pride in their hardiness.

With these outlying lands . . .

. . . It was meant to be pastoral. The result was offensive. The Quimpers had long ago driven out the poor living on the slope overlooking the port and set up their own little kingdom over the ashes. A fiefdom, Potier had thought with contempt upon his first visit, and that opinion had never shifted.

"Just a minute." Browning held up his hand. His audience paused, puzzled that they were not passing the Estate Entrance itself and headed further to the other side of Plymouth. "We're heading into the Estate," he added. "Jacobs wants to talk before he moves the corpse."

"It's still there?" Jafrez stared. "Why? It should have been put in cold storage by now!"

"Jacobs' decision, not mine," Browning said simply.

Jafrez' mouth was a tight line. Potier felt no less angry. Both men opted to stay silent for now. Drawing attention to themselves would do no good.

Chilled mist rose from the stone paths. The earth between them glistened black and soft. After just a few weeks in "The Smoke", it was strange to see buildings made of their natural stone tints, and not the black of the coal factories. He'd forgotten how the wind favoured this part of Plymouth . . . how it kept the smuts and cinders from falling save on the unlucky days.

Several constables of that tall, ever-present stock in blue wool hurried back and forth across the grounds. Potier calculated when the murder was supposed to have happened and measured it against what he was seeing. He thought some people looked edgy. How important was Ivo Quimper?

The plain-clothed detective stood apart in the crowd of blue in his brown coat and suit. Against the luxurious furnishings, he was plain as a wren. He was giving orders in a calm, low voice that was so used to being obeyed he never had to sound firm. A constable nodded and trotted off, his long legs stretching into a light run in his heavy boots.

Jacobs chose that moment to glance up. His eyes sharpened upon the trio as he extended a hand adorned with hammerhand thumbs and the negotiations – for that was what this was – began. "Inspectors," he said .
. .

. . . After they walked out of the Murder Room, matters grew difficult.

"You'll forgive me sir, but you seem to be not in the best of health."

"I'm better than I was a few weeks ago," Jafrez answered. "And I'm capable of being your translator." That quickly, he took a measure of control from Jacobs. "How would you prefer to do this? Do you want me alone with him, or do you want someone to witness? Or someone to listen where he can't see them?"

"I confess, I hadn't thought further than just getting him to talk." Jacobs was startled. Somehow he had stopped being the authority, but he didn't know how exactly that had happened. "We need testimony more than anything else. You know how men are. Once they break their private dams, more words follow the first, and more after that."

"I see," Jafrez agreed without agreeing.

Potier's sense of unease refined upon their approach of the estate's cells. It looked like a tiny stone tower, set in native block from the nearest limestone strata. Generations of rainwater leaked silent stone tears between the cracks. A policeman was standing guard and looking uncomfortable. Jacobs called him by his name, "Carpenter".

"He hasn't spoken, sir," the young man told them. "I check in on him like you say, but he hasn't said anything at all. I tried."

"Never mind, Constable, you did fine," Jacobs praised absently. "Inspector? Perhaps?"

"I'm ready," Jafrez answered firmly.

Carpenter took the nod and pulled out a ring of keys that fit upon the door. The lock squeaked. Potier watched as a smear scraped across the stone upon the door's swing . . . .

It was late into the night. Jafrez was asleep. Potier slid out of the bed with as little noise as he was capable of. Worn out, his grandson never stirred. The old man breathed his relief and quietly fixed himself a pipe. He couldn't stop thinking about the day. He was grateful Jafrez was able to put it aside for now – that or he was just too worn out – but the recollection swarmed across his eyes like gnats at twilight.

A man carved of apple wood. That was Thomas Lestrade. From the gnarled body strong as iron to the green eyes gleaming in that square face . . . Thomas looked like a man carved of a still-living tree and then filled with a shambling, wood-like life. He hunched up, those green eyes glued to his son without blinking, and his hair had turned silvery under his beaten cloth cap. A thick bandage coiled around each hand, but tiny spots of old blood had leaked through.

Thomas didn't recognize him. Potier shuddered to see a man look upon his own son with a stranger's eyes. The door's pale sunlight didn't even affect the man, didn't even make him blink. They were the violet eyes of the slightly mad . . . or at best, of a man who did not remember who he was.

"Where is Jeanne?" Thomas Lestrade asked softly. "Goulean, where is Jeanne?"

Jafrez swallowed and tried to speak. His mouth opened. He got that far.

Thomas Lestrade rose up slowly, weak as a kitten, and shuffled to the tiny beam of sunlight coming through the high window. "I wanted to talk to her," he said plaintively. "I wanted to tell her I was sorry. Could you tell her?" Blunt, work-thickened fingers spread themselves against the shaped stone. "I can't leave," he whispered. "He'll punish them. They're too old to work by themselves now. I can't leave."

He fell back into muttering to himself, tracing a single line between stone and mortar.

Jafrez backed away as if his father had become the serpent of the fountain. He fled.

Potier followed him, but did not completely shut the door. His grandson had his back to the wall of the cell, breathing from the bottom of his lungs as the constable guarded the entrance. Guard? A joke. Thomas was going nowhere. His wits were as addled as a child's when beaten too harshly.

"He thinks I am you," Jafrez croaked. He reached up and loosened his collar. Sweat chilled his face against the fog. Jacobs and Browning stood by, uncertain of what they should do, and that made them both look a little out of depth.

"Then let him think so." Potier didn't like himself for that sort of counsel, and it went against the grain of his honest grandson. "He will unburden himself, ya?"

"I'm not certain this is wise," Jacobs began carefully. "If he doesn't know who he is talking to . . . ."

"We need a confession," Jafrez strangled. "If he thinks I am his wife's father . . . perhaps that will go faster." He pulled a handkerchief out and ran it over his face. "But we need to do this now, while he's in the mood to talk about something."

Paddington Station, London:

Watson grimaced as he watched the cabs go by. Overcast it might be, but the outdoors was better than his going back inside. Paddington Station could be at times . . . a massive problem. He hated getting into the station just after the trains braked. One never knew *what* one would find.

69

He sighed and tightened his muffler about his throat in concession to the damp. A doctor had to show he was sensible after all. He squared his shoulders and stamped, half-limping back under the skylight tunnel.

Patterson's pale face illuminated in the filtered sunlight like a ghost. He pushed his way forward, slippery as an eel with his dark eyes staring out like twin lamps capable of burning a dark light against his while skin. Again, Watson wondered how much longer the man would stay on his feet. How much was even left in him?

"I just got your note," the Yarder apologized. He breathed heavily as he stopped, waiting for the crowd to split open in concession to the next approaching train.

"You're in time then," Watson answered with what he knew was sympathy under his usual British politeness.

Patterson made a face. "Do I look so terrible, Doctor?"

Watson was long used to making a smoke-screen. "It's not that," he assured quickly. "You merely look as though you've . . . well . . . ran across a few streets to get here."

"I did," was his answer. "All the cabs on my end were caught on a funeral." He rubbed the back of his neck. "Who is this fellow? Mr. Holmes never mentioned him."

"I daresay." Watson didn't know why it made him feel better – was it reassuring to know he had more of Holmes's confidence than this man? Was it a petty jealousy, or was he glad to know that there was safety in that ignorance? "Dr. Mortimer is a well-qualified expert in human bones. I can't vouchsafe his phrenology, for I am no expert, but he is enthusiastic and a thorough scholar."

"I look forward to meeting him," Patterson said slowly. He still looked slightly lost and tired. Without knowing he was doing so, he shot his cuffs to make certain they hid the scars at the wrists.

Watson's gaze had fallen elsewhere. As the detective watched, a change came over the veteran. His brown eyes gleamed, and his mouth parted in a smile. He lifted his hand and waved, determined to be noticed.

Patterson turned, seeking an invisible line that stretched from Watson and the man who would be on its other side. They settled at last on a tall, thin man. A young man for the credentials given him. Small glasses in a gold wire frame illuminated bright grey eyes, and he moved with a slightly stooped back beneath his slightly seedy coat. The posture of a man who had already been a scholar for many, many years. As Patterson watched, long spidery fingers quivered over the head of his Penang Lawyer, and suddenly lifted the stick off the ground. The man waved in turn from the swirl of the human sea, returning the courtesy of his former acquaintance.

"Dr. Mortimer, I presume?"

NOTES

1. A popular dish of cabbage and potatoes.
2. A person from Plymouth. A nickname.

Chapter VIII – Big Games and Small Games

Plymouth:

If moods were colours, the air about the inn's rented room would be swirling with sickly grey-green wraiths. The tinny chime of the inn's little clock nearly shattered the thick, drowsy atmosphere about the tiny breakfast-table.

"I'm not certain about Jacobs," Lestrade said at last.

Potier had felt the same way, but blest if he would say so. 'In what way?" the old smuggler wondered.

Lestrade was slow in his response. Not for him was the quick escape of intuition and leaps of faith. "I don't mind that he's been put upon by the Foreign Office. You get that from time to time. He's no doubt been told to come to a favourable outcome. It's anyone's guess but Jacobs' what that outcome is – for all we know, he could be told to find proof that there was a criminal ring involving forged Bibles, or something that makes even less sense." Lestrade absently passed the sugar-bowl to his grandfather, who took it without his aversion to sweets.

"The Foreign Office usually knows more about the cases than they like to tell. You never know what will happen. A poor Bobby might arrest a man caught in the act of *decapitating* another person, and it turns out the criminal is the son of some foreign dignitary – or worse, related to someone with International Connections and that usually means Royal blood or some vague tie to the Royal blood . . . We still get rumours that Saucy Jack was someone like that, though I have my severe doubts."

"Oh?" Potier was interested. "What do you think?"

"I think he was just a stark staring madman with a madman's grudge and superstitious on top of it all," Lestrade grunted. "The only thing we did right was put those dogs on the case. And the worst thing we did was pull them off it. As long as those dogs were roaming London, there were no killings. That means he believed the dogs would have found him."

"Interesting." Potier leaned his chin into his hand, elbow on table. (No women were present.)

"Well, it's beside the point . . . The point I'm trying to remember to make – I hope this coffee does its work on my head soon – " Lestrade took another gulp. " – The point I'm trying to make, is Jacobs is the only one who really knows what *should* happen. Browning has an instinct things are going wrong, and I'm not feeling too safe about it myself. I haven't been around Browning in years, but his instincts never failed him. Not even in the Hyde Park Riot. He'd be *wholly* blind now if he hadn't listened to that little voice in his head."

"Oh, I know that little voice," Potier chuckled. "It needs to speak up more. I hardly listen to it." He forked up another portion of eggs and ate peaceably. "So you're saying that Jacobs is leaning to a . . . conclusion in this case that is already bending against the evidence?"

"That's a dangerous conclusion, and I'm not taking it," Lestrade answered. "The true problem is, we don't know what the conclusion is going to be." Lestrade had finished up and was pacing back and forth with his coffee-cup in both hands. "You heard him say it yourself. They know he did it. They have proof he did it. *Do they really need to know* why *he did it?* Not according to British Law. Not yet. The *why*'s follow the *processing*. A barrister, or some sort of counselor would be assigned to this task. That's what the professional process would be. Why are they bypassing that route? Given by what we've got, and going by how the Office has worked in the past, they don't want anyone else from the outside to know what's going on." He exhaled wearily and reached for the pot. "All part of the show when you have a country divided in its politics. The Foreign Office handles the big cases and we handle the small . . . and then you have small cases that are really big cases in disguise . . . like those party-papers you unfold to find it's bigger on the inside than it was on the outside."

Potier watched his grandson take a long drink and set the cup down with unnecessary force. "So your question is, *why* is Jacobs trying to be so humane about it and get a confession?"

"Exactly," Lestrade answered. "Thomas Lestrade hasn't said anything about the murder so far. Not a thing. Not in favour nor against. He just keeps talking about the past, confusing me for you. Perhaps you'd best be the one to do the questioning." He grimaced. "Would he confuse you for anyone?"

"I would hope not. I like to think of myself as an original." Potier chewed toast, wishing devoutly that someone in the kitchen remembered buckwheat existed in the world. "I'll be glad to give it a try."

"Just be careful. Let him talk." Lestrade hovered on the cusp of speech for too long. As Potier watched, he finally caved in. His posture drooped and he looked down. "And . . . we need to find where *Mamm* is staying."

"Do you think she knows something?"

"She's a woman, isn't she?"

73

Paddington Station:

"Dr. Watson!" Mortimer puffed slightly as he came to a halt. Patterson's impression of a bright, active mind was affirmed as the man cocked his head to one side, peering at Patterson with the insatiable interest of a bird with a worm. The large beak of a nose only added to that image, and his slight stoop could have hidden wings beneath his battered coat. "You look well, sir! How are you?" They clasped hands, and Patterson was again struck by the contrasts between the two men. Watson. Shorter, deliberate in his moves, robust, and permanently browned from foreign skies was dissimilar to Mortimer: Bleached under the white northern sun, stretched thin and left to stand loose-jointed and ready as a marionette on the strings. Unlike the calm at-rest persona of a soldier who decides when to squander his energy, Mortimer was a vessel without a stopper.

They liked each other. Patterson was reassured by that sign.

"Allow me to introduce you to Inspector Patterson," Watson waved with a smile. His memories of Mortimer must be good ones, the Yarder concluded. "Inspector, this is Dr. James Mortimer – but he will correct me now and emphasis M.R.C.S. – "

"I am hardly as qualified as our fine friend, Inspector." [1] Mortimer laughed easily.

Watson flushed and stumbled a moment, taken completely aback at the compliment. " – But he is also the Medical Officer of Health for part of Devonshire."

"Grimpen,Thorsley, and High Barrow," Mortimer explained. "It is to my stooped shoulders that fall the task of enforcing health issues. I get my share of complaints this time of year for that enforcement, but boiling one's drinking water is a safe assurance against the spring epidemics!" He huffed and shuffled his shoulders within his coat. "I must say, I was delighted to get your wire – my wife had to restrain me from leaving the house the very hour I read it!"

Patterson wordlessly (but with a smile) picked up the man's travel-bag. Mortimer was a *rara avis,* no question – and it would be a long day before he would see another human being that would look so at home in feathers.

"I take it I have intrigued you?" Watson was also smiling. There was nothing contemptuous directed at the man. He was merely so enthusiastic and curious his simple joy in life was easily transferred to those around him.

"One good turn deserves the other, true? Quite so. You know I am not often at work with the *recently* departed, but there are surprisingly few differences between a man one finds in the bogs, and one finds in a broken grave."

"Allow us the time then, sir, to fill you in on the case." Patterson felt moved with hope for the first time in what felt like weeks. "May we trouble you to pause for a drink and something hot to eat?"

"Eat?" Mortimer echoed blankly, and they watched as he remembered he had a stomach. "Er, yes. That would be most welcome. I'm afraid I forgot all about my breakfast . . . I always go to the train stations much too early, but better early than late!" And despite the dubious practicality of the motion, he fished for his pocket watch, unaware that the bells over their heads were ringing the time.

"Well, the trains are reliable!" He snapped his watch shut. "So you are Inspector Patterson? The last man of the law Dr. Watson introduced to me was Inspector Lestrade. Good enough fellow . . . didn't seem too at easy in the country."

"Lestrade's element is the city," Watson smiled. "But I am afraid he is indisposed. It somewhat relates to the case that brought you."

"Oh! I look forward to it!"

"My home away from home should suit us all." Watson let his stick swing a bit in his hands. "You ought to find The Entelechy Club a haven, gentlemen. Of course, that is if you haven't been there before."

"I would recall such a name." Mortimer chuckled. "Entelechy . . . a philosophy. The perfect realization of a cause."

"Exactly. While we call it a *club*, it was based on a very valuable premise that has been the saviour of physicians since the earliest times of history." Watson had whistled up a cab and bustled them in without a seeming effort. He was the last to hop aboard and did so with a satisfied smile.

"What premise would that be, Doctor?" Patterson wondered. He was beginning to think that Watson, despite his self-discrimination, was as interesting as Mr. Holmes had been.

"That a man will speak to a waiter or his chef or even his billiards-partner with more confidence than he will to his own physician." Watson barked up a quick address two streets southeast. "Consider," he added. "London is, it must be admitted, a dreary city. We try to enliven cheer into our lives with painted tiles and enclosed porches, and stained glass at the highest points to bring some colour inside . . . but I doubt any of us will ever see the natural colour of the stone on Buckingham Palace or Old Bailey. The lack of stimulation is in part why dens of alcohol are so popular. The depressant effect of the drink unfortunately takes away the good of the surroundings . . . but the overall calculated method of drawing customers operates on a sound principle."

75

"You have a point." Patterson confessed. "I've often wondered why I go to get a drink when I don't particularly *like* the common beers and ales. Part of it is the fact that bars, taverns, and inns are lit bright as daylight with mirrors and candles. My mind craves light like a plant at times."

"You wouldn't be alone," Mortimer suggested. "Sunlight is a natural thing, and we are natural beings. At least, we ought to be. Well, Dr. Watson, you have me interested. I look forward to seeing this Entelechy Club."

"I should warn you . . . the members are men of medicine, science, and other schools of thought," Watson cautioned, but there was a glint in his eyes as he did so.

"Noted . . . but why say you we should be *warned*?"

"Because we all have the bad habit of bringing our work into the club with us."

"Coercion of a difficult client?" Patterson was smiling broadly now that he had the lay of the land."

"More or less." Watson lifted his hand into the air – a gesture that the detective had struck the target in the centre. "Except for the claustrophobe . . . We can't get his sort through the front door."

On the outside, the Club was a simple brick model that would have looked at home on any street within three miles of the Serpentine. It was nothing but normal – and that made perfect sense as Watson assured his guests that normality was something everyone aspired to achieve.

Tossing his things to the doorman, Watson kept going, letting the others follow at their own pace through a brilliantly lit front populated with milling men and a few pleasant-voiced waiters with the morning newspapers. They passed a billiards room and a darts tournament to the side, and finally came to a warm-looking library stocked with the sort of books most professional men had to deal with in their life, but not enough to go out and purchase them: Legal tomes. Medical procedure. The latest technology in glass and metals. Trading routes . . . Patterson noted a small shelf devoted just to train schedules, almanacs, and some maps of London that might (if taken altogether) be moderately accurate.

"Interesting literature, Doctor," Patterson said as they settled around an oval table.

Watson grinned quickly. "There's but one requirement to bringing these books to this room," he supplied. "They must be free or at a reduced price . . . such as an estate sale or a lucky happenstance at a rag shop. Our particular philosophy to this rule is, if we spend a pence on a book for the Club's reference, it spares us a shilling later." He reached down into his medical bag, and pulled out a long envelope. "I have here the written description of the case in question. Inspector, were you able to – ?"

"Better than photographs, though I have those as well." Patterson produced a wax-paper folder from inside his heavy coat. "I was able to get hand-prints from the man before we were forced to send him to a more permanent storage."

"Excellent." Mortimer tightened the grip of his gold-wire spectacles over the bridge of his cold-pinked nose. "If I may, I shall read the written description first . . . and perhaps my conclusions will match what I will see upon your proof, Inspector."

Patterson nodded his agreement. Watson begged their pardon and asked if they wanted anything hot to drink. The favourable response led him to rise and request a tray of hot ciders with a side of brandy, and something to eat should it "not be too inconvenient".

His task took no more than four minutes, but Mortimer was already quivering when he returned.

"Let me see these!" the tall man demanded, and nearly tore the waxpaper in his eagerness.

Watson and Patterson glanced at each other, completely ignorant but knowing when they should take hope.

"*Ha!*" Mortimer's eyes lit behind his glasses. "I was right! Patterson, your friend was a hired excavationist!"

"A what?" Patterson was afraid to repeat that word. "What is that? Like excavation? An archaeologist?"

"No, no . . . though you are thinking in proper lines, and you do have the correct field." Mortimer cleared his throat and spread out the photographs of the Wardrobe Man, along with the ink-prints of the hands. It made for a grisly impression of card playing. "Look here at the dull marks upon the hand. The fingertips here and here are worn almost smooth. That is similar to a man who grips a pen all day long, but only if they grip it in this manner . . . ." Mortimer demonstrated, showing something like a crab-pincer. "It may look as though it is unwieldy, but a man who learns this technique can be capable of great delicacy. I have a similar grip myself when I am working in the digs." He cleared his throat again. "I beg your pardon. I don't travel much of late, and I've grown unaccustomed to the fogs of London."

"Something to drink will help." Watson assured him. "What is an *excavationist*, my good man?"

"Well, a man hired to do something finer and more skilled than the blunt labor of hauling earth at a site. I pay them on occasion when I'm upon a large project . . . one of importance. When there are places that require a patient, steady hand and a sharp eye it is they who sort the bone fragments from the straw and plant fragments in the earth. To know a tarnished lump of jewelry or gem from a dull pebble. In other words, the men have trained their eyes to know the soils on a most intimate level . . . and they sort out the fragments that do not belong, for they are inevitably something of importance."

Patterson scratched at his cuff. "So he worked as an assistant of sorts in some sort of archaeological site?"

"I wouldn't know if he could be called an assistant. Think of him as a . . . a senior field hand. If something of note came up, he would be the one to notice it and draw its significance to . . . well, the university student, or the hired specialist . . . but mostly the foreman who is in charge." Mortimer shook his head and briefly lit up to thank the waiter with the drinks. When they were alone again, he poured his ration of brandy into the cider and sipped reflectively. "They're in a position of trust," he clarified. "They know not to bring anything home with them, as it would be stealing. I would say he was working at this site for a while . . . more than a year? When I supervise a large project, I conform to similar rules. But there is one thing I can assure you: He was not in my area. Not with those stains on his skin."

"It looked like tannic stains as on a peat bog."

"Exactly. I know peat stains. Excellent preservation of corpses! He was working at a site that was peat. 'Brown Coal', some call it, but I disagree with that appellation. It isn't at all accurate to my thinking." He tapped the table with his long, nervous finger. "Would it trouble you if I had a smoke?"

"Not at all."

Mortimer rolled his paper practically one-handed, and put the end to his lips in quick haste. "There aren't many bog-sites right now . . . not that I know of. Weather's bad enough in the summer with all the vampiric insects winging about and developing a taste for human flesh . . . but winter can be worse. It's too easy to be caught up in the misery of the conditions and let valuable artifacts slip through. Not to mention . . . I have been in some places where it is simply dangerous to work in the winter. Frozen crust can give one a false sense that it is safe to walk about . . . It's a mistake one won't get a chance to repeat."

Patterson shuddered like a duck suddenly drenched in water. "Dr. Mortimer . . . what sort of tool would cause those marks on the hands?"

"Well, I cannot say with the utmost certainty, but I have found it useful to use a tiny sort of billhook . . . ." Mortimer sketched the tool, so small it would have been a corn-cutting tool in the hands of pigwidgeons. "When there is a fibrous patch in the peat, it would be excellent for cutting lines here and there. One must be neat when excavating. Straight lines whenever possible." He paused and smoked frantically for a moment. "There're a few other small tools . . . Often the men fashion them up themselves, out of broken spoons or snapped knife blades. The point of the tool is to be small, versatile, and capable of long periods of work."

"So these wouldn't be tools made completely of wood, like most potter's tools?"

"Bless me, no. Wooden tools will gradually wear away from the slow force of the earth. The earth is stronger than wood, after all."

Watson blinked at the tap on the door, rose, and returned with a tray of Welsh Rarebit and onion soup. "Is there any way of learning where this man could have been working?"

Patterson had been working himself up to that question. He was starting to realise Watson was the sort to seek the core of the question and pull it straight out of the apple.

Mortimer did not answer at first, but resolutely finished his handmade smoke. When he finished, he pitched the remains into the grate while Watson silently apportioned out the light meal.

"My unofficial profession can be a jealous one," he said at last. "Jealous as women seeking the latest bolt of silk before the Season. I am not certain that any inquiry I would make, no matter how discreet and polite and innocuous . . . ." He tried again. "I could be seen as attempting to inveigle my way into someone's ambitions."

"But you yourself are not ambitious. It is the knowledge you seek, not glory!" Watson exclaimed. "Do you not have any allies in your field?"

Mortimer smiled, and accepted his share of toast and soup. "I have a few friends who understand I am a seeker of shells, not the man who wishes to own the whole beach." [2] He chewed reflectively as the others made use of their own meal. "Give me a few minutes to think," he said at last. "I shall have to put together a list for you . . . the addresses are all in my head, but I cannot pull them out just as soon as I need them." He brightened slightly as the quality of the simple food occurred to him.

"Well, you've already been a tremendous help to the Yard, sir." Patterson sighed, and allowed his spine to relax a bit in his chair.

"I can only imagine the quality of your usual informants if that is the case."

Patterson surprised himself into laughing. "All's well that works out . . . Was Dr. Watson able to let you know about some of the matters that drew him to us?"

"I caught the hint that there were some misplaced corpses." Mortimer answered. "I hope it was no more than 'some', and much less than 'many'."

Watson made a face. "That's the problem, Doctor." He sighed as he passed the cider-pitcher. "At this point, we know it's more than 'many', but as to 'how many' . . . well . . . the evidence is not encouraging."

Mortimer cocked his head to one side again, the grey-eyed bird of a man considering. "I'd be pleased to offer my assistance," he said honestly. "I rather do feel as though we never appropriately compensated you over that case . . . ."

"Ridiculous." Watson broke in rudely.

"No, I am serious. Sir Henry is a well man now, and a live one thanks to you and Mr. Holmes. But I also quite enjoyed the intellectual exercise of it all. It would be a rewarding opportunity to have another chance to help again."

Watson flushed slightly, and glanced down at his plate. "It is a strange case, and it holds its own dangers," he pointed out with a worried glance to Patterson.

"There's no question of the supernatural in it, is there?"

"Er, no . . . none whatsoever."

Mortimer sighed his contentment. "Good."

NOTES

1. Membership of the Royal College of Surgeons. Dr. Mortimer was firm in that he was a humble "Mister", but he was intelligent and experienced with an open mind and active curiosity that no doubt led to his post as the much appreciated but underthanked Medical Officer of Health.

2. "*A dabbler in science, Mr. Holmes, a picker up of shells on the shores of the great unknown ocean.*" (*The Hound of the Baskervilles*). Mortimer in describing himself was clearly thinking of Sir Issac Newton's own self-explanation: "*I know not what I appear to the world, but to myself I seem to have been only like a boy playing on the sea-shore, and diverting myself in now and then finding a smoother pebble or a prettier shell, whilst the great ocean of truth lay all undiscovered before me.*" Quoted in *The Memoirs of Newton*, by D. Brewster

Chapter IX – Saved by Liquorice

Dawn was a minimalist this time of year. Browning smoked when he was depressed. He found himself on his second pipe of the morning when Jacobs came up behind him.

The two simply watched the rolling mist of the planted estate in silence. They were hard men, but that much greenery was a strange thing to their eyes. It meant wealth and privilege and equity.

"Got a good joke for you." Jacobs said without looking at him.

"Oh?" Browning tried not to look interested.

"Mmm. How can you tell an American's moved in?"

"Umm." Browning thought about it. "You hear brass instruments playing?"

"Well, besides that."

"I give up."

"They dig up the fruit trees and plant grass."

"In't that the truth." They caught the low croak of ravens rising up and then floating across a low row of currant bushes. Small black kites following the drift of the fogs.

"I got one." Browning puffed, and blew into the fog. "How do you kill an American?"

"Lord knows."

"Take his watch."

Jacobs snorted loudly. "That's . . . terrible," he scolded insincerely.

The two men chuckled a little bit, but the silence of the estate overwhelmed them. It was all stone and clover and beautiful neat rows of fruit, berry, and nut plantings, designed to please the eye no matter what season.

"It *is* beautiful," Browning said at last. "Whoever designed this was an artist of the first water."

"It was Ivo Quimper's wife." Jacobs supplied. "I asked. She must have been remarkable. The servants still miss her. Not an easy feat for someone who has been dead, what . . . over forty years?"

"Quite remarkable." Browning agreed. "And he never remarried."

"Oh, there was one he wanted to marry." Jacobs answered. "But the lady was not willing." He traded a significant look with Browning. "Sometimes you just wonder if the rumors are anything like the truth."

"And what do you think?"

"That sometimes truth requires imagination." Jacobs folded his arms across his chest. "I talked with some of the older folk around here. Strange stuff. They don't believe their Thomas did it . . . but they go all silent, like, when you ask them who would."

"That's not so unusual."

"It is when you think of what could be causing the fright. The Master's dead. Who'd be left to browbeat these people?"

"You're right there. What about the son?"

"No one's seen hide nor hair of 'em since his ship went down in the Channel back in '84 . . . save the time he re-surfaced in Brittany last spring in time to harass Lestrade one last time." [1] Jacobs decided to smoke with Browning. "And you want to talk about rumours *there*. I've decided I don't believe eleven shill out of that pound."

"I'd heard he was killed by smugglers just last spring."

"Some were happy enough to take the credit for his vanishing. That doesn't mean they actually did it." Jacobs gnawed on the stem of his pipe. "It's a mess all around and I don't like where this is headed. Something happened that tipped Thomas Lestrade's mind over. Everyone said that man was strong, strong as a horse. Why would he go like that?"

"Strong men don't always break. They can crack first," Browning answered unhappily. "You're saying something's keeping the servants from saying something."

"If you tell me the butler's your suspect, so help me I will tackle you."

"Well, they do everything else. I'd imagine killing the master would be just another form of spring cleaning."

"Ugh!" Jacobs groaned. "I tell you, the missing son's got me worried. French gendarmes are no help at all – which is hardly surprising. He was slippery. Likely got enough on them that he could live among them in the blackmail business. We never did get a body to prove he was dead – either time we heard he was dead."

"What about the butler?" Browning persisted.

"Out of town, getting on his monthly drinking binge and there's a half-dozen witnesses to that one."

"Bloomin' lovely."

"So it still goes down to Thomas Lestrade."

"*Hsshh.*"

They fell silent. Two figures were moving through the fishy fog. Two small men, one dressed in sea togs.

"Get them back to the translating, and have Berry stand by to assist them," Browning muttered. "We're going back in that bloody Murder Room again."

"What are you looking for?" Jacobs was willing to be convinced.

"Anything odd."

82

"Well, you've certainly come to the right place . . . ."

"Morning to you, Jacobs – Browning, I didn't see you." Lestrade peered uncertainly. "When did you start wearing that coat? You look like a bruiser."

"You don't have to sound so surprised, Lestrade," Browning sounded wounded. "I'm all right in a fight."

"I know that." Lestrade shook his head. Potier was standing to one side, on occasion brushing the mist out of his beard. "What's it to be today?"

"Just sit with him for now and see if he can relax enough to start talking." Jacobs picked up Browning's request. "He never said a single word to anyone until you two showed up."

"I'll see what I can do." Lestrade and his grandfather looked at each other. "Would it be all right if he went around and asked a few questions?"

"Questions? I don't see why not, but we've asked plenty as it is."

"Not that . . . ." Lestrade winced. "We're . . . he's . . . he wants to find his daughter."

Jacobs felt the blood leave his temples as he realized the enormity of the situation. "Of course, sir, I do apologize. I . . . you ought to find her in that little cottage against the stables." He cleared his throat. "Lestrade, when you get to the cell, Berry is that big 'un with the bright red beard trying to spill over his collar. Have him help you . . . He's in need of impressing his superiors of late, if you get my meaning."

Lestrade chuckled, low and amused. "I'll see to it he doesn't make too many mistakes in my presence," he assured. "Might we go someplace warmer and . . . drier?"

"Absolutely. The kitchen's free. I was thinking some decent breakfast might help. He won't drink any of the tea we give him. Or the breakfasts . . . If you could get him to pull his strength up, that'd be half the fight."

"He won't eat or drink?" Lestrade frowned. "I'll see about that, too."

"Sorry business," Jacobs said when they were alone again.

"Let's get this over with."

A young man wearing a face drawn from grief was outside cutting windfall into manageable sticks for the fireplace. He looked up as Potier walked up, and slowly frowned in an effort to place him.

"Hello, there, Marcus. You don't recognize me?"

"Ah . . . You are . . . you are The Seagull?" The boy stammered slightly. *"You are here to see* Mamm*?"*

"That I am. Is she inside?" Potier was ridiculously glad to hear another boy call Jeanne *'Mamm.'* She had loved motherhood. Adopting Marcus would have been the right thing to do.

"*Yes, sir . . . just a moment . . . .*"

"*I'll help you there,*" Potier grunted as he let the boy pile wood in his arms. Some old pear-wood, not fit for much but heating. "You lead the way, boy."

He remembered the large, old house from one of his few visits. It would seem an ostentatious extravagance to house the horsemaster in such a place, but it was bound to the stables by a common door and frankly, it was as much a workshop and community centre as it was a house.

He remembered the large plank table where everyone gathered. And the oversized fireplace and inglenook inside. Jafrez had slept there as a boy. His mother had used the other side to sit for her sewing while the adults gathered about that table, drinking and passing jokes and gossips.

And Potier saw his daughter there now. Her hands were too stiff for sewing, but she was weaving a small carpet with black wool.

"*Mamm?*"

Jeanne looked up at her adopted son's arrival, and a frightened look passed across her face at a momentarily unfamiliar man. Then she saw who it was, and she stood, the shuttle clattering to the floor.

"*Hello, my girl. Still at the loom when you should be outside playing?*"

"*Taddiz?*" Jeanne breathed out, her hands to her face, then her throat. She watched, quite stunned. Her father flashed her a rascal's grin as he dumped the wood neatly in the corner, brushed his hands off, and buried her in a fierce hug.

"*There's some breakfast waiting . . . don't you want to eat something?*"

Thomas Lestrade remembered his manners and lifted one shoulder.

It would have to do. Inspector Lestrade nodded at Berry and quietly drew his father by the arm to the kitchen in the Main House. Of course, they avoided the front door. For all their practicality (nil), Lestrade wondered why people even built the things. Side doors were the only doors that made sense.

"Berry, if you wouldn't mind handing me that teapot . . . ."

"Tell me why people spend so much money on these things."

Jacobs shared Browning's cynicism on floor-coverings, but merely shook his head. "I suppose because they're worth money?"

"A two-foot-square version of this thing would cost more than I spend on my entire family come Christmas." Browning knelt and tugged at the corner of the carpet. He grunted. "Good old-fashioned Kabistan rugs, three-hundred-weight if they're a scruple." [2] He groaned.

"You can't possibly expect to find anything underneath that monster." Jacobs groaned as well. "We just sent the constables out."

"We're not dragging the constables into this. They've got quite enough to do with picking up after us." Browning set his teeth and squinted his one eye. "Come on, then. We're going to look."

"If there's a trapdoor under this, by Jove I'll have *you* spring it for tricks!" Jacobs swore before dropping to his knees next to his partner.

"For the love of . . . ." Lestrade stopped just short of casual blasphemy and finally just started poking about the shelves. "This isn't going to work," he muttered to himself.

"Sir?" Berry wondered.

"How's the hot water coming along?"

"Almost to the boil, sir. Good hot fire. Clean birchwood."

"Good for that. All right . . . ." Lestrade muttered some more under his breath. "I don't know how I'm supposed to feed him if there's nothing to eat."

"Sir?" Berry was startled. "There's a big platter right – "

"He can't eat that stuff, Constable. He – " Lestrade turned around, and a thought struck him. "But if you want that, go right ahead. No predicting when you'll get another meal today."

"Sir! Thank you, sir!" That easily, Lestrade made a friend for life. Berry attacked the apple-stuffed sausages and stuffed pancakes as though his life depended on it.

So nice to know that some people aren't expensive to win over . . . Lestrade yelped his satisfaction as he came across a small metal tin of groats. "Perfect! Berry, where's the – Oh, there it is." Lestrade poured two measures into a small pot with water out of the sink and a dash of coarse salt. "Just in time," he added, swinging the teapot out and replacing it with the porridge.

Berry chewed frantically – as Lestrade had said, there was no telling when he'd get another meal today, and he might get called to duty at any moment. He watched as Thomas Lestrade sat like a manikin at the table, head down and not paying attention to anything going around him. Lestrade slow-poured a steaming stream over a pile of loose black leaves and covered the lid with a clap. By the time he found the cups, they were ready to be filled.

"These sausages are very good, sir. Are you certain we can't give him any?" Guilt made all sorts of men generous.

Lestrade smiled thinly. "Your heart's in the right place, Constable . . . but believe me. This ought to be enough." He pushed the first cup forward until it touched Thomas Lestrade's fingers. "Here you are, sir." His voice dropped slightly. "Try and see if this sits well with you."

Hoary old carpets cannot be moved with anything resembling expediency. They must be rolled, and when the carpet is not to be examined so much as what's beneath it, the only solution is to roll up one corner at a time. Each roll gets heavier and heavier. By the time one gets to the center of the carpet, one may be wrestling double their own weight, as well as gravity. One person cannot do it alone. Another man is needed to make certain the carpet will not unroll itself while it is being rolled forward.

"All right," Browning gasped. "You can kill me."

"I'll have to rest up first." Jacobs' expression was rather close to the job. The men panted, sweating their collars past their usefulness in the stillness of the closed room.

"Not even . . . a trap door underneath either." Browning gave up. He sank to the floor cross-legged and let his head droop down as he breathed.

"It's . . . quite all right, Browning. You can have the next trap door I run into." Jacobs was clearly going to operate under the fuel of annoyance for some time. "Not that I fault your duty, you understand. But a promise is a promise."

"Yes." Browning sagged. "Blast it. I just think there has to be something around here."

"Sirs?" Constable White poked his head through the doorway. "Message from Inspector Lestrade, sirs. He wants you to know he had to unwrap the bandages on the accused. Something about having trouble eating with them."

"Well . . . ." Jacobs scowled his confusion. "Thank you, White. I can't see a problem with that." He pulled a deep breath in. "How long have we been fighting this leviathan?" He wondered. The clock answered for him. "Good Lord, a half-hour."

"Long enough," Browning sighed. "What do you want to do now?"

"This was your idea . . . ." Jacobs' mouth hung open . . . or rather, he forgot to shut it. It just remained frozen and half finished. Browning looked at him, then at the carpet, but didn't see what was so blooming amazing.

"What is it?"

"It's bloody right next to you!" Jacobs pointed. "Pick it up!"

"This?" Browning complied. "It's just a twig of some sort." He turned it over in his fingertips. "Chewed on . . . ." He brought it close to his face and Jacobs' saw his eyebrows shoot straight up. "Hold on," he said very, very softly.

"What?"

"This isn't a twig . . . its liquorice."

"'Liquorice?'" Jacobs repeated. "Someone was *cleaning their teeth* in a room as fancy as this?"

"Wouldn't have been just someone . . . ." Browning tossed the stick to Jacobs. "These poor folk, I don't think they'd be able to afford a luxury like that."

"No, but a butler could."

"Or a horsemaster." Browning said sadly.

"Or a horsemaster." Agreed in a like mind. They shook their heads in unified sorrow that the world had come to this. "If Ivo Quimper'd been chewing that, I would have caught that on my first night here." Jacobs climbed up with a painful grunt. "Coroner found nothing of note in his mouth when he was checking for the usual obstructions. That would have been noted."

"Best to ask him about it anyway," Browning admitted. "We need to make certain. You do admit it looks odd that the Master would let his horsemaster chew on liquorice in his presence. It's vulgar."

"It would make sense if he's permitted liberties the other servants aren't allowed."

"Yes . . . you're right."

There was nothing but the sound of that said liquorice root, being tapped like a baton against an Inspector's hand.

"Let's see if our Lestrade encouraged our Lestrade to talk." Browning said at last. It wasn't the worst play on words, but it was still weak.

They pushed the door open to find three faces look up at them: Berry, Inspector Lestrade in sharp interest, and his father, the accused, in a blank-faced response that didn't seem to care what was going on.

Lestrade said something in that language. It sounded like some version of, "Just a moment," and he was putting on his hat while meeting them at the jamb. "One moment of your time, please," he said in English.

Outside, Lestrade glanced about, plainly a little on the jumpy side. "Did you see those hands?" he asked them.

"No. Someone wrapped them up after he was found with Mr. Quimper."

"Those wounds look strange," he told them. "They look like this." He straightened one hand out flat, and pointed to the muscles, meat and skin that connected the thumb with the forefinger. "Both hands look like this," he stabbed invisible holes, "but mostly on the left hand."

"Is he left-handed?"

"No. He's right-handed. I'm at a loss to explain it. He can barely eat even without the bandages. I think there's nerve damage."

"We'll have another crow see to him." Jacobs nodded. "But you did get him to eat?"

"Oh. Yes. No problem."

"I'd like to know your secret. None of us could get him to take a thing."

"No secret." Lestrade shrugged. "He can't abide sweet things." At their expressions he blinked. "What is it?"

Browning looked sharp and startled at the smaller man. "Just like you," he breathed. "Jacobs . . . I can vouch for this. Lestrade *can't* stand anything sweet. He can take a little honey but everything else wants to come straight back up as soon as he tries to get it down. I've never seen anything like it."

Jacob's eyes had been slowly widening as Browning spoke. "An inherited trait?"

"*I* don't know!" Lestrade blurted. "We've just never liked sweet things. I can't say I thought much about it. Why?"

"You can take honey?" Jacobs asked.

Lestrade nodded.

"What about liquorice?"

Quick as lightning, a look of nausea crossed the little man's face. He collected himself and swallowed hard. "No, no thank you."

"Well . . . I'm curious, not being rude, but . . . how is it . . . ." Jacobs cleared his throat. "How do you clean your teeth when you're on the go? Most people chew on a liquorice or cane-stalk if they can afford it."

"When there's no place for the regular tooth-powder, I just chew on a stick of thyme." Lestrade pulled a narrow bundle of twigs out of his pocket. They were tooth-pick thin. "I know it's not the usual stuff, but my wife is always cooking with thyme. Might as well make use of them if they're lying around." He perched one eyebrow up. "Why?"

"Interesting . . . ." Jacobs stroked his chin. "We're just trying to account for everything in the Murder Room, Lestrade. What does your father use?"

"I don't know . . . ." Lestrade turned and went back inside. The other Yarders followed. As they settled by the table he said something quickly and explored the old man's coat pockets. A long, thin and square stalk was produced.

"Peppermint," Lestrade told them.

"So it is . . . ." Browning said in a strange voice.

Lestrade's temper had finally struck the bottom. "Will I be allowed to know what you're going on about, gentlemen, or will I just have to explode?"

88

NOTES

1. See *The MoonCursers*.
2. Three-hundred pounds if they're twenty grains – just more than 1 gram.

Chapter X – Gulls

Scotland Yard:

"Good Lord," was Inspector Gregson's summary, opinion, and criticism of Stanley Hopkins when he next stepped into the office. "You still look a little pale there, Hopkins."

"We live in London, Gregson," Hopkins told him wearily. "I'm not likely to don the rosy bloom of health – even during such a stimulating time of year as this." Despite the flippancy, he breathed as lightly as possible.

The tow-headed man grunted, his own pale face pinking at the sides. "You're well enough. I take it Dr. Watson gave you a clean bill of health?"

"Well, he agreed to let me go if I agreed to be scolded for over-extending myself and winding up in his mercies within the next week." He winced slightly. "And he gave me a snorter of a speech on how I was inviting a lung infection in if I insisted on shallow breaths . . . so I will be breathing deeply once I'm home and lying down."

"That sounds more like it. I was starting to worry about that man . . . ." Gregson was pointedly not smoking. He would be home in a few hours and owed it to his wife. "You missed Patterson, by the way. He's been working on our Wardrobe Man, and better him than me any day." He smiled at Hopkins' look of remembrance and distaste. "I know. Patterson's convinced there's something about the body that goes in with our current project."

"I'd like to know how," Hopkins confessed. "Even though I'm sure I wouldn't find the answer restful."

"Well they called in an expert of sorts to help with that . . . One of the Devonshire Health officers. Strange bird – reminds me of an ostrich somehow, especially when he looks at you with those eyes on each side of that big beak of a nose . . . ." Gregson began ruffling papers in search of a particular paper. "Said the Wardrobe Man's hands pegged him as a . . . 'excavationist'." He passed the paper over. "I made a copy of that for you. The way things are going, we should be keeping duplicates about us."

"As in someone who excavates?" Hopkins hazarded a guess. He stopped to yawn. "Well, that wasn't one of my proudest moments just now . . . ." He read through the page carefully. "Oh, dear, he's right. Those researchers are as jealous as they can be. It's like watching a rugby game staffed with professors from rival universities."

Gregson tried to cork the laugh in his mouth but failed. "That's a rich image there, Hopkins. I'm surprised *Punch* hasn't thought of it."

"Too busy having their fun with us, I suppose," Hopkins muttered darkly. He let his fingers tap on the arm of his chair in a loose musical pattern. "He mentions a list . . . do you have it?"

"He said he was putting it together today, and would let us have it when he was done."

"Let me know, please. I'd be most interested in this list . . . ."

"Speaking of Lists, how goes your work with the Burial Board?"

Hopkins just looked at him.

"Ah," Gregson sighed.

"Ever since that grave opened up under Lestrade, I've had a devil of a time getting help. You wouldn't believe the talk of curses and going against God . . . I think it's just sound and fury myself. These men don't want to work with us at all. I even promise them a better-than-standard wage."

"Now that's odd. You think there's another reason why they aren't being helpful?"

"Honestly? What if we accidentally came across the bone-thief's business? Robbing the graves here and there for medical curiosities or a gold tooth or two? Remember those grave-robbers Bradstreet found? What if it's something like that?"

"Grave-robbers charging the big criminals to let them put their murder victims in already occupied holes?" Gregson rubbed at his arms. "Wait a moment there, Hopkins. That was back in '70 . . . you couldn't have been old enough to remember that!"

Hopkins looked hurt and insulted. "Why wouldn't I?"

"You weren't more'n five years of age back then!"

"I *know*," Hopkins snorted. His glare was still young and unpracticed but it was beginning to show promise. "Believe me, Gregson, *I do know* . . . It was my birthday party ruined when everyone decided they couldn't stop talking about what was in the papers while I was trying to cut my own cake!"

Gregson looked to the ceiling. "And thus, some men choose a life of corruption and crime, while others choose the Yard . . . ."

"Oh, for . . . ." Hopkins dropped the subject – an act of will that impressed the older man. "Get me that list as soon as you can. I want to see if there's anything familiar in there." He pushed himself up to stand and slowly rubbed at his ribs. "Did anyone get the report on my accident?"

"Certainly. Not worthy of framing yet, Hopkins. You need at least three broken bones and a cup of blood for that . . . ."

Plymouth:

The day had passed without incident . . . a resting period between the squalls. Potier strolled out of his daughter's house in a mood that layered pensive thought with the relief that he was again talking with Jeanne. Poor girl. Bravery should never be rewarded with tragedy. It had been good to hold her in his arms again, and drink the tea she made with her own hands, arthritic though they were.

Her bones hurt her in part from diet, he knew. She needed more of the good fruit and food of home. Meadowsweet wines and the spicy black mustard plasters would help, and Angelica stalks candied with black cherry syrup. The size of the celery plot in her little garden spoke of her attempts to treat herself. He also saw there was a small patch of stinging nettles rising out of a warm compost-heap. Nettles were effective, but not for the timid.

He thought of how he could help as he strolled back to the big house. The ocean had warmed the land to the point that it was getting a head start on growing. He couldn't remember the last time he'd seen such a green patch of England this far from spring. Young poppies were sending out shoots with the lettuce and onions. Deep-planted leeks were just beginning to state themselves.

Night slid angles of shadow across the slope as the wet clover brushed his boot-soles. It was quiet. The folk were subdued down to the children. At one time he'd been easy acquaintance with these people, but that had passed as Quimper's control had grown. Looking back, he hadn't known if he could do anything different. One had to save oneself. And he known there would be another war someday.

A war won or lost? It seems to live as long as we live. He scuffed slightly as his feet took him off the clover and to the crushed stone and shell of the carriage-road. Potier had conducted a revenge upon the Quimpers as good as he'd been capable of giving – and that had been considerable. Smugglers weren't the sort to be crossed, and they could remember wrongs without effort. The grandson that favoured him had been the opposite. Choosing a life within the soothing straight lines of law and order and process. Life could be startling up to the very end.

Potier paused at the small lamp-post set up in the centre of the circular driveway that represented the heart of the estate. Another bit of monetary largess with the Quimpers. Potier stretched himself up, a spry old seaman, and hopped to the small flame with the end of his cigar. A moment later he was back on the ground and puffing in self-satisfied contentment.

The manor was lit brightly from within. Potier reasoned the butler – Howard – would have his hungover-hands full keeping order with all the clumsy policemen, curious newspaper writers, locals from Plymouth proper, and of course the staff that were just waiting to get their final notice for their service and be officially cast out into the wilds.

"Try it again," someone was saying.

Potier looked up. His grandson was standing in front of the library that stood by the Murder Room. The voices of the other detectives were adding in. Tense and worried. Potier gnawed on his cigar thoughtfully and decided to let himself in. They could always tell him to go back to the Inn, but he wasn't about to do that without Jafrez.

After the cool damp of the outdoors, this felt hot and stuffy. Or perhaps it wasn't illusion. The detectives looked drained and sick in the yellow gaslight. Jacobs was drinking weak tea from a tin flask.

"Hello, Mr. Potier." Browning saw him first. Jafrez was sinking into the horsehair chair with his legs straight out. Almost defeatist. "Did you find what you were looking for?"

"Ya, It was *mat* . . . ." Potier found himself grinning again. "*Mat-mat*."

"Ah. Well . . . we've been working." Browning scrubbed at his bloodshot eyes. "Geoffrey . . . perhaps you'd be the best person to tell him."

"Are we going to keep this quiet?" his grandson wanted to know. "I can assure you, he's discreet as the ivy."

"There's no worry about that, I assure you." Jacobs waved that off, stiff with his fatigue.

"*Mab?*"

"Thomas didn't kill Ivo Quimper. *He was trying to protect him.*" Lestrade felt himself losing the war with nausea. Potier's expression didn't make it any easier. He stopped and breathed for a moment, putting himself into another land from this one. As Potier watched, he went to a grotesque Baroque candlestick-holder, carved with vicious-looking spikes to simulate a real rose-briar twining up the stalk. "This is the mate of the murder weapon. You can see there's a place where the person carrying it can be free of punctures, but nowhere else." He slowly pretended to lift the thing and bring it down upon Potier's head. Potier drew his left hand up in instinct.

"Thomas Lestrade's left hand bears the brunt of the marks. He was instinctively protecting his right hand. That's the one he uses the most in his livelihood." Jacobs searched frantically for his tobacco and visibly relaxed when he found it. "Men are like bats. Most bats don't like to bite a man, even when they put their hands on them, because they can't risk breaking their teeth. They'd starve to death. Same thing here. Your son-on-law couldn't ruin both hands. He needed them to be a valued worker."

"That makes sense," Potier considered as he passed over his little match-box.

"It gets worse." Jafrez told him quietly. "The marks Browning pointed out on his hand . . . look." He held out his own hand, and slowly wrapped it around the candlestick holder. "There are no *gripping* marks. Thomas Lestrade wasn't *holding* the weapon . . . He was trying to *block* it from coming down on Ivo Quimper's head." He stretched his hand into a blocking-motion. "He probably knew he couldn't possibly wrestle this thing out of the killer's grip, but he wasn't going to just stand there and let Ivo Quimper be bludgeoned to death either."

Browning looked sick. "We have more than one crime here. *Why* wouldn't Thomas Lestrade say anything about what he was doing?"

"These people won't talk on a good day," Jacobs pointed out. "They still think they're living in the Middle Ages. If someone above them told to keep mum . . . they'll keep mum." They watched as the man paced back and forth, hands opening and opening within each other.

"Fear is its own form of blackmail," Lestrade said coldly. "If you ever worked anywhere near Saffron Hill, you'd be aware of that!"

"I'm not insulting anyone . . . I'm just saying that something's keeping these people from telling the truth."

"Jethro Quimper," Potier said it because no one else would. "He's alive."

"Why would he kill his own father?" Browning asked.

"Are you saying that one is not capable? I assure you he carries a great deal of cruelty."

"This wasn't cruelty. This was mindless rage, *Tad-kohz*, but you're right. He's cruel and he enjoys being cruel." Lestrade couldn't sit any longer. He rose to his feet and walked to the fireplace, hands clasped behind his back in an effort to hold them still. "But we can't prove he was here."

"No one else would terrify the families to that extent!" Potier exclaimed. "What more proof can you people require!"

"The testimony of one person," Browning told him. "Just one. As long as there's no hint of coercion that the witness gives and answer they think the questioners want to hear."

Potier's lips were a dark line within his beard. "Bring my daughter here. She'll tell you the truth."

Lestrade's face emptied of colour right in front of the other detectives. "Sir, I don't want her to have to do this."

"*She can. She will. She's tough as blackthorn. You ought to know. She's your* mamm, *after all.*" Potier didn't say it in English, but his meaning was clear.

94

Lestrade swallowed. "Inspectors? Your decision, not mine."

Jacobs remembered the little woman, nut-brown and drawing lines of age and fear and pain. He wasn't proud of himself for putting more on that sad face. "If she can help us come to the truth, we can only ask her."

"She can't testify against her husband." Browning reminded him. "How are we going to ask around the subject?"

"Trust me. I've had to do this sort of thing before." Jacobs did not look glad to say so. "Berry!" He lifted his voice and waited for the red-bearded man to come forward. "Please bring Mrs. Lestrade here, please. She knows enough English to know to come with you."

Lestrade went to the back without being told. He picked the chair that was almost completely behind the door and didn't move a single muscle as they waited. No one tried to say anything to bolster his feelings. It wouldn't have run true anyway.

Browning pulled out his notebook as they heard the door open and shut. Lestrade remembered he had a notebook too and pulled it out. It would help if his hands had something to do.

Potier saw how even as his daughter came into the room, her son never looked up but stayed fixed on his blank page with pencil at the ready. He held out his hand to Jeanne, and drew her to one of the settees, keeping her head aimed away from Jafrez the entire time. Berry hovered anxiously, unsure of where his duty would pull him next.

"My girl," Potier spoke in slow English. It was always better to not let people know how well you understood their language. A trick they had all played for generations. "We are needing to know a few things. Can you answer this man's questions?"

Jeanne Lestrade looked uncertainly upon the tall form of Browning, who tried to smile and look reassuring around his eyepatch, and Jacobs, who was still as grey and hard as a lean tree. She nodded nervously without taking her eyes off either of the detectives.

"Mrs. Lestrade," Jacobs pitched his voice to a low and soothing murmur. "Was Mr. Quimper in the habit of seeing guests?"

She blinked and nodded. It was not the sort of question she had expected.

"Even this time of year?"

"Ya . . . Yess," Jeanne assured him.

"Did a guest arrive the night he was killed?"

"*Nann.*"

Jacobs paused, re-thinking his question. "Did a guest arrive some time before he was killed?"

She looked confused. "*Nann.*"

Looks were traded about.

"My daughter is very literal," Potier whispered. "Very literal. She won't look for deeper meanings to your questions."

Jacobs brightened. "Thank you." He rose slowly, and stroked at his chin. "Mrs. Lestrade . . . does Mr. Quimper have family?"

"Yes."

"I see. You don't believe your husband killed the master, do you?"

"*Nann.*" She shook her head with the greatest strength they'd witnessed of her.

"Who would kill the master?"

"The master," she answered.

"The master." Jacobs repeated.

Behind his mother, Inspector Lestrade had looked up with a face white as chalk. Jacobs watched surreptitiously as he put down his pencil and slowly drew his hand up to his face, resting one fingertip to a faint scar at the left of his forehead.

Browning caught on. "Mrs. Lestrade, have you seen a man known as Jethro Quimper within the past thirty days?"

Tears filled her large brown eyes. She nodded.

"Was he anywhere near on the night Ivo Quimper died . . . ?"

"I have had my fill of this!"

Jacobs waited until Berry led a teary Mrs. Lestrade and her father out of the room before he exploded. The other detectives jumped. They'd been expecting it, but Jacobs was no ordinary man when his temper roused up.

"They knew." The grey man swore under his breath as he paced a track-line into the carpet. "I'll bet you pound to a penny the bloody Foreign Office and the Home Office knew all along he was alive, probably had their agents keeping an eye here for the past ten years . . . Saw him come in and watched him leave before the murder was reported!"

"But why would they hide that much from us?" Browning protested.

"Quimper's French connections," Lestrade spoke like an exhausted man. "There's plenty who feel the French are still willing to wage war against England."

"Oh, yes . . . the same bloody geniuses who think *you're* French, Lestrade," Jacobs spat bitterly. "Same geniuses who knew what was going to happen during the Franco-Prussian war back in '70 . . . Same geniuses who are running the show now that their sweet old papas have retired . . . ." He struck against the mantel in his anger. The clock skipped on its metal legs. "Bloody tinkers-sons set us up!" He cursed.

"Don't demean the Tinkers into this," Lestrade growled. "They've got their principles."

"I'm starting to think a Tannery sweeper has principles compared to these fools," Jacobs roared. "All this because they want to keep an eye on a man who has power in the crime rings of France."

"It could be more than that." Browning rubbed gently at his temples. "If he's come back to English soil, he's got English connections of his own . . . connections that survived Moriarty."

"And they'll be wanting to know who those connections were," Jacobs snarled. "It's all too clear. I was told . . . no, I was *asked* to keep an eye on this case. 'If he's the killer, find the proof,' they said . . . I thought it meant . . . I thought they were telling me I *had* to find proof it was your father, Lestrade." Anger and anguish mixed in equal parts across that bony grey face. "But that's just what they wanted me to do. They led me to this . . . so the real killer could run free under their eyes." He stepped forward and gripped the smaller man by the forearms. "I nearly sent your father to the rope or to Dartmoor, just so the public would think there was a nice loose end tied up."

Lestrade swallowed. "If you let my father go," He said carefully, "you might as well end your chances of advancing. Look what happened to me."

"I'll do what I was told. I'll tell 'em the truth." Jacobs' voice was chill. "I'll write up a report they won't like to hear, and they'll read it. Defensive marks on your father's hands. Servants beaten into silence. And that description your mother gave, Lestrade . . . her description may yet save us all."

"I don't follow you."

"The police descriptions of Jethro Quimper are grossly out of date. She said he limps slightly, has grey hair, and needs a cane for full support. A*nd* there's a few nice scars on his face and hands." Jacobs frowned. "He must have had a busy life since his ship went down in the Channel."

Or when he was out hunting . . . Lestrade cleared his throat. "Are you saying you're going to post an inch-by-inch description of Jethro Quimper, without saying it actually is Jethro Quimper?"

"That's mad as a March Hare." Browning grimaced. "But it's also a bit . . . clever."

"If Quimper's alive, he's active. If he's active, the Foreign Office has his real and current description in their records. Obviously we don't. They want to play us for fools. By God, I'll be their fool. I'll be a drooling, toothless gibbering fool!" Jacobs' smile was nasty. "They can't say I'm not doing my duty."

"That doesn't answer what to do about . . . Thomas Lestrade." Even with practice, Lestrade almost strangled at the effort it took to use his estranged father's name. He paused to cough. "They might want him for questioning. And . . . his wife."

"If the evidence points to another party . . . I can't exactly hold them for further questioning."

Browning reached for his pipe and started packing it. "I see what you mean." He held Jacobs' eyes in a hard light. "The Chief won't like it."

"No one will like it," Jacobs said at last. "Can you get your parents out of Plymouth, but where you can keep an eye on them too?"

"Jacobs . . . ." Browning whispered.

"*I won't have it!*" Jacobs barked. "I'll do as they say, but I won't follow them until they pull my leash. I've had it." He set his mouth. "They wanted to know if someone else was involved in this . . . That's all they wanted to know. They didn't care about that old man, they didn't care about his family . . . We're the little ones. We didn't matter . . . ." His fist dug into his palm. "I can't hold a man for a crime he didn't commit."

Jacobs spun on one foot, and stabbed the air before Lestrade with his finger. "Get them out of here. Get them out where no one's liable to find them. If we need them . . . we'll call. But it'll be me or Browning. No one else." Jacobs' glacial fury burned from his eyes. "Some people are about to remember a few things about Scotland Yard. They are going to remember we are not gulls to be used."

98

Chapter XI – Departures and Arrivals

London:

$\mathbf{M}$ary Watson was rarely as charmed at first sight as she was by Dr. Mortimer. The tall man bowed – dipped, rather – over her hand and offered sincere courtesies over the tops of his spectacles. The good humor lasted throughout supper as they traded pleasantries and she finally bade them good night and retired upstairs to Arthur.

"Patterson will join us for breakfast," John informed his guest. "He's been over-working himself of late. I told him to rest now or I'd exercise my authority over him."

"Oh? What authority do you have?"

"I'd no doubt have to make it up . . . but he doesn't seem to know that," John explained. "As it is, I'm assisting the Yard in taking up some of the cases in Dr. Roanoke's absence. His age and health are demanding either an extended holiday, or an early retirement."

"I suppose I ought to be grateful that the weather is softening," Mortimer mused as he accepted a small glass from John. "It would make field-work a simpler arrangement. A few heavy frosts can even be of value."

"Really? I wouldn't think so." John settled in his preferred chair and stretched his bad leg out to the fire.

"Most wouldn't." Mortimer chuckled. "Excellent brandy, I must say. Oh. The frost. You see, when one is working in soft soils, such as loam or humus, or something of a shifting quality, it can cause all sorts of miniscule aggravations. One has to make a much larger pit than normal to compensate for the freedom of the soil. But when you have a good, solid frost – say, a frost that would permeate the soil a good six inches or so – then you have the chance of many interesting objects rising straight out of the ground."

John thought about it, his eyes brightening with comprehension. "I see. The cold settles into the moisture in the soil, and when it freezes, it expands . . . and if there is no place for the expansion to take place, it will go up to the surface."

"I've found many curious crinoids in such a manner, as well as a few strange brachiopods that are in my personal collection." Mortimer swirled his brandy with such slight movements his hand appeared still. Only the liquid in the glass moved. "Once I discovered a fine flint-point. That led to some interesting bones. But I confess I always feel a pang to disturb the frost, for the molecules stack upon the ground like cavernous crystals. 'Frost Flowers', the workers call them. They can even tint with the pigments of the soil, so you can have crystal flowers with the most delicate shades of yellow, ochre, red, violet – even blue when I'm working about the shales. A natural phenomenon that is no less mysterious for knowing the secrets of its creation."

"A shame a camera was never around to capture those fleeting ice-flowers," John's attention was pleasantly diverted at Mortimer's ability to tell a factual story. "We had something similar when I was a boy growing up on the shores . . . small, melting blobs that shone . . . they were called moon-jellies. And we would find them upon the sands after the full moon, and we would watch them melt away with the sun. As children we would watch the scientists and researchers come to examine those delicate little foot-prints of mystery . . . but I don't believe they ever agreed what made the shimmering circles on the shingle." He chuckled to himself. "Heaven forbid we suggest they were merely jellyfish come to shore to die. I suppose their sense of wonder was diminished by having a simple answer . . . ." He leaned his arm behind his head like a pillow. "Once in a while, there would be an attempt to frighten us all into behaving with stories of the *fritteners* . . . things that existed merely to terrorize children. But it is a hard thing to be frightened in the light of the day with seagulls screeching over one's head."

"Oh? And were you still brave when night fell?"

"When night fell we were nowhere near the beach – unless there was a good catch, a jug, and a bonfire involved!"

They laughed together as the wind swept down the street and rattled a loose pane set into the wall. Mortimer lifted his glass in a toast to Watson, smiling and respectful.

"I have been meaning to write you, you know. I fear I'm just as absent-minded as ever – perhaps I am even worse!"

"I wouldn't think so, unless you persuaded me," John protested calmly.

"Why, thank you. I've been reading your articles and essays. The styles you employ are quite succinct. There's something of the Henry Mayhew about you."

John grimaced. "I should never attempt to reach his level, but thank you."

"No, no, I am serious. Some writers are resolutely trapped into one method – such as third-party or first-party narrative. They try but they cannot break the mold they set for themselves when they first began to write. A shame, for some of the most brilliant men I know are trapped so." Mortimer's long fingers rolled a slender cigarette out of a pale beige paper stamped with a tiny blue flower at the end. John watched as the spot of blue moved back and forth as if caught in a wind. "It's your ability to watch the world about you, and I believe . . . your natural affection for our race."

"Again, I thank you, but I see little point in disliking ourselves. It seems counter-productive on a Biblical scale."

Mortimer threw back his head and laughed, bright and brief. "Mr. Holmes was not the only philosopher to have lived at Baker Street!"

John smiled, glancing down at his brandy.

"I hope I do not cause you grief by mentioning him," Mortimer said quickly.

"You do not," John said. The wind was dry. The sun burned in patches and the smell of London fog and cinders was far, far removed from the cold fury of the Falls. Looking back, the depression that had crippled him in Mary's absence was a dim memory – a nightmare one cannot completely re-grasp after it frightens the sleeper into wakefulness. "I assure you, my friend deserves to be mentioned."

"Well, I most certainly agree. I don't understand why his death was so lightly observed. Poor Van Gogh's suicide took more notice . . . and the influenza epidemics." The long fingers were agitated. John watched as the emotion spread up Mortimer's arms and to his face and voice. "I don't really care about the invention of the zipper, you know. Or the Triple Alliance being renewed again – was there any doubt? But to not notice the passing of a man who gave his life for a greater good . . . I don't understand."

"Nor do I," John said gently. "I assure you . . . that will change."

Mortimer brightened. "Will you write of it, Doctor?"

"I already have," John assured him in that same calm, gentle voice. He rose to adjust the light in the gas as his guest waited expectantly. "And it will be published."

"Why, this is splendid! When may we see it?"

"Soon, I assure you." John's smile had grown, but it was very quiet, the sort of smile that a man gives when he is at a pleasant picnic, knowing that the day he planned is going along perfectly. "I must take care of my previous obligations first, you understand. Holmes gave me permission to publish some of our shorter cases after his death. I am doing just that. The public will be ready to hear of his last case . . . when they are taken care of. You might call it a final problem."

Had Colonel Hayter been in the room, his instincts would have been to shiver.

Damson Estates, Plymouth:

"Where did the bag go?"

"By the fruit-bowl."

"I found the knives."

"One each. No more. We haven't that much space."

Marcus Lestrade lowered the tiny lamp from the wall and clipped it to his travel-bag before moving to help his mother finish packing. It was a blur of activity in the cottage, as Jeanne Lestrade and Potier went back and forth, quick from a lifetime of practice and necessity. Thomas Lestrade still sat where they'd left him, his eyes vacant and his hands idle in his lap.

Geoffrey stood by the door, waiting to catch signs of something unpleasant. Jacobs changing his mind, perhaps – or someone changing his mind for him. He would have liked to help, but he didn't have it in him to move in front of his mother's eyes right now. They were both avoiding each other's gaze, unsure of what to do now that the rules of behavior had been capsized.

"Ha," Potier muttered to himself as he shouldered Thomas Lestrade's shoulder-bag upon him. Thomas didn't react. "Marcus, did you get Don?"

"I think that's him right now," Geoffrey cut in. His ear was close to the door. A horse was coming up the drive. "Sounds like a three-quarter . . . a little heavy."

"So long as he can pull us all to the train," Potier declared. "Which one are we taking?"

"I'll decide that when we get there." Geoffrey finally couldn't stand it anymore. He reached out and snagged a heavy bag his mother was trying to carry and swung it on his shoulder. She started a moment and then relaxed, moving to the wall where she pulled mufflers off the hook and passed them out.

Potier moved to his grandson's ear and whispered: "Where are we going?"

"We're headed back to Paddington Street for now. Mrs. Collins has been telling everyone that I'm still out with the quarantine . . . a day there should be long enough to decide where to go. Unless you can think of some place."

"I might – " Potier started, but a horse snorted and he stopped talking.

The drive looked as old as Potier. He carried that stubborn stamp in his hard shoulders and rocky bones. With a swing he was on the ground and approaching the door when it opened.

"Good Lord, its Geoffrey." Unlike most of the other families, the Donasians had always used good English. That priority had been a definitive moment for Geoffrey back in his childhood. "Boy, you have grown up." He paused to smack the Inspector's arms in a brief clamp. "How are things? Heard you married. When do we see the wife?"

"Don, you'd shame a woman with your gossip," Potier snipped from the other side of Lestrade. "Have you thought about giving us a hand here?"

"Yes, I did think about it . . . ." Ian Donasian smirked and stepped to the side. "Hand them over here, and I'll stow it all." He grabbed up two sea-bags by the loops and had them tossed up to the back without a pause. "How's Thomas?" He dropped his voice so Jeanne couldn't hear while she was fighting with a box.

"He thinks Jafrez is me," Potier shot back, low and sharp. "Be careful. We don't know where his mind is right now."

"Let's go, gentlemen," Geoffrey snapped. "I want us at the station ten minutes ago."

There was just enough room in the back of the wagon for everyone but one. Geoffrey took the buck-board while Potier stubbornly took the very rear, and sat in a way that would let him pull out his pistol at a moment's notice.

Don concentrated on the horse for a mile as the small bit of light melted behind them. The moon was not adequate. Lestrade's unease crept through his spine as the horse never showed a sign of breaking its slow, steady pace.

"That has got to be the most sure-footed horse I have ever seen," he said at last. He could barely see the small pool of light from the lamps Donasian had hung on flexible poles and stretched before the animal's head.

Donasian chuckled. "He's blind, that's why. I've walked him up and down this path since he was a colt. He knows the way better than anyone with eyes. But I use the light so I can see if anyone's trying mischief with us."

"It's still not much light," Lestrade pointed out. "We won't see anyone on the road unless they're dressed like Oscar Wilde."

"Good Lord, I'm doubly glad my horse is blind. The sight of that man in his velvet knee-breeches would be enough to make any mount bolt."

"The agreement was broken!"

Thomas Lestrade's voice burst into the night air like a bomb. Lestrade twisted to look behind at his estranged parents.

Stark and white, Jeanne looked up into her tall husband's face in the awful light of the slender moon. She pressed his cold, unresponsive hand between hers, but Thomas never made as though he knew it. Potier's hands were glued upon his pistol, startled by this sign of madness. Marcus stared helplessly at his parents, and then past them to his strange older brother.

103

His brother knew how he felt.

"*Hsshht.*" Donasian hissed through the gap between his teeth. Lestrade spun back to his position, hand folded over his chest as if against the damp chill as the mist settled about them. A tiny light, no smaller than a single candle-flame, was burning down the road.

Lestrade aimed with the slope of the road and reasoned the light was being held by someone. He cleared his throat to Potier, knowing the old smuggler would take his cue. In the corner of his eye, Potier was pushing the other three down out of sight.

The horse slowed for the first time. Donasian whistled softly through his short-cut beard, lifting his little whip to tap the large animal's back and hindquarters. "There we are, old fellow,' he declared. "Mind your step now, mind your step." All this for the benefit of those who didn't know the horse was blind. "Halloa, there. Are you the Canterburys?"

The man standing by the edge of the road with a gleaming new lantern (store-bought and probably never used until now), blinked in owlish surprise to be asked a question. "I beg your pardon?" he asked politely enough, but his voice was rough from lack of use and his clothing shabby. "I don't know nuffin' about any Canterburys, sir." As he turned his head, Lestrade could see a pink scar crawling like a bolt across his right cheek, dissecting the meat over the bone. The pull of the mark sent that portion of his mouth up into a half-smile.

"I'm to pick three of them up on my way to the station," Donasian declared with the proper injection of concern and annoyance in his voice. "Who are you then, young fellow?"

"I'll be the one asking the questions," the newcomer was not doing a good job of regaining his lost foot-hold. He blinked again, stern but wearing a strange confidence with his actions. "I'm here for Mr. Lestrade." He reached up and pulled back his lapel, displaying a flat metal badge.

"What a coincidence," Lestrade drawled. "I'm here to see *you*, Gordon. Been a long time since the Estuary Gang isn't it? What in the world happened to your badge?"

"What?" Confusion crossed rage over the harsh face. "I don't know what you're talking about, fellow!"

"Understood." Lestrade kicked. The lamp went flying into the darkness and burst with a sullen choke of the wet grasses. "Keep going!" He barked.

"But that was a policeman!" Donasian whispered as he clicked up the horse.

"Policeman, ha! I know a fake badge when I see one . . . You country folk aren't living that behind the times!" Lestrade cursed under his breath at both the strange man and himself. *"Keep everyone down, Potier,"* he said in the language.

"No quarrel," Potier answered.

London:

Mortimer was long abed. Watson was alone, and that was comforting.

The doctor was still considered a young man, as if his experience hadn't given him an extra lifespan and an aging of the mind. Moments such as this brought those earned years to the surface.

He'd poured one last glass for the night but had yet to drink it. The snap of the softcoal fire was far more comforting than the taste of drink in his mouth. He allowed himself the comfort of his settee slowly, thinking ahead to the next day.

Mortimer's list made little sense to him, but Watson was not alarmed to be ignorant of that sort of information. He understood the importance of archaeology, but there was still that lingering unease of tampering about with a man's final resting place.

A superstition, nothing more, he told himself. It was a rare graveyard that wasn't completely upturned every ten years. The bereaved refused to accompany the coffin to the cemetery because they preferred to be spared the sight of dislodged bones and graveclothes. A cemetery for the poor was so often a temporary house. Small wonder the soul was of primary importance.

He twirled his glass without half the grace of Mortimer, and sipped without paying attention to it. Tomorrow would be interesting . . . and important. He felt it. Like the night before a battle. Something hummed in the very ground under his feet. Something was warning him.

He could only hope Dr. Mortimer's role in this would bear out his instincts.

Time was marching. Watson sensed that as well as he did the looming fight. He reached into his desk-drawer and pulled out his notebook. His own tiny script looked back at him. Neat letters within faint lines were a code that only he fully understood.

A Study in Scarlet. The Sign of the Four – two cautious ventures into an uneasy market. "A Scandal in Bohemia". "The Red-Headed League". "A Case of Identity", followed by "The Boscombe Valley Mystery". Slow steps. Slow, cautious steps in introducing the world to a man it already knew existed.

Knew, but said nothing about. From the fine titles to the ambitious rising emperor of trade, Sherlock Holmes had been an asset to countless men and women in London and the world. But his fame had been paradoxical and ephemeral. As a gentleman, he had refused to advertise his services. As a gentleman who needed to be respected, he had never sought fame, knowing logically that word of mouth would be more reliable and a finer method of work than simply hanging out a name-plaque.

The consequence being that he had been easy to ignore with his passing.

It twisted Watson's intestines to think of it even now, for he had prevented disaster and disgrace countless times by those who would prefer to go on with their schedules and speak to their friends about the pity of having to hire the help of a detective.

It had also made it easier for what was left of Moriarty's gang to bury the past.

But not much longer.

No . . . The soldier lifted his eyes to the window, ignoring the darkness on the other side. His brown eyes stared thoughtfully through the void and all it promised.

Not much longer.

Chapter XII – Changing Plans

Potier let his body adjust to the rocking of the wagon as they neared the station. His daughter's weight was warm and slight against him.

"Remember how we'd go to the fair?" He spoke up without warning. He sensed Jeanne turn her head in the darkness to look at him. "All of us piling in, pallets in the back so the smallest ones would take a nap on the way . . . hampers of food and your cousin Marie would stop at every sweet-shop we passed."

"You grumbled every time," Jeanne told him softly.

"Of course. You women wouldn't let me visit the cider-shops. Terrible for a man like me to go without a drop!"

Jeanne rested her head against him in the dark. The tatting lace of her cap crushed against his shoulder. "It was always fun."

"Except for when your sister nearly ran off with that salt-panner!"

"I liked him, *Taddiz* . . . at least, I did at first." She smiled against his coat. "How could one man eat so many onions?"

Potier chuckled. The cloud-bank slipped in the wind and the moon came out . . . all one-quarter of it. Thomas' head was a bowed shape. Darkness against the dark.

"We'll take care of him, girl. Don't you worry."

Jeanne swallowed. "I'm not sorry he's dead," she whispered. "He's taken so much from us . . . and now he will take my husband to the grave with him."

"You don't know that," Potier corrected as gently as possible.

"*Nann*? He grew his life into Thomas' and Thomas could not leave. I saw him, *Taddiz*. I say him crumble under the years and I could do nothing."

"What made him do it?" Potier whispered back.

Jeanne shuddered.

"It's all right. We won't speak of it," the old smuggler assured her. "We'll get you to Jafrez . . . there's room at his building."

"He couldn't have that much room," Jeanne said mournfully. "Not for the three of us."

"You think? There's room, dear." Potier patted her on the shoulder while thinking ahead: Jafrez had expected trouble. One obstacle before they were a half-mile down the estate. He had no idea what the future would bring. "There are two strapping grandsons of yours that could take attending . . . !"

He spoke of them. How alike and different the boys were, their mother's house full of clumsy giants except the patriarch, a man he was pleased to call a friend now . . . Jeanne relaxed as he talked, and Marcus hung on his every word. Poor Marcus. He had never been off the estate save when he was stealing away with Jeanne. He was a grown man and knew so little of the world, save the small cruel one of the Quimper Estate.

Everyone besides himself and Potier were appalled at what had happened with the false policeman. Lestrade guessed they weren't used to crimes like impersonation like he was, and resisting anyone who *claimed* to be a policeman was a horror. What exactly the man was stopping them for . . . well, chances were Thomas was something to do with it.

A shame he couldn't even borrow one of the constables to go with them, but the less those boys saw the better. It was easy for a seasoned and corrupt sergeant or someone higher up to corrupt them in turn. The ins and outs of British Law was a snakes-knot, and a young man could be easily lost in them. The only clear path in the pitfalls was the letter of the law, and that was why a man could have hundreds of pages of procedures drilled word-perfect into his skull by the time he'd served five years.

No . . . this was an undoubted grey area. Lestrade had overlooked his duty by not arresting the imposter on the spot, but getting his parents out of this swelling zone of danger was the priority. If all else failed, he could remember that was Jacobs' desire, and Jacobs had been senior officer in this mess.

It wasn't easy to think and watch at the same time. Lestrade reluctantly gave old Don the benefit of knowing his job and gave part of his mind over to the internal world. Being a policeman meant being able to trust those you worked with. That was something he never regretted. Mr. Holmes had never understood what that meant. It was why his bones were now in one of Nature's many unmarked graves. Poor Watson had come close to saving that man from himself, but not quite.

He wished for a pipe, but the flare of the coal would just show someone where to look.

"What time is it?" Donasian asked soft over the sound of the patient horse.

"Hold on . . . ." Lestrade fished for his hunter's watch [1] and heard it ring against his grandmother's St. Anthony medallion. He snapped the lid open. Martin had painted the tips with white to help see at night. "Quarter-of."

"We'll be at St. Budeaux' ten minutes after that." Donasian assured him.

"Haven't been on that line yet. At least not from this end."

"You know how new rail-lines are. I daresay most of the mistakes have been ironed out. The last car leaves Devonport at 10:30." The old man sniffed loudly and clicked the reins out of habit. "Good to see you again," he added.

They weren't likely to be heard from up front. Lestrade sighed. "Thank you."

Donasian held the silence another minute. "We tried to take care of them," he whispered. "Both of them. And Marcus."

"I'm sure you did." Lestrade rubbed at his eyes, wishing he could see something besides that horrid yellow lamp-light. "You did everything you could for me when I was young."

"Young? You were never young," Donasian joked, but like most jokes, there was a thread of sadness within. "I'm just sorry we couldn't adopt you."

"Don't worry about it." Lestrade was growing less comfortable with this conversation by the second. "Think nothing of it, please."

"You were right to feel we'd abandoned you, Jafrez." Donasian stared straight ahead as he spoke, and he barely blinked. "Thomas . . . I suppose your father was showing signs of madness even back then. He told us you would die if you left the family."

Lestrade didn't know what to say to that – or what to think. He *tried* to think – but nothing happened. It was as if his head had become as empty and imbecilic as Mr. Holmes had always sworn.

"It's all right," he finally croaked. A lie. But it would do in an emergency. There was nothing left but to exist in a state until they managed to get to the station . . . *Train fare. The longest stretch on the line will be tuppence . . . and we'll need to switchover several times to get to London . . . that doesn't count the switchovers . . .* Thoughts of the total cost to the train seized his attention gratefully, and he concentrated on planning out the ticket-purchases with the funds in his pockets.

"Jafrez?" Marcus' hoarse voice caught his ear. He twisted around again. The boy was half-sitting up on his knees. "Is there a carpet or horse-blanket up there?" He whispered so the others could not hear him. "*Tad* . . . he's all shivered."

Lestrade thought quickly. "How long has he been like this?" he whispered back.

"Ever since . . . since it happened."

Shock. A terrible experience like that could leave a grown man plagued with unexpected chills for days afterward. Lestrade emptied his overcoat pockets to his outerwear jacket and shrugged out of his coat. "Give him this," he advised quietly. "I've got another coat in there somewhere. I'll dig it out if I need it."

"Thank you." Marcus nodded and leaned across the wagon to pass the coat on to Thomas. Jeanne and Potier managed to wrap him up between the two of them.

"Not much longer," Donasian assured them.

Jeanne had slept so little for so long she had started to fall asleep. It was warm between her father and husband and the rocking of the wagon was not unpleasant. By degrees her eyes closed as she trusted events to unfold properly. The horse slowed and lights glimmered through her eyelids, but now that she was beginning to rest, sleep tugged at her heavily. Voices rippled past her ears. People were moving back and forth, and a train was coming. A whistle sounded, long and low a mile from its destination.

She was leaning against Thomas as he too slept. The coat he wore smelled like sandalwood. Jafrez' touch. Thomas liked the cool, spicy mints and rosemarys of the garden. He could bury himself in their flavour without ever tiring. People were hustling now, preparing to get on the platform.

"Wrong train," Jafrez was saying to her father. "We'll be taking the one after this one, if I'm reading the blessed guide correctly."

"Let them rest then . . . ," her father was saying. "They are all three exhausted."

She was. It would be good to sleep a little. And she did.

"Just kindly give me the tickets, sir." Lestrade used his best Police Voice on the imbecile sitting on the other side of the ticket-gate. The fool thankfully gave up on trying to tell him two of the coins were queer and sulked as he produced the pieces of paper in trade.

"If you're worried about coiners, I suggest you take it up with the constabulary." Lestrade kept up his icy voice. Shivering coatless in the rising wind had something to do with his mood.

"Don't mean nothing by it. Have a pleasant journey, sir."

"I'm sure I will, thank you." Lestrade lied through his teeth and turned his back to the booth. He was instantly jostled half off the planks by the next wave of sleepless folk needing a quick twenty-two mile journey out of Plymouth.

Potier was standing out of the wagon and smoking. A puff of wind suddenly had him batting sparks out of his beard as he sputtered. He swore, but remembered his daughter just in time and choked down the worst of it.

Marcus grinned at him from his place by the rolled-up seabags of clothing. Jeanne had no tolerance for language, and would likely rise up out of a sound sleep to scold a man for venting.

He watched as his grandson shouldered his way through the swelling crowd on the platform and wave a harried signal. Potier tossed his cigar over his shoulder to the wet sawdust at his feet and walked forward. Donasian was still with his horse, filling its head with all sorts of cooing nonsense.

"*Train wired ahead!*" Jafrez had to speak up over the crowd and the fast-approaching steam whistle. "*Two minutes later than usual – ! Delay in picking up a truck of stone!*"

"*That'll please everyone!*" Potier shouted back. "*The rest of the train-line best remember that, or we'll be riding back on the Potluck Express!*"

"*That doesn't actually –* "

Jafrez blanched and all but trampled his grandfather to run past him. Potier was already turning with his hand on his pistol as the younger man tore to the wagon. Donasian was cursing as his horse reared up. With its trust betrayed it was now a frightened, large animal. The old waggoneer yelled, trying to reach it through its panic. A hoof struck at his shoulder and he fell back but hung on to the reins. Marcus was staggering to his feet as the wagon swayed, and – young fool – tried to calm the horse from the rear. Jeanne and Thomas were awake now. Jeanne holding on to her husband who was as unresponsive as ever and shapes were coming up behind them.

Guns were no use with so many people about them. Potier jumped to the wagon as Jafrez pulled something out of his coat. The smuggler saw the long shape of a truncheon in the gaslight before it came down with brute force on the first man. A grunt of pain blended with the crack of bone and the grunt turned into a bellow as someone realized his hand was broken.

"*Hold the horse!*" Marcus was screaming.

"*What do you think I'm doing?*" Donasian screeched back.

Potier took the horse first. It had the greatest chance of causing harm and Jafrez was doing well enough on his own – another crack of bone and an un-manly scream proved that. Potier didn't know what sort of fool would let a London peeler see them coming, but that was just a stroke of luck. He took a chance and clutched at a bit of flying leather. Marcus was scrambling to its hindquarters, his hands on the beast's tail.

Jeanne cried out in fear, and Potier very nearly lost his mind. He let go of the horse (his first impulsive mistake in years) and aimed for the wagon.

"*Get back!*" Jafrez snarled, and swung with his left hand. Dull metal gleamed and Potier made out the shapes were breaking away, retreating into the crowd with broken haste.

111

The horse dropped to all four hooves, trembling but calm. Marcus and Donasian murmured to him, patting it with their hands – Marcus was using one hand. His right was clutched around something.

Potier gasped his relief and trotted over to his grandson, who was finally turning to the wagon and asking harshly if his parents were unhurt. Jeanne managed to nod and that satisfied him for the moment.

"You dusted their coats, *mab!*" Potier wheezed. His heart was pounding like a drum. "I'm starting to get a little old for this nonsense!"

"That's the second time someone's tried to get *Tad*." In his stress, Jafrez forgot and called Thomas "*Father*". He quickly stuck his knuckle dusters back inside one pocket. The truncheon in another. Donasian was assuring the Rail Police that the horse had spooked by someone's party-snap but all was well.

"They're following us," Potier agreed. "Now what?"

"Now what? We get them out of here, that's what! We can't keep this up!"

"Calm down, *mab*." Old Potier never looked as old as now. It made him even more fierce and parochial and . . . utterly dangerous. "We need to get him out of this part of the island. *Tonight*."

"How?" Lestrade wanted to know. "How exactly are we going to do that?"

"Get him back home."

"That's impossible. There's half-a hundred train-stops between Plymouth and anywhere else in Britain."

"No. I mean . . . *get him home*," Potier repeated.

Geoffrey resisted, but the words sank in. "You mean back across the Channel."

"Perhaps not even that far. There's a little place I've had a stake in . . . Small island, sheltered from the storms, but not popular for the travelling crowd. Three houses on the whole place. We could get him there. Your *mamm* could follow once he's stabilized."

Geoffrey's head hurt. "We'd have to *get* him there first," he strangled. "And these people seem to be *a bit* serious on catching up."

"Grab my pipe," Potier announced. "I am going to think, and you, *mab* – " He pointed the stem at his grandson. " – are going to poke holes into my ideas. Once I have a boat that holds water . . . we'll take it."

Marcus had appeared by their side, his dark eyes dull with delayed fright. Without a word he opened up his hand. A sharp beechnut hull was in his palm.

"Old horse-rigging trick," Lestrade said wearily. "Put it on the soft underside of the tail?" A nod was his answer. "Tell your *mamm* it will be all right . . . We're going to move them out of here with the next train."

NOTE

1. A watch differentiated from the other pocket watches only by having a metal lid, not glass or crystal. They had to be opened for reading, were hardier and less liable to break when struck. In these days, watches were not made with interchangeable parts and any repairs would have been expensive and confined to the company that made it.

Chapter XIII – Saint of the Lost and the Forgotten

They reversed their trail starting at Plymouth. Potier found a clean inn and they transferred all their belongings to the room. Paid up for a week, the proprietors were told there was a convalescing old man who need not be disturbed. After an hour had been given to let the other three rest, they slipped out the tradesman's entrance with the clothes on their backs and one bag each.

The third time they switched trains, even Marcus was too weary to ask questions. He was the last one to fall asleep – a failure to his duty that no doubt galled as he took his protectiveness to his parents seriously. Lestrade almost smiled to see it. Poor man.

"No sign of any uninvited guests." Potier slipped into the carriage and shut the door with his back. "A bit on the luxurious side, ya?"

"Hanged if we ride coach all the way," Geoffrey retorted. "We can't keep to the same patterns, Grandfather. I learned that when I was helping smuggle a lesser noble to the Foreign Office through a ring of angry Fenians."

"What's next then?"

"I'll decide that when we get there." Was the answer. "If I don't know, I should be deuced hard to anticipate . . . Two hours ago, I would have scuttled this boat as mad," Lestrade said wearily. His eyes burned from exhaustion and train-cinders.

"Eh . . . it's better than going through Piccadilly," Potier pointed out. "Very well, we've got our boat. Now we need to take it."

"I'm not certain we've thought all the points through," Lestrade leaned forward and whispered. "What the devil are you doing with shares in *Worsley*, anyway? I thought coal mining was against everything you stood for?"

"It is . . . but there are places to hide things . . . especially in Worsely," Potier countered. His grandson snorted. "*Mab*, you have to admit, there just aren't that many coal mines connected to transport by underground canals. The potential of secreting goods away are just – " He stopped when his grandson slapped both hands over his ears. "Think of it as Patriotic Security," he pointed out. "We're fighting the enemy, aren't we?"

"I believe I'll take the higher path and not think at all, thank you," Lestrade grumbled. "Bridgewater . . . I won't be but a few miles from the

Cheatham grounds . . . Clea will put me in her roasting-pan if she finds out I blew in and through without stopping."

"Surely she doesn't want you to inflict a battle on her own family – Oh, goodness I forgot who I was talking about." Potier made a face as Geoffrey openly laughed at him. "A force of habit, *mab*. I'm sorry."

"Forgiven." Geoffrey chuckled a bit further under his breath before he fell silent. A few more minutes of the train's rock and pitch was all he could take. He got up and started walking back and forth.

"You could stand with some rest you know."

"Trains hurt my back. I won't be of use to anyone if I'm half-crippled."

"True enough."

Potier closed his eyes and dozed for a few minutes. It was deep and dreamless. When he next woke he felt much better, but his grandson was apparently working himself up into a fever pitch. He appeared to be pacing a hole through the train itself.

Potier had nothing he could say to him. He smoked and thought, while Jafrez paced and thought, and the others were silent with the sleep of sheer exhaustion.

The old smuggler watched, noticing how very different his grandson was now that he was in contact with his lost family. It was like watching a blind man re-learning to navigate.

Jafrez' step creaked the boards back and forth as the train shook their bones. His fingers went to his cufflinks. The buttons on his coat. They clasped together and opened as he concentrated on what-ifs. Potier saw how his left hand strayed to his watch as he snapped the lid open to check the time. The third time, he stopped himself and briefly touched the little medallion hanging off his chain.

Potier remembered when his wife – Jeanne's mother – had given it to her youngest grandson. It had been just before everything had gone to Hell. Before Jafrez had testified against his brothers for their part in the Aton Bank Robbery. Before one brother hung and the other went to Dartmoor for life.

They had all known disaster would strike some day. Jafrez was too much his own man to be controlled by another, even if that other was the older brother. He had known the price, and they had known the consequence. Mika' had displayed foresight in the past. Her mind had just started its wanderings to its final days . . . but she had known what she was doing when she pressed her precious medallion into his hand and chanted the little rhyme in her sweet Welsh accent . . .

"Tony, Tony, turn around, something's lost and must be found."

115

A rhyme or a prayer or a spell. Potier was not enough of a good Catholic to know the difference. He suspected Jafrez followed a similar trend. Bretons kept over three-hundred saints. Few of them were even recognized by the Church. But he had kept Anthony's medallion all those years when there was no family left. A man lost from his own people.

Saint of seafarers. Saint of the lost and forgotten. Saint of the smallest-born.

Mika' had prayed when her husband and brothers and cousins went to sea. She had always ended with the same verse:

The sea obeys and fetters break
And lifeless limbs thou dost restore
While treasures lost are found again
When young or old thine aid implore.

Scotland Yard:

Hopkins had been in the act of putting his lips to a cup (strong tea, black Assam, capable of rinsing the fur right off an alley-cat's tail) when he found himself staring cross-eyed at a piece of paper. Once upon a time, that paper had been clean bleached white. It was now quite black with grey smudges because of the massive amount of writing.

Being cross-eyed didn't help his reading ability. "What in the world is that?" he wanted to know.

Gregson grinned in that rather unpleasant way that said he had managed to find some way of transferring some of his professional misery upon someone else. "Dr. Mortimer's list."

Hopkins did not often feel the slow, sinking sensation he was enduring now. "Oh," he said faintly.

"Is that all? Aren't you going to say anything else?"

"Thank you, I suppose." Hopkins took the paper. Graphite grease left the paper slippery. "Are you certain that's Mortimer? It looks more like 'Mandible' to me."

"I have witnesses, you wag," Gregson chuffed. "I thought I'd let you have the original. I've got the copy."

"Copy? How did you copy *this*?"

"Easy. I asked him to read the list off for the record, and I took it down in shorthand."

Hopkins watched him go with a growing sense of exasperation. "Serves me right," he said to himself.

The young man carefully finished his morning's reading (nothing new, alas) and set it all aside for Mortimer's list of names. "Too bad he couldn't alphabetize," was his feeling about it all.

Coroner's Court:

Watson was going to have to give Patterson his honest admiration. Most men outside the medical profession would have lost their breakfast about now. Patterson was clearly unsettled, but determined not to let it affect his duty.

"Have you ever been here before, Inspector?"

Patterson blinked a bit. "Not often." He shifted the weight on his feet slowly. "I was usually good with people, even the difficult ones . . . so they assigned me to do the talking while someone else identified the victims we found."

"I understand." Watson wondered when Patterson had been "good with people" as the moment had obviously passed. "If you feel bothered by any of this, don't hesitate to let me know. Many of the responses that a man may feel shameful, are in truth a natural urge that can be trained against."

"That is good to know, Doctor." Patterson looked a little better for the conversation. "It's mostly the smell that gets me. I don't mind telling you that."

"One of the more powerful instincts we own." Watson shrugged, knowing that if he played it lightly, the other would see it as something to ignore too. "It did our ancestors little good to be around bodies in a state of decay. We still keep those instincts, and there is plenty of reason for it. It's our responsibility to work with our brain – " He reached up with his unused scalpel and pretended to tap his forehead. " – to compensate with Nature by practicing a greater hygiene and sense of precaution." He smiled slightly, for there was indeed something small and lost inside the larger man. Something that Watson could not help but respond to. *Trying to make sense out of a mystery. There's a thread that binds many men together.*

"Did Dr. Mortimer say when he would return?"

"Ah." Watson had found the scalpel he was looking for. "He had to visit the archives first. I believe Dr. Pennywraith is helping him."

"Dr. Pennywraith?" Patterson scowled. "Forgive me, Doctor, but one does not often hear 'help' with 'Pennywraith.'"

"Dr. Mortimer can be most persuasive, and he has quite an instinct for appealing to a man's baser flattery." Watson smiled. "If you wouldn't mind, sir, bringing the rubbing-paper over here. The sooner we work here, the sooner we can leave."

117

Patterson moved to obey. Collecting rubbings on a corpse that was just starting to collect ice was unpleasant in the extreme. They had to work quickly before the crystals melted.

Watson had to give Mortimer the incidental genius for this technique. More than soil rose upon freezing. As the cellular walls burst upon the cold, underlying traces beneath the surface wounds were showing themselves. *Except* with the parts of the hands and knees that were well-padded with the hardened tissues of a working man. Keloids were little understood to researchers who ignored an ample study field among veterans.

And a shame that is. Watson found a smile of satisfaction curling his lip as he caught an indented pattern on the rigid skin of the knee-caps.

"Pennywraith and the likes of Dr. Mortimer together." Patterson shook his head in wonder.

As for Watson, the doctor could not resist the relish at the thought. Pennywraith was old, hidebound, callous, conventionally ambitious, and distinctly a package created of many of an Englishman's worst qualities. Mortimer in contrast was young, vital, so un-ambitious Watson didn't know if the man even knew what "aspiration" meant. *And* he was intelligent to a fault.

He was also immune to disdain. Watson regretted not being a fly on the wall just now.

Gregson took the news from Plymouth with horror. "What fool put Jacobs in the same room with Browning?" he wanted to know. "They're both unbolted cannons!"

"Jacobs is due for retirement," Chief Inspector Miller said sharply. "Speak civilly about our comrades, thank you."

Gregson ducked his head – contrite, but still confident he was the Chief Inspector's favorite son. "Sorry, sir. You're right, sir."

"As I was saying, Jacobs applied to retire in June. Browning's been accompanying him on a few cases here and there that don't interfere with his own workload."

"I'm surprised to hear *Browning* hasn't retired yet." Gregson still managed to be informative and annoying at the same time. "That spooky green eye of his fair puts the countryfolk into fits."

"He tried a false eye, but that went over even worse," Miller pointed out. "Nothing out there quite matches his natural shade of green, so it was better to keep the eyepatch."

"At least he could still practice his craft." Gregson found his cigarettes and busied himself with a smoke. "Most of us'd be forced into retirement after an injury like that . . . Remind me to save the life of

118

someone important while *I'm* losing a body part . . . I'd hate to retire while I'm just an Inspector."

Miller flushed red, but had the sense to know that Gregson was being frivolous. "We can gossip about Browning and the Duke's son, or we can discuss this case."

"I'm sorry, sir. I'm all ears."

"Someone murdered Jethro Quimper's father two nights ago. Browning and Jacobs were both put on the case. I don't know who found the evidence, but they have a description of a rather disturbing individual. The servants gave testimony of a tall, grey-haired man with a limp and a heavy stick. Scars on his face and light blue eyes. Servant didn't speak a very creditable English, so it's just as well we got that much."

"Hmm. I wonder if Ivo Quimper was at all active for Moriarty when he died." Gregson blew a smoke ring, his face knit in concentration. "Makes me wonder."

Miller stuffed his hands inside his arms and sighed. "You aren't the only one. The Home Office and the Foreign Office are both watching this case. The strange thing is . . . the Foreign Office isn't giving us any grief."

"That *is* strange," Gregson agreed. "No getting in the way? No helpful advice to us? No scolding us in front of our own constables?"

"Hmmph," Miller scorned. "Nothing at all. I've seen them act this way before, Gregson, and it's reason enough to be nervous."

"I'm afraid I don't follow you, sir." Gregson must have shocked Miller with his quiet confession, but it would go over well for him later when the older man needed to be magnanimous.

"They're waiting, Gregson." Miller lowered his voice. Glittering little eyes stared hard and dark into the big man's face. "They're waiting for something."

Gregson felt his throat swell up. "For what, sir?"

"It doesn't matter, for they won't be telling us about it," Miller answered. "We just go along and perform our duties like always. But this time, we needn't *pretend* we have the eyes of the Crown upon us. This time we *know*."

"Hello, there," Watson pulled off his hat and smiled thinly at Inspector Hopkins. "Is Gregson in?"

"I have no idea," Hopkins confessed, and for good measure waved his hand around the roaring chaos that comprised the police station an hour after luncheons – and a fair bit of drink – was put into the population. The young man cringed slightly as someone was pulled to the back, singing loudly and off-key.

"I hope that wasn't an attempt to do *'The Merry Golden Tree'*, Watson said in wonder.

"You missed the real fun not twenty minutes ago," Hopkins said bitterly. "Some Highlander was singing a song about a plaid that wasn't fit for a Greek sailor's company. Even Murcher looked ready to die from embarrassment."

Watson rested his bowler in his hands. "I'll not dwell on that," he promised. "I was wondering if anyone has heard from Lestrade of late."

"His landlady won't let anyone in. But if you think you can charm her, do be my guest."

"Charm a lady for nefarious purposes? Never – thank you." Watson took the offered match and touched it to his Bradley. "But I'm flattered you think I'm up to the obstacle. I've met the good woman." He offered his tobacco back to Hopkins. "Glad to know he's still recuperating. He's not the type of man to sit idle when he feels he needs to attend to something."

"I've heard marriage has improved him in that regard," Hopkins said dubiously. "But wires and messages are all that is permitted through the front door. Do you wish us to send him any word?"

"Merely curious for now. Dr. Mortimer and I have found some interesting information from the final traces of The Wardrobe Man, as he is known."

"Patterson's informer," Hopkins said sadly. "I'm sorry for the man. I truly am. I had the impression he was of use to Patterson in bringing down the gang back in April."

"He was." Patterson was just coming into Hopkins' office. "And thank you, Hopkins. Your sympathy is most appreciated." The words were hollow and grieved still. He leaned his long back against the wall, careful not to let his hair-cream to touch it. "Doctor, I thought Dr. Mortimer was coming to meet us here?"

"He's on a wild hare," Watson apologized with a faint blush. "I'm sorry. I don't know if I truly warned you about the way the man's mind works. He is brilliant, but when one thought seizes him . . . he must see it through."

"Not so different from one of us," Hopkins soothed. "Very well. What is it the two of you found?"

Chapter XIV – Waiting

D_{r.} Mortimer had been walking with more attention to the tops of his shoes than his actual surroundings. He was surprised when a passing hansom splashed water against the kerb and just missed the cuffs of his trousers.

"Doctor!"

Mortimer blinked up, absently recalling where he was. Dr. Watson was hurrying down the street, lifting his stick in a salute. "Hullo, Doctor!" he said cheerfully. "Did you get out for luncheon?"

Watson drew up to a stop, breathing slightly from a jaunt that had taken him longer than planned. "I was trying to find you," he explained, and leaned on his stick for emphasis. "I thought you were going to come back after you were finished with Pennywraith?"

"I was, but opportunity knocked, and I simply had to take the moment," Mortimer explained. "The guard at the archives knew a fine fellow that could re-create the tools I needed . . . ." He paused and fished with his coat pockets (they were abnormally deep, Watson had already learnt), until he pulled out a small packet made of heavily oiled leather with brass rivets on the corners. Watson stared at the objects inside.

"They look like billhooks for Brownies," he said at last.

Mortimer chuckled, deeply pleased. "I hadn't the slightest notion they could be procured in London!"

"This *is* London," Watson pointed out. They fell into step together. "Are we headed back to Scotland Yard then? Have you eaten?"

"Oh, yes, I suppose I'm ready," Mortimer answered thoughtfully. "I can eat later. This was fascinating . . . ."

Watson sighed. His instincts were telling him just what the lay of the land was, as far as Mortimer was concerned. "Allow me to divert to an excellent cart of roast chestnuts," he said it as subtly as he was capable. "But pray, do not let me interrupt you. Do go on."

"Oh. Well it *is* most fascinating," Mortimer continued where he had left off. "Did you know the Museum keeps a tribe of Gipsies under contract for their tool-work?"

"*Ahem* . . . No, I am afraid it did not occur to me," Watson cleared his throat. "But do enlighten me, please . . . ."

Scotland Yard:

121

"Where did Hopkins run off to?" Gregson's mood wobbled in moments of stress – like missing Yarders. Although he didn't mean to sound quite so accusatory, Patterson shrugged wildly, his neck almost vanishing into his shoulders.

"Something about a list, sir." Constable Jeeves apologized from the other side of a yard-high stack of criminal law tomes. "And that he would be back as soon as he could."

"Which could mean anything," Gregson said under his breath. He donned a brave face before the waiting doctors, who were game about sharing handfuls of warm chestnuts with the constables.

"Begging your pardon, gentlemen," Gregson began, but the front door banged on its hinge behind, and a moment later Hopkins was floating in with that particular reek that spoke of large animals, spun sugar, roasted chestnuts, hay, straw, and filthy monkeys.

Hopkins passed the silently astonished older detective and nearly collapsed into the empty chair set up in his honour. He looked utterly exhausted and he was pressing his arm against his ribs but he smiled from ear to ear in his triumph. "I found your friend, Patterson. His name is Laurence Johnson, called 'Louis' for short because there was a *second* Lawrence (spelled with a '*W*'), last name Jones, and he was a hired worker for the Natural Sciences division in that London Museum." Hopkins paused to suck in breath after that impressive little speech.

With just a slight flourish, the young man put down a small packet of papers before the astonished Gregson's gaze. "He was working for the Museum of late, assisting in the removal of human remains from a block of prehistoric bog. What do you say to that?"

"*How did you find him?*" Patterson stared at the papers, and then at Hopkins. His skeletal face was tinted with the unusual colour of emotion.

"By our new friend here." Hopkins beamed in the direction of the pleasantly surprised Mortimer. "There was a name on your list, sir. That seemed familiar to me. I went to investigate. I have to say, I found my answers sooner than I expected." He grinned, stopping short of smug self-satisfaction. "Would, by any chance, a piece of real estate known as the Isle of Streat be familiar to any of you gentlemen?"

Marcus Lestrade was completely taken aback by the crack of thunder over their heads. He jumped on pure reflex and nearly knocked his adopted older brother off the train's shelter and to the swampy earth.

"Easy – !" Jafrez – *Geoffrey*, Marcus corrected in his mind, exclaimed as he steadied them both. He must have felt the younger man trembling, but he said nothing about it. "*Tad-kohz!*" he called. "*Did you find that canvas?*"

"We must have left it behind!" Potier called over the drum of the rain – a steel drum. Rain hammered into the tin roof like thousands of long-fingered witches above their heads. Rain from the outside glistened in his grey beard like mercury. "I can't find it!"

"All right!" Geoffrey bellowed back. They were the only ones misbegotten enough to be trapped in the deserted train station. Everyone else (it would seem), had the sense to take the leap and run for their homes or the nearest pub. He turned again to look at Marcus. "Are you all right?" he asked bluntly.

Marcus shuddered. "I was just surprised," he lied. "I didn't expect it to storm this soon in the year."

"Yes . . . ." Geoffrey spoke with too much of a drawn-out syllable in his words. He was accepting what he was hearing without putting all his faith in it. Marcus huddled inside his heavy coat and tried to think of something pleasant. "Don't you worry none," he said carefully. "We'll be getting into some hot tea and a clean bed soon."

"I hope so," Marcus blurted. "I'll . . . I'll see to *Tad* . . . ." He flinched again at another bolt from above, and nearly tripped in his haste to get to Thomas Lestrade.

Lestrade watched him go, huddled into his too-thin coat. Potier came up behind him, his stride heavy and oddly clumsy on dry land. *He must be too tired to keep it up,* was the detective's thought.

"All right, *mab?*" Potier asked softly, barely heard over the baritone patter of raindrops.

"Marcus is close to having a nervous wreck," Lestrade answered in the same tone. "What's happening?" He paused. "Why didn't you tell me his parents died?"

Potier winced. *"Mab* . . . ."

"Don't, Potier. *His mother was my sister.* I had a right to know." Geoffrey's voice was cold and controlled. "My sister Jenny."

"I didn't know myself until recently. I just heard they'd adopted the boy. I didn't know it was because his parents died." Potier thrust his large hands inside their pockets. He looked down to the smeared planks of the train platform. "A fire. That's all I knew."

"Hell enough if you're a boy. *Look at him.* He can barely move. When the lightning hits . . . he's in pieces." Geoffrey's mouth was set hard. Angry.

"He's brave. He'll stand by us. We need to get them all out of here," Potier half-groaned. "Where can we go that would be safe?"

Geoffrey took so long to answer, Potier thought he hadn't been audible over the sound of the rain. Tired out, the old man had sunk into an empty bench. When he opened his eyes his grandson was moving back with his strange, lilting stride from the barely staffed office with a receipt in his hands.

"What is that?" he asked groggily.

"I sent a wire for help." Geoffrey left it at that.

Potier didn't need long to figure it out. "The Cheathams?"

"They are vacationing here," Geoffrey said quietly. "God forbid someone challenge them on their own sod. They'd likely welcome the challenge."

"I can see that," Potier admitted. "Did you tell them there would be company?"

"I told them enough . . . ." was his answer. "We just have to wait . . . and see . . . if the wire got to them intact."

Marcus had been uneasy at the very start.

Jafrez – *Geoffrey* – took Marcus aside and quietly introduced himself before the storm hit. They shook hands. Marcus still felt it was all a bit eerie, but there was little choice but to accept it. He hadn't seen Uncle Geoffrey (now Brother Geoffrey) since boyhood. He'd been *much* bigger. Marcus remembered him dimly through a frosted glass. It would be important to remember him, now that it seemed he was family again.

He remembered a younger man, tolerant of the children and their misdeeds while couching his lower tolerance of the adults in polite restraint. He remembered a picnic on the grounds. Before his first mother and father died. It was before the fevers, but after a war he knew nothing about.

"What do you expect? They signed up to fight for the French, like the trusting fools they are."

And that bitter conversation at the table was his clearest memory of the whole event. What they were talking about . . . Marcus had learned since it had been the Franco-Prussian War of '70 and '71. Cousins, aunts, uncles, entire branches of the family had been struck down in that war, all because they had been foolish enough to place their trust in the French, and the French had repaid that trust by making cannon fodder out of them.

When he was a boy, he wondered about the dead. When they walked among the crowds he thought of the spaces between, thinking they might be actually the ghosts of the relatives that should be alive. While his adulthood could logic that thinking away now, he still carried some of the shreds of fear with him. Any large sounds of storms brought back the old sounds of the burning house about their heads, and the roar of flames, like the *"sound of many waters"* of the Bible as his mother picked him up and threw him out the window into the shallow pond splashing against the foundation . . .

Marcus had squeezed his eyes shut.

His grandfather was shaking him by the shoulder.

"Boy?" The old pirate asked him. (Smuggler).

"Yes?" Marcus asked stolidly. He was a grown man. Men didn't quiver at storms.

"Stay close to your parents. We have help coming."

Marcus watched the little old man go. He had paused to press his hand upon his mother's head gently, like a priest's benediction, and his face had creased with a strange, silent sorrow upon his father. But with a businesslike squaring of the shoulders, he had turned aside to stand with Geoffrey.

His strange older brother was staring out the narrow door to the wet curtain pelting down about their heads. He didn't look like he was waiting for help, Marcus thought. He looked like he was waiting for trouble.

Chapter XV – Isle of Streat

"Isle of Streat?" Watson frowned as the name meant nothing to him . . . overtly. "It's a small isle in the North Sea. Some old Viking ruins and traces of Pictish settlements, but that was before the climate changed for the worse." His frown deepened as he pulled at his memory. "Name derived from its unusual shape, which is uncommonly narrow and straight, but that was largely to do with the fact that the isle was originally the top of a mountain-range that has long since sunk into the sea. Just like the Channel Islands were once the land connecting the Thames with the Rhine."

The Yarders paused just slightly, impressed.

Mortimer was also impressed. "Have you been there?" he asked. "I doubt you'd be interested in the peat bogs, but I've heard the duck-hunting is spectacular."

Watson chuckled easily. "I enjoy duck, but not the getting. If I'm to tramp out into a marsh in the chill months for dinner, I would like it to be something with a little more meat. A goose, perhaps . . . the plumper the better."

Hopkins smiled thoughtfully. "The block of peat was from Streat. So was that Loseth fellow whom Lestrade ran afoul of."

"I'd say it was more like he ran afoul of Lestrade," Gregson smirked insufferably.

Patterson nodded the truth of *that* statement. "I don't understand why the Museum would pay so much to have a block of that stuff sent to them. Wouldn't it be cheaper and with better results to have a dig on-site and ship it down that way?"

"*Ahem.*" Mortimer lifted his hand, politely begging for attention. "Not in such a way. You see, the Museum has been quite jealous of previous discoveries by other countries. The Woman of Haraldskær – originally thought to be Queen Gunnhild, murdered over eight-hundred years ago – was an accidental coup for Denmark. There are leading scientists in this country that would dearly love to re-capture what they feel is a lost corner in the field of study."

The tall man blushed, an action that tinted his face from beneath his collar all the way to the roots of his hair. "I'm afraid matters were exacerbated on a professional level with the fact that a rather young archaeologist by the name of *J.J.A. Worsaae* furthered his career by proving it was not the lost Queen of the *Jomsvikinga Saga*." He sighed and pressed his glasses further up the bridge of his nose. "Worsaae's future was cast in stone from that point onward. He has many envious rivals in this country. I'm ashamed to admit it."

"Why ashamed?" Watson wondered. "Rivalry can be healthy, and if it can spur further research, the outcome can only be positive."

"One would think so!" Mortimer exclaimed. "If the field was populated with distracted, un-ambitious dabblers such as me, then I would agree." His long, nervous fingers could no longer bear the inactivity and he reached for his tobacco and papers. "But there are too many brilliant minds who seek more than enlightenment with knowledge. They seek prestige and authority . . . frills and bodkins." That last was said with strength of emotion unusual to the man in their limited experience. "Until recently, the possibility of human remains in English peat bogs has been an intelligent theory, but it has not been recognized as a fact." He lit his cigarette with relief while they waited in fascination.

"England has the climate, the geography, and the cultural history to be a very rich source of sacrificial victims. Consider our own history: Caesar and Strabo both spoke of the pagan necessity to offer up human lives in order to correct an imbalance on the gods' scales. Queen Boudicca, who once walked in this very city, impaled victims, and there was more than one Druid in the histories that read prophecy in the writhing of a victim, or in the splay of his intestines." He smoked a moment more. "Bogs, according to the way the early mind worked, were sacred, for they were *gateways*. Bear in mind that for all their superstitions and the romantic mind of the Celt, they had a fairly orderly and organized mind that was capable of some flexibility. A bog was neither water nor land. One could drown or suffocate in its depths. A *between*, or a conceptual grey area, was important because it possessed more than one spiritual quality . . . the *genius loci* was thus extensive and powerful."

Patterson wondered if anyone else saw how Dr. Watson had drawn up an immobile and wooden face as Mortimer described the mind-set of the Celt.

"So far the finest examples of early murder are found in bog areas of a colder clime and within distance of salt water. One would think with this combination we would be the leading authority in the field! But no. England is sorely lacking in that sort of scientific discovery. Possibly because peat is a slowly moving material, but it does move. The patient accumulation of plant material every year gathers like layers, or rings in a tree-trunk, and some bogs gather faster than others. It is far from an exact science, finding these old victims."

Mortimer's sadness had its unique affect upon the policemen. Watson could see them pass swift glances upon each other, and he knew what they were thinking: That finding the truth in murder was hard enough when the body was still warm.

"And there is hope Streat will bring England to . . . this sort of . . . scientific glory?" Gregson spoke hesitantly. He looked like he would be far more comfortable facing down an angry mob or three.

"Artifacts have been found in its bog against the Neolithic ruins since antiquity. Silver coins. Gold relics – though for the most part quite small. A few ivory pieces were preserved in the oxygen-free atmosphere of the peat." Mortimer was rolling his next cigarette as he spoke, the old tobacco still dangling from his mouth. "Due to the personal nature of most these pieces, it was believed that the bog has smothered up an old burrow or mound. A few years ago . . . I received a report from an old colleague. A human body had been found, but the quality of the corpse led to authorities believing they had a modern victim of murder." Mortimer lit the bare stub of his old cigarette into the new one and placed it into the sand-bucket without a hitch. "It was most embarrassing for the government. What is now believed to be a well-preserved Bog-man had been given full burial honors and a coffin in the small cemetery against the castle chapel."

"Oh, my word." Hopkins blinked. "And they thought it was a murder victim? I'm sure I missed that."

"Well, as I recall the Home Office decided to keep it a little quiet . . . partially because it was most embarrassing . . . but mostly because a local man stood up and confessed he had killed a neighbor in a dispute some time ago. He thought the bog-man was his former comrade. I have no idea what the baronet will decide if that man will ever show up!" His eyes widened as a thought struck him. "Good Heavens. For all anyone knows, he could be in that block of peat at the Museum!"

Patterson paled by at least three shades. "So all of this is so the Museum can personally . . . take apart a block of peat that would ordinarily be used for fuel . . . in hopes that something important will be found and identified within the Museum itself? But what a long reach that is!"

"The block would have been selected for a variety of reasons, and cut out of the peat after it was decided it was a suitable example. But there is another method in the madness. You see, a skillful bog excavation takes practice and time. The Museum is weary of the lack of skilled labour." Mortimer blinked, remembering something, and patted at his pockets before saying 'A-ha!' and going to the haversack at his feet. "I beg your pardon," he began, and pulled out the objects Watson had seen earlier. "These are some of the tools that are used in such an activity. You can determine for yourselves the purpose they fulfill."

The Yarders silently passed the tools around. Gregson never quite lost his faint air of skepticism. Patterson adopted a bit of a curious look and

128

turned each tool over and over. Hopkins shared Patterson's curiosity but not his world-weary demeanor. He glanced to his older and more experienced comrades on occasion.

"This looks like the sort of wooden knife a potter might use," Patterson offered.

"And this one – " Gregson held up the tiny "billhook for Brownies". " – would be for cutting and slicing plant materials . . . no doubt a small amount at a time to perform the job."

"I've seen something like this at an old wood-carver's shop . . . Constable Culpepper's father the oakwright." Hopkins brightened as he caught on. "He called it a 'scorp' and used it for scooping out long segments of soft wood."

"It takes practice to perform swiftly and efficiently with any excavation tools." Mortimer was pleased. "Why not perform two duties at once? Train the rising experts in the field, whilst they are on the premises of the Museum, and take away any question of their education?"

"I see. This would be a prestigious sort of schooling." Hopkins did not look very happy about it. "This would be a popular sort of training, I presume?"

"Oh, very. If you like that sort of thing." Dr. Mortimer shrugged. "I can't speak for the personal attractions myself. Give me a good, clean skeleton to study, with nicely defined phrenology traces."

Watson had flinched. Gregson cleared his throat. "I didn't think we'd find a thread so quickly, sir, but your list appears to have done some good . . . Will you be able to stay here in London for a bit longer?"

"Oh, I plan on being here!" Mortimer assured him cheerfully. "I travel to London but seldom, and there is much catching-up to do. My wife wants books, and I thought I would assist Dr. Watson in this little incident with the bones."

"That would be most welcome, but we can't ask you to overtax yourself – "

"Think nothing of it. As I said, I prefer to work with bones. They're so much cleaner and neater. I never much cared for examining skeletons with their window-dressing still on them . . . distracts from the true story underneath."

"Whew!" Hopkins stared at his comrades once they were alone. "That Dr. Mortimer . . . he's a character to witness!"

"I hope he never has to stand as a witness for my character." Patterson made a very rare joke, but shuddered. "He knows his work. Why did Watson flinch just then when he was talking about skeletons?"

"Took me a moment to catch on," Gregson admitted. He found a cigar in his desk-drawer and was lighting it with an indecent relish. "Couple of years ago – before you made the grade, Hopkins – Bradstreet and I took Lestrade to Watson for a patchup. I noticed at the time that there was a large phrenology chart on the wall of his office, and it was being used as dart-practice." He blew a smoke ring. "Something tells me our doctor doesn't think so much of reading a person's character with bumps and fault-lines."

"Doesn't keep him from using him." Patterson noted. "That would suggest Watson trusts him."

"Watson has good instincts, and he doesn't disagree with someone for the fun of it." Gregson drummed his fingers on his blotting-paper. "Which is why I'll trust him."

Marcus Lestrade flinched at a large hand on his shoulder. Geoffrey was shaking him gently. "Get the others up," he said quietly. "Our cab is here."

Cab? Marcus stirred himself and complied, hating how his mother's face was drawn in sleep.

"I thought we'd be getting snow this time of year," Potier was saying as Geoffrey pushed open the door to the outside platform. A few bedraggled stragglers were hurrying off the mushy street and into the warmth of the station. Mud and water was flung about like spaniels.

"*Mmmph.*" Geoffrey sighed. "Looks like we're doomed to be damp."

"Let's clear the path first," Potier shared his resignation. They watched as the cab-driver huddled into himself, poor fellow. Through the curtain of rain inside the car sat the unmistakable form of a Cheatham – it looked like Robert. The poor sot was the kindest in his family, and the advantage his siblings took upon him was shameless.

"That's the largest rain-coat I have ever seen," Geoffrey said under his breath at the driver. "It looks like something from the Australian closets."

"You'd never pay me to drive one of those things," Potier sympathized without thinking. "Oh. I forgot you *did* drive one of those things."

"Not for long, I didn't." Geoffrey sighed. "I don't miss those days."

"We're ready." Marcus had come up from behind them, his arm around his mother. Thomas lagged behind him, his mind and eyes politely distant from the events swirling around him.

"There's not going to be enough room," Potier noted, just as the sky darkened to consommé under a clap of thunder. He groaned. "*Why* couldn't it be snow?"

"I'll stay behind." Geoffrey had already decided. "I want to make certain we weren't followed."

Potier didn't like it, but he was tired and feeling his age. "Get yourself hurt this close to your little wife and she will not be happy," he warned.

"I'll be careful." Geoffrey tried to smile. "And if something happens . . . well . . . I'll just camp out with the Gipsies a few weeks until her anger cools. There's a camp they keep just outside the city limits." He kept the smile as he watched them all hurry out and bundle into the cab –

– and then his father's large boot stepped out and Geoffrey watched with a mouth full of dust. Thomas Lestrade shambled carefully, like a man on eggshells, across the street riddled with puddles and mud.

His father's head was down, and rain slickened his bowler, but he made his way back up the steps one foot before the other until he was standing just underneath the lip of the eaves. The only time Geoffrey could look his father in the eye was when he was on higher ground.

"Triaged." He spoke firmly, like a sane man would. "Here. Take my coat." He'd forgotten they had traded coats at Plymouth. He unbuttoned the heavy wool and held it out as Lestrade calculated the odds of his getting physically ill on top of everything else in the cold and wet. He mechanically obeyed.

"Thank you," he said evenly. "Take good care of Jeanne, would you." His throat felt like it was going to split in half. He didn't know how much longer this deception would have to happen.

"I will, sir." Thomas took his old coat back. They were at least similar in the shoulders and he turned to make his slow way back to the waiting hansom. Robert was holding the door open. Someone must have told him the extent of Thomas' madness, for he ignored the older man. His Prussian blue eyes were dark with worry on Geoffrey.

Lestrade waved them to go on. The sooner they vanished, the better he would breathe.

Chapter XVI – Trouble

Barts:

"If your patients have a genuine desire to help themselves, you must try not to discourage them."

Dr. Mortimer had found his quarry: Dr. Watson was instructing a young trainee in his Art.

The humble scientist paused behind a potted lemon-tree, wondering how it had gotten to the hospital intact, as Watson continued his conversation with a much-younger man. Not that Watson was particularly old. His obvious love of life continued to shave years off his face.

"But spring water is no better than any other water – if it is clean!" the young man protested.

"That isn't the point. When you look at it, nearly everyone believes in the powers of spring water, and on some perspective holds it to have more healing qualities than well water. From a medical standpoint, we cannot discount this belief. If a patient believes it will do them good, then it can at least do no harm. On the other level, look at the number of springs that carry sulphurous elements. A sufferer will find some relief from a wound with this water, as you and I know sulphur is an effective wound-cleanser. Warm springs such as at Aquae Sulis at Bath . . . well . . . thousands have visited that shrine in our lifetime. No doubt the total number is in the millions."

The young man pondered his shoe-tips a moment, thinking hard. "But where does the authority come in?" he almost blurted. Mortimer instantly felt proud of the youth for finding the one true detail.

Watson smiled too, just as pleased. "The patient wants to know what his doctor believes in, Roland. It takes time to develop your ear and your instinct on that sense, for it will not be found in many classrooms. What if you have a contrary man, who thinks that if you prescribe two grains, then four grains would be better? Do you write a false prescription? Do you speak to his chemist and have them divide the strengths of the drug? Do you take the time to explain to him the consequences of not adhering to his regime?

"Or do you," Watson lowered his voice with a twinkle in his eye, "sidestep all of the above and make certain his wife is in charge of the medicine?"

Roland stifled a laugh.

"Or you have a patient that is afraid to sneeze without his doctor's permission. How much leeway do you give? This skill isn't about to happen overnight, like mushrooms after a rainstorm. You are feeling your way, and developing your skills."

"I wish I could be as correct as Dr. Bell," the younger man confessed. "He is an amazing man."

"Dr. Bell is like no other." Watson agreed. "When it comes to diagnosing illnesses or conditions, or even an entire life history, he is unmatched, and Edinburgh is more than fortunate to have him. But I would advise against pure emulation. You are young and in possession of a warm demeanor. You should use that quality to inspire trust. Dr. Bell uses his cool, occasionally callous air to his patients, and they trust him for that *because that is his natural person.* Were he not himself, he would hardly be entrusted to be the Queen's personal physician while she resides in Scotland." Watson shrugged. "He can reveal the most humiliating details about his patients' past before the lectern. It displays his skill, but I do not advise that practice." Watson's good-humored face had softened along calm and thoughtful lines. "I would prefer to employ his sense of humor, which is rare and marvelous, or his ability to step apart from the subject and analyse with his brain first – " Watson tapped his temple before moving to his breast-bone. " – and the heart second."

Roland, whoever he was, sighed slightly. "I'm afraid I haven't much of a back-bone, Watson. I once said we needed to listen to our hearts, and my instructor nearly bit my head off. I was treated to a speech on how there are no synaptic nerves in the heart. No connective paths leading to the brain that would allow the heart to think."

"Let these men have their say, for they are literal-minded. The heart is your barometer, Roland. Your brain thinks faster than even you know. Your heart is reacting to thoughts that have flitted by so swiftly you may not even know they were there. When you look back, do you think you were wrong to feel that a patient would inexplicably recover . . . or a strange notion that there was a hidden disease, or that perhaps the man you were working with was not to be trusted alone?" Watson tapped his chest again. "Barometer, Roland. We know in our bones that a storm is coming in, or that the air is damp. But the barometer refines that knowing. Gives us the degree of humidity and the percentage of pressure."

Mortimer burst into applause, causing the doctors to start in astonishment. Behind Mortimer, a few other physicians had collected and were joining in. "Bravo!" Mortimer exclaimed. "A deceptive bit of brilliance, Doctor Watson – and I call you *Doctor* out of personal admiration. The Royal College would do well with a man of your calibre behind the podium! Have you thought of lecturing?"

Watson's mouth opened and shut like a fish for a moment before he rallied his composure. "I thought I just did!" He exclaimed, creating a bomb-shell of laughter about the hallway. The lemon-tree's leaves fluttered.

Roland grinned openly, and it was easy to see why Watson was pressing him to enhance his natural qualities. The boy was handsome on a level that could be called noble. Well-shaped if not finished in his growing, and possessing a strange scar like a small crescent on his left cheek where the muscle was the thickest. The flaw only enhanced his handsomeness. *And named Roland, too. A bundle of advantages . . .* Mortimer privately prayed the boy had a strong wife and mother at home. Someone that compelling could be considered fair game in the social circles, or become the oblivious light-house around which unpleasant moths would circle.

"Dr. Watson, it is always a pleasure to hear you, even when you're scolding me." He held out his hand and Watson laughed, taking it firmly. Low laughter hummed about the hospital, and still smiling, the crowd went on with its duties.

He is a gifted physician, Mortimer thought. *And he comes alive when he is with people. This is the man who could counterweight Sherlock Holmes. Salt with pepper.*

"Dr. Mortimer," Watson had put his back to the wall and leaned on it. His arms folded across his chest. "My word."

Mortimer sighed. "*Please*, Doctor. A humble '*Mister*' will do." [1]

"I speak your title out of respect for your medical acumen," Watson riposted blandly. His smile continued. "Were you successful?"

"I went straight to the Museum after our meeting with Scotland Yard." Mortimer agreed. "The block of peat is hardly the first ones taken out of the Isle of Streat. Depending on whom one asks, it is the fourth or fifth. Three times some intriguing example of bog-victim has been found." The tall, thin man rubbed his chin in a fantastically quick motion. "Remarkably fresh corpses," he added almost under his breath. "A few have exposed skeletons underneath the skin – well, might as well call it leather." He sat down at the proffererd wicker chair by the potted tree and leaned back, absorbed in a thought while Watson waited patiently.

"You know, a lemon tree *isn't* the sort of foliage one expects to find at Barts."

Watson had half-expected the man's mind to temporarily veer. He was like Holmes in that respect, but Holmes's mind had been ever so much faster that he would have observed the tree, reasoned out the cause, and then returned to his conversation before anyone had suspected his mind had ever wandered in the first place. Mortimer was a refreshing conversationalist.

"It was grown from seed by one of our returning Army surgeons," Watson explained. "It stands here as a lesson to us all, for a man can return from a strange climate with the seeds of a disease or condition. Some may take years to emerge, just as a lemon tree will take an inordinate amount of time to sprout and mature to the point it bears fruit."

"Interesting." Mortimer's intelligent face was charmed by the story and its example. "Would that all our morals were so pleasantly stated." He paused to sniff a waxy flower. "Strange to think of something flowering in winter."

"Part of the lesson, I fear. A condition can flower when it is least expected."

"One might go on indefinitely with these examples – I'll overlook the obvious ones with the thorns, or the resemblance of tumors with the lemons." Mortimer poked one with a smile and that quickly, he was back on track with the original conversation. "The peat-bog corpses are quite unusual. The first one to be pulled out was clearly an example of Celtic nobility. Such a marvelous round head! But I must not dwell on that."

"No, no, if you believe it is of use . . . ." Watson protested.

"You believe, my friend, that phrenology is no more than moonbeams and bad science." Mortimer chuckled at the other man's quickly disguised embarrassment. "Have no fear, Doctor. I am hardly bothered by another man's honesty. But I must put it to you, your deflections are so graceful and gentlemanly, one might think you were actually in agreement with me!"

"I confess, I have little time to study phrenology." Again Watson deflected with good manners. "The studies that directly involve my duties are enough."

"Such as the cemetery cases?" Mortimer guessed. "From my studies of the three skulls at the Museum, I would have thought they would be unanimously short, dark-haired, and with a sturdy musculature. It is the type one may expect from the early Celt."

Watson had been described as a Celt before from Dr. Mortimer, and had not been altogether pleased at his summary. In his personal view, a "romantic" was someone who was not in control of their emotions. Watson saw himself as a being that enjoyed his emotions without apology, yet did not seek to let them control him.

"I confess I am fascinated at the idea of viewing a Neolithic people as they were when they died. Phrenology is all well and good, but seeing them in a preserved form is – well, it isn't an opportunity to be taken lightly." The two paused as a knot of students flurried out of the stairwell and across the hall. "The peculiar thing is, the following two examples found in the peat-blocks have little or nothing to differentiate them between a person in London."

"Interesting." Watson looked drawn in despite himself. "Examples of an invading population?"

Mortimer was vastly pleased. "An excellent premise. There were different sorts of sacrificial victims in the Celtic world, Doctor. The most favoured, if one is to go by the ancient Romans – Why do we call them 'ancient Romans? There aren't any modern Romans! – is the criminal guilty of shedding blood or a thief. Thieves were *remarkably* despised in that world. But these sacrifices were burnt alive with animals and one can hardly reconstruct a skeleton from a bag of ash.

"The other sort would be nobility, someone giving their life for the gods. They would show signs of being well-nourished and well-taken care of, if we are to go by the scanty accounts and scantier examples found. The last possibility would be an invader. A leader from the enemy partition, who would be sacrificed to appease the gods of the land and perhaps persuade them to strike down the newcomers."

"What of barrows?" Watson had taken the other wicker chair by the tree and was now leaning forward. "You said there was a suggestion the bog had swallowed a barrow."

"I refined my questions," Mortimer assured him. "There actually is a barrow on the Isle of Streat!" Mortimer could barely contain himself. The long fingers rubbed together. "Sir Niles, Baronet of Streat, is most determined that this discovery is kept under the control of the island. He is most set against any unauthorized grave-robbing. I admire that approach." The tall man's eyes glittered grey and fey. "It just so happens, he is hosting a celebration of the isle's recent discoveries in a few days. I have been invited . . . Would you like to come with me?"

It was a marvelous thing how Watson's warm brown eyes lit up, like a candle in a glass bottle. The flame banked, and he carefully chose his words.

"I would have to make arrangements with my work and my family first," He lifted his hands. "And the Yard may be less accommodating than my old friend. But I shall see what I can do."

Mortimer also leaned forward, and grabbed his knee in his excitement. "Bring your notebook, my friend!" He exclaimed. "I shall certainly bring mine!"

Clea Lestrade was as good in emergencies as any Cheatham. Within minutes of their arrival, Geoffrey's family was plied with steaming hot soup and a little bread to counter the shock of travel in such miserable conditions. The Lestrades were either too mannerly or two benumbed to react much to the usual overwhelming presence of Cheathams (who held the average height at six feet, and dominated most species for the amount of muscle on their bones).

Elizabeth, Robert's wife and Louise, Bartram's wife, were the quickest to jump in with assistance. Elizabeth always knew where clean clothes, blankets, and carpets were in any of the households a Cheatham resided in. Louise stepped to with a gratifying speed and a willingness to help.

If things were not so sad at the moment, Clea would have laughed long and hard at the Cheatham reactions to Thomas Lestrade. He was as unlike his son as night to day, with a build that must have rivaled her brother Andrew's back in his prime, his glossy hair the colour of red oakwood with a fine sweep of pewter displaying his age upon his temples. His ponderous deliberation was also a contrast, for they were used to Geoffrey's perpetual motion and indefatigable presence.

Old Potier paused to scoop up a grandson in each arm (briefly) before retiring to the sides for a talk with Clea's father.

Geoffrey's mother and Marcus were familiar to Clea. She personally took care of them and they were grateful. Marcus needed a few sips of soup before he recovered himself enough to sit with his father on the other fireplace settee. Thomas remained within his own private world. Or dreaming nightmare.

"That's that." Clea brushed her hands on her apron a moment. "Excuse me a moment, Mrs. Lestrade . . . I need to speak with my brother."

Bartram Cheatham had been about to help himself to one of the hot rolls on the kitchen table. The cooks had long ago given up with holding their own territory with any of Charles Cheatham's sons. Andrew was assisting in the crime by riddling out the latest hiding-place for the sweet butter.

Both brothers tried to adopt innocence as soon as their tiny sister swept in.

"Bartram! Andrew!" Her face was pale, chalky against her blue-black hair. "How fast can the two of you sneak out the door?"

"Sneak out?" Andrew exclaimed – but quietly. One didn't protest the frantic whisper in Clea's voice. "What is it?"

"Something's wrong. I know it. There's trouble. Geoffrey's as big of a fool as the two of you at times. He's alone at that station and there's already been two attempts on his father's life. Go get him, and – " She put her hands on her hips and iced her brothers over with her glare. "*Go looking for trouble.*"

Bartram, the big lug, accepted this declaration by stuffing a roll in his mouth and hunting for his coat. He was big, he was strong, and it rarely occurred to him to question or argue with his sister.

Andrew was made of sterner stuff. "You're telling us to get into trouble?"

"No. There's already trouble. I feel it. But the two of you are tops in the field of trouble, and I can't think of anyone else who'd be able to handle it when someone's giving you nonsense."

Andrew was still staring.

"Andrew, you'll never hear this from me ever again, so make the most of it." Clea's mouth set like a clamshell. "I know Geoffrey. He would've rode on top with the driver if it meant getting back to us. *He didn't. Something's wrong. Go get him.*"

Andrew swallowed hard. Bartram had returned – he could be fast and silent for such an inhumanly big man – with their coats. He grabbed one last roll out of the bowl as he threw Andrew's coat over his head.

NOTE

1. Despite the amazing level of respectability of the Royal College of Surgeons, its members are addressed as "Mister". Mortimer was not exaggerating his humility in *The Hound of the Baskervbilles.*.

Chapter XVII – Conflict

Andrew Cheatham thought of lounging in the shelter of the kitchen doorway while Bartram brought the rented carriage about. No such luck. His youngest brother was larger by far and knew more of their father's illegal moves than anyone else on the island.

"'*Geoffrey's as big a fool as the two of you at times,*'" Andrew sulked into his waterproof collar. On the other side, Bartram didn't even bother to grunt. "What the devil does she mean by that? Woman's going to jigger [1] herself with all that fussing."

Bartram did grunt then. It could mean a multitude of things. "You let your Lanky out," he said bluntly. "You always forget your schoolin' when you're worried."

"I'm not worried," Andrew contradicted rudely, though there was a tiny bit of alarm in his face that Bartram enjoyed.

"Good." Bartram was content to drop the conversation.

Andrew held the silence for nearly a quarter-mile. Bartram grudgingly gave his fop-of-a-brother credit for having some strength of will. "What do you think is happening?"

"Dunno." Bartram chose to worry when he was faced with something to worry about. "All I know is, his *feyther*'s not right in the head and they think its shock from watching a fellow getting murdered before him."

"That's not 'a fellow' – that's Quimper's father," Andrew scorned. "So he was born of man after all . . . Well, we still can't rule out a serpent in the tree until we learn about his mother." He crossed and re-crossed his long legs in an effort to be comfortable while the poor driver earned every shilling of his contract. Rain spattered against the small glass panes, but it was growing thick and trailed down the window sluggishly. A bad sign. Andrew knew the rain grew dense before it turned to mineral form. Ice or sleet or heavy snow would be the worse thing to happen on top of all this. He felt sorrier for the horse than he did the driver.

Bartram dealt with the deadly mix of boredom and apprehension his usual way. He started rolling his broad shoulders back and forth, his trademark warm-up before a fight.

"Did you see how he acted when he saw Martin?" Andrew asked softly.

"No."

"Called the poor boy 'Geoffrey'."

Bartram's midnight-blue eyes deepened to bottomless black. Andrew was sorry he opened his mouth at that point. Bartram's last memory of their mother was being confused for their oldest brother Myron. The fever had taken her in more ways than one, and she had not known her youngest son at the end. Andrew could only imagine the scalding pain that must have created, though Bartram typically never spoke of it.

"What'd Martin do?" Bartram demanded roughly. His large hands opened and shut, as if he could physically yank that experience out of his nephew's viscera.

"Boy's smart as his mother. He looked the man dead in the eye and pretended along." Andrew smiled wryly. "Fetched him some tea and nodded when Thomas told him to practice his English."

"Wonder how much those boys'll understand," Bartram rumbled. "They're both smart, but Nick's a bit on the lazy side."

"He's a Cheatham. He can afford to be lazy. There aren't going to be many people out there who can take him on when he finishes growing." Andrew reviewed the obvious. "You watch. He'll snare a rich widow. Martin's going to stay small, but he's clever and he's quick – quick as his father would be if he didn't have that bad foot."

"Foot was good enough when he put it on you, Andrew," Bartram taunted with a gleam in his deepset eyes.

Andrew could have wilted with relief to see things were back to normal with Bartram. "I was surprised," he shot back. "He wouldn't beat me in a fight now."

"Uh-huh." Bartram retorted. "And I suppose Dr. Watson hung you up by those antlers because you didn't want to fight a veteran?"

Andrew sputtered like a Clyde Engine.

"Well, he's crippled too," Bartram continued smoothly along his sadistic course. "Leg and arm. Good of you to let him think he could win again' you – "

"Now see here, you great big noddy – " [2] A cherry-faced Andrew tensed as the horse slowed. The rain had almost stopped but the glass was turning pale and misty from a drop in temperature. "Here we are." He grabbed Bartram when he started to get up.

"S'wrong with you?"

"Clea told us to go looking for trouble. You go on in the station and I'll ride with the cab to the livery."

"Why the livery?" Bartram wanted to know.

"Because when Geoffrey's in trouble, he goes to the nearest rat-nest he can find. He doesn't stick to open spaces where he doesn't feel safe."

Bartram muttered something but nodded his agreement. He clumped out, rocking the cab-section from side to side with his weight and shut the door after him.

Bartram looked from side-to-side as the rain picked up about him. It pelted straight down over his wide-brimmed Australian hat, adding to his naturally dangerous look. He pulled his boots out of the suck of the street and clomped fountains of water as he made up the short steps of the train platform. Smells of unwashed people and even a few animals, pine-tar, and the reek of the coal industry struck his nose before he pushed open the door. The knot of people inside were a pitiful lot. Someone sneezed constantly, and a woman huddled by the tiny stove, her face bright with a fever. No wonder she was the only one by the heat.

Bartram turned his head slowly on his thick neck. He didn't see his brother-in-law anywhere. A few people were taking his arrival in, mouths dropping open. He ignored it. He was used to it. Normally they'd be wanting his signature or to talk to him or offer to buy him dinner, but Bartram's expression was discouraging of that right now.

The ticket-gate man looked up as footfalls vibrated to his ankles. The view of the lamp-posts were blackened by a gigantic man. "Oh," He blinked. "Mr. Cheatham. Good to see you again, sir. Are you heading back home so soon?"

"No."

Hands that could have substituted for badminton-rackets plopped on the sill as Bartram of Lancashire leaned forward. Wood and nails creaked within each other.

"Lookin' for my brother-in-law."

The ticket-gate man didn't know why he felt a sudden sting of sweat on his face. It could be just the way his customer was talking. "What does he look like?"

"Short little fella." Bartram indicated with his hand leveled to a height that would be considered average to many. "Dark hair. Dark eyes. Kinda Welsh-lookin. Bowler hat probably." The wrestler paused. "Likes long coats."

The ticket man, who went by the name of Bates, cleared his throat. "Are there any distinguishing features on him besides that?"

Mr. Cheatham thought about it. "I broke his hand once. That wouldn't show though."

"Er, no. No, I'm afraid it would not."

"Sharp dresser. Always neat. Kinda dapper." Bartram tried again. "Like my brother Andrew, but not as bad."

"I see."

"Has a voice on him." Bartram had struck a seam. "Stern when he can't get his way."

"Oh!" Bates' face went from confused to relieved. "Well, he was here for nearly an hour. I suppose he was getting warm from the wet. He left not a quarter-to the hour with some men."

"Some men." Bartram repeated, and it was not in a nice way. It sounded ominous and happy at the same time. "What d'you mean?"

Andrew took delight in being the family toff, but even the pleasures of civilised refinement couldn't take the Cheatham out of a Cheatham. He opened the door and hopped out of his seat to the mews before the driver had finished slowing. His tall, strong form was nipping into the shadows just as quickly. Bone-cold and exhausted, the poor man was thinking more of settling his horse to the rented stables and drowning his aching sorrows at the greasy little pub across the street. At least until they called him again. Good luck to him.

Wrapped within his MacIntosh, Andrew would pass for a cleaner version of the hardened crowd that crossed his path. With a cigarillo between his teeth he didn't have to wrinkle his nose at the ripe stew of odours rolling off the many unwashed bodies. They were all a rough sort, nipping gin because a little went a long way, or circling around a large jug of what Andrew hoped was not juniper beer. The stuff seemed to make a person want to fight. They jostled each other and tossed small boxes and traded filthy jokes back and forth that weren't even imaginative. Their idea of sports ranged from subjects as diverse as cards, dice, mumblety-peg, and small animals. Despite the fact that hay and straw was everywhere, there were *a great deal* of smokers. Finally, Andrew had enough. He stubbed his own out on a wall-plank and repocketed it. Whoever burnt down this wooden fire-box tonight, it would not be he.

Andrew put his back against a timber-pillar and pulled a small packet of dried leaf out of his coat. He rarely indulged in chewing-tobacco, but here it was best to fit in. With a grumpy look on his face (a look that was hardly feigned for being out in this muck), he chewed with mulish determination.

"Lookin' for someone, fellow?" The speaker was a leathery Geordie [3] doling out cards at a barrel-table. What he was doing with two Jackeens, [4] Andrew couldn't imagine unless it was business of an unsavoury nature.

"Lookin' for a mon, no crime." Andrew used his parents' old accents and his natural sulkies. "Tha moitherin' me for business?"

"Plenty o'men pass thru." One of the Jackeens turned to spit tobacco juice out of his mouth. All the better to keep smoking. Andrew had heard of men who were truly addicted to the weed, but that was beyond his self-indulgent nature. "We're not bein' anyone's mother . . . or nursey."

Without a doubt, suspicious and hard-eyed.

142

"Don' throw tha toys outta tha pram. Mon owes me. Worth tha time if tha seed im." He rested his hand at his side-pocket, where a confident man immune to pick-pockets would keep a purse. "Tha ha'nt seed im, nay brass. Tha seed him, I get mi'brass owt' back." [5]

A fourth man, no more than a part of the stinking shadows of the mews, detatched from the murk. He was smoking something cheap, like a hard-up's cigar, and his left hand wanted a few fingers. Andrew narrowed his eyes at the newcomer, which was simply good business sense and a sign of respect among dirt-water toughs.

"Tha chats good Lanky," was the cool observation. "An who tha' mon? Friend?"

Andrew snorted. This one was in control. The card-players had slowed in an affectation of nonchalance. "Na *friend* owes me." He chewed and paused to spit, deliberately breaking gaze. "Small fellow. Hast mi'brass. Seed here not long by."

"Good luck. This is a place to find jockeys," one of the Dubliners cracked.

Andrew didn't bother with false manners. He took one long stride and brought his brass knuckles down on the smiling face. Decent fight manners meant knocking teeth out was a bad idea, but Andrew had already pegged him for the sort who should have pulled them out anyway. Before the blood had finished landing on the barrel the others were scrambling back and reaching for knives, short clubs, and whatever toys they kept.

Andrew was disgusted at the unprofessional level of thuggee he was facing. He hauled his victim up like a shield or storefront display. "I want mi'brass!" he roared. "Tha' takes a *Cheatham of Lancashire* issa putty-brain?" [6]

The effect was electric. Andrew might have to work harder to prove Cheathams had table manners and conversational skills, but no one had to prove the family was a force of nature in a fight. They left their friend for dead as they back-treaded away from the centre of damage. Andrew rather enjoyed himself, but business was business. He slung up the gasping Dubliner and gently tossed him out the nearest horse-window. A slimy splash and a groan was his reward.

"D-didn't noo ye was a Cheatham, shir . . . Now that I look upon ye, I see the stamp o'yer fine father," the other Jackeen stammered. He traded alarmed looks with his remaining mates. "There was a little gentleman answering to your description, but he was . . . conducting business with some other gents before you showed up."

"If thust a saucin' be mi'hand!" [7] Andrew raised that hand in question and again enjoyed the reaction. "He'll be shived!" [8]

"They went to the back-alley." The Geordie lifted both hands (one still clutching his knife.) "If you hurry, they ought to let you have your satisfaction out of him before they finish up their business."

Andrew solved the problem of turning his back on them by grabbing the Geordie and using him for a cricket-bat against the others. His roar of rage ought to suggest he was a madman incensed at having his satisfaction taken from him by someone else. Madmen were usually left alone, more was the pity.

Still, he was Andrew. A quick glance over the others relieved them of anything useful and he hurried off down the mews.

Bartram pegged the knot of stable-scum at a glance. His large presence alerted their attention away from something very fascinating on the other side of the wall. They looked up. A crowbar? Interesting. Someone was trying to break a door down. Wonder what was on the other side?

He jerked his thumb.

"Off."

They recognized him, which was usually fun. They didn't run, which was surprising. And they must have already been paid, because they ran for him.

Bartram had time to ponder the waste of it all. His father might take on something like this with glee, but the son didn't see much joy in fighting without pay. Once you did that, your reputation as a professional might suffer. Or it might not. His audience was fickle and there was no point in taking chances.

A greasy little man that reminded him of a whipcord grinned, showing a mouth of broken teeth. Bartram noted that and let him swing his knife. He deflected it with his arm, and the edge of the blade failed to penetrate his quarter-inch thick coat without the speed built up behind it. The wrestler calmly picked him up and threw him with little finesse into his friends. *Bad form. No time to spin the little fright around a bit first.* This crowd wasn't using firearms, which might be lucky. A gunshot this close to the train station would send every railyard-copper and regular bluecoat running like cats.

"Get him!" The little man spat blood. His broken teeth were poor friends in a fight, as he cut his mouth easily. "Streuth, men! He's ours!"

"You ain't from around here," Bartram grunted. He grinned at last, and that must have frightened them, because Bartram still had all *his* teeth. That more than anything attested to his skill as a fighter.

Someone else started to come up, but Geoffrey popped up from behind the door and cracked him with the truncheon. *Oh, good. There he is. Thought so.* Clea wouldn't kill him for losing her husband now. Fighting close, but then, little people didn't have long reach. He had the loop around his wrist so he was meaning business. Bartram took the distraction and knocked out a man who was trying to sneak away. "Can't stand yellowbellies," he muttered.

"Don't let that one get away!" Geoffrey nearly screamed. His face was ghastly white in the murk of the mews. "Sit on him if you have to, but don't let him go!" He promptly launched himself back into the capers.

Bartram lifted an eyebrow at that, looked at the groaning man, and came to the conclusion that Geoffrey had his reasons. He bent down and grabbed the little snake by the collar. Another groan, louder this time. The big wrestler calmly waded through the muck and hoisted the man on a large metal hook that had once been for hanging tack. Why no one had stolen the hook for the scrap he didn't know, but any port along the cut, as they said in his family. [9]

"Bloody Hell." Andrew had shown up. "What do you call this mess?" He waded in on Bartram's left and the brothers initiated a bewildering mop-up.

The problem with being big is, too many people mistake it for being slow. Cheathams come into the world fighting, and they never expect things to change.

Lestrade would later describe it as watching two cowcatchers sweep dull-witted tramps off the tracks.

"You're in trouble with my sister, you little glock!" [10] Andrew delighted in crowing. "She says the next time you get into a fight, be polite and bring it home with you!"

Lestrade had (after eight years of marriage) gotten used to Cheathams. "Didn't want her to make me look bad!" he panted.

Bartram roared. A seedy looking groom took to his heels. "Hard to feed anyway." He grabbed a knife out of someone's hand and rapped them on the skull with the handle. "Messy. She hates messes." He grabbed Andrew and pulled him back against the next wave. "Where were *you*, Andy?"

"Working." Andrew glared pure poison. "I took care of *four* of them before I got here."

"You mean *those* four?" Bartram mused as the gang suddenly got reinforcements. "When I get 'em, they stay down."

Andrew growled in exasperation and pulled out his brass knuckles again.

"Cheater." Bartram jabbed.

Crack. Lestrade sent another one off to dreamland.

"He's a mean little sandman," Andrew noted. He broke someone's jaw with a nice little punch.

Bartram was holding the last man. He scowled and tossed him aside. The crook staggered in his haste to get away. The rest were (mostly) moving but discounted.

Bartram's first victim had freed himself in Bartram's blindside. His coat torn in the back. He realised the way out was blocked. Geoffrey was in the process of turning but not in time. He froze at the touch of a knife against his throat.

"Everyone just stop it now," the greasy man advised.

"Blast!" Andrew cursed. "You cut him, the only way you leave here is for the road to Hell."

"No need for that." The knife pressed deeper into Geoffrey's neck. As Bartram and Andrew watched, barely breathing, he started edging his way to the open alley-way. Outside the rain was coming down even worse. Footprints would be obliterated in minutes.

Geoffrey lowered his hands down and let himself be pulled reluctantly backwards.

"Now, Geoffrey," the knife-man shocked them by using their brother-in-law's Baptismal name, "We're going to take a walk, aren't we? Just behave yourself this time and we won't have to hurt each other – "

It was like watching a cork explode from a bottle. They saw his eyes go black at the conversational tone of the attacker, and just as he stumbled, the knife-edge slipped from against his skin to the stiff cloth of his collar. It was all he needed. Geoffrey twisted down and to the side. The knife caught on his tie and sliced it almost in half. By then the knife was worthless, because a hard fist was blacking both eyes with a double strike.

Lestrade surprised them. The normally controlled little man was lit from within by his fury. One fist went into the man's gut. The next his ribs. Another strike, then another. He wasn't using *savate*. [11] He was causing hurt.

"Woah!" Andrew gasped. "Geoffrey! I think you have him!" No response. Geoffrey kicked into the groin. The man was huddled into a muddy ball, too pained to scream.

Bartram was slow to act only *outside* the mat. He assessed the situation with his unique talent and reached past his brother-in-law, grabbing the lump and tossing him into a pile of mucked straw.

Geoffrey looked like he'd been mesmerized, and the conjurer had just snapped his fingers and commanded, "Wake up," he breathed unevenly. Face draining of its unhealthy colour. Sweat shone on his face.

"Geoffrey." Andrew risked grabbing his shoulder. "Who the devil is that man for you to hate him so much?"

146

Geoffrey was trying too hard to control his breathing to talk for a moment. Bartram silently kept one eye on him, and the other on the moaning victim.

"One of the Aton Bank Gang," Geoffrey said at last. He found a handkerchief from somewhere and ran it over his face. "We never found him, never arrested him for his part in Constable Cooper's murder."

Andrew and Bartram didn't know the whole story, but they knew (thanks to heady London gossip) that Cooper had been Lestrade's closest friend before he was murdered. The gang had been under the control of a certain Jethro Quimper back in his early days of criminal activity.

"He gave the gun to Armoricus," Lestrade was saying. "He gave the gun to him, told him to shoot . . . and he did. He killed him right in front of me." His breath was stumbling down, slow to calm. "He fled when we got help. I've been looking for him ever since."

"Well, now you found him," Andrew said gingerly. "You can arrest him."

Geoffrey began to laugh. "Oh, you think so?" he wanted to know. As they watched, he kept laughing. "I can't turn him in without people finding out I'm here! I'm in hiding, you sot! Hiding to get my parents as far away from London as possible!"

"And if you arrest him . . . Oh, dear." Andrew whispered.

"I can't arrest him." It was painful to watch the conflict crushing him. "I can't arrest him, but *I can hurt him.*"

NOTES

1. Lanky slang for wearing oneself out
2. Noddy = fool
3. From Newcastle-on-Tyne
4. Dubliners: Derogatory
5. Don't get in a huff. The man owes me. Worth your time if you saw him. You haven't seen him, no pay. You seen him, I get my money owed back.
6. I want my money. Do you think I'm an idiot?
7. If there's a scolding, I'll be the one to do it.
8. I'll slice him!
9. "Cut" is Lanky for "canal". The Cheathams see themselves as slightly nautical.
10. Half-wit.
11. Savate is a French hybrid martial art and full-contact combat sport that combines principles of western boxing with a wide variety of kicking techniques.

Chapter XVIII – Respite

It was Andrew who hatched the plan.

Geoffrey had given up on being polite at this point. "You're a sodding lunatic."

Andrew sniffed and re-arranged his necktie using only his fingertips. They had escaped the worst of the stable muck. Lestrade pulled his sliced tie off with a sigh. As far as the dapper contest went, Andrew had won the round.

Bartram grunted. "He'll pull it off," he told his brother in law. "Andrew's the one for stupid things. Gets away with 'em half the time."

"Now." Andrew bent and heaved up the muddy gang-man with one hand. By now they knew from Lestrade his name was Tarby Baldwin, nicknamed "Bold Tarby", but that hardly stood now. The man had given himself up for dead and was doing a fair impersonation. After the pounding they'd just witnessed, he was entitled. "We're going down to the Rail Police, my fine fellow. And I'm going to turn you in. You don't have to admit to anything, I do hope you realize." He pushed his face deeply inside the other's face. Black eyes managed to widen despite the swelling. "Anything."

"Never saw you before, sir." Baldwin rasped. Andrew gave him a tiny shake. "*Sirs,*" he corrected.

"That's better. Whether or not you get out of prison, that's up to the jury. Whether or not you get killed in prison . . . I'm sure that depends on how you comport yourself in front of your employers."

Baldwin looked terrified and bewildered at "comport". Geoffrey sighed and translated in Breton. If anything, his version sounded simpler and worser. The brothers had picked up a few bits of the language here and there around him, but not the really interesting bits.

"I told him to keep his mouth shut and he probably wouldn't get his heart carved out with a sharpened spoon at Newgate," Geoffrey said.

Bartram grunted. They watched Andrew go, dragging the smaller man after him. It was a failure, as Andrew's legs were far longer and his stride matched. "Now we hide you," he said. "I'll have the carriage brought 'round. You nip in."

Lestrade did as he was told, rightfully concluding that Cheathams had mastered a thing or two about being hard to see when they needed. Bartram had the carriage park back at the small tavern across the train station, and soon emerged with a large mug of hot syllabub.

149

Lestrade took it without a word. He winced as the heat pressed against his aching hands. They were swelling. Bartram examined his own marks critically, flexing and unflexing his large fingers to test their abilities. He looked like he'd done nothing more than take a walk and get caught in the rain.

"Your *feyther* thinks Martin is you." Bartram decided to get on with it.

Lestrade froze and slowly melted enough to close his eyes. "Marvelous," he said under his breath. "I'm my grandfather and my son is me." The strain of the day – several days – was starting to tell. He took another gulp. "Just perfect. Fitting and perfect and I don't know why I bothered."

"Huh?"

"He never saw me when I was his son," was the answer. "Stands to reason he still wouldn't, eh?"

Bartram was still pondering what the right answer to that would be when Andrew bounced into the carriage, pleased that Baldwin had been recognized by the Rail Police without his help, and the fact that he'd helped himself to the pockets of their so-called attackers. One of the objects, an obviously stolen little box for cigarette papers, put him in raptures because it had delicate scrimshaw of French lilies on the cover and his wife was sure to like it.

Cheathams. Lestrade again pondered the cleverness of marriage vows. They didn't point out that a person married an entire family, not just one, at the altar. Had that been emphasized, there would be many a panicked dust-up in the church.

Clea had set up a long buffet-style feast for the family by the time they returned. (Cheathams preferred to eat at their own leisure, not anyone else's.) She waited for them by the kitchen door, her hands tucked neatly inside her apron-pockets. Geoffrey hung back, motioning the brothers to get out first.

He stepped out wearily, his fingers dragging against the wood as if reluctant to let go. Bartram reckoned he was thinking ahead to seeing his father again – a man that didn't see him either.

"I stink like the mews." He held up both hands as she made to step closer.

"You aren't the only one," her nose wrinkled up. "Well, you know where the washroom is. Come on down when you're finished and we'll put something into you."

"So long as it's not your apron-knife." He half-heartedly dodged her friendly little smack.

"You first, seeing as how you need it first," Andrew called after him blithely. He dropped his pose when Geoffrey was gone. Bartram lingered too. It didn't take long to outline to the bones to Clea.

Clea shook her head, not afraid but angry. "I knew it wouldn't last," she said bitterly. "Mr. Quimper would return sooner or later." The little woman reached up and rubbed her forehead. "It couldn't last." Her lips set thin. "Blast him to the Hell that made him."

"Clea – !" Andrew could still be shocked at his baby sister's language.

"I mean it. I should be thinking of my second wedding anniversary, [1] not my chances of being a widow." Clea stamped over to the table and started shiving a cold ham. "If he was ever in the same room with me again, I'd do more than what I did last time."

Andrew and Bartram traded looks. Clea was furious. Before the children, she probably would have run to the rescue with them. It occurred to their slower male minds that staying back had been a heavy toll on her nerves.

"Mr. Quimper wouldn't hurt you." Bartram felt useless as he said it.

"Not directly, no," she answered.

Martin and Nicholas Lestrade were sitting at the bottom of the wide staircase and playing a game of draughts. It was the one thing that obsessed Nick's attention outside of animals, engines, and basking sharks.

Martin grumbled as his younger brother took the board again, but his heart wasn't truly in it. They were setting up for a new game when their father walked out of the side-door underneath the staircase. Seeing them, he quickly held his hands up in a familiar gesture: *Don't touch, I'm filthy, let me clean London or whatever this is off me first so your mother doesn't skin all of us.* The boys settled for grinning at him.

"Did you like your present?" Nicholas beamed mischievously.

"Yes, and I suppose your cheek is a bonus?" Lestrade tapped a single fingertip on his largest son's crown. "That poor cook! And thank you too, Martin. I'd thought you'd use that paper on yourself."

"I did." Martin protested. "I made up myself some cards."

"You mean, 'I made myself some cards,'" his father corrected. "Now, who am I going to give them to?" He tapped Martin. "I'll be down as soon as I give it a wash." He ruefully *tsk*'d at his hands. They were definitely swollen, and he didn't want to think about the hot water in the bath.

"I like grandmother," Nicholas blurted.

"I'm glad to hear that," Lestrade answered gently. "Why don't you go talk with her? She won't be visiting much longer."

151

Lestrade wondered if this was what war felt like. He couldn't relax enough to stay in the tub. He still had the urge to round them all up and keep going to some vague place of safety. He force-dried his hair in a towel, smothering it all in that unspeakable lavender hair-cream Andrew stocked. Then again, Andrew was beyond description in every aspect of his life that Lestrade had witnessed.

Oh, well. At least it keeps book-lice out of my hair. He tried to adopt the best possible light on the situation.

Clea hadn't shown up yet. She could tell he was desperate to think uninterrupted.

The Policeman's Prayer – one of them at least – surfaced in his mind as he worked the comb through his hair and pulled on the spare suit Clea kept on standby.

Someone knocked on the door with a two-tap he recognized. "Come on in, Martin."

His older son stepped in a little slowly. "I thought I'd come down with you," he said carefully.

"S'all right," he said. Clea had squirreled away his other pair of shoes under the bed. Martin reached in and fished them out. "Thank you . . . ."

"Are you getting Grandfather and Grandmother and the Seagull out of here soon?" Martin sat on the edge of the bed next to his father. "And Uncle Marcus?"

"Yes. Does that upset you?"

Marcus answered thoughtfully. "I suppose I'll miss them a bit. But it sounds like you have to."

Geoffrey felt something strange and put his arm around his son's small shoulders. "I remember when you were born, you imp. How did you get older than your *Tad*?"

"Maybe it happened while you were off at work." Martin smiled faintly. "But I'm sorry for Grandfather. He doesn't know me. And for Nicholas. At least he thinks I'm you . . . but he thinks Nicholas is someone you used to play with in the summer."

Potier insisted Martin was like him. If this was what his parents faced every day . . . no wonder they didn't understand him. Geoffrey didn't understand it himself. Which meant Martin most likely didn't either.

Thank god for Nicholas. He didn't care that his brother was smarter than three grown men put together and found fun in calligraphy. He just wanted someone his own age to play draughts with and give a helping hand in his godawful animal collections.

"I'm sorry he doesn't know you, Martin."

"I'm sorry he doesn't know you." Martin was still young enough to have that wonderful ability to cut straight to the bone with his innocence. "Dr. Watson said it was normal."

"Dr. Watson? How did that happen? I don't remember that conversation."

"He came by to see Nick when it looked like he might be getting what Mum had." Martin was still young enough, or honest enough, to enjoy leaning into his father's half-embrace. "Tip and Devon were picking on me and it made me mad."

"Your cousins have to make fun of everything," Geoffrey sighed. "Cheatham blood doesn't mix so well with your Aunt's old military stock."

Martin snickered at the truth of that. "Dr. Watson stopped to say hello to me on his way out. He asked how I was doing and I . . . well, I complained a bit."

"And what did he say?"

"He said at least they were smart enough to make fun of me in ways that showed they actually knew me. I had to think about what that meant." Martin confessed. "He also said that he spent most of his life not even being John Watson, but John, the brother."

"Now that's a shame, because Dr. Watson is a remarkable man, and I've said it many a time."

"That's what I told him."

"Of course you did, you imp."

"Well, it made him smile. He said I was lucky because I had a father who saw *both* his sons, not just one." Martin looked up, with a spark of mischief in his deep blue eyes. With age they were turning less blue and more into some shade even darker. "I'm glad you're like that, because I wouldn't have a chance against Nick. He sucks all the air out of a room when he comes in."

Geoffrey was surprised into laughing. "If you want Nick off your back, just wave a salamander or some sort of horrid insect in front of him. It's like a string in front of a cat."

"That's why I got him a spider for Christmas."

"Oh . . . I didn't know about that." He ought to have caught his wife's outraged shrieks from the heart of London.

"It's a special spider," Martin explained. "It came over from South America with some bananas. Don't worry, it was already dead."

"I hope Nick appreciated the thought you put into that gift."

"He was thrilled. But now he's wondering what sorts of birds over there are big enough to eat that kind of spider."

153

"Big enough? How big are we talking?" Geoffrey felt his eyebrows shoot up as Nicholas indicated a fiercesome size. "Oh. Does that include the legs? *Oh.* Well . . . no wonder he was curious."

"Dr. Watson said they get even bigger in Australia."

"Good thing we sent all our best convicts there, then. Spiders like that could use some humility . . . ."

Geoffrey wondered at himself at that moment. Talking with his son, somehow finding something amusing, thinking ahead to what had to be done . . . and realizing Dr. Watson had found the time to travel all the way over here and soothe the fears of his wife over a trifle.

He probably wouldn't even charge them for the trip, the noble idiot. Just because he knew Clea had a fear of nearly all doctors and he was the exception.

Sherlock Holmes was a larger-than life brain. John Watson was a larger-than-life heart. If the two had ever been combined, the result would have been a modern-day Charlemagne. Just as well.

NOTE

1. Geoffrey and Clea Lestrade were married on Leap Day, February 29th, 1884. (See *Test of the Professionals: Leap Year.*) Thus, as Leap Year only occurs once every four years – 1884, 1888, and 1892 – this is technically their second anniversary.

Chapter XIX – Collusion

"John, for mercy's sake. Is this what you were looking for?"

John Watson looked up from his packing to find his wife in the doorway. A familiar-looking journal was in her hands. "You found it!"

"Of course, dear." Mary smiled at him and held out the small book. "But if I may, why are you so determined to bring a never-used journal? Wouldn't it be practical to take the one you're still working on?"

"No, not for this, dearest. Thank you – " He bent forward and gave her a quick kiss. "It helps me compartmentalize my thinking." He stuffed the book into the top of his small suitcase with a click. Mary imagined the house-brownies breathed a sigh of relief now that the man of the house had no need to continue ripping their domicile apart.

"Ah. A book of the case, the whole case, and nothing but the case?"

"So help me." John lifted his hand solemnly and they both laughed before the smiles faded. In the grey light of London, the slow-freezing rain was casting black streaks of weeping smuts against the glass. Tomorrow's weather would be Biblically wretched. Poor travelling weather for John. Poor air for the health of Mary. It was too soon to tell yet if Arthur had her lungs.

They loved London, but this was a worrisome time of year for Mary's stamina. Her lungs had never had cause to show anyone concern when she lived abroad, for the warm coastal air and lack of fog had been medicinal in nature. Here was different, and her duties with Mrs. Forrester had been out of the main reach of London. She was simply unaccustomed to this air.

"The Yard will keep an extra watch on things in my absence," he said at last. "But I wish I weren't leaving you here."

"Arthur and I will be fine." Mary took up his large hand inside her smaller one. "I am quite aware there are no answers for the strange attacks. That does not mean that I believe nothing will happen, nor is there any point in living as if one is already being victimized." She pressed his hand and he returned the pressure. "Theresa is staying the nights here, as usual. Her father will be shuttling me back and forth with his cab, and I will be visiting my friends at least once a day." The strength of a colonial upbringing, their first common ground, allowed them both a degree of understanding and trust that they understood was unusual to English normality.

"Too many threads, not enough warp to hold them," John answered ruefully. "I shan't be long. A few days with Dr. Mortimer and I'll be back to the two of you by Friday."

"I worry about your taking a trip to a place like the Isle of Streat this time of year."

"It couldn't possibly be any worse than taking one of the old freighting-ships to the Arctic . . . not that I ever did, mind you," John smiled. "But one would hear the worst things where the men congregated at Edinburgh." He slipped his other hand around her waist. "I wired for the weather report. The more northerly the route, the drier the clime. We appear to be getting our punishment from the southern coast. And the south, I'm afraid, can outmatch us for geography any time!"

"You'll be taking The Flying Scotsman, then." Mary nodded. "Good. It's cleaner than most." She *tsk*'d. "I wonder why they call it The Flying Scotsman?"

"The Flying Dutchman was already taken, nowhere near Scotland, and has a terrible reputation?"

"You forgot the passengers probably won't get sea-sick on The Flying Scotsman." Mary laughed. "Why do I have the feeling that you would have ridden The Flying Dutchman on a dare?"

"Because I would have. Youth is for squandering. Maturity comes later when all other options are exhausted."

"Then I am indeed blessed," Mary teased. "Shall we celebrate with a cup of tea before supper?"

"I would enjoy it." When Mary started to pull away, he held her grip.

"Mary, dear . . . look to the police wives." John's strong face had adopted a rare expression, both solemn and gentle. "If you need anything . . . look to the women who married to the badge."

Mary didn't know what to say for a moment. She'd heard him talking with Patterson, of course. The two men were united in the combined sorrow for Mr. Holmes's death, and John had a gift for pulling the best out of people. She knew that whatever was happening, she and Arthur were not considered the targets. John naturally was not taking that pattern to heart, as anyone horrible enough to devote their life to crime would also be dishonourable enough to change their plans to suit themselves.

"I will be careful, John," she promised. "I know several of the Inspectors' wives . . . I even work at the same charity as Mrs. Gregson does, and Mrs. Lestrade sees me in her little charity at least once a week. The Constables' wives see me the most often, for they know I can find the tea that helps their children through the common stomach ache or teething or some other ailment. But I . . . . ." She tightened her grip. "I know they are honoured to help when help is needed."

"That is good to know." John looked upon her with pride. "Bring Arthur down, sweetheart, I should like to enjoy my time with both of you before I leave."

Worsley Outskirts:

Again, the sensation of war. Lestrade felt it was helped along by the fact that his grandfather was sitting at the guest's chair at the table with his hands on the surface. The candelabra cast twinkles into the silver hairs of his beard and danced something a bit more profane into his dark eyes. Against the collapse of daylight, Potier looked like someone that should never, ever be crossed. It was all his eyes. They were too dark and could easily turn into a bottomless criticism.

If that's the effect I have on those poor constables, I should try to be nicer. Lestrade slowly evaluated his own standing. If he carried a fraction of that look, it was no wonder his superiors were so determined to lean on him.

Charles Cheatham reigned on the other side of the table. Somehow there was room for his legs and the dog.

Myron Cheatham sat by his father. As the eldest, he unquestioningly performed as his father's eyes and human escort. Clea sat across him. Poor Marcus had the second chair over, next to Potier.

Lestrade couldn't bring himself to join the table. Not yet. It was easier to walk back and forth before the fireplace, and smoking, he had realized, eased the swelling in his hands a bit.

"The problem is getting to the island from here," Potier began. "It's difficult. Far easier to get there from the peninsula."

"What of paying for passage?" Marcus queried. He was slowly gaining his confidence in this crowd of familial strangers. Clea and Potier were a help. "Whatever the fare would be, it will cost us more to keep the questions out."

"We have the money," Potier cut in before Charles Cheatham could offer. "I set aside plenty enough for the future. The problem is *getting* to it in this weather." He sniffed and jerked his head to the window, where bits of ice were congealing against the dark glass windows. "Does anyone feel like joining me for a bath in the canals?"

Lestrade groaned softly. "*Tad-kohz*, please don't tell me you hid your smuggler's toll inside the Duke's canals?"

Potier smiled contritely. "It isn't as though a person would think to hide it there."

"Can't imagine." Myron shuddered. "Well, you're a braver man than I am, and that is a fact." He poured himself a glass of yellow wine and sipped reflectively. "I would think you do want some assistance in a place like that."

157

Potier nodded by shrugging. "I had to leave it in a hurry, but it isn't as though I can describe where I put it verbally. I have to do it myself." He smiled apologetically at his daughter-in-law, who had certainly seen much worse than this old rascal.

"I'll help," Marcus said softly. "The sooner we have it, the sooner we can get them out of here."

"No matter what, we can't stay here," Geoffrey said heavily. Lack of sleep burned in his eyes. "Mrs. Collins can't hold off the well-wishers forever. The sooner they're off safe and I'm back home . . . the sooner I can help out with Jacobs and Browning."

"You know they could just be the latest sacrificial calf in this," Potier said soberly. He hated to think it, and saying it was worse.

"There aren't any sacrifices just yet," Geoffrey muttered. "With any luck, we'll keep that from happening. *Tad-kohz*, your hideaway truly is safe?"

"It isn't important, and the maps miss it half the time." Potier lifted his shoulder. "Eventually, I can move them elsewhere even deeper. Your *mamm* needs good food and the sun of her home. The Quimpers have learned not to approach my lands. We'll work it from there."

Lestrade sighed. "We don't know where he is. I wish we did."

"We can only stay sharp. He doesn't seem interested in announcing himself." Potier accepted a measure of wine and passed it neatly to Marcus.

"No, that would be quite against his intentions." Clea spoke carefully. Everyone stopped talking. Clea's brains rivaled Myron's, but not always in the same areas. "From what you tell me, he killed his father in a fit of temper."

"Nothing else would accommodate the marks I saw," her husband said softly. "It was without any logic to it. He *knows* how to fight. This wasn't a fight. It was a bludgeoning. It was like . . . like a mad dog."

"He's lost control." She took the wine and finished pouring it for Myron. "He's a man of patterns, Inspector. He's pulling back under for a while . . . turning turtle. He won't come back out until he's done with sorting it all out in his head."

"He must have said something to his men." Potier stroked his short beard. "They seem determined to settle Thomas."

"That could be what he commanded in anger." Clea's mouth was set. She rarely discussed "that man" and everyone tiptoed around the subject, but the indigestible truth was, Clea appeared to have that man's measure more than anyone. During her enforced courtship, Quimper had, she said once, "confided" to her in a show of his willingness to trust her. She rose and joined Geoffrey by the fire with his wine glass. "Best to get them out

158

of here. They must have gone after Geoffrey because he knew where Thomas was."

"Baldwin was one of Quimper's trusted men. I felt he was the one in control of the Aton Bank Gang. Armoricus had been put there to learn from the master." Geoffrey felt the cool of the glass soothe his hands. Now that his head was cool too, he could barely believe he'd been so stupid as lose control like that. And put his hands at risk. Barking mad.

"What is it about that man?" he whispered to his wife. "He makes me Hatter-mad. I can stay calm around anyone else . . . but not that man."

"I suppose that's only fair," Clea said reasonably. "Because it's quite clear *you* have the same effect on *him*."

New Scotland Yard:

Inspector Gregson wondered why he was doing this to himself. There was no need to keep up this unholy level of ambition. His status was settled and secure as far as the Old Man was concerned. Some long-ago investments were slowly starting to prove their worth with their three-percent interest with his parents' care, and Lestrade still didn't have a prayer of ranking up before he did.

Their truce was still fragile. After eight years of careful avoidance, it still felt peculiar to have to work together and not against each other. Gregson's work with organized crime had given him a taste for something truly challenging and heady. Lestrade's lack of interest – utter lack – was surprising, but Gregson was beginning to see that as a gift horse. Lack of interest meant no competition.

The big man sipped his tea (watered down in concession to the late hour) and riffled through another quire of paper. Even absent, Lestrade seemed to be able to cause some sort of mess. Case in point: The thorned horse that nearly made the end of Hopkins' quite promising career.

Thank God the lad came out all right, because no one else is mad enough to take on this problem with the Burial Board and the grave vandalisms . . . Just the prospect of taking up the young man's rope made him slightly sick inside. This was a case for the younger, energetic crowd. Not the older folks like himself, who knew too much about preceding cases to have an original thought . . . Gregson sipped tea and picked up the last bit of the incident. PC Burke had said something about Lestrade in it. He wondered if there was enough to rag on Lestrade later.

Well . . . no way of knowing unless one looks . . . .

Gregson smiled to himself. Besides, if he didn't torture the little rat, Lestrade would think for sure he was gravely ill . . . He found the cabbie's

159

verbal report and read it (slowly) through Burke's staggering and cramped shorthand:

"I didn't know it was him first, sir. I thought it was Inspector Lestrade, the way he stood up from the table like that, leanin' his weight in, like you know, he does because of that inturned foot."

Gregson spluttered. His tea patterned over the desk and he wiped it with his sleeve with a curse, but it didn't change the facts before him or slow the pounding in his heart. Ice crawled over his cheeks.

Hopkins. Hopkins was coming out of The Elegant Barley, a tavern famous for its patronage of policemen. Hopkins was alone that night, unusual for him.

Lestrade tended to drink alone. One or two mates as much as he'd wind up with. Circumstances brought on by his late hours.

Lestrade and Hopkins were both similar in height and dress. It was dark. Hopkins had been, to the eye-witness account, tired and shuffling. Hunched over slightly.

Lestrade's outerwear was cut just slightly too large to allow for freedom of movement. It made him look smaller than he really was, and when he was tired he had the impression of slouching.

"Bloody Hell!" Gregson whispered. The facts were right there – cold and sharp and bright as lightning in the sky. "They weren't after Hopkins at all." He stumbled to the doorway and leaned out. *"Colin!"* he rasped. The young constable at the desk looked up in shock. "Find me Bradstreet. Tell him it's vital. Tell him someone's after Lestrade!"

Colin took off. Self-exiled as the big man was, Bradstreet would come running after that message, and woe to anyone who stood in his way.

Gregson could only wait. He lit a fag with trembling hands. Nausea was coming in now, cold and self-appointed. How could he have missed such a thing? It was right there in front of him!

Lestrade was home alone with that dragon of a landlady, but once he stepped out of his rooms . . . *What then?*

And what, he wondered, *what did this have to do with Dr. Watson?*

The late Mr. Holmes would gibe him all he wanted. Gregson didn't care. Somehow the past events with Watson and what was happening now with Lestrade were tied in. Somehow. He felt it, but he didn't have the map to lead the way.

Watson must know something, he smoked frantically. *Somehow, he must know. He acts too calm. You can't fake that kind of cool. It's when he's worried about something that things crash down . . . What's he doing right now? What's he planning to do?*

He stuffed the cylinder of tobacco in his mouth and ripped through another stack of paper until he found a copy of the Police Surgeons' schedules.

Pennywraith was serving tomorrow. And the next day. And . . . Gregson's eyes scanned the paper in bewilderment. Until the following Saturday when Watson was scheduled to return.

"What is going on?" Gregson whispered under his cigarette. "What exactly is going on?"

Chapter XX – Worsley

If an underground canal was man's imitation of nature, man still needed practice.

A year ago, Lestrade would have been impressed, amazed, and in awe of the English engineer to fashion a canal of brick and mortar all the way back to the centre of the eighteenth-century, and with the tools of that era, create a working channel to connect the coal of Worsley to the surface.

But a year ago, he'd had his first experience with the natural caverns of his grandfather's land, and he was more impressed with the tools of Nature: Stone, water, and patience.

A single spider's net hung over their heads, anchored by the tight mortared line between the bricks of the ceiling. Too dull from coal-grime to shine, it hung like a black thread in the arch of the wet tunnel. A thin breeze following the slow movement of the dull water beneath made the thing wobble and waver like a living thing.

Marcus had opted to pole their boat. He was younger, more resilient, and he most certainly did not possess aching, swollen hands. Lestrade gave in with a display of good manners that he hoped didn't reveal his case of the sour grapes. He hated being idle. It made him think out of boredom, and his thoughts weren't usually good ones.

"*Ugh.*" Marcus whispered to himself, uneasy and chilled as the lamp-light caught grotesqueries against the slope and spans of the underground canals.

Geoffrey lowered his head and lamp as well as he could as the boat floated them underneath the tattered silks. He hated spiderwebs far more than he hated the spinners.

Ahead of them, Old Potier was poling on ahead with his disheartening energy. Geoffrey wondered why anyone bothered to compare him with his grandfather. The way things were going, he was far likely to beat the old rascal to the bone-yard. To make matters worse (or at least brag about his ability to recover), Potier was whistling a snatch of tune about sea-farers and some woman pirate queen. Probably an ancestrix.

"*Mamm* used to say the spiders taught us to knit," Marcus whispered. His breath steamed like a train in the dark of the tunnel. The young man was clearly whistling past his own graveyard as tiny white balls of ice from the outside melted in the creases of his outerwear. He was trying to be a man about the fact that he'd never seen the earth over his head before.

"I remember when she told me that too," Lestrade admitted. Watching a spider at work on her web in the garden . . . the little children had been allowed that before they were deemed old enough to work with the men. Finger-knotting and the string crafts as a wise past-time. Purses by girls, nets for boys. *Mamm* had told them the spider had taught the first people the trick, and to simply watch a spider spin if they didn't believe her story.

Marcus' innocent memory had triggered a landslide of his own. The garden had been a safe place because it was Jeanne's. He and Jenny had woven grocer's bags and pouches together in the garden. The whole garden had been a tightly ordered sort of community, where peas never associated with beans, and broken flower-pots made housing for the small brown toads and larger natterjacks. Above their heads, strings of bird houses made use of the insects, and the estate's honeybees had pored over the blooms.

Looking back, it was the fascination of an industrious world within a world that drew Geoffrey to London. He'd been interested in the business within small spaces. It helped immeasurably that all the Quimpers (and thus his brothers) held that there was nothing good about cities. Filthy, cramped, and populated by the poor unfortunates who could wrest nothing better out of their lives . . . the list went on forever. Their philosophy had implied it was better to serve the Quimpers in Plymouth than it was to rule alone in poverty.

Better the devil you know than the devil you don't know . . . What a convenient saying!

Of course it was all part of their work to keep everyone in servitude. It was a fine art form, delicate as a spider's web and as difficult to extricate.

Friendships were cultured within the approval of the Master. Grudges too. It kept the twelve families fighting amongst themselves just enough that no one would ever be able to organize themselves up, union-like, against the ruling party. And it kept them all united when something outside the estate threatened their "safe" world. The Baldwin who gave the gun to Armoricus had been the great-nephew of the old Baldwin who was such a friend of Potier back on the Peninsula. All connected, like tunnels inside ant-hills.

Better to reign in Hell than serve in Heaven? Poor quarrel, that.

Lestrade thought of Plymouth as Hell, and London – if not Heaven – was surely salvation. He'd wanted to go out and meet that devil of London and see if it was as bad as the one he already knew. It wasn't. He left.

Reign in Hell . . . a good thing? Doubtful.

Milton had said that blasted line first. Lestrade barely knew the classics, and concentrated on the English skills that would improve his work. But one could hardly avoid hearing the betters talk amongst themselves. They enjoyed words that had showed off their schooling. Mr.

163

Holmes and his use of foreign words was a perfect example. It was a separate language all its own, and it was a language of *battle*.

The battle went to not the person who was right or wrong. It went to the man who knew words the best. Police constables never spoke better than the Inspectors. Inspectors never, *ever* spoke better than the people at the Home Office. And the Home Office was the direct wire to the government. One never faced them on their own ground.

If this is Hell, it at least has some rank and order to it . . . .

Water dripped from the sides of Potier's boat. He'd shifted his weight, making the whole thing tremble. Lestrade stopped thinking for nearly a minute (bliss) as he waited to see if the old pirate would fall in. That earlier remark about being put in an unmarked grave was suddenly worse than ever.

Then things arighted. They kept going.

And he started thinking again.

Too-often he'd heard Milton's words from another's lips. *Better to reign in Hell . . . .*

Did you ever try to reign in Hell? Damson Estates would still be Hell, no matter how high one would aspire.

It made about as much sense as another quote, one he hated even more because people were determined to use it the wrong way:

Am I my brother's keeper?

Rot.

After the anger of the mews-fight had ended, Lestrade had been forced to stifle his natural urges on Baldwin. The anger was still there, just hiding. Marcus' comment about spiders had pushed his mind to places and a single moment in time he no longer wanted to remember.

They'd told him he was his brother's keeper no matter what (as if that argument had worked against God), and in ways that suggested it made everyone happy to make Armoricus happy. If the Pope was Peter's successor on earth, then Armoricus was the Master's Son in human form. *Follow. Obey. Questioning is rude. Questioning is impertinent.* No philosophy should justify slavery within the family. Martin and Nicholas took care of each other because they wanted to. Duty was a hollow burden in childhood if there was nothing to feed it.

A house divided cannot stand – That proverb makes sense.

Even Andrew, who was as petty and mercenary as a banker's wife, would never think of joining a family fight (and he'd just proven it).

Next to him, Marcus made a faint sound and pressed himself closer into the little boat. A punt would be easier to use than this clumsy brute. Lestrade thought of the horrible little coracles of his childhood. Their shipworthiness had improved the swimming skills of more humans than any other thing in his experience.

And I think I'd prefer a coracle right now . . . Lestrade swallowed and tried not to think of how the tunnel-arches were getting closer and closer to their heads as the water level continued to rise.

The canal-water didn't even look real. That was the worst of it. They'd gone past the dark red vein of iron water into a slender seep that showed a strange sort of miracle: Past the bloody run of mine-water, a clear spring had flowed innocently over the cobbles on its way to the deeper water of the channel. It was pure. A strange thing in this place tainted by honest workmanship. Like a lens it magnified the earth beneath: Common grey stones were tainted like rubies and garnets from the iron. Older stains were darkening like the dull lumps of coal here and there. With age the false gems had grown black and blue-black, and marked eerie trails upon the greenish cobbles and broken brick. Lestrade had stared at the sight upon their passage, for the lamps cast a strange illusion, making the surface of the flowing water appear as tangible as gossamer silk. [1]

Things had only started out bad at the entrance to the mine. Potier had begged a moment's leave to bribe the lonely (and miserable) guard at the opening. Lestrade didn't know what the selling point was: The shillings or the free flask of American bourbon.

But to do the man credit, it was doubtful either bribe would have worked at all if Potier hadn't produced papers to prove he was a part-owner in the coal.

"Is he really?" Marcus whispered.

"With him? I'd just assume yes." Lestrade put his back against the damp perch of stone, wishing that they could find a shelter out of the just-forming ice storm. Prickles of tiny white marbles stung their exposed ears and dug long fingers inside their collars. Marcus shuddered as if in pain and balled up tight as boiled wool yarn.

Their shelter was thin but at least it did not have to do with going into the black opening Hell of that underground canal.

"We're supposed to go through *that*," Geoffrey spoke as calmly as he could, but this looked like the worst thing his grandfather had come up with, bar none. "That . . . there."

A round-eyed Marcus silently assented. The entrance to the Worsely Mine was full of water. The typical orange tint was diluted from the high amount of rainwater adding to the mess, but it was still appalling to think of getting into something one didn't know the bottom to.

"Don't worry about it." Potier shrugged as he slogged back in his water-proof boots. It must have been simple to read their eyes . . . or else he was used to the experience. "We have boats."

165

". . . don't really care about boats." Marcus said into the collar of his loaned raincoat. "Care about learning how to breathe underwater." Geoffrey awkwardly patted him on the back.

Marcus was breathing easier again now that Potier was back on a smooth trail of water. He kept glancing upwards, and the lamp-light reflected the whites of his eyes.

"It's all right, Marcus," Geoffrey told him under his breath. "The tunnels've been here since the 1700's."

"They look new," Marcus admitted. His voice hushed out in the quiet drip. Bricks passed their floating heads, still tight and cleanly mortared. Icicles made of water and the calcium in the mortar created a strange, dripping thread here and there.

Geoffrey chuckled. "A good bricklayer is never out of work."

Marcus nodded, but he swallowed and looked a little sick. "Does he have to whistle that?" he wanted to know through his teeth.

Geoffrey listened and sighed. "He probably doesn't know what he's whistling, Marcus."

"How can you live in England and *not* know the tune to *London Bridge is Broken Down*?" Marcus whispered back.

"Our grandfather is strangely selective about what he wants to know. But he's never lived longer in England than he has to. I find it safer to assume he knows very little about England." Geoffrey yawned. It was a bad sign. He was tired and increasingly broken down from his day. Potier at least had been able to grab a bit of sleep at the Cheathman house, the old pirate . . . .

"I suppose you're right." Marcus gingerly touched his pole to the watery ground. Something gave under the tip, like a grainy lump of coal. "It smells like a fruit-cellar in here," he whispered. "Like mushrooms."

"No mushrooms I'd eat here."

"Nor I. I prefer truffles. Nothing here looks like the right sort of tree." Geoffrey smiled despite himself.

"All this for a bag of money." Marcus sighed. "I hope it's still here."

"That makes the two of us . . . If it isn't, I won't be pleased." Geoffrey wondered if it were possible to go mad from inactivity.

"I don't like thinking he's spending his money on us," Marcus confessed. "He should be saving it for his old age."

"I would have agreed with you a year ago, Marcus." Geoffrey picked up his pole and gently pressed it against the sides of the tunnel. They were a little close for his comfort. "But I've come to the belief that our old *Tad-kohz* is doing exactly what he planned to do with his old age."

"He says *Mamm* will improve once she gets back home . . . to her old home," Marcus murmured. "I suppose we'll find out if we improve too."

166

"You'll do fine," Geoffrey assured him.

"I'm more worried about *Tad*. Do you think he'll be better in the Channels?"

"Positive."

"I wish I could share your optimism."

"That's got nothing to do about it. It's common sense. Once they get on the island, I won't be around to reinforce his madness."

Marcus made a strange clucking sound. "Maybe there's room for a horse over there."

Geoffrey found himself smiling thinly. "There's a thought."

"But his hands . . . ."

"I know."

"Pity without help does little good," Marcus decided at last.

"Yes."

Up head, Potier gave a happy shout.

"Here we are then," Geoffrey whispered.

"What now?"

"We get it out of here, and pack the three of you up to one of the old rascal's ships."

"Will you be going with us?"

"It looks like it . . . ."

Geoffrey sounded sad even to himself. He shut up. Marcus didn't need to know how he felt to see his mother's smiling face underneath his skin.

Reuniting with Jenny and her laughing husband had been a slim fantasy over the years. The people who had liked him best deserved better than that. They were gone now, and their son was now his last brother. It was hard to see the young man, but the thought of *not* seeing him was even harder.

I think I'll be glad to get back to work at the Yard. I wonder what Dr. Watson's doing?

Miles away in London, Inspector Gregson was wondering the exact same thing.

NOTE

1. Without the spectra of sunlight or an illumination from multiple locations, underground water has an eerie, two-dimensional appearance as if it possesses a different texture and property. This is because water will partially reflect light, and not penetrate.

167

Chapter XXI – Chess Games

John woke up to find Mary's side of the bed already empty. (The advantage of having a maid around – she could help with the buttons.) He smiled and stretched slightly, noting it was still dark. Mr. Jefferson's curses were already muffling the pre-dawn as he delivered the milk.

At least he doesn't curse in a language most people can fathom, he remembered, knowing the old veteran needed to express himself – and after Africa, he was entitled.

The doctor rose and went to the wash, where Theresa had already set out his shaving-shelf. It was the work of a few minutes to crisply strop his cheeks and set a small amount of wax to his moustache. (It kept his upper lip clean from London.) A shame there was no counter-part for the rest of the body, John mused ruefully. *Now to see the verdict for the fine outdoors* . . . He dealt with window and sash, leaning his head outside to make out the foggy world below. Halos of grimy street-lights created a soft fuzz of illumination, and made a lumbering-shadowed giant out of the patient, slow-stepping constable in uniform.

"Morning, Doctor." PC Lions tapped his brim. "Fine morning, eh?"

"Fine enough for this time of year!" Watson joked back. If a policeman didn't say something to someone once in a while, he felt he was ignoring his duties. Watson closed the window, glancing at his watch as he set it at his waist-coat. Lions and his *compadres* passed their house every quarter-hour, and tried to be as punctual about it as possible. If there were no crimes or quarrels, he ought to be able to pass on his messages without delay.

He passed Theresa coming up the stairs, a basket of clean wash in her arms. "Good morning, sir. The Missus is downstairs with Young Arthur, sir."

"Thank you, Theresa." John gave his tie one last adjustment as he slipped down and paused to give a perusal of the coat-tree. Theresa had put out his travelling-clothes as directed, and even polished his spare shoes.

"I can tell you're already upon a case." Mary rose from the little breakfast table. Her hair was still tied loose in the back in concession to the morning. Later she would have Theresa bind it all up in a plait and finish it with a delicate cap. Behind her, the first tips of dawn struggled to paint cheer into the sleeping remnants of her garden. John could see a valiant war of alpine strawberries trying to bloom even as they froze under a glaze of ice from the roof. It was beautiful, but somehow John felt a chill as he looked upon the clear sparkle of the trapped blooms.

"What is the matter, John?" Mary had come to his side. A cup of coffee was in her hands – *his* cup.

He shook himself and did not answer directly. "Your strawberries are inundated."

"Oh . . . ." Mary looked over her shoulder and sighed. "It can't be helped. My own foolishness. I shall move them in the spring."

"If they survive, dear heart." He put his arm around her and they both leaned into each other. Arthur slept on in the day-crib Mary had set up by the window so the baby could "get the benefit of the sunshine when it comes." In the new glow of the day, he was pink as a rose petal.

"Strawberries are hardy plants. The plants you see in ice may not survive, but they may survive you. They are beautiful cased in the ice like that, are they not? Like Snow White in her glass case, the beauty is preserved forever . . . or at least until the apple falls out of her throat."

"Or until the sun melts the ice." John smiled and kissed the top of her head. "You sound like someone I once knew . . . ."

"You once knew? And you no longer know them?" Mary's blue eyes teased with the deepest affection.

"I'm not certain how to answer that . . . It was an artist. Does a person truly know an artist?"

"Now that is an excellent way of answering my question with a question. Not that I regretted our visit to Elizabeth Cheatham's showing!" Mary stood on her tiptoes to give her husband a kiss. (Theresa was nowhere near to be scandalized.) "In fact, I would enjoy one of her paintings someday. Though not the one of Old Father Thames – not unless I wanted to frighten small children and wandering missionaries."

"Mary, you have a bit of a hoyden in you!" John laughed as they re-settled about the table. "Arthur's sleeping a great deal, isn't he?"

"You say that because you slept through his nocturnal adventures." Mary's kind face was a little tired as she dished up eggs with dill. "I'm pleased he is growing so quickly, but why must he be entertained when I'm ready for a little rest?"

John sheepishly smiled. "Give yourself a nap later. You'll need all the rest you can take while I'm gone. Are you certain you don't need me?"

Mary chuckled. "The fort is under control, Major. I have plans to stay busy and – " She examined the framed calendar behind John on the wall. "I even have an appointment with Mrs. Lestrade tomorrow."

"Mrs. Lestrade? I hope she's doing better. Her fear of doctors is understandable considering her past experience, but it might help if she spoke about it a bit."

169

"I can't say if she has a particular motive in seeing me. We do try to say hello every now and then. She does marvelous work with her charity. And that would be Dr. Mortimer."

John had paused in the act of buttering his toast. "Who would be Dr. Mortimer?"

"That would be Dr. Mortimer," Mary said serenely as the door-knocker clapped. "See to our guest, Theresa," Mary lifted her voice just enough to carry.

John stared at his wife, butter knife in one hand, toast in the other, as Mary sipped her coffee pleasantly. "Good morning, Dr. Mortimer," Theresa was saying. "Shall I take your coat, sir?"

"Mary . . . how in the name of Heaven . . . ."

Mary chuckled. "You do love a mystery, dear . . . ." She reached over the table and patted him on the wrist. "I shall leave this one for you to solve."

John collected himself barely in time. Mary set out a third place from a covered dish – John had completely missed it, absently assuming it was something to eat for breakfast. Dr. Mortimer was chafing his hands together from the slight chill, his face pink. Cold followed in his wake. He smelt of the rising odours of the London streets.

"Well, a good morning to the two of – I mean, the three of you – " Mortimer absently nodded to the still-sleeping Arthur. "You have an interesting door-knocker, John. I was half afraid to use it. The teeth on that chimera looked ready to bite me."

"Yes. I'm afraid it came with the building." John sighed. Why was he not surprised Dr. Mortimer had failed to notice it until today? "I must get it replaced someday . . . It frightens away more than a few children and the occasional timid adult . . . Feel free to use the doorbell."

"No, no . . . I never remember doorbells. They're always so tiny."

"Oh."

Mary passed him a plate as he sat down. The man blinked his surprise before thanking her. "Will you be taking my husband soon, Dr. Mortimer? He is most anxious to see the Isle of Streat."

"To be truthful, my dear lady, not many people can say they're anxious to see Streat. It's so . . . ." Mortimer searched for the right word. "Dull? Monotonous? Monochromatic. All grays and browns and a green so dark it might be black against a slatey sea. Very flat, but you do have what looks like a regiment of Neolithic remnants to enliven the monotony. Not interesting like Dartmoor."

As Mortimer sipped his coffee, his hosts silently traded looks: Dartmoor could have many deserving appellations, but *interesting* would likely never occur to either. They would have used many other words first: *Looming, pensive, gloaming, primeval, mirksome . . . .*

"*Madescent,*" Mary whispered.

"*Maliferous,*" John whispered back. That was all either dared of the game. He cleared his throat quite loudly and wiped his hands on his napkin. "There are a few gentle swells of slope and a tiny fishing-cove or two, are there not?"

"A few. Rather difficult to tell this time of year when you have alternate snowfalls burying everything. Even the ducks put low and give the impression of burrowing underground, so sincere are their efforts to avoid the weather. Legend has it one of the baronet's guests shot a seal, thinking it was an especially clever drake." Mortimer shrugged his bowed shoulders. "But as to travel, Sir Niles has arranged an excellent ferry for his guests. We needn't worry on that score."

John hadn't been worried, but then, he had never been afraid of shipwrecks, capsizing, or even swimming in the North Sea. It was one of the many things that he didn't know set him apart.

Instead of the expected blue-coat approaching, Inspector Hopkins was pausing in his walk.

"And good morning, Dr. Watson." The young man grinned in a friendly manner despite his apparent fatigue. "I hope you aren't out here to chase me down over these ribs." He touched them with a grimace of self-mockery. "The others down at the Yard are telling me I can't brag about this unless I can prove I'd drunk a barrel and fought a priest first."

Watson was surprised (in a delighted sort of way). He laughed. "I'm afraid I can't help you, Mr. Hopkins. I was your attending physician, remember?"

"Better luck next time, eh?"

"One can only hope . . . Are you off to the Yard then?"

"On my way back to it, actually . . . Another fine job at the Burial Board." Hopkins stepped out of the way so the lamp-lighter could continue on with his inspection of the lamps. "I've been up for hours."

"You met a member of the Burial Board . . . at this hour?" Watson reflected that his imagination would always prove lacking against reality. "Is the man an insomniac?"

"Nothing so mundane. He's an albino. The strictest albino you ever saw. Can't stand any sort of sunlight at all, so naturally he works at night." He shrugged. "You'd think London would be soft enough on his eyes. Especially this time of year with the nights long and the factories belching."

Watson shook his head. *Once again, my imagination falters before the variances of reality.*

"Anything I can do for you, sir?"

"Actually . . . yes. I am taking a few days from the Yard. My regular practice will be handled by Doward. He's a good *locum* and interested in working with the police so you needn't worry about frightening his sensibilities if Constable Edwards falls down another basement-chimney and breaks his leg."

"Well, that's good to know, but to be fair, I don't believe Edwards broke his leg falling *down* the basement chimney . . . He broke it when we were trying to pull him out. *Lions!*" Hopkins lifted his voice. "How did Edwards break his leg?"

"Which leg was it, sir?"

"Ah, never mind," Watson said hastily. "At any rate, I would be most gratified if someone could help keep an eye on my practice."

"And your family of course." Hopkins smiled a bit wistfully. "Understood, Doctor. We'd be pleased to keep a watch. They'll be safe with us."

"I'm sure of that, Inspector." Watson answered. "But that's no license for you to overstrain yourself, or to forget your breathing exercises! Now if you would be so kind as to pass on some messages to the Yard for me . . . ."

London is getting crowded, was Hopkins' involuntary thought as he rounded the corner and collided. *And that hurt . . .* For a moment Patterson's shocked gaze bored into his own like a drill made of moonlight, then the tall man was hastily backing away, his hands steadying Hopkins as he wheezed for breath.

"Dear me, I am very sorry, Hopkins! I didn't see anyone . . . ."

"It's all right . . . ." Hopkins clutched for breath. After the initial blow, the pain was subsiding in his ribs. "It's all right . . . How . . . are you?"

"Er, unharmed. For all that I nearly took home an Inspector on my shoulders."

"Oh, not all the way, surely, Patterson. I'd've hopped off once you got to my street." Hopkins could finally stand upright again. He took a deep breath and held it with relief. "Much better," he decided. "I didn't keep you from anything, did I?"

"Not at all. I'm just trying to find out something about . . . ." Frustration blackened the tall man's voice. He paused and rubbed at a throbbing vein in his forehead. "*Why* is it so hard to get a funeral director to speak? Would it help matters if I swore I wouldn't arrest him?"

172

"Only if you wore a priest's collar and conducted services in the church of his choice," Hopkins answered soberly. "I'm just back from the Burial Board Chairman. Would you like to trade?"

"Surely you couldn't be as fruitless as I was just now."

"Come around and have a cup of tea with me, and let's discuss it."

The cup of tea turned into something a with a bit more breath to it for Patterson. Hopkins merely shrugged to himself as the other man tipped his hip-flask into the cup in question. Patterson looked as though sleep had been a stranger to him for the past decade.

The older man lived in a very simplistic set of rooms. (It was literally a "set": A room for sleeping and a room for living.) Both rooms were decorated with the old sort of wood paneling that came into vogue before wallpaper was so popular. A folding bed rested against the wall in a large oak cabinet – it must have cost at least seven pounds. Hopkins found himself sitting on what was called an hygienic couch with a heavy, removable cover for washing.

The older man's rented rooms were actually what Hopkins had expected. He was proud of himself for being spot-on: Minimal, simple, but with an eye to harmony. That lined up with what Hopkins believed was Patterson's personal tastes: Patterson would far rather do without than have something clash within his living quarters.

Which makes sense . . . Patterson doesn't look as though he cares for any sort of stimulation once he gets home.

This was his first actual conversation with the man since his voluntary retirement, and subsequent return. Hopkins better remembered him as the man who panicked during what was now called the Estuary Affair, where Lestrade and two of their best constables wound up as temporary hostages. Patterson's control had shattered like a lamp-globe in front of them all.

Not that *Hopkins* had been all that British that night. His memory inevitably returned to the moment where a spent bullet struck his leg and left him writhing on the stinking boards of the warf. Gregson or Bradstreet had pulled it out of him on the spot and he might have fainted, because all he could remember after that was Patterson screaming and Gregson putting him to sleep with a single blow to the face.

It had been a terrible night, but it certainly had inflated Gregson's reputation . . . .

"Gregson isn't telling me everything." Patterson paced back and forth in his small room. (Not even a window, but one gargantuan wall-lamp.) "To be fair, I didn't ask, but . . . ." Patterson sighed. "I didn't know what was going on with the Colonel and Dr. Watson."

173

"What do you mean? You have me a bit in the dark there. I know the Colonel holds Dr. Watson accountable for some verbal slander against the late unlamented brother the Professor . . . ."

Patterson's eyes had gone black. "We're not talking slander, though you've seen as many people kilt for it as I have, I'm sure . . . ." He lowered his voice. It still shook. "The Colonel is setting up for all and out war with Watson. *War*. And I'm convinced Dr. Watson knows it."

Hopkins gnawed his lip and caught himself. He stopped. "Tell me more," he said softly. "I never really knew Mr. Holmes much, but he was fair to his own lights, and Watson's working with us now."

"I'm not sure what exactly the *why*'s are, but the Colonel seems to want something out of Watson. As far as I can tell . . . ." Patterson picked up his drink from the sideboard sipped at it slowly, with no appearance of tasting. "I had to research everything I possibly could on the Professor to bring down that wretched Family," he said at last. "Had there been two of me, I would have spent some of my hours with the Professor's blood-kin. His brother the Army Colonel had a stain about him. People were afraid to say anything overtly against him, but at the same time . . . Well, you know how it is when you're asking an officer anything."

"They turn discreet," Hopkins nodded. "Very discreet."

"The Colonel's peers were as discreet as they come. There was a dust-up against him during his service abroad. It involved a bit of India and a good portion of his term in Afghanistan. At the time, I thought it was just an interesting coincidence that Dr. Watson was in the same area as Moriarty. Then . . . it turned out Dr. Watson's brother, who was also an officer, had been courting Hayter's daughter."

"I can only hope the courtship was approved-of."

"It would seem so. But the girl up and married a man completely against her father's wishes, and he lost his zest for the life, so they say. Dr. Watson's brother went off somewhere outside of Edinburgh and died a few years ago, to all accounts a broken man. Now, the man Miss Hayter *did* choose, was some Northerner named Grover. He was a *protégé* of Colonel Moriarty . . . in the same way Watson was a *protégé* of Hayter." Patterson had almost finished his glass. "You can smell the hate in those reports. The sheer restraint makes you want to just jump out a window to get away."

"I'll take your word for it." Hopkins was silently shocked. "This is a delicate affair, Patterson. What makes you think I'm your man for this talk?"

"You're smart, Hopkins. But that's besides the point. There's something binding Colonel Moriarty's business interests with Afghanistan somewhere. It's somehow with the burials of the men who were brought

174

back." Patterson finger-stabbed the air in front of Hopkins' necktie. "You've been working on these burial cases."

"Working and getting nowhere!" Hopkins protested. "Many of the people who would have been there ten years ago are dead, or moved to parts unknown. Some of this mess has to do with the cremation folks, and you know as well as I how popular they are right now! Cremation is about the only thing that will make the Catholics and Protestants rub elbows."

"Blast," Patterson said wearily. He shot his cuffs and made another drink.

"Well, if you're getting nowhere, what if you tried to find something on Moriarty? What about this Grover?"

"Grover comes from an old family with more age than money. Which is ironic, considering they were purveyors and barristers specializing in property. He started out as Moriarty's secretary. Not long after his marriage to Miss Hayter, the two appear to have had a falling-out. They aren't socializing together nearly as often."

"Cold comfort to Hayter, I'm sure." Hopkins sipped his tea, thinking hard. "Is there any light on his war against Dr. Watson?"

Patterson shook his head. "Not enough to fill a ladle. He issued some sort of challenge to Lestrade to find Watson guilty of hiding the truth of his part in Maiwand, but as soon as Lestrade showed his teeth . . . Moriarty backed down. Gregson feels the whole thing was a test to see how the Yard would react." Patterson sniffed his drink. "I can't say I'm surprised. Moriarty thinks in terms of the world being a giant chessboard. Life really is no more than a game to him."

"I suppose he'd want to see for himself if we cared about a man who wrote about us in such . . . flattering tones," Hopkins offered.

The two smiled at each other.

"Strange, isn't it?" Patterson said softly. "People ask me how I could stand to work with Mr. Holmes, for all the things he said about us . . . but Dr. Watson gave as good as he got and showed Mr. Holmes as having as many flaws."

"People remember what they want to remember," Hopkins shrugged. "My old Sunday School teacher said that four times a week."

"He was right. They do." Patterson set his cup down and absently rubbed at his wrist. "Mr. Holmes always struck me as that Irish proverb . . . '*Speak with a mouth of ivy, and carry a heart of holly.*'" He smiled. "I'm certain he did just that when he thought about it."

Hopkins laughed softly. "I miss the man. We never had anyone helping us like that before. Bradstreet said he was like one of the old thief-takers back to life. He had the time to *read*. He had the time to *research*.

175

He never understood everything we went through, but then again, we never understood him. It was the results that mattered."

Without planning it, the room was put into a pall as both men thought about Sherlock Holmes in his own way.

"I suppose," Hopkins said at last, because the silence was hard, "Colonel Moriarty went for Lestrade as his challenge because he wanted to see if Lestrade wanted to find Dr. Watson guilty of tale-telling. An opening move?"

"Mr. Holmes never once held back when he was chewing out a man. And Lestrade got the rough end more than any of us," Patterson agreed soberly. "I don't think he *particularly* singled him out. Lestrade just consults – *consulted* – with him more than anyone else."

"So Moriarty was testing our mettle too. We're not the corruptible sort we were back in the seventies. You'd think he'd know that. On the other hand, he's a military man. Change comes slow to his species. Quite slow." Hopkins realized the tea was actually quite good. He rose for another cup.

"And we have veterans in our force. Moriarty had plenty of reasons to fish us out. I wonder what he found?" Patterson asked rhetorically.

"Hard to say. A tactician never reveals all his moves, even when he wins. And the best tactician doesn't have an 'end' to his games. They're constantly going on."

Patterson slowly set his cup down. A faraway look filmed his eyes over. "Now you may have something there," he murmured.

"Pardon?"

"Moriarty's a chess player. Collects sets from all over the world. Plays games with almost anyone . . . and he never gets tired of them. He's a fine manipulator, and it stands to reason his methods in life would be the same as they are on the real board." Patterson hurriedly refilled his cup. "It would just be like that clever woodscolt . . . ." His knuckles struck the tabletop. "Blast it, I am going senile. It was right in front of me."

"I'm glad, because then you can explain to me what you're talking about!"

"I'm sorry, Hopkins . . . ." Patterson dug deep into his eyes with the heels of his hands. "Moriarty likes to set up the board in ways that if you capture one of his pieces, there will be at least one piece waiting for you to do exactly that so he can capture yours . . . ."

"So he might be the one sending these low-cut villains after Dr. Watson the night of that Mummers' Parade – and Montgomery's attack!" Hopkins caught on. "If the worst members of his gang achieve his goals, excellent. But if they are killed or arrested . . . they're out of his way."

"Betting you it's also a way to weed out the factions that are loyal to someone else in the gang." Patterson gritted his teeth in disgust. "We're helping him, aren't we? We're helping him!"

"You're saying – " Hopkins had suddenly forgotten the tea in his hands. "You're saying that . . . Lestrade is playing right into Moriarty's hands."

"Not just Lestrade," Patterson said heavily. "We all are."

Chapter XXII – The Cult of the Dead

The Flying Scotsman arrived in a shriek of steam that felt as though it fell upon their faces already freezing. Watson coughed faintly. He hefted his luggage to test its weight. Dr. Mortimer was moving ahead, gaily waving through the white steam-bank as a last shrill took a nip out of their eardrums.

"Edinburgh should be a change from King's Cross!" Dr. Mortimer proclaimed gaily.

Yes . . . colder. Watson kept the unworthy thought to himself. *Edinbugh is eight-and-a-half hours away . . . Conservation of one's strength is absolutely necessary . . .* He ought to be grateful for the especially timed Scotch Express for cutting *two* hours off the travel time . . . but he was not fond of particularly long journeys. They made his shoulder ache, and thus his leg.

Thank the mercies for the half-hour stop in York.

"Here we are . . . all to ourselves." Dr. Mortimer put his single suitcase down with relief. It was a heavy looking thing contrived of crocodile leather, and so solid it never once wobbled. He propped his Penang Lawyer against it and looked out the window with satisfaction. "Such a joy to ride in English trains! I shall never take them for granted again."

"Did you use the rails so much on your trip abroad?"

"In some parts of the world, it is the only reliable method on land . . . outside of the ox-cart which I cannot recommend during the monsoon season. Each country seems to deal with the inevitable train-breaks in a different matter. Whilst in India, we had a minor technical breakdown, and – "

"Allow me to guess!" Watson laughed. "The paperwork acquired a timeless sort of importance!"

"It was most surreal. The official didn't want us to just walk across the field to the other train station, as it was operated by a cousin he disliked."

"I once saw a clerk take ten minutes to write out the word '*India*' on a relief form," Watson sympathized. "There was a ceremonial mask hanging out of the top filing-cabinet, and torn mosquito-netting hung off the chandelier."

"Obviously I did not have a novel experience! But that one was not my only experience." Mortimer easily tucked Watson's two small bags against his large one. "There was an actual train derailment when we went to Sasketchewan. Do you know how Americans deal with train delays? They have picnics!"

Watson thought about it. "I take it the trip was a success anyway?"

"Sir Henry is a much improved man," Mortimer assured him. "If he were not, I would not even venture to London on a Sunday jaunt." The tall doctor's grey eyes sparkled kindly. "You really must think of coming up to visit him. You and the family. He would be delighted."

"As would I," Watson answered softly. He liked the young baron, who had no rank save that of his natural talents. Unaffected, unpretentious, strong, and confident, Sir Henry was impossible not to like and even more impossible not to respect. It had been easy for the two of them to strike up a friendship in that rambling old house.

Watson had been a little afraid of following-up on him after the closure of their case. Had he returned to the affections of Beryl Stapleton? That question haunted him, for the man had been struck hard in his heart over the young woman. But Beryl Stapleton had been so cruelly used . . . Would she fixate upon him as her salvation? He pitied the woman for giving her heart to that monster of a husband so completely, and to be coldly used just as wholly. Had she waited for Sir Henry's return, or had she left that lonely cottage on the moor and its memories?

Memory could be a terrible thing. All the warm, sunlit moments where Beryl Stapleton had been at the peak of her beauty against the moor at its loveliest had been crushed at the sight of her swooning at the bottom of the pillar, her body marked by violence.

Lestrade had said later the sight of that room with its specimens preserved in glass had unsettled him as badly as anything else in his career. "Mrs. Stapleton had been one of his collections, it looked like." The little professional had made certain Holmes was no place near before he unburdened himself of that thought.

They both had shuddered. What a night that had been! A part of Watson was still amazed at the heights they had all achieved in the midst of the tragedy. Lestrade's nerve had held out, though he had to stay in that dreadful house with its dead butterflies and torture-marks and a half-mad Beryl Stapleton . . . the only other person under the roof had been that half-deaf, half blind old servant who was useful because of his worthlessness. The poor old man, with no place to go, had waited pathetically waiting for the Master to come back and give him orders.

Sir Henry had taken the news about Beryl with an admirable calm and acceptance. But he'd overheated in his run from the Hound, and that over-heat had led to a too-rapid cooling on the damp moor. The wracking fever had not been a surprise.

Holmes had blamed himself for that too. He shared his victories far better than he ever shared his failures . . . .

"You look thoughtful."

Watson shook himself back to life. The train was picking up to its maximum speed. "I was thinking," he apologized. The nearest alternative topic came to his mind and he took it gratefully. "You have the appearance of being an expert on bog-remains, for all that you seem to prefer skeletons."

"Yes, I do. They're so much . . . neater. And to be truthful, more efficient. To be able to see the face and not the skull is a distraction." Mortimer glanced at the closed door before rolling himself a cigarette. "A sad distraction." He sighed through his nostrils. A grand, defeatist gesture. "I did study them most assiduously when I was younger," he confessed.

"Oh?" Watson found himself smiling slightly. The writer in his brain scented a story. "Do tell me."

"I used to summer with family friends upon the coast overlooking the shores of France. I doubt you would know the name of my hosts. They were the utterly honourable Lockwoods. Content to rule within the small confines of their smaller chapel – Mr. Andrew was the sexton – and I daresay his wife, a grey tigress of a woman that went by the unlikely name of Heaster, [1] could have rivaled any man on her self-taught education. Indeed she was even able to teach in a few schools as guest-lecturer from time to time! The will of an Amazon with the brains of a man. They were an excellent match, for she was shrewd enough to marry a man who was able to stimulate her intellect as well as she did to his. I remember the garden they kept together. A lovely sculpture of texture and colour against the cliffs. It was a marvelous playground for a young boy. I'm afraid a part of me found so much delight in being a boy during those summers, that I remain a boy inside."

Watson was smiling so hard his face hurt. Mortimer was a delight. It took only a few words to paint a world anyone would want to be a part of. "I can hardly fault you for that, if your presentation is an accurate one."

"Oh, they were childless, so they incorporated the lives of all the Dover children into theirs. I couldn't tell you how many young ones were effortlessly convinced of the value of a good education, pride in honest work, and to remain curious if one was to keep one's intelligence. Needless to say, we were constantly exposed to a variable populace: Wandering Tinkers, Gipsies, *carnivale* workers . . . a few half-mad monks on self-imposed sabbaticals . . . We even had a self-proclaimed Druid show up once, a green dowsing-hazel in each hand – 'following the ley lines', as he put it. Spiritualists, mediums . . . and of course the usual pedantic researchers and scientists who were never without their rock-hammer or digging trowel, or their guide book and a fond prayer-book or two. A week digging on the grounds, and Sunday at chapel. That was the routine, enlivened by whoever would show up for dinner – or *what*, for that matter! I was helping press brick into the old patio-walk when a full-grown *sturgeon* was transported to the estate as a gift. How they managed to get a *four-and-a-half yardlong fish* to the Lockwoods before it spoiled is a mystery to me to this very day! 'Fisher's secret!' I was told. Heavens!"

Years later, Dr. Mortimer still conveyed the frustrated admiration to the men for such a trick. Watson was chuckling now, enjoying himself immensely.

"I don't suppose you would know how they did it?" Mortimer asked hopefully.

"I haven't a clue!" Watson said around his laughter. "Pray continue! I am hanging on your every word!"

"Well. One needs a pit to roast a sturgeon adequately. Mr. Lockwood was fearful of achieving the project before His Magnificence spoiled. It was Mrs. Lockwood, or course, who came up with the bold genius of using an archaeological pit that had 'played out' of interesting artifacts, as it were . . . ."

"I deduce," Watson was holding a hand out before him as he chortled, "that the pit performed one last use?"

"Yes, and that was the finest sturgeon I have ever eaten." Mortimer smiled, slightly wistful. "Childhood is a golden thing, is it not? When I was sitting on the clover in the middle of that bright day, gorging myself on that fine fish with all my summer-friends, I truly thought life could get no better, no more vivid and full of life."

"It sounds as though it was fine enough," Watson pointed out.

"It grew even better that evening. We were still eating that fish, as well as whatever vegetables and savouries thrown in for good measure, and gallons of water-cider. Mr. Lockwood's guests that night were a lifelong team of amateur diggers. They created an informal lecture for the children as the stars came out and I can to this day re-create large portions of their speech, for it affected me so deeply. It was this speech that led me to the path of scientific research, knowledge for its own sake." Mortimer's long, hawklike face was soft in memory, and Watson could well believe the man was comfortably reliving that warm, soft evening in Kent, oblivious to the biting cold that hammered against the window of their train.

"They spoke of Dover. How the ancient name for England itself, *Albion*, came from the white cliffs that faced France. They spoke of how the name of *Dover* was not even English, but Brythonic, for *Dubrās*, a word that means '*the waters*'. The Romans called it *Porte Dubris* in tribute, and to this day the River Dour's name echoes that old-standing title. Fascinating people, the Celts. A name is so much more than a name . . . it is also a title. A function . . . a statement of existence. Our guttural Anglo-Saxon with its borrowed Latin melodies simply isn't suited for that sort of concept."

Mortimer had smoked his cigarette down. Without an apparent thought, he disposed of it and created another. Watson had almost forgotten to breathe. Mortimer had without knowing it woven a spell of uncommon colour and power.

"Dover may be the longest-operating and most important point of commerce *in all of Europe.*" Mortimer added thoughtfully. "Every year, we find artifacts of such age we cannot identify them. Think of it! What did the Romans think when they stepped their two-inch sandaled feet upon that earth, look down and see flint points capable of piercing even their armour? Or the wealth of tin and bronze that passed through at this very port? It must have been as sacred to their eyes as it was to the little people who lived there. They built one of their greatest roads to connect Dover to their great centre of communications: Iter III, claimed by the following Anglo-Saxons and dubbed, 'Paved Road of the Foreigners' – The foreigners being the very Bretons that witnessed the Roman construction! Watling Street. Did you know you still can find people who don't know the name of the Milky Way? They call it 'Watling Street' to this day."

Mortimer had finished his second cigarette. "And the first inhabitants remain foreigners and strangers, for that is the root of 'Welsh'. Who is to say if we aren't the true strangers, to insist on that division between fellowship for so long? The Danes battled here after Rome. The waves of Normans, later the French. And some of the original people sailed across that narrow channel and created their own lands, kept their language. Do you not find it ironic that their language is relatively intact compared to ours? But that isn't even the half of it. Night had fallen at this point. And that is, as you know, the traditional time to tell a ghost story."

Watson remembered his back hurt. He leaned himself back carefully, taking the strain off his bones. *I would have Dr. Mortimer by my camp-fire any night*, he thought. "I am all ears, Doctor."

"It was inevitable, I suppose, with the sea before us and the black strip of land that was France, that the ghost story would be Breton.

"Perhaps it was because they were pushed out of this land to another one, but the Bretons had a cult about them, which I can assure you is far from extinct. It is called colloquially *The Cult of the Dead*, and from the stand of the scientist, a fascinating living relic of the days of Roman occupation. They cast auguries with nuts, and passed their cattle through

182

fires in June, and all the stuff one reads about in books, but the Celtic mind is so romantic it cannot release itself from its emotions."

Again, Mortimer had casually expressed his opinion, but Watson was willing to overlook it for now in the interest of story-telling.

"The Bretons, we were told, have no difference in their mind between this world and that of the afterlife. Enemies stay enemies. Friends remain friends. But the afterworld was a tangible thing. When the fisherman or farmer in France looked across the water to where we sat with our fire . . . he saw not the land of Britain, but the very land of the Otherworld! And while that belief has eroded some with time, one can yet hear stories of the Dead Ferries on winter nights. Though it was a warm evening, I can feel the chill yet. Here I cannot give justice to what I heard, for I do not have those powers. Imagine yourself a young boy again, drunk with history and its traces all about you. And then imagine the image that is being painted for you: Of a tiny port somewhere, some secret place in France, where men gather with their boats and wait as the boats sink deeper and deeper into the waterline as the weight of the dead collect. And at last, when the boat can hold no more of its invisible passengers, the ferryman begins his silent journey across the Channel to the port of Dover."

Watson shuddered, for he was not familiar with that particular story. "Suggestive of nightmares," he said at last.

"Oh, indeed. But the story is even more fascinating with the truth," Mortimer supplied. His grey eyes burned with a zest for the moment. "The ability to ferry the dead was so firmly believed in that the Franks overlooked the Bretons' tribute to their king because they were already bound in service to a greater one: Death. And why would he contest their servitude? Even the Romans acknowledged that the Celts claimed ancestry from the Lord of Death himself, the *Dispater*."

"*Brrr!*" Watson rubbed at his forearms. "So you spent part of the night waiting to see if a fleet of black boats were coming for you?"

"Not all of us." Mortimer smiled thinly, for the memory had power over him yet. "For while the boats stopped at Dover, *the dead did not*. Their final destination was to rest in the hands of the Keeper of the Souls at a large, black bog not far from the shore, which was the true entrance to the Otherworld where they expected to rest . . . save the parts of the year when they were permitted to return and celebrate the holidays in the houses of their living descendants. The approach of winter was said to drive the dead to Britain like the flocks of geese. But now that spring is approaching . . . they should be on their way back home."

Mortimer leaned his chin in his hand as his story wound down. "There was a bog, you see. A large bog not so very far away from us." He paused. "And the next day we went there on a search. We were successful, very successful . . . but I tell you frankly I haven't any desire to recapture that sort of success ever again."

NOTE

1. Heaster means "be silent", and girls were once given that name in the hopes they would be biddable.

Chapter XXIII – Riding With the Dead

Watson knew when not to pursue a topic. He diverted Mortimer to milder queries: How did they dig when the weather turned foul? Surely a popular site would attract all sorts – did they ever struggle with a language barrier? How did relics record under personal property and Crown property? Did the Lockwoods keep an exhibit?

Mortimer was relieved Watson did not seek further questions about the bog. He was pleased at the intelligence of Watson's questions. Gradually they moved from the dig to more ordinary subjects. Watson was personally curious about Mortimer's duties, and Mortimer proved an interesting conversationalist when it came to explaining the stilted and dry world of borough health. Until this moment, Watson had never thought that a Boil-water Advisory would be deleterious to the commander's health, but he soon saw that Mortimer carried his Penang Lawyer for less than ornamental reasons.

Watson dozed in snatches. Being warm and dry without exposure to the elements made him appreciative of the true comforts. Mortimer proved himself in possession of peaceful silence. He read from a thick newspaper and then a journal when he finally grew tired of the former. He also appeared content to watch the world whistle by the windows as the landscape grew whiter and the weather worser.

Eventually, even a thick-walled roof would be unable to hide the creeping cold of winter. Watson shifted slowly, feeling how his toes were beginning to ache inside his boots and wool stockings . . . .

"Edinburgh!"

Watson jumped out of an exhausted fugue at his companion's exclamation. Mortimer was eagerly peering through the filthy window in hopes of seeing Auld Reekie. He grimaced as his bones protested movement. *Too long asleep . . . I feel as though I've been riveted in the same spot . . . .*

"Shall we find lodgings for the night?" Mortimer wondered. "Do you have any recommendations? I confess I'm rarely this far north."

Watson stifled a yawn as he managed to un-bend his bones enough to stand. "There's an excellent tavern not far from here. The meals satisfy and the stout is worth writing about."

"Then we shall only hope there are rooms." Mortimer sighed and paused to yawn himself. "A good meal and a stout would be an excellent prescription."

Feeling as though he had tried to race the train halfway up Scotland, Watson picked up his lighter-weight bags and they threaded their way through a confusing crowd and out of the station where a man in a thick Lallan accent was protesting the demolition of a town's historic fixfax.

"Which is what, exactly?" Mortimer muttered.

"The pillory," Watson explained under his breath as he pointed them down the connecting road with his chin. "Which, I might add, might be historical but has been outlawed since the thirties."

"Good to know," Mortimer passed one last askance glance to the raving man.

"I wouldn't concern myself. His family was probably the town's official warden or guard for the shameful thing, and he was making a few pence by demonstrating for the tourists."

While it had been some time since Watson's last return to the city, he remembered the streets with ease. Edinburgh had been built with some plan for the future, and businesses tended to stay in one place once they were successful. It was a few moments' work to find the tavern in question.

Mortimer, as Watson had half-anticipated, hung back a moment, taking in the unmistakable sight of the battered tavern-sign hanging above the door. A large fat man with a cherry for a nose was smiling and about to snuffle down the contents of a foaming tankard before his fat hands.

"The Grog-Blossom?" Mortimer read aloud. His brows fluttered up. He looked at Watson, who was smiling.

"Never judge a book by its cover, Doctor!"

"I assure you I try not to. But I *have* been influenced once or twice . . . ."

Settling into home again was much more boring than it was leaving. Clea accepted the stack of letters, wrote her own to the shop to ensure all was well, and to also warn them she would be by in the morn. After that, there was nothing to do save putter about in the kitchen while Mrs. Collins took her own leave to see some old friends.

Women did not always want to rule a kitchen single-handed, especially a large one like this. It was potentially lonely, and inspired one to compensate with too much cooking. She set aside bread sponge for tomorrow and put out a batch of chickpeas to soak. Mrs. Collins' large cat tried to come in from the garden with a very dead rat – killed all over, Clea had to give the furry brute credit for a thorough job.

It felt a little strange to be glad to be away from the family that gave her life, sheltered and loved her for so many years. There must be more of a private streak to her than she'd known. Nothing else made sense. She might be alone, but Geoffrey was coming home soon and the boys were off catching up on some much-needed time with their cousins, aunts, and uncles – not to mention their grandfather. With any luck, they wouldn't return too spoilt from the overbearing affections that came with being a Cheatham . . . .

Someone knocked at the tradesman's entrance. Clea wiped her hands dry and went to the knob, forced to yank it out of the frame as the cold settled into the wood.

"H'lo, Clea." Roger Bradstreet swept in with a peruke of light spring snow on his shoulders and cap. Flakes drifted in his wake to melt upon the stone floor. "I came to see Geoffrey. It's a bit of an emergency."

"Well, I'm sorry to hear that, but you can't see him." Clea set her hands on her hips and narrowed her blue eyes as Roger spun on his heel to gop back at her. "He's recovering, and I don't want to see widowhood before my time, Roger Bradstreet. You aren't going to give him any news, any information, anything about whatever cases you're chasing right now!"

"But – !" Roger's face (even his moustaches dripped melting white bits), was a comedy of indecision. He even looked up at the ceiling as if he could peer through two floors of plank and one expensive carpet to their living quarters. "I know he's in here, Clea!" He protested. "The blues haven't seen him out in days!"

I'm so glad to know I married a man clever enough to sneak out of his own house. Clea kept the thought to herself. She sniffed. "Be that as it may, I'm not about to encourage a back-set of his health. Not after what happened, and I'll have you know he's *almost* sleeping normally again."

That made the big Borderman hesitate. Another minor capitulation, but the war was hardly Clea's yet. He yanked off his wet hat and gripped the brim in his large hands, twisting it in ways that would not reward him once Hazel noticed.

"I'll pass on a message, but no more, Roger. I am not swaying."

Roger looked quite ready to take the blacksmith's nails and chew them into good-luck rings for the local children. "Clea, if you've ever believed me on anything, I need to talk to Geoff."

"Roger." Clea said it as gently as possible. "I'll pass the message, but you will not see him today. I have my duty too, and I hope you don't think I'm the sort to disapprove of my husband's work."

That reached him, to Clea's relief. He sagged and wiped at his melting face. "I need to see him as soon as possible," the big man said. "Tell him – and this applies to you too, Clea – that one of his old . . . ." He gulped convulsively. "Shall we call it an old client . . . wants to kill him? See that he doesn't leave the building, would you? At least until I've spoken to him."

187

He waited for her reaction, but it was hard to feel surprise after the past few days. She nodded quietly.

"Give Hazel my love, Roger," Clea said firmly.

Roger was exasperated, but he knew not to cross her. Better cross the Chief Inspector than this little long-clawed cat.

"Come and see us some time, Clea," he managed to get out before it choked him.

She permitted herself a smile. "That I will, Roger. Dust think I've forgotten Hazel? That would be a bit on the impossible half."

He struggled to smile, but he was sick with worry. "I trust you to keep him in hand, Clea. Don't let him out."

"I promise," Clea said. *As soon as he comes back inside, that is . . . .*

Roger turned then, pushing his big body out the door. Clea watched him go. The cold draft of his passing sent a chill across her feet and up her spine.

Geoffrey Brock Lestrade, come back here soon. Come back here now.

Inspector Patterson leaned back in the very hard hardwood chair and rubbed the sleep back out of his eyes. "I need to make some coffee," he announced.

Hopkins blinked up from the other side of the table. Bloodshot or developing a case of conjunctivitis. "That would be a very good idea," he mumbled. "The next time, I'll bring some good tea."

"Make it Ti Qwan Yin." Patterson joked wearily [1], and let his fingers bumble their way to putting a large amount of strong coffee into a small basket suspended in the tall metal pot inside his fireplace.

Patterson's living room no longer looked so neat. It might even be classified as slovenly. Hopkins promised himself the fortitude to help clean up the layers of paper that now lined the floor, shelves, and desk. The books Patterson had grabbed down and requisitioned from the library for reference . . . he could deal with those, as he knew where they went.

Patterson was either tired or focused enough that he no longer tried to hide the scars on his wrists. After a few hours of being around the pale marks, Hopkins was able to ignore it. He knew the story like everyone else, and was willing to believe there were worse wounds lying underneath his shirt . . . but he wasn't going to ask about them.

If Moriarty's men had even indirectly been the cause of that sort of pain . . . Hopkins could not fault the man for trying too hard to bring the gang to justice.

"Ready for the summary?" Patterson wondered.

"Well . . . here's what we've been able to agree on . . . ," Hopkins said doubtfully. He cleared his throat. "Blake is a cutter for the funeral homes that have suspicious ties with some charity ventures that create affordable burials for Afghanistan veterans. You were able to prove they weren't interested in veterans of any other wars. Thank you, by the way, as that both narrows our search and adds to the strangeness." Hopkins drank the glass of water by his elbow with relief. "Blake's history is a bit on the odd side, and Lestrade was able to prove he was without a doubt the youngest and prospectless brother of the clerk at the First Bank of the Thames."

"And it was *that* Bank that was sponsoring so much of this charity," Patterson pointed out. "The more I think of this, the less sense it makes. It cannot be coincidence. It would be too strange."

"Even though we can't find who the real backers are," Hopkins reminded him with deep disgust.

"We'll save that for later. For now . . . keep reading."

"Right. George Blake was a cutter for the Army Medical Corps." Hopkins absently scrawled the insignia on a piece of stray paper before he caught himself. "Excellent work and he could have risen far, but his superiors and peers admit he has an . . . *Ahem!* A problem with fathoming certain issues. In other words, the man is a dot shy on his dice."

"Seems to be what everyone else thinks." Patterson sighed. "Does whatever the first person tells him to do, and doesn't change his plan."

"It was likely how he was raised," Hopkins pointed out logically. "A way of controlling the strong but somewhat unintelligent member of the family."

"True. At any rate, he seemed to like the regimented life of the military, and gathered a reputation as a good worker."

"And he set into Colonel Moriarty's people." Hopkins drew a series of arrows on the paper as he spoke. "I don't really want to know what he was doing, but it seems to have to be one of the reasons why Colonel Hayter was at war with Moriarty."

"Which led him after Maiwand to do something else . . . Something to do with funeral homes. And dead veterans."

"Blake's family was tied to the First Bank of the Thames . . . and . . . asset appraisal."

The silence grew slow, and thick.

"Patterson," Hopkins murmured, "I do not like to think of where this is headed." It made him swallow against a rising sickness beneath his ribs.

"Nor do I." Patterson looked just as ill. "We're going to need Lestrade back for this . . . and . . . I hate to say this, but Gregson's the one who can tie all these threads together. The man is cool enough in his head to ignore distractions."

189

"We will . . . but I want to know what the Burial Board has to do with this first." Hopkins stood to stretch and rub his aching neck. "When we have everything we can show Gregson, then we give him something to think about."

The kitchen clock was beginning to chime the eleventh hour into the night. The knock against the thick wood was barely heard against the silence of the growing ice-storm.

Clea had been listening for it.

"Geoffrey . . . ." Clea hurriedly set the hand-towel down somewhere and quickened her steps to the tradesman's door. Her husband was leaning against the frame, slowly stamping his feet against the new-forming ice at the step. Clear glaze crackled against the worn mortar.

"How are the boys?" he asked with a voice sandpapered down with exhaustion.

"Still with their grandfather. There was a travelling show coming in and they – "

"Say no more. I hope they know to keep an extra eye on Nicholas."

"I don't think he'll run away without his brother, dear, and Martin has more sense."

"From your mouth to the ears of God," Geoffrey prayed fervently. He huddled half against the wall, holding one arm as if it hurt him.

"Let's get you taken care of," Clea suggested softly, and gnawed down on the urge to talk about that arm. This was not a night for nagging any more than joking. She pulled him away from the door and hung up his travel-stained coat with a practiced flick. The tweeny could sweep that up tomorrow . . . It was too late to care about that just now.

"I am not walking upstairs in *these* shoes," Geoffrey protested, pointing downward with his good left hand as he did so.

"I see." Clea looked and couldn't blame him. "Well, hand them here. I've got a box . . . Once we're upstairs I'll run the water. It's going to take more than the usual wash to deal with this."

"You are so very, very right," he answered, with a voice slurring from exhaustion.

Clea knew he meant other things than laundry.

"Roger stopped by, Love." Clea caught his arm. She stared into his eyes even though he was too tired to hold her gaze longer than a few seconds at a time. He smelled of salt-water, and oak-tannins, and something sea-watery and strange that made her unsettled and against her ease. "He said to be careful. Someone was trying to kill you."

190

"Just someone?" he mumbled. "That's . . . an improvement." He closed his eyes. "I'm sorry," he apologized. "That's . . . unworthy."

"You're asleep on your feet. We get you to the wash and take some of London off you. Once you get some rest I'll bring Roger here." Clea prayed the problem would be as simple as her advice. But looking at her husband's sallow pallor and his half-useless arm . . . she very much doubted it.

"Lock the doors," Geoffrey was muttering. "Lock the doors . . . set the wires across the doors, Clea. I don't think anyone followed me . . . but . . . I can't be sure."

"If they knew they were following you, they'd know where you lived, wouldn't they?" Clea slipped the wire across the door that connected the door-handle to the electric door-bell. One sly attempt at moving the door would trip the wire and send a screech halfway to Saffron Hill.

"Not if they thought I was someone else." Geoffrey sank down into the nearest chair by the table, and remained unmoving while Clea saw to the rest of the doors.

"I don't understand, Geoffrey . . . ." Clea hurried to his side and put her small hands on his shoulders. He blinked up into her face, aware of her but little else. "Geoffrey . . . where did you go?"

"Where I'd never planned to go, Clea-*bihan* . . . ." He reached up with a slow-moving hand and gripped hers. "I wound up in the middle of the sodding Channel, but that wasn't the worst of it." He leaned his head forward until he was using her apron-band for a rest. "There was only one ferry back to England tonight. I rode back here with the dead." Half-hysteria lit his voice. "Not particular about the company they keep . . . but they're *heavy* . . . you'd think they'd lose some of the weight they carried around in life . . . *You'd think it, wouldn't you?*"

Clea felt cold and still inside, like a frozen cave. "Upstairs, Geoffrey," she whispered, stroking his hair. Now she knew what that scent was. He'd brought it home with him before Christmas. It was the smell of the grave. "*Upstairs.*"

NOTE

1. Iron Goddess of Mercy tea.

Chapter XXIV – Africans and Indians

Shaftesbury Avenue:

"**B**ut *why?*" Patterson slammed his fist into the quarter-oak desk with a bang. Papers slid off the top to add to the growing layers at his feet. "The numbers aren't adding up, Hopkins! Why such an elaborate, monstrous scheme for a handful of dead Afghani veterans? *What* would be so valuable about these poor men that they'd be used for this sort of purpose?"

"I know. It can't be for their personal belongings . . . *soldiers aren't rich!* They barely have a duce in their pockets at any given time . . . ." Hopkins was upset too, but trying to be the calm one in the room.

"They aren't rich . . . neither are their families. How many of them were like Watson, taking the Queen's shilling because there were no other paths in their future? We're a nation of volunteers!"

"Offhand, I'd say most of them, but Watson was luckier than most. He was a Major, mind you. It's not like being a policeman at all." Hopkins had found something to do with his hands, for his relief and Patterson's. He rose and tapped his pencil into his palm like a drum. "Policemen must start at the very bottom. You can't go up until you've been down. "

"Well you can't just rise fully formed to Major . . . ." Patterson pointed out reasonably. "Even if you did purchase a commission, and that's been illegal for twenty years."

"Medical officers were different," Hopkins said slowly. "I mean . . . you hear the veterans talk. There's a sense of isolation between the regular soldiers and the medical soldiers. They were without a doubt treated different from the others."

"There must be something here." Patterson sank down, rubbing his chin. "Let's look at it this way: Watson as a medical officer would be forbidden to give another 'regular' officer or soldier an order. That makes him to all purposes, powerless. He wasn't allowed combat medals or any other marks of achievement if it could be construed as being warlike . . . so that leaves out the power of ambition. So . . . .if there's no power, and no ambition . . . what's left?"

"Subterfuge?"

Hopkins had meant it as a joke. As soon as it escaped his lips they both realized it was truth.

Patterson's eyes resembled golf balls. "Subterfuge?" He repeated in a whisper. "He'd be perfect."

"The man can't lie," Hopkins blustered. "He's too honest."

"Honest people make the best liars," Patterson snapped. "They're used to being credible. Watson is a smart man. Smart . . . but overlooked. I don't know if it's his nature, or if it's to do with those rumors about being shadowed by his brother . . . but Watson tends to be overlooked. He does nothing to stop that from happening, mind you. It's as if he feels another man's shortcomings aren't his problem." Patterson clasped his hands behind his back and paced jerkily back and forth – he looked like a broken puppet.

"I can see the map, Patterson. Something was going on. Watson was a major. Granted it's war-time, but how could he make rank so quickly?" Hopkins felt his heart beat faster.

"Several reasons," Patterson said bluntly. "*First:* he was known as a man to be trusted even when he was a boy. When he joined, his Recruitment officer added a letter of recommendation to his signage. He was a natural athlete. Played for the good of the rugby team and not his personal achievement, and he threw himself into his residency at Barts and it was partly on their recommendation that he joined the Army on the Netley course for surgeons. He was promoted to Corporal as soon as he finished, and by the time he was posted to the Fusiliers he was an assistant surgeon." Patterson remembered he had a pipe on his desk. He started fishing under the litter of paper for his tin. "*Second:* the man is stocked with courage. He has confidence. He has nerve. It didn't take long for the Army to realize what they had with him. He wasn't *real* military like his brother, but his brother had a reputation too. It isn't fair, but brothers tend to be judged against each other."

Hopkins nodded. A part of him was frankly curious as to how much Patterson had learnt about Watson. The doctor wasn't . . . well, secretive. He simply didn't talk about himself and that was not the same as hiding something. Once in a great while, one did encounter a man who thought of himself as a boring subject. Watson's preference for writing about Mr. Holmes would put him by default into that category.

"A Corporal can be a long toss from Major," he pointed out, gently prompting Patterson to go further.

"Umm," Patterson agreed with the stem of his pipe hanging off his mouth. He scrabbled with the tin in one hand, the other caught spidering about the desk for his matches. "I think it was the third point that did it. He had a reputation for being able to take orders and follow them sensibly. That requires more than bravery. Letters from his superiors are rather clear that Watson would never send one of his orderlies into a situation that he

193

wouldn't put himself in, and he was often right there with them. He had – has – a fine eye for organisation and detail but he doesn't bog down in it. His men were a well-oiled machine, even in the thick of things, and while Maiwand was as bad as it could get . . . I think it bears mentioning that Watson's men were ready for disaster when it hit. Hard to say just how many lives were saved by his training. It also bears mentioning that he trained them to operate with or without him. That lack of arrogance most likely saved his own life when his orderly had the withal to get him to safety without being ordered to do so."

"I remember hearing that story," Hopkins admitted. "The veterans were proud of him and liked to talk about it."

"Had he joined up before '71, I'm sure he never would have made rank, as people were still purchasing their commissions, up to the point it was outlawed. But the military finally became a meritocracy like the Yard. Talk about opening the field! I'm sure the Moriartys of the world were foaming-livid to see their most convenient method of controlling folk and power-plays were gone. Imagine how well you could command your own kingdom if you purchased a man's rank for him?"

"I shudder to think," Hopkins said honestly. It was coincidental that he rose to put a few lumps of coal on Patterson's fire.

"Hopkins, I'm afraid I'm going to put you to sleep within the next few minutes, but you absolutely must understand this background first." Patterson sighed and touched his match to the tobacco bowl. A tiny red flare illuminated his skeletal face for a moment, highlighting a wire-thin scar under his eyes. Hopkins had never seen it before, or anything like it. *What in the world could have caused a mark like that?*

"There has always been some sort of rivalry and enmity within any war-oriented organisation – common sense when you think about it. Lambs do not make good commanders, and many fought themselves into their position. The British Army is still divided up along the lines of 'Africans' or General Wolesley's crowd, and the 'Indians', who are General Roberts' boys. Unfortunately, where you served says which side you're on. Watson is by geography, one of the Indians. Colonel Moriarty and Hayter are Indians. This means whatever personal warfare is going on . . . Well, it's going to stay with the Indians, even though I can think of a good number of men on the side of Africa who would be splendidly qualified to settle the mess."

"From what little I understand," Hopkins snorted, "they wouldn't even think of crossing the party lines, and the lines are going to last as long as one on each side remains alive." He shook his head and fumbled in his coat for a bit of dried apple. "You had better resources than I did, Patterson. All I could find out from Watson's life that was in any way

194

interesting was that he'd transferred from the Fusiliers to the Berkshires at record speed. No explanation was ever given that I could find. Is that normal?"

Patterson shrugged in a strange way. It was not meant to be encouraging. "His brother was in the Berkshires. For whatever reason, our Watson signed up with the Fusiliers. If you ask me, that's something to do with the need to be separate. They were twins, and alike in every aspect. How tiring must that be, to be so alike and so often confused for one another? I don't think I could stand it myself." He smoked some more. His pipe commented with him with soft whispered chuckles of fire eating the dried leaf.

Hopkins was chilled to silence in the face of Patterson's matter of fact coldness. Twins were supposed to be special. Set apart. What they lost in their identity was supposed to be compensated for in their unique closeness. Twins were supposed to be one person in two bodies. He wouldn't have thought along those lines at all, for it would have felt . . . disrespectful to Watson somehow.

"No matter where we go in this . . . no matter how often we dance around the mess . . . Watson's our closest link," he said at last. "Let's take this one thread, this tiny, thin thread, and see where we can go with it. Somehow, this leads to the Burial Board. I can't prove it by logic. But it's my gut telling me and it's high time I started listening to it."

Paddington Street:

"Hold still."

Geoffrey wasn't about to be recalcitrant with his wife – and never with that tone of voice, but Clea Lestrade's worries grew when he succumbed to her direction without even a joke.

"Careful with that," he managed to mumble. The cup of red tea she'd offered was lowered back down to the floor. He didn't feel like drinking it just yet.

Clea blinked at him, set her lips, and concentrated on sponging the arm. Once the sleeve was off she saw the reason for his favoritism of the limb. She just wasn't certain what she was looking at.

"Geoffrey, did you fall off a ladder . . . or get hit by something large and wooden?"

Her answer was a half-amused snort.

"Well? I might have an easier time taking care of this if I knew what caused it."

"A moment, dear," he answered wearily. "I need to think of a way to relate this in a way that makes sense."

195

"Oh, dear," Clea said without thinking. "One of those stories, eh?" She rose up from the edge of the tub and rummaged in the medicine cabinet for a particular tin and the little bottle of spirits.

Geoffrey merely leaned back and shut his eyes. They'd needed to rinse him off *before* the tub. The grave residue had gotten beneath his clothing and onto his skin. Clea had seen her husband in various states of fastidiousness during their years of marriage, but she rarely saw him scrub out his hair with such mindless vigour.

She toed the small footstool back to the tub and pulled Geoffrey's arm slowly back, swabbing a light amount of spirits on his arm first. Geoffrey had his eyes closed. He was pressed the wash-cloth to his forehead as if steam might drive the day out of his mind. If only it were that simple. She shook her head to herself and selected the round-tipped tweezers.

"*Ow!*" he opined without moving.

"That was the worst one." She held up the offending splinter before her eyes. (She had a feeling she was destined for near-sightedness in her old age.) "You were successful, then." Clea added quietly.

"If you can call it that." Geoffrey did not open his eyes. "The old pirate did it, Clea. He got them all to safety."

"With your help." Clea pointed out, still gently. She searched his arm for further marks, but nothing quite matched up to that first one pulled out. The rest came out smoothly. She set them aside for disposal and massaged the spirits deep into the muscle, hoping she was cleaning it properly. Splinter-marks had a nasty tendency to infect within a matter of hours.

"Getting them to the isle wasn't the problem." He did open his eyes then. They looked bruised in the low light of the bath. "They'll be fine . . . I think. I won't be there to keep his madness going."

"Ah, Geoffrey . . . ." Clea swallowed. His own father had looked upon him, and saw someone else. She couldn't imagine what that truly felt like. "They'll be safe then . . . but how did you get back?"

"I rode with the dead," he said flatly. "I can't believe . . . I used to think that was just an old story to frighten the children." He swallowed hard. "I thought I *knew* the real story . . . smiled when people put it out as a ghost story . . . ."

It wasn't like Geoffrey to ramble or repeat himself in words, even when he was tired. Clea took the wash-cloth and simply took over. He couldn't get that spot on his neck with his arm stiffened up like that. *What if lockjaw sets in?* She sponged something like a bit of tar off his skin, and was grateful it wasn't real tar or she'd need something worse to remove it. Well . . . tar was antiseptic . . . .

"You could just pull out the horse-blanket . . . ."

"You are not sleeping on my floor, Inspector!" Clea tapped him on the head.

"Yes'm." But his smile faded to a shudder.

"Go on, Geoffrey," she urged softly.

"Smuggling ships," he said at last. "It's the old stories, you know . . . how the ferries would take the dead from the new land back to the home land. The boats would look empty, but they'd be weighed down from the sheer number of the ghosts." He reached up and rubbed at the tight band across his forehead. Clea picked up the red tea and put it in that hand so it had something more useful to do.

He humoured her by drinking half before returning the cup. "If you look at those old boats," he whispered, "you see nothing in the seats . . . nothing to explain why the boat rides so low to the waterline. And they will tell you it's the weight of the dead that pulls the boat down on its way to Dover . . . whichever part of Dover or point on the coast the dead wish to go."

Clea wordlessly found the towel and gently scrubbed the arm until it was dry. It would be a few days before he could lift it normally, but overall it wasn't a terrible wound. Satisfied the marks would not open up, she rubbed some of her father's "wrestler's salve" into the skin. Geoffrey's nose tried to close up – he could barely stand the odiferous blend of camphor, wintergreen, cayenne, arnica and calendula that Charles Cheatham had invented.

"What causes the boats to lie low in the water, Geoffrey?"

"Whatever they're smuggling," he answered with his eyes closed. "Mostly, it's food. Or some supplies that the Families need that they can't afford elsewhere. Quimper's control isn't absolute over them. I learnt that tonight. It was worth it. They still slide trips back and forth across the water . . . ." He laughed without a sound. "Quimper uses superstition to control people with his Wild Hunt. But superstition works both ways, doesn't it? He can't do anything about the smugglers using superstition to their own ends . . . They've been moving goods back and forth since before King Charles. He can't do anything about it."

"So . . . they have false bottoms?" Clea reasoned. "Where the cargo is being hidden?"

"Yes. I had to ride in the bottom with the cargo." He had stopped laughing, but his eyes had opened up to a horror she could not see. Clea lost him then, as she was wont to do when he had to re-live a memory he was afraid to forget.

She waited, rinsing out the tub and drying the water-marks while he combed his hair out by the mirror. He suddenly pulled up the towel and

197

frantically scrubbed his head until it was as dry as it could get. With studied calm he re-combed everything back in place.

"Geoffrey, where were you?" She put her arms about his waist and leaned her head on his shoulder. When they were both out of shoe, they were less equal in height.

"They don't always smuggle goods across, Clea. That's . . . that's what I learnt the hard way." He rested the comb by the sink and leaned forward on his arms a moment before reaching around to hold her with his better arm. "Some of those elders . . . *they really do come back to Britain to die* . . . or at least . . . ." He swallowed. "To be buried."

Clea swallowed hard to think of Geoffrey, who had no love of being helpless or in a place like an airless cargo, sharing a space with a corpse.

And she knew that the hard-earned work of weeks was about to be undone again. Geoffrey's nightmares might not start up tonight, tired as he was . . . but the respite was over.

They were back where they started.

Chapter XXV – Johnny,
I Hardly Knew You

Edinburgh:

The stout was remarkable. The dark beef stew had simmered low until the meat fell apart from clean white bones. Mortimer was delighted. He had two helpings and declared his journey was so far justified.

Watson smiled to see the easily distracted man so swayed by cooking, and lit a Bradley while the latest knot of diners tromped within, bee-lining to the fireplace. He'd insisted on a place by the wall, and not close to that soothing fire. Mortimer now knew why: The hot food heated them from within, and it was difficult to enjoy the fireplace with all the human traffic.

"I do not believe," Mortimer confessed as his tankard was filled to the brim with white ale, "I would have chosen this establishment without your word. I stand scolded for judging an eatery by its sign."

"If you knew the story, you'd understand." Watson delicately maneuvered his cigarette to hover over a tiny ceramic dish filled with beach-shingle. "Some families labour beneath a curse, such as that of the Baskervilles. Some families labour under the more insidious curse of grasping and disputatious relatives. And some establishments . . . labour under a combination of the two." He puffed with a bland smile on his handsome face as Mortimer sipped his new drink. "The property is under a clause in the deceased owner's will that it must be re-leased back to the owner's family – who do not even want it – after a three-year term. So every three years, it is sold back for one pound, and the name changes along with the sale, and it is bought again for the same amount of money . . . Every three years the name gets worse. Last time . . . I believe it was called 'The Collapsing Telescope' . . . or something just as bizarre. Still . . . it made it briefly popular with the astronomy students."

Mortimer blinked like an owl behind his glasses – an owl suddenly startled awake with a lantern into his eyes. "What a sadistic will."

"It was. The tavern is considered the bad luck of the family, so of course they don't want to mess with it . . . but four more years to go and the will can be changed forever. The deceased sorely underestimated the grim stubbornness of his relations." Watson chuckled softly at Mortimer's face. "Welcome to Scotland. What do you think of the white ale? It's a local specialty, very seasonal."

"Quite good. I've never encountered this particular bouquet . . . earthy with a nutty tone. Barley?"

"A very old barley. I thought the Neolithiphile in you would appreciate it. According to the learned men in University, this is a Stone Age species, called the '*bere*'." He mused, "To hear the crofters complain, it is a real 'bere' to thresh out."

Mortimer laughed. "Your wit is dry as the winter wind, Watson. I'm fully aware that 'barley' comes from 'bear-grass'." He lifted his drink in a toast. "So I am drinking the same nectar the ancestors enjoyed? I'm hardly surprised they kept the recipe."

"For all its frustrations. I can't say we'll get as good a fare as we will on Streat."

"It will take the day to ferry over on the steamship." Mortimer sighed. "But we'll arrive in good time for Sir Niles' celebration." He took another sip, as if to wash a future taste out of his mouth. "I haven't seen that man in years . . . I can't say I completely missed him, though he was always good about scientific discovery . . . kept meticulous notes." That last was said in a peculiar tone.

"Is there anything I should know about?" Watson ventured cautiously.

Mortimer was feeling the flush of drink. He leaned his head into the heel of his hand on the table. "You can know a man for decades without really knowing him," he said at last. "Sir Niles is *without a doubt* in that category." He thought for a moment. "The man probably has an envelope somewhere with his first attempts to write the alphabet. Never throws a single thing away, and that is commendable, but I declare quite honestly without any exaggeration . . . he is a compulsive list-maker. You smile, but I am serious. I spent a week at a flint-mine with him once . . . by the end of that week he'd gone through *four* notebooks."

"Four . . . what did he do with all that writing?"

"He gleaned a fifth notebook out of the contents of the first four. How the man accomplishes anything, I couldn't tell you. Sir Henry is an admirable baronet, capable of balancing his books and maintaining his assets whilst seeking new ones, and he even has the time to visit the races a fortnight while swiving the Devonshire widows . . . But Sir Niles . . . I believe the minutiae is the man's first love."

"Other than his love of writing . . . ."

"It isn't writing, my good fellow. It is lists. Time. Weather. Location. Who is working at the dig and where. Comments overheard. Soil temperature. Local birds . . . all this before he gets down to noting the artifacts recovered. The man must drink tincture of *polygonatum* [1] every night to stave off the arthritis certain to come. He's older than myself by a good twenty years, but . . . while I am picking up a seashell here and there, whilst the great ocean of mystery lies before me . . . Sir Niles is the type who would happily spend his entire life cataloging the sand and shells on the shore with his back to the ocean."

"Has he made any scientific achievement?" Watson was a little nervous about asking a question that could be construed as personal, challenging, and probing.

Mortimer snorted delicately. "He has a love of the bog-people, which is just as well this discovery has shown itself by his door-step." He shook his head in a strange motion, like a dog finding water in its ears. "Perhaps he'll find a way to turn it all into financial asset. He could use the money."

"Another member of the impoverished gentry? I hear there's a cure for that," Watson said with a straight face.

"There would never be an American desperate enough to marry his daughter off on Sir Niles." Mortimer looked Watson dead in the eye. "I know they're supposedly less choosy than English fathers . . . or that perhaps they're in love with our titles . . . but Sir Niles rules the worst island to satellite Britain, and there is no society worth speaking of outside of the smallest fishing-village south of the Norway fjords and a population largely comprised of ducks. The store-house for the nets doubles as the chapel. That is a late development . . . one would actually have to join society to get anywhere in that field . . . and he would have to pull out of his notebooks and surveying equipment to do that." He took a more fervent drink. "His people have traditionally been well-shored up with the good old money . . . held many fine old pieces from the Viking days . . . a few salvers and cups buried by monks on their way to more Christian lands. One can't keep up a crumbling old manor with a bag of silver and a bit of Baltic amber."

"How disheartening," Watson mused. "I suppose there comes a time when everyone faces the prospect of selling the family plate."

"If they have it to begin with . . . Still much of it was his fault. No forest for the trees." Mortimer regarded the last of his bread thoughtfully before glancing about him for censorious women. Finding none, he swiped his dining-plate clean in triumph.

"As famous as the ducks are, one would think he could make some money off them." Watson wiped foam off his lip. "But the bog-people may be a hope more close to his heart."

"And that is the core of it. If only something could attract more guests to the island. We aren't talking something as advanced as one of the penny-ferries on the Thames. One would need at least a shilling to pay for regular transportation. Sir Niles has been seeking a paying solution for years."

"I'm not certain how antique remains can be that solution," Watson mused. "Unless there would be some sort of . . . ." He frowned. "Equity up front? How often does the steamship go to Streat?"

"Once a month, which is quite the improvement. Other boats, such as fishing and passing craft, show up more often. The island is not self-sufficient, and that is the problem. Visitors can provide money and the northern isles of Little Britain aren't complicated by the sort of laws in the Channel. Landowning isn't feudal up here. Its Viking and Athling and *thing*-laws." Mortimer was content to signal for another ale.

"Visitors such as . . . visitors to see the bog-people." Watson's face lit with understanding. "I believe I see what you mean! Sir Niles has sent those blocks of bog with human remains to the London museum, in the hopes that the London intellectuals take notice!"

Mortimer chuckled and lifted his drink in a salute. "Very good! While I can only share this suspicion, it fits with what I know about the man."

"But . . . this adds problems as well! What about the need for extra police . . . extra security against grave-robbers and unlicensed pot-hunters?" Watson answered his own question: "If the site is important enough . . . there would be assistance from the government on adding to the police force . . . ."

"I'd heard Streat does plan to expand its greater-than-one police force." Mortimer smiled dryly. "Sent one of their young men down to train up on better procedures for a while . . . and the fishermen who live on Streat have to volunteer so many hours a month to help patrol for things such as shipwrecks, signs of ships in distress, or natural disasters. When a storm hits Streat, it hits like a cricket-bat."

"I have no desire to find out," Watson admitted. He was down to the bottom of his mug. "Well! A good night's sleep should have us up by six . . . and if I read your schedule correctly, we'll need at least half-a-day to get to Stewart's Point for Sir Niles' steamship. I wonder how much it cost him to contract the ship?"

"Dear me, more than what I've got in my pockets!" Mortimer exclaimed.

Clea was unsurprised to see Geoffrey had fallen asleep before she finished laying the coals into the fire.

She was tired, but her nerves hummed with a restless energy. Her father and brother Bartram had always been so before a fight. Her other brothers also when they faced some sort of challenge. She was no different. She was a Cheatham. But this was no enemy or challenge or riddle or whatnot.

She paused at the vanity table and sat, sighing at the need to pull forty-two pins out of her hair (one by one). In the lamplight, she looked even more tired and was beginning to show some of her age. The blue-black hair with its heavy gloss felt a bit more brittle to her fingers . . . and her nails were starting to crack. Stress? Likely . . . .

Clea ran her fingers through her starboard locks when a soft rustle caught her ear. Geoffrey stood behind her, sleepily giving her a hand. He extracted a handful of pins and held them in his palm. She murmured a thank you and let him concentrate on that side while she did the other.

"I'll be in soon, love. Why don't you get your sleep?"

"It's all right." After a minute (and four more of the slippery pins), he added, "You looked troubled just now."

"Mrs. Watson is coming to visit me tomorrow," she said softly. "And Roger is coming to see you. He wanted you to know that someone is after you."

"Again?" He breathed wearily. "I'm sorry, *ma-mel*. I'm not being flippant."

"No, you're just too tired to hold back. Your manners are the first line of defence between your honesty and its recuperations." Clea stood, one last pin in her fingers. She dropped it in the trap with a sigh. "Stay in bed tomorrow. That ought to convince Roger you haven't been going anywhere and you'll be able to catch up on all the reading we've been collecting on your behalf."

"Oh, dear . . . ."

Edinburgh:

Mortimer was pleasantly contented with the hearty fare after the strain of the trip. Their rooms were a split, with a door between each bed.

"Which do you prefer?" Watson asked him. "I confess I'm not the particular sort so long as there are no uninvited companions already crawling about the linen . . . ."

Mortimer chuckled. "I am easily disturbed by light, so I'll take the darkest room."

"Which would be that one." Watson nodded to the connecting-door. "Then I shall have this room." He dropped his luggage to the floor and stretched stiffly. "I told the maid we would need breakfast as soon as we arose, and they agreed to wake us up at six. I hope you enjoy their morning cuisine. They have a quick hand at journey-cake and sweet milk. Which reminds me . . . ." He yawned behind his mouth while loosening his tie. "Beware of their tea if your nerves are easily taxed. They have a strong hand in the brew . . . very strong."

"A northern affectation," Mortimer assured him. "I can adapt. For all I know, a strong tea will be needed to keep my strength up in this cold weather."

"It will be even colder tomorrow. My old wounds are quite firm upon that."

"I shall leave you to your rest then. Good night, Watson. I trust you will sleep well."

"As you, sir." Watson smiled with his warm humour as Mortimer shut the door.

Alone, Mortimer dressed quickly for bed and found his room even more comfortable that he had expected. The other side of the wall was plastered against one of the many chimneys, and drowsy warmth permeated the chamber. He slid between the sheets with relief, wondering what the long-suffering Mrs. Mortimer would think to be faced with a journey such as this. She disliked anything that took her away from her work in the charities.

Mortimer woke several hours later. He was too hot. The warmth of the chimney had built up into the room with the door shut, and the doctor felt as though he were being roasted into an airless mummy.

Not wanting to wake Watson, he slipped as quietly out of bed as possibly and by memory found his hand on the door-knob. Again, he moved quietly, thinking that a veteran like Watson needed as much rest as he could get.

Moonlight spilled like icy milk across his stockings and the carpet, cast a black shadow behind him. Cooler air swirled, and he took a deep breath of relief.

And held it.

Watson was wide awake, and standing with his face to the window, staring at something Mortimer could not see.

He was singing.

"Where are your legs that used to run, Huroo . . . Huroo?" [2]

Watson's voice, so suited for rich tones, was warped and weary within that melodic whisper. Mortimer's hackles lifted to hear it.

He could see Watson clearly, his lean shape blocking the moon and the night-lights of the city, his good right arm flung up to lean against the window-frame.

It was a bitter song the soldiers sang upon their return, and sung by their loved-ones. Sad and full of longing. Mortimer knew many families that forbade it among their children.

"You haven't an arm . . ."

Watson reached to his bad shoulder and clenched it, fiercely, as if he could tear the wound out of his body.

"You haven't a leg . . . ."

That same hand went down and strike his thigh, the source of his limp.

"You're an eyeless, boneless, chickenless egg . . .

And you'll have to be given a bowl to beg . . . ."

Watson's voice trailed off, dark and venomous and self-recriminating under the music. It was not his inflictions . . .

. . . He was singing in the voice of another man . . . a man who must have used the song as a weapon to harm.

"Johnny, I hardly knew you . . . ."

Mortimer quietly shut the door and went back to bed.

NOTES

1. Solomon's seal.
2. The song used in this chapter may be familiar, or it may not. In America it is "When Johnny Comes Marching Home", and is so patriotically and saccharine sweet it does no justice to the original song, a much more realistic view of the horrors of war. The modern version is, I'm afraid, the only version school-children are taught now. The old one was sung extensively during the American Civil War, especially by the Irish Americans.

Chapter XXVI – Revelations

The sea rolled before Mortimer's eyes. It heaved and tossed, and threw against the steamship as it churned merrily to a foggy bank west of the Stewart's Point. Mortimer found the tarnished rail a slender comfort as he hung on and thought of a different sea: The moors under moonlight, silver and slow-moving geology, so slow to human eyes it would appear to be frozen in time.

The moors were an ocean sculpted of land, and the source of his deepest affection. He had not married until he found a woman who loved the land the same way he did. Poor Gertrude would not care for this liquid ocean at all. Nor did he, to be honest . . . .

"Dr. Mortimer!" A familiar, blessed voice at his arm: Watson was holding a battered tin cup that smoked a sweet-spicy cloud. Hatless, the sea-air tossed the man's brown hair like a child's when stroked by a playful guardian. "The captain strongly recommends this for stormy weather and choppy seas!"

Mortimer noted that Watson had no apparent effects of sea-travel and took the hot cup. He felt the acid of sweetened ginger beer and lemon scald all the way down to his toes.

"I've never had ginger beer this strong!" He fought for breath as his eyes streamed.

Watson grinned. "Does it take your mind off the sea-sickness?"

Mortimer sniffed loudly. "Is that what that was?" He tried to joke.

Watson laughed, a flash of teeth and bright eye. He was nothing like the man of last night, crushed by his old wounds and bitter memories. To some men, the ocean was invigorating. He even looked younger.

"I've never been on this stretch of the North Sea," he explained. His eyes gleamed as he peered across the sloping triangles of waves. "I see why Sir Niles has troubles with steady transport."

"I'd forgotten the waves were this colour." Mortimer sank back into a waiting chair that was thankfully bolted down. "Grey as a slate roof!"

"Just not as immobile." Watson took a chair next to him with a contented sigh. "You might feel better if you just set your mind elsewhere. So this is your second visit to Streat?"

"Yes, and the summer voyages are much calmer! At least to go by my one example." Mortimer sipped the brew and felt his internal organs settle down, bit by bit.

"You are a most patient man, Watson. My compliments."

Watson had been watching the curls of fog. "I beg your pardon? I wasn't aware I had just done something that required patience."

Mortimer laughed. "I mean the other day. When I so gracelessly dropped the end of my story about the ferries of the dead."

"Oh." Watson didn't know what to say, other than a reassurance. "Think nothing of it."

"Still, I should pick up the chapter that followed in the interest of fair play."

"If it is disturbing . . . ."

"Not in the light of day." Mortimer answered succinctly. He shivered slightly as the bracing sea-breeze became a bullet-sharp gust. "I told you there was a bog nearby."

"Yes."

"We went there, and we found human remains." Mortimer burrowed deeper into the heavy blanket set out for the purpose. "Well preserved . . . remarkable remains. The problem was . . . they weren't very old." He looked wryly at the surprised doctor. "It would seem the bog was being used as an . . . impromptu graveyard of sorts several hundred years ago. It was certainly not in the days of flint spears and atlatls."

Watson pondered that in silence while the ship rumbled its way through the cold waters.

"I am puzzled," he said at last. "I have been to France, and walked in the forests of Broceliande . . . You say the ferries of the dead were to send their loved-ones home. But I was under the belief . . . when I was in France . . . that the dead are buried as close to home as they could possibly be."

"And so they are. On the peninsula, the graveyard is the center of life." Mortimer pulled off his glasses and hurriedly cleaned them against a sudden spray.

"Well! I cannot fathom it. The bog is a sort of church-yard . . . ."

"A church-yard without a morsel of stone to mark human passage. I am puzzled as well. But I cannot find the truth of this matter. The people were so well preserved, one might think they were still asleep. I can't really bear that, and I shan't make an apology for knowing my limits."

"Not at all." Watson mused. "Were they all the same people?"

"Now that you mention it . . . they were all sailors. They were buried with their sea-togs at their feet. And most of them were men, a few women . . . no children at all."

"Some mysteries defy an unriddling," Watson said at last.

Mortimer laughed kindly. "The more a mystery defied, the more your friend took offense! I see some of that in you, Dr. Watson."

Geoffrey groaned and rolled over at the sharp porcelain clink of the china tea-cup lowering to the bed-stead. "Oh, no."

"It's Assam." Clea chuckled and rubbed his good shoulder. "Brewed only once. No sugar. Drink it up and you can have breakfast. Any suggestions outside the usual crepes?"

"Carbolic," Geoffrey said into the pillow.

"Carbolic what?"

"After the night I've been through . . . is it possible to dilute some carbolic to the point where I can drink it, kill everything in my system, and manage not to die?"

"I've no idea, but I can ask Mrs. Watson when she comes."

"Dear me. I forgot." Geoffrey staggered half-upright. "And Roger's coming . . . ."

"And we both agreed you'd stay abed today." Clea rapped his thick head with her knuckles.

"I thought I agreed," he corrected weakly. But the pillow . . . and linens . . . and comforter . . . felt very good. He felt his bones settle into a resting position again as Clea laughed. "Make it toast and add enough for Roger too . . . he's gotten a taste for chestnut honey."

"I thought one had to be a full Celt to eat it." Clea smiled.

"Roger's sense of adventure extends to his meals," Geoffrey answered sleepily. "Hence the size of his waist-line."

"No doubt inspired partly by Hazel's accomplishments in the kitchen." Clea bent over and kissed the top of his head.

Geoffrey hadn't even known he'd fallen back asleep until an all-too-familiar thud of a battered boot-tip caught the edge of the rug at the doorway.

"Sorry, Clea," Roger was saying. "Everything's all right."

"Oh, dear," Geoffrey said for the second time that morning. He groaned as he levered himself upright, knowing his hair was a fright and his face was probably good for nothing more than frightening children with.

"Hullo, Geoff. Nothing's spilt."

"I'm shocked," Geoff mumbled. "You're getting light-footed in your old age, Roger." He groggily pulled the pillows up behind his back and inclined against the headboards with a sigh.

"You don't seem to have gotten much rest, old fellow. Aren't they feeding you well enough downstairs?"

"The feeding isn't the problem . . . and speaking of . . . give it here."

"Hang on there . . . ." Roger set the tray on Clea's little side-table and poured the tea. "Your little wife has set up quite the arrangement. I should eat over here more often."

"Feel free . . . but you'd best bring Hazel with you."

"Not likely. She wants me to extend my pinky when I drink." Bradstreet made a terrible face as he made the motion in question.

Geoffrey found himself laughing. "That's only because your hands are too big for most cups."

"Handles like mouse-traps, for the most part." Bradstreet snorted through his thick moustache. "Some of that butter and honey combination you like?"

"Yes. Yes positively. I am ready to eat something."

"Here you are then . . . ." Roger gingerly handed the little plate over. "What exactly do you do to let your wife permit you breakfast in bed? Anything less drastic than being at death's door?"

"The knowledge that if I ever make a mess I'll be doing my own laundry for a week. I don't think you're up to that."

"You know me too well," Roger joked a moment before he could stop himself. Both men hesitated. Geoffrey hadn't known Roger too well at all. If Roger had let him know what he was up to with the strike, he would have stopped him.

Geoffrey finally sighed and chose to ignore the thick air. "I need a knife, Roger."

"Oh. Sorry about that." Roger took to his own plate with relief. "I suppose I should say you're looking a little better . . . but honestly, I thought you'd be ahead of the game by now. It hasn't taken you this long to recover from any sort of disease before."

"I never fell into an open grave before. Speaking of which, I don't advise it as a way of getting out of work." Geoffrey calmly drizzled bitter honey over his toast. "I'll be glad to be back at the office, I tell you. I'll even enjoy whatever Gregson's slipped under my files. The fool thinks I'll never notice."

Roger kept from spilling his tea over the carpet just in time. "Geoffrey, I swear the comedy theatre lost a gem with you. Are you certain you aren't Welsh?"

"One of my grandmothers was Welsh."

"There you are then. Two-hundred-per-cent Celt. No wonder you and Gregson hate each other."

"We've decided to postpone our hatred, Roger. We're saving it for the next generation at the Yard." Geoffrey sighed as the tea glowed through his bones. "Oh, Lord. No one brews a cup like Clea."

"I don't know . . . Mrs. Watson has quite the touch."

"True, but Mrs. Watson has teas from around the world. Clea can make any leaf taste like it came from any country. Now if I can just convince her we don't need to haul out that bloody great samovar every Sunday."

"She's a Cheatham, Geoffrey. A Samovar is a Brown Betty to that lot. I once saw her father drink a quart of black at a garden party."

"My father-in-law at a garden party is the worst of the two images."

Roger sighed. "Still. I'm not here just to socialize and steal off your plate . . . ."

"Clea said someone's out for me again."

"Yes." Roger set his cup down and looked him dead in the eye. "Someone tried to run Hopkins down while coming out of the Barley. Gregson's convinced they thought he was you."

Geoffrey absorbed that, too surprised to blink.

"How is Hopkins?"

"He had a close call, but he's back to duty. Bruised ribs mostly, and his brains were knocked halfway to Bethnal Green when he got to Barts. Gregson got to thinking about that and a few other things . . . those little things that kept happening to you . . . Well . . . he doesn't think it's all a hodge."

"You mean hodge-podge," Geoffrey corrected automatically. "And he's probably right . . . Gregson always was good at drawing the missing pieces back into the puzzle." He sipped his tea, thinking hard and Roger, bless him, allowed him the moment.

Every time they attacked my father . . . they attacked him when he was wearing my coat. His mouth dried up at the realization. They could have killed him by accident. *They could have killed him because he was wearing my coat.*

"Oh, you've brought him!"

"But of course!"

Clea laughed and held out her hands for the baby. Arthur was so swaddled about his face to protect his lungs from the soot she had to unwrap him one-handed. Mary quickly freed herself from her travel-wear and swept her veil off her face.

"Such a lamb. He has the shape of your eyes, how fortunate!"

"And I think there's a bit of his father's nose coming in."

"Just adorable." Clea kissed the nose in question. Arthur loved the attention. He boxed Clea's chin with a gurgle.

"Oh, dear!"

"That's how a Cheatham baby says hello, Mary! Shall we take him to my old crib? I have it set upstairs in the guest room. There's a good bit of morning sunlight this time of year."

Mary followed up with a smile, knowing Clea was delighted to hold another baby in her arms again. They passed the landing where the murmur of men talking crossed their ears and continued on. The guest room was indeed as Clea had promised. Arthur took in the new surroundings with wide-eyed curiosity.

"You'll have your hands full when that one starts crawling!" Clea warned. "My first was like that!"

"But not your second?"

"Heavens, no. Nicholas was so much calmer we found ourselves rising in the night to make certain he was still in there!" Clea brushed her hands in her apron briskly, and moved to the tea-set. "Do you still take the orange?"

"Yes, thank you." Mary smiled beautifully in the morning light. "This will be a pleasant change of pace. Theresa is conquering the dust in my house – every inch of it – and I soon realized I'd have a better time breathing outside in the streets!"

"You have a good girl there. Do let me know if you come across an empty post. I still have some excellent girls that need a respectable establishment in which to work."

"I did bring a list . . . ." Mary pulled a small piece of note-paper out of her sleeve and Clea courteously took it without reading the contents. That would come later, when Mary was well out of the house. She took her cup of tea in trade, with a small plate of scones drizzled in orange. Still warm, the tang of peel married to the sweetness of the icing, and the low bite of fresh ginger and cinnamon.

"Clea, if the Palace knew how you cooked, we'd find you shanghaied and secreted away in the kitchens."

Clea laughed. "It's not my recipe, dear. Very few of my cooking comes straight from me. It's what someone's showed me here and there. The world has a wonderful palate. It just takes a bit of patience for a great reward." Still, she was pleased. "Geoffrey never fails to praise my hand in the kitchen. For a man who loathes sweets, that's quite a sincere endorsement."

"I would imagine!" Mary sighed in the comfort of the wicker-backed chair. "I trust he is recovering."

"Well on his way. He'll be back on duty by Friday. I know he's anxious against the bit, but this time of year it's mere foolishness to overstrain one's strength."

"Yes, I hear there's another storm on its way to watch for."

"Not another one!" Clea protested. "We've barely gotten our feet back from this one!"

"John's friend Lomax receives wires on the weather in the Continent. There's quite the swirl building up. He says it's doing nothing now save spinning and marshalling its forces, and it will either continue across the Rhine or straight to us."

"Brrr . . . I'll send my own note to the school and see the girls check the coal-reserves." Clea shuddered. "Thank you for the warning."

"Not at all. I suppose it isn't a London weather if we're not led to bow to our superiors once in a while!" Mary offered. "But I am still surprised."

"Your John is away on a trip, is he not?" Clea wondered.

"Oh, yes. He and Dr. Mortimer went to that pleasant, pastoral land known as the Isle of Streat for some sort of celebration. It was good to see John in such high spirits. I daresay he'll get a story or two out of it for publishing. He took much paper with him!"

Clea smiled. "Then we look forward to reading it. On top of the next story to show in *The Strand* . . . Will there be one?"

"Oh, yes."

"Well, that one with the beggar certainly made Mr. Bradstreet happy. He was in it." Clea's lapis eyes sparkled. "May I inquire for details about the new one?"

"You may. It's one of the few cases John brought to Mr. Holmes's attention . . . and the villains are a most terrible sort. Counterfeiters. Perhaps related to the sort that the Yard ran afoul of last year."

"I will indeed look forward to it!" Clea exclaimed. "Thank you for the advance notice!"

"Not at all!" Mary laughed. "It's a small enough thing."

"Well . . . perhaps to you." Clea's humour softened gracefully. "But it would be a welcome change of pace among us all. It . . . ." She sighed as the purpose for inviting Mary returned. "It has been a difficult year for all of us," she finished.

"I understand." Mary murmured. "If I may be of help , , , in any way . . . ."

"Perhaps a suggestion . . . if you had one to give."

"Do tell me."

And Clea took a deep breath.

Chapter XXVII – Thinking

"**H**ere we are!"

John Watson barely heard Dr. Mortimer's triumphant shout over the howl of the ocean wind. He narrowed his gaze to the thin strip of dark, smooth grey mottled with white upon a choppy sea. Seagulls cut through the air with the same energy, their wings imitating the play of the water below. They shrieked. Below them, on a tiny pinprick above the water, ant-like men were scurrying about.

"Fishermen?" Watson shouted his guess.

"I would say," Mortimer yelled, just as the wind dropped. They both laughed their relief to be out of the nonstop slap of air against their numbing cheeks. "There's always some sort of fishing going on . . . the cold water brings the deepest catch, you know."

"I do know," Watson admitted. He wondered what sort of rewards would be in the nets today. Scotland alone fed much of England and her lands from her chilly currents. Salmon and trout might be the most glamorous . . . but the range of saltwater fish was enormous and the prawns were outstanding.

Watson was one of those few people who could eat from the ocean for the rest of his life and never miss a side of beef.

The sun staggered out of the cloud-cover for a few moments, dazzling their eyes against the ice-capped rocks rising to the top of the sea. The steamship was unimpressed, and continued to chug arthritically against the push of the current. About them, short, wind-blackened men in oiled togs clumped about in heavy boots against the deck and occasionally cursed from behind thick black beards.

"I feel as though we've been shanghaied by early Picts," Mortimer mused, which anticipated Watson's thoughts by a scant second. Possibly the inspiration was influenced by the large number of knitted-pattern jumpers and mittens. The language that floated down seemed to be the universal language of explicative and imagination.

Watson chuckled behind his glove. "Stranger things have happened," he pointed out, and rearranged his muffler to hide his inevitable glances at the sailors.

Mortimer gave him a kind look. "I'm certain you of all people may make that claim with some veracity. I, however, a humble Royal Collegiate, cannot be as free."

"You think too lightly of yourself, sir," Watson started. With a bone-jarring crunch of gears and one last flurry of foul invectives, the steamship had slowed and was attempting to turn leeward. Watson grabbed the rail and peered best as he could, but for the life of him he could not see anything resembling a port, dock, or sheltering cove suitable for a craft of this size.

"Where are we headed, Mortimer? Do you know?"

"There's a frightening channel of deeper water that partially rings the isle," Mortimer explained, but his face had paled again, and he kept glancing above his head as if to ask the gulls not to hurry up and dine on him just yet. "They have to slip inside the channel, and go to the other side of Streat by those means. Too many feet on the outer side, and the ship might scrape against one of the rough chunks of reef." He sighed. "At least there are no fishing boats this time. When I was here last, there was quite a war between my ship and a small navy of fishers . . . who accused my ferry of stirring up the shoal of fish they were bent on capturing."

No great love lost between Sir Niles and some of the people . . . Watson filed that away for future reference. *One never knows, does one?*

And then the wind returned, the sun vanished, and the first lace of snow spun like paper doilies over the world.

Mary listened without a single interruption and waited until Clea was thoroughly finished before she spoke. Even then she concentrated until it came out of her face.

Clea felt oddly emptied after her confidence. Normally it was Hazel who heard the brunt of these things. She busied herself with filling her arms with Arthur, who was happy to renew his punching-bag acquaintance. She chuckled into his little face.

"I miss having a baby in my arms," she murmured. "There's nothing like it."

"I know. They're so precious." Mary shared the smile that mothers knew. She stirred her tea as she thought, and it occurred to Clea that Mary was one of the most beautiful women she'd ever known. Rarely was a person matched from the inside and the out, but Mary was without a doubt as good on the inside as she appeared.

"My John is no stranger to the strains of his profession . . . or his life," Mary murmured. In her mind she was thinking backward: To her witness of Mr. Forrester, the people who had taken care of her as a child, what little she knew of her father . . . of John himself and the husbands, brothers, and cousins of her many friends. John often observed (with a smile) that hearts in need flocked to her like birds to a lighthouse. "He has things he enjoys doing, especially in times of overwork. Does your husband have something similar?"

Clea smiled and winced at the same time. "His work is usually all he does . . . ."

"Does he read?"

"We have a purchase of a few magazines. He reads them when he has the time."

That didn't sound like it was enough. "Physical activity?"

"Usually it has to do with the house. If he's home in time or long enough, he works on a few repairs, or painting-jobs. I'm sensitive to the poisons in wall-paper, so it's a lot to work with."

"Perhaps he would benefit from having some sort of hobby . . . or something he enjoys doing."

Clea sighed. "There's little enough," she said at last. Arthur had quieted, his eyes sleepy and fascinated with a little chime hanging from the ceiling. The smooth metal pipes gleamed as they slowly turned with the air currents. "Nearly everything he does has something to do with his work . . . and he does nearly everything around the building. Masonry repairs, concrete . . . whatever Mrs. Collins can't do . . . he usually does it. He even makes the netted grocery bags for shopping." She was silent as she thought. "He likes people," she said at length. "Which is somewhat remarkable, considering he's usually seeing the wrong side of them." She sighed. "He doesn't seem to mind being around my family, which is more than I can say for most of Lancashire."

Mary discreetly swallowed her smile.

"We've had good years and we've had bad years . . . but of late, he's spent too much time working long hours. When he comes home, it is mostly to rest in some fashion. When he wakes up, there is time for breakfast and then a return to work. It's been that way for too long."

"I am sorry to hear that." Mary answered. "Is it a matter of waiting it out?"

"If so, I hope the wait is short. It's been too long as it is." Clea spoke softly, her deep blue eyes a little bleak.

"Then let us think," Mary offered. "Between the two of us, there should be some sort of solution or palliative."

"Gregson's put Patterson on with Hopkins." Bradstreet dropped the minor bit of sensationalism into the middle of the conversation. Lestrade's hands palsied over their task of spreading butter.

"Gregson and Hopkins together are bad enough . . . Now they put Patterson in the mix? I'm too old for the End Days." The smaller man grunted. He bit into the salted butter viciously. "Hopkins with his funerary duties. Patterson with his under-the-cover work with organized crime, and Gregson . . . who would prefer to know everything and all at once . . . I'm not often grateful for being off duty." He stopped as Roger went utterly still for a moment. "What is it?" he asked with deserved suspicion.

"Well . . . that's the thing. You've been out for close to a fortnight . . . ."

"A fortnight-and-a-half, Roger. Out with it."

Bradstreet did just that. "How soon can you come back?"

Lestrade dropped his toast. "What's going on?" *Pretend to be shocked about Baldwin . . . .*

Bradstreet took a deep breath. "A few days ago, the police grabbed Mr. Quimper's old friend Baldwin for trying to attack your brother-in-law, Andrew Cheatham. He was instantly sent up for Cooper's murder."

"Imbecile." Lestrade didn't have to think of the right word for that situation – or lie.

"I agree. But last night he died in his cell."

Lestrade sat upright, coming close to knocking his tray over. Bradstreet grabbed it out of reflex.

Lestrade had never been slow to act. He was fully dressed in minutes, and doing an admirable job of ignoring Bradstreet's anxious hovering until it was time to pull his shoes on.

"For the love of Heaven, Bradstreet! Hazel's not the only broody one in your house!"

Bradstreet sniffed, relieved that Lestrade was back to his strait-laced self. "Where's your coat?"

"Hold it, I'm putting on my second-best . . . ."

"In this weather?"

"Shoulder's popped a seam. No use to have a leaky roof on a day like this . . . ." Lestrade found one of Elizabeth Cheatham's hand-knitted mufflers and pulled out matching gloves. Not even water could get through that woman's stitches.

"Get one of her Jerseys on then, and perhaps your wife will actually let you outside." Bradstreet was doubtful.

"Don't be ridiculous. She'll let me out."

"Will she let you back in?"

Lestrade snorted. "Talk to me," he ordered. "How did he kill himself? Was it like Loseth?"

"Hung in his cell. Just like Loseth, by the way. Appeared normal enough . . . calm . . . collected. He even passed a few jokes to the guards about the new taxes."

"And he appeared normal in every way?"

"I heard the physician checked him over a few hours before . . . seems your Andrew is quite humourless to being robbed."

216

"He is not 'my Andrew' you priceless . . . ." Lestrade yanked the door open and picked up his pocket notebook. "Let's go."

Bradstreet had borrowed one of the police-wheels for the job. Lestrade fidgeted as they settled on their way to New Scotland Yard. "Not that I was feeling comfortable about this, but the fantods are getting worse."

Lestrade glowered from the tops of his eyes. "Not much to do then but go see what the rest of the Musketeers are going," he grumbled.

"Well, I advise you right now to walk in quietly. Gregson's head is pounding like a drum against the weather, and it has sweetened his mood to such an extent we're going to nominate him for sainthood."

"Roger Thomas Bradstreet, you wouldn't know a Catholic saint from a Roundhead. And bearing in mind that I'm probably the most ignorant Catholic in England, that should stand for something . . . ." He switched the subject. "What's going on with your end? Last I heard, you might have to enact your extradition duties with the Irish property."

"That only worked as far as getting there." Bradstreet grimaced, showing his teeth. "You know how the Irish are whenever someone from English soil comes to take care of one of 'their' people. Forgetting the fact that Blake family involved in the bank and the funeral home used to be one of the outsiders a few generations ago. Short-term Irish is better than any English, any day."

Lestrade nodded. The Irish were still liable to riot over the topic.

"A few years ago, the Blake ancestral home – very small, but old – enjoyed a slow but steady stream of repairs and renovations. The property is hardly bigger than one of the wealthy properties off the southern edge of London, but we're not talking cheap work." Bradstreet fiddled with his gloves. "It's one thing for a family who's biggest money-maker is a bank clerk . . . put up the funds to have the stonework refurbished. It's another when they also put up a new roof, trim the greeneries, renew the orangery, and glass up the old solarium."

"Did they explain to anyone where the money was coming from?" Lestrade asked without any hope whatsoever. The mere discussion of money was supposed to prove one's ill-breeding.

"Not directly, no," Bradstreet answered. "It would appear there was a . . . ." The Runner suddenly cleared his throat. "Well. There was an investment they took a risk on, and it returned most generously."

"Do tell." Lestrade's eyes narrowed. "And what was this risky venture?"

"They purchased a few shares into a Neolithic dig that was partnered through the London Museum."

"Roger . . . ." Lestrade closed his eyes. "I don't like where you're leading this."

"No . . . ." Bradstreet whispered. "It's pretty clear the Blakes are one of the silent parties enjoying something illegal and monstrous with dead Afghanistan veterans."

"Blast!" Lestrade swore. "Men who fought and died . . . men who were Dr. Watson's friends and companions . . . Has he been told anything about this?"

"We thought it best to wait until we had as many of the shots lined up first." Bradstreet shrugged bleakly. "Well, Gregson thought it best to wait . . . No matter what, it's going to be a dreadful thing to talk about, and I for one would rather put it off a bit."

"I . . . I can't say I blame you," Lestrade answered.

"Well, it's going to be a terrible shock to the man." Bradstreet pointed out.

"Yes . . . ." *That is, if Watson didn't already know about this . . .*

The slippery, dark sensation was back. This was part of what Watson couldn't talk about. He knew, but he couldn't say anything without betraying some person or persons.

Just because a crime existed didn't mean the laws that outlined it were simple. Blackmail, extortion, or just plain fear led to more burial of evidence than anything else. There were crimes that happened outside London. Inside London. On foreign yet English soil. Within the British government. Within the British military. Within, Heaven forbid, the British and Foreign Embassies. All of these separate-but-supposedly equal areas were their own jealous divisions, hostile of any 'outside' influence, and capable of throwing taffy into the works, extending something as open as a public knifing for months or years.

Lestrade hated suppositions. So many times, *a crime was actually straightforward.* You had a witness somewhere. You had footprints. A murder weapon, or an incriminating letter. Records. Photographs in the archives. A well-oiled machine in the Bobbies who went out every day with a list of wanted men and women. Railyard workers, port authorities, depot guards, and even the Beefeaters were eyes and ears for the information of London itself. The overwhelming majority was a matter of just rounding up the perpetrators and bringing them in without too much damage to oneself.

I'm such a fool. I'm a damned fool. Mr. Holmes is laughing in his grave . . . or else he's screaming names at me I deserve.

Watson was a Surgeon-Major! He would have been right alongside whatever illegal horrors were going on around the dead soldiers! He would have been working with the dying, trying to save them . . . He would have been on the outlying fringes, but he still would have been in a place where he could observe something! And that dead brother of his . . . the one who supposedly drank himself to death . . .

Whatever Watson was involved in . . . as an officer and undoubtedly a gentleman . . . had to be very, very thorny.

With all of riding on one tangible clue of gibberish on an officer's sabre:

Cave of the Dead Druid.

Chapter XXVIII – A Master Blackmailer

Gregson's mood was actually much worse than what Bradstreet had told Lestrade.

The big man was chilled to the bone, his hands ached, and there was something wrong with the draft so he was hovering closer to the coal than was dignified. Their "conference room" was nothing more than one of those small rooms things tend to get lost in until they're needed, and in this case it was an annex off the Missing Items Claims.

Hopkins made no particular contrast in his own misery. The young man had been developing a chest cough since the previous night, and Patterson (who looked ill enough when he was supposed to be having a good day), sat on the other side of the card-table, caught between a potentially catching comrade and a big man who wanted to pace incessantly.

Bradstreet was in temporary disgrace. Lestrade was still out from the effects of his accidental invention of the sport of graveyard-diving, and Montgomery was taking a much-earned vacation in the south (no doubt drinking his way all to Nantes).

They were a sorry lot.

"I agree with what the two of you are saying." Gregson folded his aching hands under his arms to pad them with steady heat. "There are just too many coincidences."

"Blake's our man," Hopkins persisted. "He's got to be."

"Hopkins, *we know you're right*," Patterson lifted skeletal hands in exhaustion. "The problem is mapping out *why* he is exactly the key."

"He's not the key," Gregson retorted. "But he's one of the underpinnings." He pulled out his throbbing hands – Elise would have the hot water ready as soon as he got home – and counted the points on his fingers. "He was a cutter for the Army Medical Corps. If that didn't give him access to some unpleasant stuff, nothing would."

"Not to mention his brother and father both have significant posts in the First Bank of Thames, the same wonderful people who supported the burial charity in the first place." Gregson opened his mouth to add a rather important point, but all three men wound up jumping instead at the sound of a body striking the door from the outside. The wood rattled in its frame. "Bloody Hell!" he swore.

Bradstreet's large hand punched the door open and held it as a frozen-countenanced Lestrade came in, propelling a white-faced Pennywraith before him. The old man's arm was wrenched behind his back.

"There you are, Doctor." Lestrade gestured to the stunned Inspectors as he shoved Pennywraith forward. "They're all there, and you needn't try to listen through a half-inch of pinewood door . . . You can just sit down and spy on them the old-fashioned way."

"No doubt, he's been playing the crooked cross," Gregson explained to the Chief Inspector.

Miller's blotchy face was close to repeating the attack of last spring. He ignored Bradstreet's presence in the room – he could hardly get rid of him, seeing as how the Runner had witnessed Pennywraith's defection as well as Lestrade.

Gregson pondered how it must completely gall the old stick to face the fact that a man he trusted was not only corrupt, but that he was exposed in that corruption by two of the Inspectors he hated the most.

He felt a little sorry for old Miller, but he also knew he could afford the sympathy. Miller had never personally crossed him, like he had most of the others. For all his flaws and horrid desire to prick pins into the men around him, Miller seemed to want to regard Gregson as his successor.

The Chief Inspector paced in the confines of the room, and if he looked sleepless he was in good company. None of them looked like men who ought to show up before a journalist's camera right now.

Gregson was shocked by the sudden emotion in his breast. Miller was living proof a human being could cross-breed with the stinging nettle, and he was probably as ugly on the inside as he was on the outside. At the same time, there was something sad and pathetic about the old man as he struggled to swim upstream against his upbringing and his training to face the truth.

What would happen to the old man when he retired? – a movement that would happen soon, surely! Not outside the next ten years . . . .

Miller was so old he could resent the French for the murder of his grandfather back in the last sea-war with France. It was the first of three reasons why Lestrade and his Frenchie surname would never rise higher in rank than plain Detective-Inspector . . . but at least Lestrade had the sense to ignore the other man's failings.

Perhaps it was because Gregson was childless too, but he could glimmer something of Miller's world. Whether or not you were a father, there existed some sort of desire to leave some sort of legacy behind . . .

Miller was looking at him.

Gregson carefully schooled his thoughts. It was time to put them aside and tend to business. Even as his mouth opened and assuring plans of attack came out, the big man was thinking ahead of his lips, to the strange and disturbing future that lay before them.

"The garden."

Clea said it so abruptly, it surprised Mary. The thought must have percolated unawares while they dipped into more restful topics – the uses of sweet almond oil being the current one.

"The garden?"

"When it's in bloom . . . he goes there. Even when he's tired out, he tends to it a bit, and when the weather's wretchedly hot he almost sets up a desk outside." Clea sighed. "It's taken me longer than I like to think to remember that . . . ."

"I thought your husband was indifferent to the country."

"Believe me, he is. But Mrs. Collins' garden has him absorbed. He's always doing something with the fig-trees, or the stone walk." Clea's deep eyes were surprised. "I never really thought about it before, Mary, but he's always doing something with it. Except for now . . . there's not much anyone can do."

"So we need to think of some way to work the garden into the house for the winter." Mary mused. "Is it the plants he likes? Or the architecture?"

"I couldn't tell you. He doesn't talk about it . . . ." Clea shrugged helplessly.

"Men can be unfathomable," Mary decided. "I'm aware that's a trite observation, and something that allows one to blithely drop a matter, but there are some things they do that I'm sure I'll never follow, should I live to be a hundred."

"Hold the light."

"I'm holding it, Ratty."

"Then hold it *still*, would you please, *Euclid*?" Lestrade shot back.

"Temper, temper," Gregson scolded but without heart. Lestrade had the worst of the job, combing over the smallest nooks and crannies of Pennywraith's desk. The room was stifling-hot, but the floor was ice cold and Lestrade's back had been on it for nearly an hour. "At least you can lie down. I'm the one bent half-over."

"Gregson . . . ."

Gregson grinned, mostly in the luxury of Lestrade's ignorance. He couldn't see him from several layers of pressed wood, could he?

"Oh, dear me . . . ."

It was the rat's worst invective. The flat and empty way Lestrade's voice turned was enough to deaden anyone's heart. Gregson lowered the little lamp with an equally sinking heart.

"What is it?"

"Give me a hand and . . . dear Lord, I hope I'm wrong . . . ."

Gregson complied. Lestrade pulled out from the desk, rumpled and pale. A sheaf of tightly stuffed letters rumpled in his fingers.

"Where's the good light?" Lestrade wanted to know.

"What's wrong with you?" Gregson demanded. "Anything good?"

"Look for yourself . . . Where's the water-jug?"

Lestrade pushed the paper into his startled rival's hands, got to his feet, and went for the pitcher resting against the wall, muttering softly to himself.

Gregson opened the first envelope with a shaking hand. Even though it was unadorned on the front and back, the sender's address rested neatly in the upper left-hand corner in a beautiful flowing hand.

A hand no one at the Yard had seen in two years . . . and had no desire to see.

Charles Augustus Howell. [1]

"Damn," Gregson breathed. "Oh . . . *damn*."

"Careful, Gregson," Lestrade's black humour emerged as he poured water. "There might be women present."

"Not likely, as they're filing our reports right now." Gregson disliked men who preferred the peaceful life of clerical joys under a roof.

Charles Augustus Howell had been one of London's *special* scourges. He was a master blackmailer who hobnobbed with the art-patrons and artists (all the better to find incriminating materials). He was most famous for illegally exhuming the grave of Dante Gabriel Rossetti's wife in order to recover the unpublished poems Rossetti had placed inside her coffin in a fit of artistic grief.

Even Mr. Holmes had run afoul of the man – repeatedly so if there were any truths within the rumour-mill – but events transpired in a strange way and the Great Detective had at least lived long enough to see the satisfaction of the blackmailer's death.

Lestrade held part of the correspondence in his hands, thinking of that particular case.

Gregson sat down next to him with the other half, and lit up a smoke. "You think Howell *really* died of pneumonia?" he wondered. "Or was it the slash over his throat?"

"I don't know. It wasn't my inquest," Lestrade sighed. "At the time, I was just happy to be nowhere near Chelsea . . . ." He poked open the flap

223

of the envelope and wondered what would happen when they read the contents. "Funny when you think of it."

"How so?"

"All that wealth he amassed . . . gaining it by hurting other people who must have made just a simple bloody mistake . . . ."

"Language, Lestrade."

Lestrade ignored that. "Mr. Holmes tried hard to get evidence on him, so I suppose it shows how oily he really was. But what good did it do him? He still died."

"Dunno, Ratty." Gregson smoked. "You have two choices. The first one is that he really *did* die of pneumonia, and one of his victims hauled his corpse out to Chelsea, slashed his throat, and stuffed the ten-shilling piece in his mouth for the police to find. The second is, he was *really* killed by a slash across the throat, in which case he was also stuffed with the shilling, and tossing his body by a public house was icing on the biscuit."

Lestrade had to agree. Howell's fastidious arrogance would have hated to be associated with a public water-hole. In comparison, being murdered would be secondary to the man's horrendous pride.

"Choices aside, Gregson, there was *still* a dirty ten-shill in his mouth. The righteous dead are given pennies over their eyes, or under their tongue to pay the ferryman. But it's the traitors we find with thirty silver pennies in their hands, or the slanderers with ten shillings in their mouths." Lestrade had drooped like a grass-stem, and was now sitting on Pennywraith's blotting-paper with a cup of cool water against the back of his neck. "So what now, genius-Inspector?" he asked too tiredly to be wholly sarcastic.

"What now?" Gregson repeated softly.

"Yes, I believe I just said that." Lestrade spat even as he heard how fruitless and petty the words sounded when coming out of his mouth.

"Good question," Gregson answered in that same colourless voice. "First of all, if Pennywraith had been in communications with Howell . . . who *else* was he in communications with?" He didn't wait for an answer. "You remember Howell as well as I do. Hell, man. You probably gave people the same speech I gave 'em when I was telling 'em to stay away." He leaned back, eyes closing for a moment. "We're going to have to read this garbage," he said at last. "Go over it for names, and I hope to God there's nobody mentioned in here that we like."

"Howell didn't target people that were despised," Lestrade reminded him.

Gregson sighed. "And here I thought Blake would be our ticket . . . ." Both men looked up as Bradstreet's heavy tread neared the door. He poked his head in, hat in his hand.

"Just thought you ought to know," Bradstreet began, "but Pennywraith was the physician who saw Baldwin the night he died. I'm still trying to see who saw to Loseth before he died . . . but . . . still . . . ."

"Pennywraith wouldn't have any call to be all the way down *there*!" Gregson exclaimed.

"Dear Lord." Lestrade closed his eyes. "Roger, get Patterson. We need his gimlet eye on this."

"What are you thinking?" Gregson asked as if he already knew. Lestrade slid off the top of Pennywraith's desk and began slowly pacing back and forth.

"I'm thinking that Pennywraith's been ensconced for a long, long time. I'm thinking that we need to see if Patterson recognizes some of the names that come up."

He did.

So did they.

There were many names.

Patterson was still finding them when Lestrade gave it up for the evening. He bade them a decent evening and donned his hat and coat. There was less rain, but the wind was biting, and there was that particular scent in the air (underneath the flying smuts) that suggested snow was coming back.

I know this is still winter, but this really and truly is ridiculous . . . .

Clea met him at the door, flour-dusted and smiling. "Welcome back, love," she paused to look him over. "What's wrong with you? You're not covered in London!"

"Stayed inside today," he explained. "How are things?"

"Very good. Had a good chat with Mrs. Watson . . . ." Together they hung up his street-wear and went up the steps. Clea pushed aside a flurry of papers done up in coloured chalks to make room for a light meal. He saw a lump of green on the corner of one and picked it up.

"Designing the gardens?"

"I think it's the effect of too much ice and rain and snow." Clea explained. She frowned her concentration over pouring the tea. "I want to see something green again."

"It'll be a miracle if Mrs. Collins figs survive," he mused, and set the paper down. "Too bad my mother couldn't be here. She liked nothing better than to work over a garden in paper."

"Really?"

"Probably has plant-juice instead of blood . . . Oh, that's good." He relished the first cup.

"Don't fill up on tea . . . We have chowder soon!"

"Yes'm . . . ."

"So she has a hand for plants?"

"You've no idea. The floor in our kitchen was an awful exposed plank ... She had us paint it up so it looked like the bottom of an herb-garden." He grinned at his wife's expression. "Even painted a few Apothecary Roses in the corner. Still, it was the only garden we were allowed to just walk in."

Clea was turning thoughtful.

"Oh, no you don't!"

NOTES

1. Yes, like Charles Augustus Milverton, Charles Augustus Howell, a master blackmailer, did exist, and the subject of his life, and death is an absorbing one!

Chapter XXIX – Ravings of a Madman

Watson considered himself a man who was not shy of adventure, but he had to admit to a startled gratitude when the steamship stopped at a stone-and-wood dock against a tiny spur of sea-rock. Large iron bolts were set into the stone: Mooring anchors. More men dressed like fishers swarmed about, hauling heavy goods and crates stamped in a dark blue ink.

And the wind grew bitter. It picked up like a sleeping dog that has suddenly awakened, jumped up, and threw itself at them. Sand from the small shore kicked up with grains of ice and snow from the clouds.

"We're headed that way!" Mortimer nodded to show a large grey lump of what Watson had mistaken for some sort of geological mound, but when he squinted his eyes he saw it was a manor. He spoke with the waiting carter, and they piled in with great relief into the back of the covered wagon.

"Whew!" Watson batted at his numb ears. "Are we the only ones attending this open house?"

"Oh, no . . . but we're probably some of the first," Mortimer answered. "Sir Niles will be bringing the guests in over the next two weeks." He burrowed deeper into his coat, hat, and muffler. "Once or twice a year he has seasonal guests, but they can easily make themselves into the proverb about fish and guests after three days. Not that the island is that small, it's just that the weather is often this . . . bad. Even the ducks go to ground, so there's little in way of sport."

Watson wondered what was so very sportsmanlike about going after ducks in marsh grasses, on an island smaller than half of any of the Channel islands.

Mortimer chuckled at him. "Wait till you try the duck."

"They can't be that good!"

"Wait till you try the duck."

"Well . . . ."

Watson had gone on strange escapades than this one . . . surely. *Just not recently . . .*

They both settled into the thick carpets left for passengers to the manor. Watson could see the sense in not having anything more elaborate than a trap. The weather and the roads were just too unreliable, and the manor was only a quarter-mile as the crow flew.

On the other hand . . . he shifted his weight to ease his old leg wound as the wagon jolted over a frozen puddle. Ice ground under the wheels loudly, like the sound two icebergs make when shaving together. Watson hadn't expected to hear a sound he associated from his childhood that strongly.

He'd been no more than a child when the ship took them to Australia . . . Was it a memory of the journey out, or the journey back?

Watson did not have time to resurrect facts from his mind. Mortimer was sitting upright, his beaky nose pointing forward in his anticipation.

Watson followed his gaze. A tall man in a thick fur coat – not a luxury so much as common sense here – was standing by the stone gate. The gate must have been a fortune in ironwork.

"You really have to wonder," Mortimer mused with an utterly unconscious sense of humour for his statement, "how much architecture changed once the Vikings stopped all the raiding."

Watson laughed. "Looking at those walls, I must wonder if they were worried the Vikings would invent cannonballs!"

"The nice thing about living on a peat bog island instead of a forested isle," Mortimer joined the game. "No one, not even a Roman, could fashion a trebuchet or catapult out of a block of peat!"

"Is that human bear our generous host?"

"None other."

Watson tried to see the man, but it was difficult through the copious amounts of black beard and moustaches. His hair – every bit of it – was similar to the thick bearskin he was wearing.

"Well, Doctor?" Dr. Mortimer had slid up beside Watson as discreetly as possible. Knowing grey eyes twinkled from behind the lenses of his gold-wire glasses.

"Well," Watson cleared his throat. "Sir Niles appears to be . . . ." He cleared his throat again. Behind Mortimer, a flock of waterfowl took wing. "A bit of an odd duck?"

"This is *without a doubt* the island for it." Mortimer didn't even blink.

It was Bradstreet who found the notebook.

Gregson was caught up in transactions, looking for something – anything – incriminating. Hopkins was going through the fatalities reports in the hope of finding a familiar name with his Burial Board search. Patterson was going through the punishment of the file cabinets.

So no one noticed until the oxygen suddenly turned blue around Bradstreet.

"Topping's too good!" [1] The Runner slammed the notebook down on the doctor's desk before a surprised Gregson. "That filthy . . . Gregson, tell me this isn't work capital?" [2]

"What is it?" Gregson gingerly picked up the fat little volume.

"Remember that patch of bad morphine back in '83? We knew someone from the inside was giving it out through Barts and a few other hospitals – "

Gregson cursed out loud. "You mean the fool *kept track of it*?"

"More than that." Bradstreet's face was the colour of a heart attack. He sank into his chair and put his hand to his face. Hopkins and Patterson crowded around Gregson. "He kept the records of who got the bad doses, where they lived . . . ."

"Their age, sex, families . . . how much money they made? Why would he – "

"Look." Patterson's sharp eye picked out a notation in the bottom. "He even wrote down how long it took the drug to take effect . . . ."

"He marked where there were unusual effects . . . ."

"We need to find proof it's the same batch that poisoned Lestrade," Hopkins coughed weakly.

"Well, let's see . . . ." Gregson held out his hand and Patterson put a cigar in it. Gregson sat down and let Hopkins light it. There was no sense in continuing their searches until this seam was played out.

"A-ha," he said some minutes later. "Evening of December 15th to the morn of the 16th . . . administered one full dose . . . demonstrable effects delayed . . . he thinks it's from '*exertion*', which I suppose is a fool's way of describing being slowly drowned in a fishpond while Jethro Quimper lectures you on your flawed breeding . . . ." He gnawed the end of the cigar for another moment. "Hallucinations of burning and drowning, imitations of drowning, gasping for air, ripping at shirt-front . . . ." He ignored that Bradstreet looked away with a stricken face. "The rest of this is medical doo-dad language for 'racing heartbeat, sweating, panic, and inability to eat or drink anything larger than a few spoonfuls at a time for the next three days . . .'" Gregson suddenly brightened. "Oh, this is marvelous. He spends some time cursing out Dr. Watson for interrupting the experiment and leaving the results unsatisfactory!"

"I owe Watson a drink." Bradstreet prayed out. "I owe him several."

Gregson frowned. "If I'm to understand this at all, then . . . Watson did more than possibly save Lestrade's life. He also ruined quite the cold-blooded experiment."

Lestrade faced the news carefully, and several times glanced to the safely shut door that kept his wife from hearing anything. Bradstreet didn't blame him. Clea's temper was rare, but when it went off, it was the stuff of legends.

Clea Lestrade née Cheatham had been courted by only one other man besides her husband, and that had been the man who tried to kill him various times in his life.

"Mr. Holmes was righter than any of us knew," he said at last, when Bradstreet ran out of steam. "I wish I knew how he could get his facts. I used to think he just had a better blow [3] than we did."

"I wish it were that simple," Bradstreet agreed. They both looked at each other in mixed silence. "I can't even fathom what you're going through right now, Geoff."

"It isn't a complete shock," Lestrade answered slowly. "Quimper's friend Griox tried to get me to talk over on the peninsula . . . ." He picked up his drink, set it down, and picked it up again. "I thought a lot of it was just flamming . . . he was *wanting* me to talk, you know . . . ." He laughed. "Wanted the names and descriptions of the men who were with Patterson on that raid . . . ."

"Leastwise you had the sense not to give them to him," Bradstreet offered.

"Sense didn't have a thing to do about it," Lestrade protested. "I wasn't going to give that killer the colour of the sky if he asked for it. At the time I didn't granny [4] what was going on . . . ." He took a sip. When agitated and *very* far away from the ears of women or superiors, his English slipped to the more typical forms of the twenty-mile bobby. "Griox and Quimper were the same kidney. I tell you. I'm not sorry Griox is dead. But Quimper . . . I suppose it's been too quiet for too long. He was just . . . incubating."

"Or fermenting."

"Ha. He's gone to vinegar decades ago." Lestrade paced slowly, the little glass tumbler rolling from one hand to the next in an absent juggler's motion. He really was upset to do that. Lestrade hadn't shown anyone any of his "tricks" since the CID tapped him for his connections with the Tinkers.

"I didn't know . . . everything that happened," he said slowly. "I suppose I wasn't interested in knowing what had happened while I was in that . . . fog."

"Did you remember anything at all?" Bradstreet found it hard to believe, but he was admittedly ignorant about drugs.

"Just the burning . . . I remember thinking I was on fire . . . and there were flames everywhere . . . it must have been the trauma of the warehouse going down around me . . . and then the cold of the Thames . . . I swear, I must have picked up someone talking, because the Thames was speaking to me."

Bradstreet shuddered.

"The Thames was saying, '*The hour is come, but not the man.*' And that's all I remember, but the drowning feeling followed after that. And then . . . it would be back to the burning. I'm thinking that the fever I had was why I felt like I was burning up . . . ."

Bradstreet found a circle of moisture on the library-desk from the bottom of his glass. He absently traced it with his little finger.

"Do you feel better knowing that Quimper had a false account of what you feared the most?" he wondered.

"I feel better any time something slips by that rabid fox."

"I wonder if he ever caught on."

It was a good question. Dr. Roanoke, in Watson's absence, had agreed to take time off his convalescence to review the notebook. Within minutes he'd ripped a supposition to shreds.

"*Aconite, morphine, traces of cocaine, nicotine . . . It is capable of inspiring nightmares. Do not be mistaken.*" *The old man's eyes had a strange twinkle to them as he pulled his glasses off the tip of his nose and polished his pocket lens.* "*You say the purpose of the drug was to reveal the victim's deepest fears?*"

"*Yes . . . I know it sounds like something out of a fantasy book,*" *Gregson started, but his apology was cut off by Roanoke's uplifted hand.*

"*It is quite capable of doing so, but I'm afraid Mr. Lestrade was an exception to the other cases in this . . . log of poison.*" *The old man tapped his chin thoughtfully.* "*Not on purpose, mind you. I doubt Pennywraith or anyone else in the gang would have thought to catch on . . . .*"

"*Please, what do you mean?*" *Bradstreet asked with a very pale face.*

"*I mean, that the trauma of falling through a burning warehouse, getting doused by the Thames eleven days before Christmas, and also endurance of a second, deliberate murder attempt by drowning . . . it was all so strong it overwhelmed the purpose of the drug. The hallucinations were completely ordinary nightmares, and the concoction no doubt exacerbated the effects, even though Dr. Watson's suspicions were roused and he was able to further reduce the drug.*" *Roanoke neatly folded his legs and started polishing up his glasses.* "*I can tell you that due to the confidence between a man and his physician . . . his deepest fears are actually nothing at all to do with burning or drowning.*"

Bradstreet heard his jaw click open. He wasn't alone. Gregson and Patterson were equally flabbergasted.

231

"I think the Yard owes Dr. Watson a thank you." Roanoke added thoughtfully.

Gregson shook himself. "He'll get it," he vowed.

Pace, pace, pace. Lestrade looked willing to walk the night away.

Bradstreet sighed. Lestrade's life circled with Quimper's since the day of his birth. Something always pulled him back to that rotten man. It was ironic that Quimper had won the majority of their battles, but Lestrade had won the most important one: The hand of his wife.

How it must canker and fester Moriarty's agent to know that the one time he lost against a man he had nothing but contempt for . . . it was for Clea's hand. Bradstreet doubted the man really cared a whit for Clea – he had the taste but not the heart. But the man had his pride, and –

"Look on the bright side," Bradstreet tried to joke. "At least the rival for your wife's hand wasn't related to you."

Lestrade's glass shattered on the floor.

Bradstreet frowned, uneasy and worried because the poor joke didn't warrant such a reaction. "Geoffrey?"

Lestrade was standing stock-still. His eyes were stuck upon the broken glass shining through the pale liquid. The sharp tang of dry applejack filled the room. He made no mood to pick up the mess. That scared Bradstreet.

The Runner moved to pick up the shards. That spurred some movement from Lestrade. He found a cloth and concentrated on pulling up the brandy from the floor while Bradstreet collected the glass on a piece of paper, carefully tipping it all into the rubbish.

"Geoffrey . . . stop. You'll cut yourself. Geoffrey . . . *Stop!*" Bradstreet realized he wasn't being heard. He reached over and simply closed his hand around the smaller wrist, immobilising it. "Geoffrey Brock Lestrade – *Stop!*"

Lestrade stopped, but his eyes were someplace far away.

Bradstreet was close to swallowing his tongue from worry. "Geoff . . . . ."

Lestrade mused (from a distance) that it was a sorry thing when it took a moment like this to make them forget they'd ever been at odds. Roger was an idiot, but he was still a friend.

"I'm . . . I'll be all right, Roger . . . ," Lestrade whispered. "Help me up." He collapsed into the chair and buried his head in his hands. "I'm sorry, Roger. I just . . . I didn't see that coming."

"I'm the one who is sorry. I didn't think you'd be that upset over a stupid joke."

232

"It . . . it isn't a stupid joke, Roger." But Lestrade spoke faintly. "It was just . . . I didn't expect to hear those words . . . ."

"I don't understand . . . you mean because you and Quimper shared a brother with Armoricus?"

"No." Lestrade let his hands hang off his lap as he stared straight down to the carpet below his shoes. "It was just . . . ravings of a madman, Roger. Ravings of a madman . . . ."

NOTES

1. Hanging's too good
2. Commit a crime punishable by death
3. Slang for informer
4. Understand or recognize

Chapter XXX – Frozen Truths

"**D**r. Mortimer!" Sir Niles lifted his hands in a smile that did not allow his lips to part from his teeth. A shyness? Or just the cold? "It's been too long, sir. I was delighted to hear you responded to my invitation."

"Only just, I fear," Mortimer blinked as the wind battered against his glasses. "I was visiting friends, but my wife had the foresight to send word ahead . . . ." He grabbed at the gold frames against another gust. "And pardon my manners . . . Sir Niles, please allow me to introduce one of my aforementioned friends, Dr. John Watson. He has quite the egalitarian approach to medicine and science. I daresay we shan't be running out of things to talk about!"

"I assure you – damn!" Sir Niles swore. "Hang this mess, let's get inside!" As he turned to go, a book toppled from its hiding in the folds of his coat. It fell, as books were wont to do, spine-down and cracked on the frozen earth. The pages unfurled like bird wings and with a hurried oath the baronet scooped the damaged volume back to safety. "And if that isn't the luck!" he mourned. "I was almost finished with it, and now I shall have to start all over."

"I beg your pardon?" Watson asked in an understandable confusion. "The spine is damaged, but it surely isn't ruined . . . ."

"No, no . . . it's no good now. I can't have a book in such condition . . . it simply won't do. Just think of how it would look on the shelf with the others . . . ." Sir Niles brushed snow and sand off the cloth cover. "It wouldn't look right. I shall have to begin transcribing tonight in-between our visit."

Mortimer caught Watson's eye from behind the broad, wooly shoulders. A lesser man would be patiently resigned and perhaps a bit condescending. Mortimer merely shrugged as if to say, "*This is what to expect.*"

"May I ask of the other attendees?" Mortimer rubbed his gloved hands against the cold.

"Oh, about half the old crowd out of London . . . not that they're often in London! Duty calls with the spring thaws, as those old diggers say." Sir Niles laughed self-consciously, is if he were quoting a joke made by someone else. Considering the snow and icicles around them, there was at least an awareness of irony.

"That sounds like Haversham," Mortimer said to Watson. "As soon as the icicles change colour, he's off with his rockhammer for the nearest chalk-bed of fossils."

Watson chuckled into his moustache, glad again he had something to keep his upper lip from freezing.

A butler with a greying blond spade beard met them with silent solicitousness and the heavy door clapped shut behind them.

Watson's cheeks stung. His ears rang. The butler took his heavy coat and thin shreds of ice glittered to the stone floor. Another servant swept it up before it had the chance to melt. A footman emerged from a rabbit-warren of darkly shaded doorways and announced the dinner was prepared to the butler, who nodded with regal courtesy.

The baronet's manor was nothing at all like the gloomy largess of Sir Henry's. Where Baskerville Hall was full of that dark, opulent form of corruption favoured by the worst sorts under Hugo Baskerville, Streat Hall was ancient enough to dwarf the importance of a powdered court. There was little of the Baskerville civilised brutality and cruelty that the notorious Sir Hugo had forged. Here one felt the eras were much older and crueler without bothering to seek apology.

The usual tapestries of the gentry hung on the stone-cut grey walls alongside hunting trophies of stag, red deer, elk and what Watson was shocked to recognize was a European bison.

A wild contrast to the red cows of Devonshire, and Sir Henry's hedged fields were no comparison to the slight rolls of Streat. Watson thought of the thick ferns and moss that clustered against the moors and felt a longing for that difference. *There* the only ocean was in the play of moonlight upon the grassy land. *Here* a man's walk was ringed by a frozen devourer of life.

"You both must be frozen," Sir Niles announced. "I had the butler set out the dishes for your arrival. It shall be our last calm meal before the hoard of scientists descend."

Watson found the meal – White Windsor soup and jugged hare – exactly what the doctor would order, and murmured so when their host rose to see to the wine. Next to his plate rested the broken book and a clean replacement. Sir Niles had eaten one-handed while transcribing the old one while he talked. Watson was torn between amusement and amazement at this display of operation.

Even though his voice was pleasant and his manners impeccable, there were traces of the baronet's slight madness in everything he did. For the most part, his fingers ached to do something, and when they were free of the pencil they moved restlessly upon his lap like a small animal. The hand holding his drink was completely calm and still.

"You should see him during the busy season," Mortimer whispered. "He truly finds serenity in the making of lists and organisation. I wonder if the butler has much to do with such a master."

"A decent enough ale to finish off the meal?" Sir Niles wondered as he poured a familiar-looking liquid into large mugs. "I made certain to grab a few barrels as soon as the harvest was put up."

"Twice in two days." Mortimer smiled his appreciation. "I am most content."

"So long as we stick to the usual fare." Sir Niles shook his head. "There's a stronger variation out there, and if there's something to getting the sacrifice to the gods drunk before they head off to the otherworld . . . it would be a brew like that." He lifted his glass reverently. "I had a small glass of the stuff and lost track of what I did for the rest of the night." He shuddered at the loss of data. "Well!" He exclaimed as he set the vessel down. "Now we can speak of pleasantries. Dr. Watson, are you still writing?"

Everyone asked that. "As much as my schedule permits," Watson answered. "I just finished a dry article about the Temperance Societies."

"Dry? That's a delightful pun, Doctor." Mortimer laughed.

Watson blinked ruefully. "Serendipitous. I'm not that clever."

"But the article was." Mortimer explained to Sir Niles: "He pointed out that the salons and bars and drinking establishments are more successful because they are attractive to all classes. A man may vow to end his drinking, but the bars are bright, well-lit, hung with mirrors and lights of all assortments, and the profitable establishment is constantly cleaning them. The Temperance Dens, for the most part, keep morning hours, are not as well-lit, and frankly have less to do in them – I suppose because many people associate drink with all the other evils, like gambling over a game of darts, cards, or billiards."

"And books." Sir Niles struck his thigh with a slap. "I've been to a few of them on business. The libraries are worthless. Most of them religious tracts or a few journals of exploring the world – some thirty or forty years out of date! I wonder why?"

"Because few individuals can start up a Temperance Bar on their own recognizance." Watson drank his ale with no guilt for the topic. "Everyone needs backing. Banks are often leery of such an unfriendly sounding venture, and the churches tend to control all aspects of the business once their money is put into it. There is one establishment that sits against the rule, and it will be the subject of the next article to be in *Beecham's*.

"The Wooded Glen." Mortimer sat up in his chair. "You're writing about the Widow Arbuckle?"

"The same."

"Excellent!" Mortimer explained to the fascinated host: "The Widow's fortune came from her husband's death by dissolution. She couldn't afford to keep up her property, so she transferred it all to a drink-free business, though she does serve near-beer."

"And it is a clean, well-lit place, with a section for the men and the women," Watson added. "The men have their interests, while the women have theirs, and a large library sits between the two sides – a common ground, as it were, with a librarian to serve as chaperone in case the socializing gets out of hand by two earnest young bibliphiles."

Sir Niles laughed hard at the image Watson painted. "By George and his dragon, that would be a treat to see! And she is successful?"

"Extremely. She had the sense to partner with The Lancashire Rose charity so her maids are skilled in the kitchen, sensible, and of good habit. Mrs. Lestrade, the Rose's owner, has them 'pass muster' before they go out into the world with her training, and Mrs. Arbuckle tenures them for half-a-year as a trial. If they do well, they enter the work force with excellent references."

"Mrs. Lestrade?" Sir Niles frowned lightly. "That's not a common name . . . I think I've encountered it perhaps twice in my life. It's *Lestrahde* in France, but I suppose it's *Lestrayde* from the Cockney influence." Sir Niles' far too active mind had seized upon something to do for the moment. "And there was a horseman in Plymouth . . . his master called him 'L'estrade' – pronunciation between the other two. It's intriguing how the miles can shift sounds . . . or is it the other way around? As a Baronet of Streat, one can pronounce it 'Street' or 'straight' and it still means the same."

Watson remembered the first time he had asked the little detective about his name. He could admit now, with the curtain of years between them, that he had been fishing for clues the way Holmes excelled. Lestrade had sworn he didn't care what he was called so long as the letters were strung in the right order – and that most people mangled the pronunciation anyway.

Watson had no desire to parse a man's ancestry in his absence. It happened on a daily basis, and it was considered a natural form of conversation (the male version of polite gossip), but Watson never liked talking about other people. One small mistake and one's credibility could be shot out of the water.

"I've been devouring your stories as soon as they wash ashore, Dr. Watson." Sir Niles returned to the subject. His "ill hand", as Watson was beginning to think of the right, twitched and moved with the buttons of his waistcoat. A man who knows of his disorder is a rare one. Sir Niles had learned to school his relationship with it to the point where he could function well. Watson made another mental note, then caught what his host was saying.

237

"Oh. No, Sir Niles," he said quickly. "I find no difficulty with my schedule in my profession and my writing. It's the mixed blessing of my location, you see." Watson explained wryly. "My portion of London is turning into quite the new address for new surgeons and physicians. I've never seen so many red lights installed in the past ten years as what is being put up now!" He shrugged lightly. "I could be bitter, but to be truthful, I am enjoying the quiet. I worked hard to be where I am today, and if a fretful hypochondriac or two wishes to sample the skills of my newer colleagues . . . who am I to begrudge them?"

Sir Niles chuckled. His restless hand moved into his thick beard. "I've noticed your discretion in a few of your stories . . . I'm certain to have missed many of them. Tell me, what does Scotland Yard think of the rather unflattering portrayals?"

"They simply retort is it sensationalist literature – a claim my late friend would support wholeheartedly."

"Ah. There is where I met the Mr. Lestrade of your acquaintance. I wonder if he even remembers?" Sir Niles passed that odd comment off and promptly forgot about it. "I wish you all the joy in your writings, Doctor. You have a gift for making one feel for all the characters in the play. I certainly did not expect to see so many . . . sympathetic characters in villainy, nor see so many exposed grey areas in the battle between the law and justice."

"The two are not always compatible."

"Oh, quite," Sir Niles said with a sigh, "And then, if the winters get any worse, we'll have to stop burning peat and cut down my forests!"

Watson lowered his dessert fork slowly. "Forests, sir?" he inquired puzzledly. "I am afraid I completely missed the sight of any forest in Streat so far." He looked to Mortimer for help, but the doctor was just as stymied as he.

Sir Niles laughed lightly. "I'm afraid most people do! But come, if you're finished, I can show you the forests in question." He rose to his feet, flinging his napkin down after him. Watson and Mortimer traded glances, bolted the caramel, and stood to follow their host.

They had not far to go. Sir Niles merely walked them through a high-ceiling library to a narrow door at the end and paused, fishing for his keys. They rattled with a peculiar sound, and Watson realized one of the keys was carved of wood. He was so amazed he barely noticed when the door opened on its hinge.

Mortimer gasped faintly. On the other side of the glassed-in solarium rested a magnificent vegetable-plot. It must be truly remarkable during the growing-season. As it was, earthen pyramids to store the autumn's cabbage heads and carrots rested smoothly over the soil. Remaining to vanguard the winter snows were rows of delicate-looking leeks, perfectly sound despite their broken and sere tops. Behind it all was the kale, and that was clearly the prize of the plot.

There were at least three acres, the stalks betraying their particularly primitive and hardy ancestry. Like walking sticks they grew, and at the top of each yard-long stalk a scraggly bonnet of dark green leaves waved.

"My forest," Sir Niles explained. "Black Kale. When they mature, they certainly rise to walking stick height, and I swear they're about as woody in the stem as any coppice!" He chuckled. "I'm told they make creditable walking sticks."

He chuckled to himself and turned, setting the broken book into a cabinet underneath the library shelf. Inside, Watson could see countless such volumes. The clean, "correct" copy was placed reverentially on the shelf.

"He is an unusual man," Dr. Mortimer felt bound to explain as they settled into their rooms. The storm had quieted. Nothing penetrated the ink of the night, and Watson had given up trying to see something, even a spark of light from the mainland. "On occasion he says more than he means to, but there's rarely any harm in the outcome. His mind is brilliant but not . . . completely orderly, I suppose. Hence his need to be orderly in other things." He ruefully regarded his necktie, which had gone limp, before putting it aside. "Very different from Sir Henry's humble quarters, are they not?"

"It is . . . ." Watson searched for the words to come out in his mind. "A most compelling contrast to Baskerville Hall." He watched as Mortimer suspiciously tested the quality of his bed-mattress. "In Baskerville Hall, we were surrounded by rich oils and tapestries while portraits of Sir Henry's forefathers glowered down upon us." Mortimer smiled at the aptness of this description. "One could feel that by some misfortune of fate, time could unravel itself like one of those tapestries and the bloodthirsty Lord could ravage the countryside again."

"And here?" Mortimer looked as if he half-divined the answer.

"Here I feel as though we're back in an earlier, rawer time that makes no attempt to hide its bloodshed with lace and velvet. Baskerville Hall was protected in part by the cuplike depression in which it rested. It . . . implied a sort of discretion. But here . . . the manor is standing proudly upon this jut of stone, as if defying the elements and human hands to attack it."

"I admit I understand you wholeheartedly," Dr. Mortimer said. "Ivy may seem cruel in its ability to tear down houses, but at least it breaking up the sharp outlines of the structure beneath." He sighed a little. "Oak." Was his final reflection. "The Baskerville crest was boars' heads, but I always felt that the age-blackened oak was its true emblem."

Watson had to agree. Sir Henry's Hall had been clothed in oak's many forms, from the dark paneling to its blackened rafters and pillars, hard as limestone from curing. Here the walls *were* limestone.

It was all a little too strange for his tastes, and Sir Niles, to his credit, had made a conscious effort to relate to him as an outsider and as a man who was not on his level. Watson disliked criticizing the ways of his own people, but he had enjoyed Sir Henry's Canadian casual friendship more than he could explain. There were no barriers between himself and Watson.

"How is Sir Henry?" he finally asked.

"Doing well – or rather, doing quite well to judge by the numbers of hopeful mothers at the outlying society events." Mortimer rolled his eyes briefly at the maddening optimism of mothers, and Watson caught himself hiding a chuckle. "He's got his sights narrowed to two prospects, and with any luck we'll get his invitation to the wedding by spring."

"Is it down to the last lap, then?" Watson grinned from ear to ear. This was more pleasant than thoughts of sleep in a strange bed in a stranger manor hosted by an odd man in a cold island named after a road.

"Very much. I'm afraid the one who answers his affections the most openly is the one least suited for him, but they still have their common grounds. Good, healthy family and a stable income . . . The lady who would suit his temperament was in frail health as a child, so of course that would have to be considered."

"Of course," Watson agreed politely. He was again glad to not be in a baronet's shoes, where one grew up knowing one's duties to the family history.

"Still, I think spring will be the deciding factor in more ways than one . . . It isn't just a young man's fancy that turns to love when the flowers are in bloom."

Watson was still chuckling as he climbed into the sheets and blew out his bed-stead candle.

Chapter XXXI – Cold Truth

Paddington Street, London:

Lestrade saw Bradstreet to the door and was silent for some time, watching his friend's cab disappear into the glassy street. He thought of his past as an ordinary bachelor and Roger would come on occasion, split a few bottles of beer, and chew the fat. Those days were long gone. Once in a while he spent the night at Roger's when duty called, but never without alerting Clea with a wire (and thank God the telegraph station was a hop to their home). Roger too spent the occasional night-over here, once he got through the mob of two little boys, but those nights were rarer than they used to be. He couldn't regret the march of time, but there were moments when he wished for just one of those old nights back, when they were both less weighed down by the past.

Roger Bradstreet wasn't the same since he'd lost his three youngest children to the epidemics. He was harder for a man to befriend, while at the same time doubly protective of the friends he had. Perhaps some of that fear would go away once Hazel ended her confinement . . . .

His thoughts shied off that topic with the speed of reflex. Hazel had wanted more children. So did Clea. When they were all younger it had been easier to be reckless with the dice.

He saw a spot of mud, well-dried, on the sleeve of his jacket on the coat-tree and busied himself with working it off. Mrs. Collins' new maid was better at cleaning the house than she was the clothes. His mind was still free to think.

This wasn't the London of sixty years ago. No one had been safe. No one at all. Even the gentry could have faced an accosting, and hired guards were common. Still . . . the world was changing. London changed with it. And the face of crime changed with London . . . or, to be honest, it was the criminal that changed first. London followed suit, adapting laws, making new ones, and evaluating the old ones – some traceable to 1066.

London would never be a safe city. Never tame. But for some it was safer. He reminded himself of the differences people had made. Slavery abolished. Food protection laws. Ragged schools. And more policemen than ever, with far less suspicion and accusation than ever before. The Met was his world, so he could track those changes the best. From his own view, the Yard was strong and gaining in strength . . .

. . . Only they were up against clever and resourceful criminals that too often outranked them in society. Poor Inspector Wicher. Solved the most heinous of crimes, but because the killer had been inside the well-connected family, his own career had been forfeit. What fame had been left him? Not much more than the fact that Wilkie Collins had openly based his character of Sergeant Cuff after him in *The Moonstone*.

It was possibly the only work of fiction everyone in the Yard had taken the time to read. Not just out of respect, but because it reminded them that there were consequences to doing one's job. Wicher's fate could be any of theirs. They could all be ruined by the blow of someone above, someone with connections and money . . . .

Had Roger directly joined the strike, Lestrade would have understood. There were times when you had to take a chance. If all else failed, he supposed he could return to his family's district and take up some sort of farming to get by . . . At least he had that to go by. Lestrade had much less. His wife ran a charity, and his own people were malcontents and smugglers. Old Potier was wealthy by their terms, but not for much longer if he kept spending it on his children and grandchildren.

Twice he'd offered his grandson land in the Channels. It was attractive only because it was nothing like the world he lived in now. Lestrade figured he could deal with a population comprised of birds and fish for about two weeks before he started talking to them.

People wanted what they didn't have. You could rely on that. He smiled at himself and went back up the stairs.

It was quiet by the fire. Clea bent over her sewing with that deep frown scoring her forehead, and allowed him the solitude to fix his last pipe before bed.

"How goes the charity?"

"Well enough, but I'm having the usual troubles convincing the good households to take on some of my girls." Clea fished for her tiny sewing-scissors, which were shaped like a crane. Geoffrey wordlessly took them from the top of the mantel and handed them to her, holding them by the beak-cut blades. She smiled as she took them and began snipping threads. "So many of them think the *workhouse* means one is *workless* . . . and it doesn't."

"You needn't convince me." Wanting to avoid a woman's private contemplation with her needlework, he took the couch on the other side and slowly stretched his legs. Clea thought he looked tired, but strangely at peace over something.

"I hope Roger was doing well."

"Well enough. It was luck that sent him on an extradition job at the time of the strike . . . ." Her husband sighed smoke. "He had an inkling but no proof, as they say. And likely he would have joined them had they asked."

"He has too many childer to feed to join that sort of crowd," Clea criticised, but the usual tart was out of her voice. Roger Bradstreet had been thinking of his children in the first place. Money was never in long supply for a policeman. Less so when there were little ones to feed.

"It will all sort out . . . sooner or later." Geoffrey fell into a brown study over his pipe.

"You're thinking hard," Clea observed.

"More like recollecting," he admitted.

Whatever was plaguing him, Clea waited for it to come out. It did once the pipe was down to warm coals. He drew a long breath into his lungs, so deep he had to hold it a moment before he let it out. Clea took the cue and set her sewing into her lap.

"He shocked the living daylights out of me."

"*Roger* did?"

"It wasn't deliberate. He was trying to jolly me out of a mood and made . . . ." He cleared his throat. "He said . . . 'at least the rival for your wife's hand wasn't related to you.'"

"Oh," Clea whispered. She rested her hand over his wrist. "Well, of course he didn't know what he was saying."

"He will soon," Geoffrey said heavily. "I'm going to tell Gregson and the others first thing tomorrow."

"Must you?" Clea said without thinking.

He flinched as if she'd openly slapped him.

"Geoffrey, I don't give a hang what people think about me – I'm a Cheatham and you married me anyway – but won't it open up more upset for you?"

"It's been hidden too long," Geoffrey answered. "It's been too long. I can't . . . put this off any longer. I've known all this for what? Three days? It's a millstone about my neck."

"But there's still no solid proof to what your father was raving about."

"There's a small piece of evidence. Not much, but . . . it's something."

Clea swallowed. "Why must that man have the need to hurt others? Why must he be so good at it?"

"I don't know." He let his pipe down without looking and leaned back, briefly closing his eyes.

Clea pulled his head down (checking for needles first) and let him rest in her arms.

"I don't want to believe it," he said at last. "Who would? This isn't something I was taught in the CID. How to believe a madman who also happens to be your own father."

Clea was out of depth there. Even Andrew, who was incurably selfish, was appalled at how Thomas Lestrade treated his only decent son. Perhaps that had hurt her husband's pride, for who wants the sympathy of someone who likes to give you trouble?

Like it or not, Geoffrey had proved himself with her family years ago.

"Sometimes a madman has only a twisted truth," she pointed out.

"Yes . . . Now those I've had to deal with. It's no simpler."

Clea had heard enough. She rested her hands at his temples and leaned back in a comfortable position. The blackwork could wait. "Tell me what it is," she insisted.

"I can't prove *without a doubt* if it's true or not," he protested, "that's the problem!"

"Then trust yourself. I don't know any other way. You knew that when you married me, Inspector."

Geoffrey's response was to say nothing, close his eyes, and shake his head. "It's the ravings of a madman, Clea. I don't know how . . . how right he is, because I don't want to believe it . . . or if they'll believe me tomorrow."

"They'll believe you." Clea thought for a long time in the silence of the room. The only conversation was being held up by the crackle of the coal-fire. "Remember when the boys came home with that cart full of wood-scraps?" she asked suddenly.

"Yes, and I also remember the hiding I gave them with the rough side of my tongue for doing such a foolhardy thing."

Wood-scraps were precious in London. The boys hadn't had to compete with just the street-urchins, but also the larger and brutal homeless and the starving. They had decided to take the horrific risk to search for firewood because they'd heard their mother fret about the price of coal against the strain on their budget. Eight-year old Martin came back with a bruise on his cheek the same size and shape as the edge of a broken board. Nicholas, younger by a year but heading to twice as big, bore terrible rends in his coat and trousers.

Naturally, neither boy had "seen a thing" to explain their rough state. Their father hadn't known if he should laugh, cry, or give out medals.

Clea reached out and squeezed his hand. "You've trusted me where many a man wouldn't," she said quietly.

Geoffrey flinched. "None of my business," he mumbled.

"Some would say it was completely your business." Clea nestled her head against his shoulder. "After all, you were about to marry me."

"I would've been a hypocrite if I'd taken you to task for what Quimper did to you and your family." Just saying that name made him look knotted and ill inside. He pulled his arm around her and they rested in silence while the fire snapped. "Clea . . . it really was none of my business."

244

"I am glad of your sentiment, Geoffrey . . . but am I wrong to think you have that understanding because of what happened to your mother?"

It was a delicate subject. He said nothing, but his anguish said it all.

"Speak to me when you're ready." Clea left it at that. "I assure you, I'll be here to listen."

Thankful beyond words, he squeezed her fingers within his. "When I'm sure of the truth . . . I will."

"But you'll be going to them anyway?"

"I know it's the truth, Clea-*bihan*. The problem is proving it. They'll take my word for now . . . but you deserve the facts."

Clea said nothing, but she squeezed his hand tightly.

New Scotland Yard:

"I believe I know why Jethro Quimper killed his father."

Gregson faced this news first thing in the morning stolidly, but astonishment lurked on the other side of his face.

Lestrade was pale and ill at ease, but the usual energy he carried was gone. For a man who could barely endure a stakeout without checking his watch every ten minutes it was a bad sign. He was saving his reserves for later.

Hopkins and Bradstreet traded looks of unease over Gregson's head. Lestrade had something personal to tell, and it couldn't be good.

"Have a chair, Lestrade. There's lots."

"I've been down for days." Lestrade remained standing, but he had his back to the wall in a defensive position he probably didn't know he was employing, and toying with the battered watch in his hands. "Gregson, you may want to have me off this case. I've gotten too involved with it."

"You've been personally involved with worse cases than this." Gregson reluctantly invoked the case of his murdering brothers.

Lestrade merely lifted his gaze until he was looking at Gregson through the tops of his eyes. "No, I haven't," he answered back evenly.

Gregson wordlessly reached for one of his cigars. "I'm going to have a smoke, if no one objects."

No one did.

Lestrade pulled out one of his own cigarettes, and took three long draws before he started speaking again.

"Everyone knows Jethro Quimper hates me because I sent Armoricus to the gallows. It came out in '83 that my brother was really my half-brother . . . Armoricus was Jethro's brother through Ivo Quimper."

"I remember he took a lot of joy in telling you that," Bradstreet answered soberly. "He must have saved it up for years, waiting for the right moment to stab at you."

Lestrade grunted. "Once the shock wore off, I could see he was telling the truth."

It was the common knowledge no one talked about. It was no fault on Lestrade's part – and certainly not that of his poor mother's – but society was rarely so sensible. Lestrade's professional reputation was sterling. His unprofessional reputation was a disaster. And it was the latter that created – or prevented – promotions, recognition . . . and respect at the Home Office.

"It's all water under the bridge," Gregson argued. "Why would that be an issue now?"

"Because Jethro Quimper, when he was telling me all the sordid details, *thought* he was telling me the whole truth," Lestrade answered tightly. "He told me because he wanted to see the horror on my face when I realised I shared a brother with him." Lestrade's hands were starting to shake. "He didn't know the whole story . . . just the parts his father told him."

"Lestrade, sit down," Gregson repeated.

Lestrade ignored him. He was staring at some point on the floor between the lines on the cold floor of the cramped conference room.

"The night Ivo Quimper died, he chose to tell Jethro about the *other* Quimper family scandal, and that one I'm afraid hit a little too close to . . . the centre." Lestrade shook his head. "It wasn't what he wanted to hear. He must have gone mad with it, and beat his father to death. My father tried to stop him, but he didn't have the strength, so he just blocked what blows he could with his arms. It nearly crippled him. So Jethro left his father dead, and Thomas Lestrade was left to take the blame."

They were all dying to know what it was, but they all kept their mouths shut. Hopkins had grown very pale, and Bradstreet's hands had frozen at his sides.

"Ivo told his son that . . . just as he had shared a brother with me by Armoricus . . . ." Lestrade suddenly swallowed. "Jethro and I share the same great-grandfather – a *Lestrade*, and not a *Quimper*."

Bradstreet sucked in his breath and nearly lost it.

Gregson went a little white about the chops but kept his composure. The cold demeanor that kept him calm and level during disaster was doing him well now. "You don't have to talk about this," he pointed out.

"No, I think I do." Lestrade shot back. "If I ever get promoted or dismissed, it won't be for what I've hidden. Better to tell the truth than to bury it. Look what burial's done so far." He smoked furiously in the silence that followed.

"How?" Bradstreet finally croaked.

"Luke Quimper died a few months after his birth. This upset his parents, for he was already promised in marriage to his third cousin Anna." Lestrade looked at the bottom of his cigarette before throwing it away. "But there was a child of the right age born to the Lestrades."

"Is there proof?"

"Not much. I don't think it will be recognized in court." Lestrade sighed and pulled out a beaten flat tin. He prized the lid up and held out a piece of parchment paper, folded for so long it had torn along the fold-lines. Gregson had to rest the pieces side by side.

"I can't read it, Lestrade," Gregson said at last. "Except the . . . date? Seventeen . . . fifty-three?"

"It's a bill of sale," Lestrade answered succinctly. "There was never a birth-record outside the family Bible, and that's supposed to be lost. The bill of sale is the only proof of Daniel Lestrade. His name was changed to Luke Quimper soon after . . . a year later his natural parents had a second son, who was my grandfather James Lestrade."

Bradstreet caught on. "And marrying the cousin, Daniel's children would be seen as being Quimpers, eh? It doesn't matter how thin the blood flows, so long as it's Quimper blood."

"Two drops would be enough," Lestrade nodded. His eyes were quite flat and dead.

"Luke's son was Ivo Quimper . . . and Ivo's sons were Jethro and Armoricus . . . ." Hopkins scrubbed his weary eyes. "No wonder your father tried to protect Ivo Quimper . . . ."

"And no wonder Jethro went mad with fury." Gregson handed the papers back. "It's motive enough for murder, and no doubt."

"Not that it'll go anywhere," Lestrade agreed heavily. "Because it won't."

"We'll keep it quiet," Gregson said at last. "If word leaks out, it'll just distract from the facts of the case." He held up the notes he'd taken from Lestrade's words. "But I'm keeping this in the vault. You never know. It might save us all someday."

"That is just what I'm afraid of."

Chapter XXXII – A False Grave

Isle of Streat

Dr. Mortimer stared out the window of his shared room with Dr. Watson. In the light of day, Streat was a confusing smear of grassy greys, whites, and the black of broken wet soils. He could see almost to the very tip of the land where it met the ocean. In the soft grey veil of the sea, a tiny cluster of fishing-ships collected over a profitable shoal. Gulls wheeled like spring toys over their heads.

Close by, Dr. Watson was falling into an exhausted sleep.

After the entire day in the field, Dr. Mortimer held no blame for the man's early retirement. Sir Niles had typically not noticed that he'd driven his guests to the limit of their energies. At the same time, Sir Niles had dropped everything but his watch and went to greet the steamship as it unloaded a portion of his expected guests, starting the whole cycle of hospitality all over again.

Ordinarily, Mortimer would have been pleased to meet all the half-familiar faces and the more familiar names, but a vague sense of unpleasantness had sunk upon his breast to see Watson so pale, and how he had withdrawn by degrees from the conversations.

He knew the doctor was limited to some extent from his war injuries. Marching across the bog to view the frozen dig sites had hardly been necessary. And then to cap it all with a show of a few relics under a glassed box? Fine as the bits of blue glass, hammered metals, and Baltic Amber were, they were hardly enough to justify all the fuss.

Mortimer told himself it was his own professional prejudice. He preferred the relics of *humans*, not the relics the humans left behind.

Watson stirred an hour or so later. Mortimer checked the time.

"Just in time for our 'early sustenance', Mortimer announced with a slight trepidation. "I wonder what the evening's entertainment will be?"

Watson slowly sat up, groaning slightly as he tried to stretch protesting muscles. "I hesitate to consider," he confessed. "Is your friend always so . . . enthusiastic?"

"Only when he's in the very teeth of an interesting case. And I can't say I can call him a friend. A fellow colleague in science perhaps . . . As far as friendship goes, he has been nothing but a proper baronet to a humble MRCS such as myself." Mortimer looked uncomfortable. "I can't say why he's acting as though the Crown Jewels of Ys were dug up on Streat. A few shards, bits, and some interesting bone tools with a few articles of leather clothing are interesting, but hardly enough to throw a party over and refurbish an entire wing of the manor into a museum!"

"Perhaps we will know more when we tour that aforementioned wing tonight after supper." Watson very slowly bent and touched his toes. He grunted in self-disappointment.

The manor of yesterday had been quiet and stately with a slight savage undertone. Today, the manor had released that savagery to that unique form of thuggery. The English intellectual away from home, family, church, and University. Surrounded by others of their own ilk, the twenty-some men were clustered around a raucous contest of some sort of bragging that seemed to be a debatet on who'd had the worst vacation abroad within the past five years.

"This is not our manor anymore," Mortimer murmured into Watson's ear with a smile. His breath smoked slightly in the chill.

Watson smiled back. The brief nap had refreshed him and he was clearly back to normal. "I feel as though I'm back at school, touring the pubs and other less-respectable places."

"Sir Niles is a confirmed bachelor, so that's unlikely to change."

Watson was surprised. The gentry usually had more pressure to marry than the poor.

Mortimer caught his puzzlement. "Sir Niles always swore he liked a woman at his side, but not on his hands."

"His loss, I'm sure," Watson answered back without rancor.

"Or his limitation," Mortimer snagged two glasses of a dry sherry from the sideboard and handed one to his companion. "We are most fortunate in our wives, and I am not bragging. For my part, a woman who can tolerate my unique mixture of foibles on my income is rarer than a perfectly preserved Viking longship."

"I can think of no man better . . . *equipped* to find her." Watson clinked his glass to Mortimer's with a straight face. Some men measured their women in gold. Some in pounds sterling. Some compared them to pearls or a summer's day or diamonds.

Dr. James Mortimer, MRCS, compared his wife to an oaken lapstraked ship of war.

Well, he did have a point. Those things were in exceeding short supply these days.

"You have a remarkable wife yourself, I noticed." Mortimer's kind face wrinkled in his usual smile. Watson thought to himself that this was the true Mortimer, not the harried and concerned friend of the Baskervilles who sought advice outside his usual skills.

"That I do, but it was a near thing for my nerves." Watson took a drink at the memory. "I don't have the slightest idea why a man is lauded for his bravery when he faces down screaming savages, or heavily armed criminals, or even a burning building. His true mettle comes out when he finally has the nerve to propose."

Mortimer slapped his good shoulder, barely hanging on to his sherry. "We make a terrible pair, don't we?" he asked under his breath as the party about them picked up in pitch and fury. "I tell you, my childhood was spoiled for the delights of a good sturgeon-roast in the open air." He glanced up automatically to the high stone ceiling, where the smoke of many fires had blackened the stone beyond restoration. "But I'll admit, the ceiling's high enough, and the atmosphere's chilly enough to pass for an open-air party."

"Halloa!" Their genial host bellowed. The big man looked less civilised by the minute. Watson wondered if he unconsciously adapted his personality to fit the majority about them. His large hand waved in the air and the crowd (Watson calculated there were a good twenty men), stilled.

"Everyone, I'm certain we're all in the process of acquainting and re-acquainting ourselves . . . ." There were a few chuckles. Watson recognized a few faces from the museum back in London. "But as your host, I thought I ought to give my distinguished guests a choice for tonight's entertainment. Shall we have supper before or after the tour of my new museum?"

"After!" cheered the crowd.

"Scientists," Mortimer said fondly. "They know they can sit and discuss the importance of their own findings in leisure afterwards, and work Sir Niles' accomplishments into their own."

"Economical," Watson observed. Privately he was thinking that intellectuals were the same the world over – with the exception of Mycroft Holmes, who was an exception in everything, they all chose knowledge over food. At least temporarily.

"Very well!" Sir Niles was saying. "Gather up, gentlemen, and I ask you to pay close attention, because I want you to pick out any errors in my speech tonight! This is your chance to correct a baronet in his own castle! I trust you are all up to the challenge?"

"As you wish, Sir Niles!" A stick-thin man with ferocious red hair – Watson recalled him as one of the hangers-on at the art show – lifted his glass in a toast. Watson found himself lifting his glass along with the rest.

Mary Watson stared at the print before her, and finally pushed the budget papers away. The storm was affecting the gaslights. Either too many people were drawing on the lines, or the sheer numbing cold had forced a greater drain on the city than normal. She rubbed her eyes – lightly, of course. She was tired. Arthur had perked up like a flower that has just been watered, and his constant chirrups and self-amused noises had filled the house like a family of sparrows. His stockings were a constant source of amazement to him. One of her school-friends (Helena? Vicky?) had knitted little balls of brightly colored yarn on the edges like a clown's shoes, one red, one blue.

"I don't know if the magazines approve of having a child wear their toys." Mary teased of the gift . . . Vicky, that was it. Gracious, but she was tired to not think of Vicky! The girl's sense of mischief was unquenchable.

"I'm practicing for my own, you know," Vicky had answered. "A house with babes and laughter can hardly go wrong, can it?"

Arthur certainly vouchsafed that sentiment!

Mary rose from the little desk and bent over the edge of the crib. Arthur gurgled up at her, and some of her fatigue lifted. The trust in those large, deep eyes was pure elixir. She was in the process of speaking to those lovely eyes when her expected visitor rang.

"Oh, Kate!" Mary swept her little friend inside and had her coat off her shoulders before the small woman could finish chafing her hands. "You're chilled to the bone! Come sit by the fire. There's a pot of cider mulling up."

"Oh, thank you, Mary," Kate Whitney breathed. She was Mary's age, but was starting to look older. Being married to an opium-addict was a strain for anyone. Mary caught that her hair was plaited inaccurately, and privately vowed to have a quiet but firm word with that maid. Too many servants took the example of the master and matched slovenly for slovenly.

"This storm is dreadful!" Kate Whitney waited until she was warm from fire and cider before she picked Arthur up and put him in her lap. Her face instantly grew young as a girl's again. Poor Little Kate. She'd wanted nothing more than a loving husband and children in her arms . . . but with opium came many prices. Vile whispers suggested Isa was incapable of fathering children.

Even if they were true, Mary's first reaction would be to slap the source of those whispers. One had to have principles, after all.

"Such a love," Kate cooed and played with Arthur's tiny hand for a few moments while Mary picked up her sewing with relief.

"Do enjoy him a moment, Kate! I've been trying to finish this hem for half the week!" Mary held out the troublesome four inches of linen with a sour expression that made her friend laugh. "Is it any chillier in Hanover Square?"

"It is universal!" Kate exclaimed. "This is the storm that proves the payment to the brickmen! I declare, if the slightest gap remained in the

251

mortar, these winds would betray the mistake!" She shivered. "But I'm grateful you're here where it is warm and safe."

"It is more than many people can say now," Mary admitted sadly. "I shudder to think of the poor people out there tonight with nothing but the clothes on their backs to keep warm."

Kate glanced down and studied interest in Arthur. Her natural and large heart was enough to encompass the world, but she rather struck Mary as a bird inside a cage. She would enjoy keeping busy with the charities, but her family felt it would be in poor standing for one of the Whitneys. Take away a bird's wings, and you have a timid thing indeed. She was supposed to centre her entire life on poor Isa, but what to do when he never came home? John had rescued him from himself night upon night for her sake, and never a complaint from his lips.

"So," Mary concentrated on her stitches while she spoke. "The storm is supposed to stay with us a few days. Do you have any plans?"

"I'm afraid not." Kate answered. "Isa is off with his brother at a conference. They're staying at George's, and goodness only knows when they will return. It takes a good day for them to get as far as the other side of London!"

Mary chuckled. "Well, there's no sense in you going home to an empty house! Why don't you stay here tonight?"

Kate's reaction was a sad mixture of hope and gratitude. "Oh, I couldn't impose."

"Not at all. My John is off on his own business, and even with a baby in the house it is a bit lonely. We can stay up with the cider and catch up on all our business!" Mary snipped a thread off the edge and glowered at it. "All we need do is send a wire to your household so no one need worry."

"That would be lovely, Mary . . . Thank you." Kate spoke to Mary, but her adoring eyes were upon the baby in her arms.

"And here, the *piece de resistance* . . . ."

Watson nearly fell backwards in shock. A corpse was stretched out on a wooden waggon, arms folded neatly over its breast. As his heart settled, he realised he was looking at a cleverly made-up manniken.

"Whew," Mortimer said behind him. He had no love of skeletons that still had their clothes on them.

And the image was clothed in every sense: Finely woven cloth adorned the imitation body, the threads cleverly dyed in a soft grey-and-white plaid reminiscent of Watson's old home-colours. A circlet graced the wax brow, and rings studded the false fingers. Leather boots were handsomely stitched in a primitive design with elaborate stitches of dragons and ley lines upon the calves. A short sword, a gladius, rested its

252

hilt underneath the hands. Under the hem of the short sleeve, hammered arm-bands gleamed over an intricate knotwork of woad that matched the style of the painting upon the face.

"Our first discovery was that of a warrior-prince," Sir Niles announced. "Feel free to step across the ropes. You have the privilege of your peers, but the common viewing public will be forced to admire our masterpiece from a short distance."

Watson complied with the others, but his mind was barely on the excited murmur and babble as men commented on the period jewelry and the woad painting. Yellow had been used on the trim of the pale plaid shirt, the gold mingling with a single stripe of woad in the cloth to make Saxon Green.

He looked not at the false corpse, but in the artificial room. The walls had been sculpted with a type of adobe and painted to simulate the inside of a barrow. In an artistic touch, the labourmen had added bits of chaff and tiny stones, layers of carefully stacked logs, fragments of wood and peat into the material before it cured. It really did seem to be a hollow bubble of earth.

At their feet rested clay and glass jars of whatever the dead nobleman would need on his way to the Otherworld. A stuffed horse in a position of sleep, save the gash in its throat, was supposed to join its master. Watson realised he devoutly disliked this. Devoutly.

"I say there, Sir Niles," a blocky man with a red face piped up. "This is a replica of what is now at the museum in London?"

"In every respect save one: My version is much better!" Sir Niles waited for the laughter to die down with a smile, his "mad hand" clutching at his new writing-book. "I re-created the pigments and the jars, the woods and goods, in their original glory. Everyone may rest satisfied with my solution: The original remains may go to the institutions who can plumb the secrets from the depths . . . but I have the artistic inspiration for visitors here." He swept a large hand across the room in a panorama. "The public is hardly allowed to see what rests behind the vaults and back-rooms of London . . . or even Edinburgh. We are finding steady supplies of bog-men in Streat, and not only is it giving my poor folk an opportunity to give me useful employment, but it is also giving them something better than fishing and netting."

Watson thought of the proud old leathery faces on the steamship, and wondered if Sir Niles had bothered to consult with his people before he went about "improving" their future.

"My museum will temporarily house the original relics and discoveries under an officially trained member of the police force, which

I am sure will add to the safety of these valuable." Sir Niles stopped and brushed his palm lovingly against the false earthen wall.

"How will you bring a copper all the way over here?"

Now that voice, Watson knew. Professor Emile Dover, attached to at least three Universities and an eternal guest-lecturing circuit. A man known for his speeches and his ability to hold a conversation on anything under the sun. The doctor sneaked a peak through the crowd: Stocky, pink, white hair thinning on top, strawberry birthmark . . . yes.

"As I recall, it's difficult enough to have a policeman come up here whenever there's a problem."

Problem? Watson's mind grasped that eagerly.

Sir Niles was unruffled. He was even pleased at the opening. "Not to worry at all. I have several of my own island residents sent into the world for a better education. Two of them were sent to be trained in policing my island for the future needs of security and safety." He paused and sighed. "I am afraid one of them fell afoul of the pitfalls in the Main Island, but the other is most promising and he will be returning to us soon with his excellent training under his belt."

Inspector Loseth.

Watson's mind spun like a child's top. The baronet had sent someone else besides Loseth out for training . . . but . . . how did Loseth reach the rank of Inspector so quickly, unless he had already stood in a post of law enforcement to begin with? Loseth was clearly the one who had failed . . .

.

"You look a little troubled," Mortimer said in his ear.

"It's . . . nothing, I suppose." Watson shook himself. "It's the plaid." He nodded to the finely woven jacket and trousers of the imitation dead man. "Northumbrian pattern. I didn't expect to see it up here."

"Well, that's a question easily settled," Mortimer turned and lifted his hand before Watson could stop him. "Excuse me, Sir Niles! I couldn't help but notice the weaving on your barrow-prince. Isn't that the Northumbrian pattern?"

"That it is . . . one of the oldest plaids in Great Britain. There were enough scraps of cloth to identify the pattern." Sir Niles' hand shook on his book. "One of my men believes the prince in question was from the Northumbrian region, and died in battle. Being Celt, they chose to intern him here in the place of his demise."

"Most interesting!" Mortimer said gaily. "I knew the plaid was ancient, but I never thought to put it all together."

"Life is fascinating, is it not?" Sir Niles mused. "As much as death is. Dr. Watson, you served with the Northumbrians, did you not?"

"Fifth Fusiliers," Watson answered automatically.

254

"Who knows, sir? The man could be an ancient kinsman."

"Who knows indeed?" Watson answered back, just a little too quickly and too cheerfully for his personal ear. It would do no good to display his growing sense of unease.

The room made him feel as though they were entombed. But the conversation and the body at the table . . . He finally forced himself to stare at the wax face. The face was mostly clean-shaven, so there had been time to be influenced by Roman fashions . . . but the thick moustache under the lip could have been a modern style.

He disliked it immensely. *The dead man looked a little too much like himself.*

Ch XXXIII – Conclusion

"There we go." Mary leaned over and blew out the candle. After what had seemed like an agonising period of an infant's complaints, Arthur had simply closed his eyes and gone to sleep. Kate envied his ability to find rest when he wanted it.

"He'll be sleeping through most the night," Mary explained as she settled herself comfortably. "It's much of an improvement over before. His nursery overlooks the garden, but the sounds of the paper-men come through in the morning and before you'd know it, he would be awake and cross as a little bear."

"Poor thing!" Kate was ready to feel sorry for the baby.

"Not to worry, dear." Mary was quick to reassure her. "He'll be quite all right. He just needs an appropriate place to settle down . . . not too different from his father. I hope John isn't aggravated tonight . . . the cold always makes his wounds ache."

John was not aggravated. He was furious.

Wild horses couldn't take a true gentleman from his manners . . . but his unease had grown over the course of the night. After the chilly exhibit and the false corpse, John was glad of the dinner table. Candlelight was better against Pictish oil-lamps any day.

One of the guests – an overly polished idle son with hair the colour of a winter-blasted cattail swamp-had started it all halfway through the courses with an opinion on writing. John now knew him as the brother of a periodical editor, so his assumption of expertise was inevitable. (John never liked the periodical anyway.)

"Writing should be in facts, not fiction," Giles Andrews persisted. "Our work as researchers and explorers is too important for distraction . . . but here we are competing in the market-place for whatever tripe is being printed on cheap paper! Or what about the installments in the newspapers?"

"Fiction is a matter of life," a fat man with curling white whiskers against his florid face pointed out. "I know you dislike the sensationalist 'historical fiction' as well as I do, Giles, but it is there, and we can hardly eradicate it."

"We can at least stop supporting those rags and encourage others to do so." Giles was well on his way to being the first drunk of the evening. "Look at the trumped-up false Druids running about, claiming to be the inheritors of the Celtic mentality! Shall we all re-write actual Roman history on the island and pass it off as fact? How many minds are warped thinking it is all genuine history?" A mutter of low humour fluttered through many of the men there, but there was something ugly and too-smug about it.

"People want to believe what they're reading. That's why they read it. But most people have the sense not to grasp fiction or a fantastical work as if it actually happened."

"Most? That's a generous estimation!" Giles was growing angry. His eyes settled on the half-expectant Watson. "Shall we ask the *writer* among us?"

Watson mentally sighed. "What shall you ask of me, sir?"

"You have experienced the realities of life in war. You write quite excellent articles on the life of London, as well as the occasional medical treatise – "

Watson jumped slightly. Someone noticing his medical papers was an unexpected shock.

" – but if you are to be remembered for anything, it would be as the observer of Sherlock Holmes." Giles hesitated a moment, perhaps to allow his point the time it needed to collect the appropriate drama. "You cater to different audiences, Doctor, unlike anyone else in this room. How does it make you feel to know you will be known for your sensationalist literature, and not your more *important* writings?"

Very rarely did a man's honest opinion make Watson see red. When the brown curtain dissolved before his eyes, he was standing on his feet with the wineglass creaking in his grip while Mortimer peered worriedly up into his face.

Calm down, he advised himself. *Calm down. A man who speaks in ignorance is a poor target. And Holmes wouldn't even understand why you're upset.*

"I would humbly submit that there are two perspectives on writing," he said at last. In a way, he already knew what to say – this was the same old question, only phrased in an unusually clever way. "The message that the author is earnestly attempting to convey . . . *and the message the audience believes.* It would be tempting and simplistic to say that the author truly owns his work. I do not believe he does. When Robert Browning was asked what was meant by a line of his poetry, he kindly told his questioners to 'Ask the Browning Society. I'm sure they know all about it.'"

Still too angry, John. Calm down . . . He took a sip of his wine as the silence about the hall grew thick.

"A writer by nature is fluid. He writes what he has to say . . . and he moves on. *The reader does not move on.* The reader catches what he can

257

from the words, draws his own meaning from it, but the words are frozen. They are memorized in order to make a point in a conversation, or perhaps inspire another man's work of literature . . . How many of us have read a book where Shakespeare was quoted or even the point of the conversation?

"I humbly submit to Lord Openshaw that my sensationalist writings were disliked by many, including Mr. Holmes himself. He wanted to demonstrate to the world his methods by which he solved problems – the difference between seeing and observing, and indirectly, the benefit of a trained education. Over time, I fear, he grew a bit annoyed at the reactions of the people he aided. Their admiration for him was the admiration the audience gives an illusionist or a conjurer. Once they knew the methods that Holmes employed, they instantly devalued his work. The audience may wonder how the magician can levitate the sleeping lady, but do they really want to know?"

He took another drink. "Mr. Holmes was at heart a most logical and forward thinker, and the reaction to his life's calling caused him no end of bafflement. At last, he granted me permission to publish his work, under certain stipulations. They would only be remarkable cases of note containing an apt demonstration of his powers. He also preferred cases that demonstrated a social or economic problem, for that was the root of many crimes. Lastly, he granted me permission to publish these cases after his death, and I believe that was partly to avoid the inevitable pestering of the curious and the bored. The good magician reveals his tricks at the end, after all." His throat threatened to close up for a moment. By dint of will, he forced it from happening.

Not a sound.

John regarded the large table, stuffed with enough food to feed the crawlers of London for a week, and yet it was just a casual display of hospitality.

Dear God, they wanted him to keep going.

"I would not call my own accountings of Sherlock Holmes sensationalist, although many elements of his adventures were sensational. I have my own methods of writing, and I chose the form of language and atmosphere that would . . . *convey* some of what we encountered. The vast majority of my readers have never been to Dartmoor. They have known France only by a map. The King of Bohemia rules a land they will never see, nor would they know how to address such a man. I tried to let them see what I was seeing and feel what I was feeling. In a way, I write for everyone who has ever wished to have the company of a person who is . . . good at solving problems, for problems are a fact of life, and we are often overwhelmed by them. To know that *somewhere* there is a real, live, flesh-and-blood man who is a problem-solver for his career . . . who has the wit to take what confounds us, make sense of it all, and leave the world a better place for his interference . . . well . . . that is a good medicine, gentlemen. A medicine that gives that rare elixir of hope and optimism – qualities that we must have if we are to survive in adversity.

"If it appears sensationalist to contemplate that a man would murder his own step-daughters with a poisonous serpent, it is only sensationalist because poison is considered the murder weapon of women, not men. His readers were not astonished at the cleverness of the robbers in The Red-Headed League, but they were more surprised that a man of noble blood would be the intelligent force behind it. And thus you see the problem I grappled with. My audience reaches sorts I could never predict.

"I would seem to be not the only one with this phenomenon. There is a writer I feel who is much more talented than I, and I am certain some of you have read his work: Dr. Arthur Conan Doyle. He is a natural detective, a skilled doctor, and he has pieced together intelligent, gripping accounts of crime as well as the mental process that makes the victim and killer tick. But right now, he's unfortunately more famous for *The White Company*, serialized last year in *The Cornhill Magazine*. It grieves me to say that while I enjoy *The White Company*, his worthwhile articles and observations from a scientific viewpoint are ignored." He sighed. "Dr. Doyle was upset and concerned at the renewal of the Triple Alliance last year. I know from my personal meetings with him, as well as the quality of his research, that his concerns of war are legitimate. But will he be listed as an expert? I do not think he will be given the respect he deserves."

Watson tried to ignore his rapt audience. "My medical articles are received by the medical eye. That is to be expected. My articles of London are received by the dwellers of London first, the rest of England second. But it is my . . . sensationalist writings of Sherlock Holmes that I am the most fond of, for I cannot tell you who will read them, nor who will enjoy them. Hardly a day passes when I don't hear something from one of those readers . . . and be they rich or poor, their appreciation for my sharing the stories is heartfelt and honest. Even their criticism is welcomed, for they feel strongly about the great man they remember. We share that strong feeling. And while I know I am no resurrectionist, I feel as long as the methods of that great man are with us, his legacy will ensure he is remembered for a long time afterward . . . ."

Watson had meant to finish, but the clapping overwhelmed him. Astonished, he took in the sight. Over twenty men, whom he would have tagged as sour academics, were rising to their feet, pounding their hands and slamming their palms on the tabletop.

"Quite beautiful," Mortimer repeated for the unknownth-time as they prepared for bed. "It is to balance between two wires to be an author: To write for oneself, or to write for the praise of the public? You reminded us all that one motivation is incomplete without the other."

"I swear to you, such was not my intent," Watson confessed with dissolving enthusiasm. Against their ankles a creeping draught chilled the skin and slipped icy fingers upon the floor where even the thick carpet could not shield them. He pulled on his bedroom-stockings in hasty relief. "I wasn't even speaking with an outline in my mind! I was just . . . speaking intuitively, I'm afraid."

"You shouldn't be ashamed of speaking intuitively." Mortimer spoke with a firmness outside his usual manners. "You are a Celt through and through. No one could ask for a better friend, alive or dead."

Watson sighed and brushed at his moustache. "He would have spoken differently."

"Of course he would have. He was different. As different in his way as one continent is to another . . . but Russia lies within view of North America, does it not?" Mortimer shuddered as his warmest night-clothes failed to take effect, and he paused to stand before the peat fire with his hands outstretched. "This will be the last time I forget my night-cap," he muttered under his breath.

Watson chuckled despite himself.

"As I was saying, you have your own talents, just as he did his."

"I assure you, I have no desire to bury my own identity in someone else's." Watson spoke softly. "But still . . . it was good to be a part of something larger . . . ."

"And if anyone was larger than life, it would be Mr. Holmes." Mortimer smiled at fond memories.

"Yes . . . Good night, Doctor."

"Good night."

Watson did not allow himself to relax as Mortimer's occasional toss turned to idle snoring. He felt wide awake – as if he'd drunk coffee instead of wine.

He'd felt this sensation before. In the starless, humid night of India after a tiger hunt he did not to this day choose to recollect. That night was followed by his boarding the next ship to the Berkshires. The sensation came back many times after that – sometimes strongly, most times a glimmer of awareness or an echo thrumming behind the ear. He'd looked up into the brilliant Afghanistan starlight and known if there was such a thing as destiny, he would meet it that coming day.

He had never shied from that sensation. It had grown less common . . . but it was there.

The night at the Roylott mansion had been his worst experience after Maiwand. A mere blink of his eye and he would be back in that cold, half-finished room with the dreadful bed that could not be moved.

Holmes rising up in that darkness, seeing what Watson could not as he struck upon the bed with his cane . . . seeing it because he knew it could only be a snake in the light of his match and the snake would be . . . *there* . . . upon the bedcovers . . .

The terrible scream that magnified the darkness.

Holmes pale as marble, his sharp eyes glinting in the gloom as his chest heaved with the effort to calm his breathing. His face had never been whiter, and the loathing in his face had yet to be equaled in Watson's memory.

"You see it, Watson? You see it?"

No. My eyes were not as keen as yours, and they were tired from being open for so long. The paltry light of your match was enough to blind me . . .

Watson sighed to himself, for it was no light thing to admit his vision was not what it had once been. The desert had burned the best of that gift from him, though nowhere near as badly as it had for his brother . . . . [2]

"You see it, Watson? You see it?"

No . . . but I am beginning to . . .

Mortimer was completely asleep, so deep in his dreams that his fingers twitched above the covers. He never stirred when Watson slipped out of his bed and dressed in the dark.

It took him less time that he estimated to reach Sir Niles library room. As he had suspected, the library was unlocked. There had been little need to lock it. None of the books looked particularly valuable in Watson's casual glance.

The cabinet beneath the immaculate rows upon rows of the baronet's diaries was unlocked too. Watson risked a single match in his hand but glanced away from the bright little flame as it flared. He avoided setting his eyes upon it the entire time he peered into the little wooden cavern.

A man who collects things with such fervent need ironically demonstrates a lack of strength in his character. Watson had known too many men and women who made a fetish out of their possessions. *They invariably found it difficult to make decisions.* The greater the need to keep things past their usefulness, the stronger the degree of their unnatural attachment.

And as he suspected, Sir Niles had his old "imperfect" books all stored in the back away from his "perfect" books that were worthy of perfect view. Judging from the musty smell, none had been opened since their incarceration.

It took but a few minutes' work to find the book he wanted. A brief perusal of its contents tomorrow would return the diary to its rightful spot. Breathing a sigh of relief, he quietly closed the door on the cabinet and returned to his room.

Kate Whitney awoke to the easy warmth of the feather bed. Next to her, Mary was just sitting up and pulling off the covers.

"Get yourself some more rest, dear." Mary smiled at her. "I must see to Arthur." The baby was whimpering from the crib in the warm corner.

"Oh, the poor dear." Kate whispered. "How is he?"

"He's just hungry . . . and I daresay a bit damp!" Mary chuckled softly, but pinned her dressing-gown in place swiftly. "Shush, dear . . . your mother's here."

Arthur squirmed as his mother quickly popped him into clean hippens and settled into the rocking-chair with the baby in her arms. "Never much sleep in the world with a baby in it," she whispered. "You needn't get up on our account, Kate. It's still early."

Kate couldn't quite explain that she felt completely rested in the peace and quiet of this household. Here there were no sulky maids who forgot every other thing they were told. No sound of late-night traffic or the worry of a husband coming home in pieces from his nightly revels.

"I slept deeply, Mary. I'm wide awake. Shall I tell your maid to fix up some tea?"

"Mmm, some rose-hip tea would be a delight . . . Oh, there you are, Theresa."

"I heard you were up, Ma'am, and wanted to see if there was anything I could do."

"The usual morning cup of tea, please, and the usual hand with these dresses!" Mary's smile of mischief startled Kate, for she had long been told that one could not be at all frivolous with the work. Theresa smiled as she ducked her head and agreed to tend to things at once.

"Why is it all my prettiest dresses require another person with two working hands to button me inside them?" Mary sighed. "I wish my dresses buttoned in the front."

Kate blinked. "It's hardly respectable, Mary. A woman who can simply pop in and out of her dress whenever she wants – "

"Cloth chastity belts," Mary said firmly, and overlooked Kate's fierce blush. For that matter, so did Theresa. "Bad enough we can't even lift our arms over our heads . . . We have to have servants to help us! I suppose I'm fortunate in that I enjoy the maid we do have . . . Her father's a cab-man so I never have to worry about her being able to come to work."

262

Kate's mind whirled slightly, but she was already on the fringes of respectability thanks to her husband. "I would be afraid." Kate confessed. "I don't think I would feel safe."

"Forgive me. When I least expect it, I think of my childhood abroad." Mary's smile was warm with memories. "It's so different over there . . . sometimes I wish I were abroad again, but it's the small things I miss about it . . . the sunshine, the rain that won't turn you black . . . ."

The air that won't make you cough . . . Kate looked into her tea. *Surely you miss the freedom of breath . . . but if you left I would be heartbroken.*

"You look sad, Kate."

"I suppose I'm thinking of today." Kate lied easily, though she hated to. "The weather's so vile. They say it's going to get worse before it gets better."

"I hope it isn't that way where John is," Mary frowned out the window as she tucked Arthur into a light blanket. "The chill always aggravates his wounds." She sighed as if to herself. "Nothing for it, I suppose . . . and I do need to go outside today." She gave Arthur to Kate, who was all too happy to cuddle the baby.

"What a mess," Mary said at last. Kate looked up from Arthur's attempts to lift and twist his head like an owl's to find her friend staring out the window. "There's no doubt you're right about the weather, Kate! Just look at those clouds! You can't even see the church from here!"

"Are we to be snowed in?"

Mary sighed again. "No . . . it's clear enough in the streets . . . but I do need to get some things. Theresa's father is an excellent driver and I trust his skill." She looked better for having come to her decision. "Do you fancy a short drive out before the storm?" She smiled.

Still no time yet to go through the book. Watson was careful to secrete it behind the false backing of his locked bag. It was a simple-enough measure, and the lock was small but difficult to prize. In the light of day, he could admit to a thread of absurdity . . . Still . . . .

Still there was something. Sir Niles had been trying too hard to be his friend, trying too hard to get his agreement to return for another visit, or stay a bit longer . . . .

Perhaps it was as simple as being discomfited at the sight of a sacrificial manikin that looked too much like himself. He was hungry and tired of the rabid eagerness of their host and their fellow-guess who lived to approve of everything Sir Niles did in the name of "Bringing discovery to the visitors." They had seen the old dungeons. The torture room – and what was a dungeon without one? A nearby bog-dig where a wind with teeth and death from freezing temperatures was more interesting than a well-preserved left shoe from some forgotten pagan . . . .

Watson's battle-sense was not going away in the face of all this hectic science. He'd had enough. It was time he went home to Mary and Arthur, and he was thankful that Mortimer had only pledged two nights on Streat.

"He won't get many visitors in the winter," Dr. Mortimer said from behind him. The hawk-like man was perched on the edge of his chair like a long-legged bird, inspecting his boots for fresh blacking.

Watson snorted. "The problem is, most of the weather on Streat seems to be winter."

"Oh, I have it on good authority the sun shines at least twice in June . . . ."

Watson was chuckling when a timid knock at the door drove it away. "Not again," he whispered.

"John, I promise you, Sir Niles is not keeping us. As soon as the ship docks, we will be there waiting – " Mortimer whispered as he stepped out of the chair and across the room to the door. "Yes?" he asked, expecting to see one of the pages.

It was Sir Niles himself, and the man was pale beneath his black beard. "I . . . forgive me for troubling you, gentlemen . . . and . . . ." He set his mouth. "Dr. Watson, it is my duty to bring you unfortunate news. I just received a wire from Scotland Yard. It concerns . . . your wife and son."

Watson slowly stood upright. The look in the baronet's face was unique to one subject. "Sir?" he whispered through lips of wood.

"It is . . . I fear the cab holding your wife and son . . . was in an accident . . . ."

The story continues in:
A Fanged and Bitter Thing

264

MX Publishing

MX Publishing is the world's largest specialist Sherlock Holmes publisher, with over six-hundred titles and over two-hundred authors creating the latest in Sherlock Holmes fiction and non-fiction

The catalogue includes several award winning books, and over four-hundred-and-fifty have been converted into audio.

MX Publishing also has one of the largest communities of Holmes fans on Facebook, with regular contributions from dozens of authors.

www.mxpublishing.com

@mxpublishing on Facebook, Twitter, and Instagram

www.ingramcontent.com/pod-product-compliance
Lightning Source LLC
Chambersburg PA
CBHW071129260626
47162CB00003B/722